Tales of Br

in Niðavellir

A stirring dwarf we do allowance give before a sleeping giant

Troilus and Cressida: William Shakespeare

Copyright

Foreword

I would like to thank the many people who have contributed to the creation of this book. I would also like to thank my early readers for their perseverance in reading the various drafts of the stories.

In particular I would like to acknowledge the contributions made by my wife and daughters and my good friends Dez and Margaret who have supported and encouraged me throughout.

******

Where do Vikings go when they die ? Valhalla or Hel...or is that just Christian propaganda?

Some scholars of the old Norse religions think that it was more a matter of individual choice. What's it to be? Endless Rugby club dinners or wall to wall repeats of Eastenders. Maybe you'd prefer something different... Welcome to Niðavellir.

This story takes place on another world very reminiscent of one of the worlds in Norse Mythology. In keeping with dwarven values I would like to say that I have taken this mythology and re-worked it into a real physical world for the sake of the story.

In reality the dialogue, vocabulary and commonplace items of a completely different world would be different to our own world. However I have used English terms, names and concepts to tell the story. In keeping with the Mythology, wherever I have created something particularly unique I have given it a name that might have originated in the language of the Scandinavian and/or Icelandic regions. I have assumed that I will be allowed some indulgence by the reader in this as most of the names are made up for the purposes of fiction and are not direct translations. However, for English readers, some of the letters that make up these words may be unfamiliar (e.g. ð in the title) and their presence may hinder reading. In an attempt to overcome this I have taken the liberty of reducing the alphabetic content in parts of the story so that these words read as a transliteration into English. I apologise if this offends any Icelandic/Nordic readers.

I have included a glossary of terms. The reader may wish to consult this if he or she encounters an unfamiliar word or concept. Alternatively, a full discussion of cosmology, ecology, habitation and social mores is available on the website: Https:/www.blank-books.co.uk.

Map

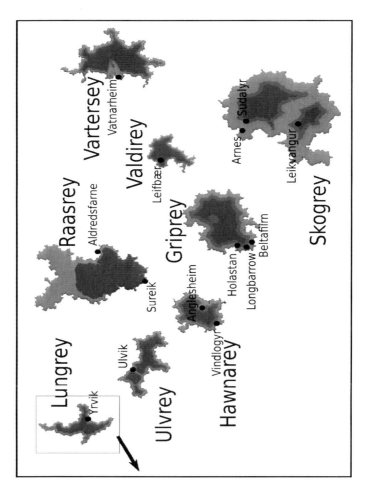

The Home Islands

Glossary

This is a list of specific terms that the reader will encounter in the text and that may require further definition. The pronunciations are approximate: they are meant as a reading aid only.

Álfur; the dwarven name given to the Álfurapa. The term is used as a generic reference to the fey races that migrated to Svartalfheim at the same time as the dwarves. They consist of four sub races each aligned to one of the elements Lorelei (water), Troll (Earth), Aeriel (Air) and Lampad (Fire) and each sub race has many variants.

Barr; A baar is a predatory creature that inhabits the mountains in the Northern islands of Svartalfheim. It is superbly adapted to life on ice and snow. Its large feet and flat tail can act as skis and its arms can be used as ski poles. When it descends from the snowfields; in times of food shortages etc. it is far from helpless on ordinary ground. It has multiply jointed legs driven by powerful thighs and it can leap from considerable distances onto its prey. The arms and feet are tipped with substantial claws and it has an impressive array of teeth. When it is in its normal posture on snow and ice fields it stands about 1.3 metres tall however when it unfolds on ordinary terrain, it stands over 2 metres.

Brockviken; a cat-sized predator common in forests.

Browth; the common name for the Vatnsbragð (Pron: Vat-nis-browth). It is the tuber of an aquatic plant which is rich in carbohydrates and soluble minerals. It grows naturally in vast groves in the shallow waters of lakes and sea coasts. It is one of the staples in the dwarf diet and serves the same function as cereals such as wheat, maize and rice. It can be dried and turned into flour. When processed as food it is commonly known as 'Brot'. There are two main varieties one derived from freshwater, (Ka-), and the other from salt-water. (Ni-)

Bru; a herbal infusion. It is a non-alcoholic alternative to beer, mead and wine. It has a considerable social history and its consumption is often formalised in association with a set-piece social event. Thus there are inns which serve Bru with small meals to workers (Gistiheimbru) who cannot, or prefer not to, eat at home, and there are very formal occasions, mostly involving the upper classes, where dancing (Skrefbru) or eating (Hárbru) are involved.

Byrjunarstormur; the first storm after a period of fine weather. These are usually severe and include lightning and heavy rain, snow, ice or sleet.

Draugr; also known as a Revenant or Barrow-Wight. Usually the remnant of an evil sorcerer. An undead spirit with corporeal form.

Dwimmerlaik; An undead servant similar to the ring wraiths in the Lord of the Rings but much less powerful. Usually subservient to an undead master such as a draugr.

Elgrott; a large rodent-like deer

Ethlabarn; the generic name for the hatchling stage of any of the sentient reptilian species that make up the Skógurlifa that inhabit the southern continent.

Firedab; a pidgeon-sized fire-breathing flying lizard

Fiskur; the common name for the Eðlafiskur (Pron: Ethla-fis[as in fish]-cur) are small carnivorous lizards that inhabit lakes and rivers. There are several varieties. Some are akin to crocodiles and alligators others are more like miniature plesiosaurs. They infest the waters of lakes and are responsible for many of the occupational injuries sustained by dwarves who gather the Vatnisbrowth.

Fljúgbátr; a vessel akin to a large racing catamaran. When driven by a strong wind it is capable of rising above the sea surface on hydrofoils. This allows it to travel much faster than a conventionally hulled boat. They are extremely expensive and are only capable of carrying passengers or small loads. They are popular with pirates and smugglers.

Framandi; a term for an outlander or alien. Someone who is not part of a particular culture.

Golden ones; machine intelligences evolved from dwarf engineers. These operate at petaflop rates (10^{15} floating point calculations per second) they have discarded human names in favour of single letter designations A to Z and use regular expression syntax in place of case and verb agreement thus \A means the individual "A" and [A-G] is a group of individuals comprising of the individuals \A,\B,\ C,\D,\E,\F and \G.

Holastan; the capital city of Dwarfish civilisation. May be loosely translated as 'hole in the stone'. The word is used in two contexts, Holastan is the name of the city itself but when used with the definite article 'the' as in 'the Holastan' it refers to the cave in the old part of the city where the original settlers made their home and where the dwarf aristocracy now reside.

Jötunnfiskur; marine reptiles and, as their name suggests, they are the larger cousins of the smaller, freshwater Eðlafiskur, growing to twelve metres in length. They roam the seas and oceans but they are not the only inhabitants. Ordinary fish and marine mammals compete with them for marine resources and it is not unknown for the body of a Jötunnfiskur to be washed ashore covered in scars from encounters with large squid and massive sharks.

Justiciary and the Justicers are a quasi civil service that is based on a theocratic organisation. It's structure and organisation is split into factions

The Healers: the medical establishment.

The Priests: clerics who oversee the Temple and its functioning and people who do charitable works.

The Justicers: the police and military who keep the peace and enforce the Laws

The Administration: the civil service. A hierarchy ranging from humble clerks to the powerful Council of Justice. This college consists of a council of Lords who are effectively both the establishment elite and who make policy and law.

All factions show allegiance to a nominal 'Temple' and this is where novice justicers are raised and indoctrinated before being dispersed to one of the factions.

Many justicers are obsessed with power and the control of others due to their years of indoctrination. This can manifest as arrogance and cruelty in their dealings.

Kattdaun; a herbal extract from the plant of the same name. It grows wild in the forests of all the home isles and it is particularly associated with the dens of wyre whose smell it resembles.

Kraftmoot; A competitive showcase or festival where maker dwarves show off their skills in various crafts.

Menntunleit; a quest and coming of age trial undertaken by all dwarves. There is no specific age when this takes place; readiness for the quest is judged by the individual's teachers and parents. It consists of the dwarf youngster setting off into the wild country of their choice and fending for themselves for a period of time until they are ready to return to normal dwarf society. The youngsters are only permitted to take a single pack on their quest. The contents of the pack are controlled, no weapons or money are allowed but other items may be chosen by the youngster. Most include food and some items of rugged clothing. However, to ensure the safety and to assess progress and performance, each participant is issued with a scrying stone. This stone is monitored by the teachers and, if danger threatens or an accident occurs, aid can be dispatched. Most dwarves undertake Menntunleit in their late teens or early twenties.

MHD; Magnetohydrodynamics: in this context it refers to the machines that generate electricity via plasmas and have virtually no moving parts except the plasma itself.

Mnemnosynth; A device that alters or erases memory

Pilot Islands; the name given to a series of tiny islands that are dotted between the main land masses of the home islands. They gained the name pilot island because ships used them as navigation points and relatively secure stopover anchorages where they could shelter from heavy storms. Most of them are formed from the peaks of extinct underwater volcanoes. They are largely uninhabited and uninhabitable except for a hardy breed of dwarves who are akin to lighthouse keepers on earth. These individuals maintain the stores, the magical scrying links and semaphore relays that provide fast global communications.

Sap; the name for a form of mental magic where the wizard takes direct control of a person's mind and/or body to use their skills.

Sjálitla; literally a machine that sjá (see) litla (small) i.e. a microscope.

Skog; the short form dwarven word for the race called Skógurlifa. Skogs are reptilian hominids evolved from the original dinosaur inhabitants of the planet. They are akin to the monkeys and great apes of earth and have a similar range of intelligence.

Smygl; beasts of burden, they perform the same function as horses do in human society.

Sting; the street name of a highly addictive drug made from a plant called Kanis Frábærtis. Its name derives from the sensation experienced when it is taken which is not unlike the electric shock from a stingbush. The drug and the stingbush are otherwise unrelated.

Uteligger; swearword meaning person of no value.

Wyre; a cat-like lizard domesticated for use as a general guard and pest control animal. It has a sinuous body covered in fine, overlapping scales. It hunts in packs and is seldom seen as an individual creature. Its behaviour is also cat-like in that it assigns its current loyalty based on whoever is providing it food and shelter. It is, however, a voracious hunter and packs of wyres have been known to attack large wild elgrott and bring them down. In domestic situations a small pack is often used to control vermin in food storage barns.

<u>Calendar;</u>

There are sixteen, twenty-day months and both are referred to by numbers. For convenience the story uses ordinary English numerals. A list of the Norse numbers can be found on the website Https:\\www.bank-books.co.uk

Each week is divided into five days ; Mani's day, Tyr's day, Woden's day, Thor's day, Frigg's day

They are derived from the names of a god or goddess from ancient Aesir lore. These were adopted before the Dwarves migrated to their new world and remain in use;

For example *Mani, níu - tólf* :i.e. the first day of the week that is the ninth day of the twelfth month (in autumn).

Prologue

Plintz was in the lead armoured car as it turned off the road and started up the war torn slope to the castle. He felt, rather than heard the tremendous blast as the castle collapsed in on itself. The column of tanks behind halted and watched. The building was burning but it wasn't like any fire they'd ever seen. Huge gouts of white flame shot skywards. A pall of jet black smoke and dust circled like a tornado in the sky above. Lightning bolts descended from the cloud peppering the ground in front of them with craters the size of bathtubs. Dazzling actinic light from the sagging towers testified to metal heated to the point where, it too, burned.

******

It was exhilarating, the power made me feel god-like. I directed it, destroying a tower here and a wall there, like some child trampling a sandcastle on the beach. I sat there, in the midst of it all, swirling the energy around me. The energy sang to me and I played it like some huge musical instrument. My mind controlled it all; Sally revelled in it, and joined in the fun. I hardly felt the mundane world slipping away. I can't say when I lost awareness of my surroundings, or when I lost awareness of my body. Only the energy was real. I knew that the energy playing around me was twisting the dimensions. It was easy just to embrace the energy; to become the energy. Slowly, or maybe quickly, for time had lost all meaning, I left the material world behind and became a being of pure energy. There was no going back now. (*The Quicksilver Wyrm*)

Day One

Einar Balder peeped around the curtain at the audience. There were hundreds of them and he swallowed the lump of fear that had risen in his throat. What could they do? He was a famous poet and bard. Even if they didn't like it, it would bring publicity and being in the public eye was paramount. The master of the stage was settling them down now and silence began to fall around the auditorium. Einar checked his costume, it was a copy of some ancient battle armour and it looked the part; but it wouldn't stop a stick of celery, never mind a spear. He wore it for the look, going on stage in full battle armour and delivering an Edda length poem would have been extremely uncomfortable and it would have prevented the easy gestures and dramatic poses that gave his performances life. It wasn't all smoke and mirrors, he did believe his new work was a worthwhile tale and it was fresh in the collective imagination of the dwarven race. A tambour thumped and a horn sounded; his cue. He stepped from behind the curtain and strode to the centre of the stage accompanied by a roar of applause.

He waited for the applause to die down and the ensuing silence to build. He timed it perfectly; before the first cough, his voice rang out.

"Lords, Masters, Makers and Commoners, dwarves of all paths, I come before you tonight to tell you the tale of Brannhår Dagmarsdóttir. You all will have heard of her, some of you might even have met her but her tale reminds us what is great and good about Dwarf-kind. Even though she was low born she embodies the true nature of a Dwarf. My tale seeks to explain that being a true dwarf is not about birth but is a path that can be taken by any soul. I truly hope that we can all learn from it," he paused for a second, "I give you; Brannhår in Niðavellir"

Ch 1: Overture and Beginners

The dwarf climbed over the rubble. As always he was looking for metal or its traces. He and his wife had wintered in the high mountains and had come down when the spring thaw had started. The winter had been hard and they had expended most of their energies just keeping alive. The area had been abandoned by free living dwarves; most people had congregated in the dwarf village before the true winter had set in.

His wife was about twenty yards behind him at the edge of the lake harvesting the starchy tubers called 'browth' and she called him over, "Look here, there's something in the water."

He went over to her and saw a shape floating just below the surface of the lake. He waded in and pulled the thing to shore. It was the size of a child and it looked like one of the álfurs, spirit beings belonging to the fey races. Possibly an undine or lorelei. Her form was too slight to be a dwarf. She was naked and appeared uninjured but she wasn't breathing. Her red-gold hair streamed behind her in the water but fell into a tangled wet rope as he lifted her clear. He laid her on the bank. His wife said, "She's got something around her neck. It's gold."

The dwarf smiled, gold was always welcome. The festival of Kraftmoot was in a few weeks and he hadn't had time to create anything for this year's event; he wondered if it would be worth re-working. The fine chain ended in a talisman; a gold disc holding a deep red gem. He examined it, the chain was too fine for it to be common work but he frowned in distaste as he saw that the setting and talisman had been cast. He thought that he might be able to do something with it. Of course he'd have to enter it in a rework category rather than as an original but it would be better than nothing. The gold setting dangled from the dwarf's hand by its chain and the red gem seemed to pulse in the bright sunlight.

Since the creature was clearly a water spirit he was about to push the body back into the lake to be claimed by the other water spirits when he noticed something. Her body was warm even though she must have been in the freezing water for a long time.

"We will take her back to the cave and see what can be done," he said.

His wife nodded in agreement; "We must preserve life; it is our duty to the world."

Norri agreed and they took the tiny creature back to their cave and put her into the bed that Norri had built years before when they had been young enough to hope for a child of their own. "We will care for her until she is well," he said as he laid the small unmoving form into the cot.

The girl didn't stir for a week and the dwarf's wife, Dagmar, tended her; trickling water into her mouth every few hours. Water spirits had to be kept in contact with their element.

After a week the creature was still not of the world. Dagmar noticed that she appeared to be shrinking and the warmth that her husband had detected when they'd first found her had now cooled to an icy chill. She discussed this with her husband, it looked like the creature would fail after all. Then Norri had an idea, "Perhaps she is not what she seems. Perhaps she needs some warmth. We will move the bed over beside the hearth to counteract the chill."

Within a day the warmth from the hearth had driven the chill away and the spirit-girl appeared to have grown back to her original size. Two days later her eyes opened.

The spirit girl's awareness came back in fits and starts; it emerged from the void as consciousness but it was without substance. She became aware that she had a location in space and time and that she had a functioning set of senses. She could hear someone speaking nearby and feel the cool sensation of water being poured into her mouth. Opening her eyes she cried out. Dagmar put down the water and took the small form out of the cot and held it to her gently. The dwarf made soothing sounds and rocked back and forth until the spirit girl calmed and slipped back into sleep.

Norri had come in from the workshop at the sound of the girl's cry. "What happened?" he asked.

"She woke and I think that she couldn't understand where she was. She's gone again," the wife said, "but we know that she is living and she'll be back."

The second time that the spirit girl woke she made no noise but watched the outlines of the two people moving about the room. She could see their lips moving and she was listening to the unfamiliar sounds. After a little while Dagmar noticed and came over to her. Dagmar made more noises but her expression and tone were gentle and the spirit girl was comforted and appeared to go back to sleep.

Dagmar told her husband later in the evening when he returned from his workshop. He was distracted because he had been intent on the task of re-working the spirit-girl's talisman and he said, "That's a good sign, it seems that she understands that we mean her no harm even if she cannot speak. However, I am worried that, in my eagerness to re-work the necklace, I may have destroyed any clan mark that it bore. I would hate to think that I might have destroyed her only link with her clan."

"I am not," Dagmar assured him, "It is clear that she was abandoned by her clan or lost to them in some other way because they would surely not have left her for the fishes. I think that fate has smiled on us and given us the chance to have a daughter of our own."

Norri frowned, "I will agree that the idea is tempting but how will we manage? We had to work so hard to survive last winter. The high forests are getting more dangerous not less. That sloth-bear tore off the cave door as easily as if it were made of leaves. It was lucky that all it wanted was the honey pot that I threw at it. If it had been really hungry we might have been killed by mistake when it raided our larder. Besides, I have a feeling that my re-work will not be good enough and we will have to take commonplace jobs during the rest of the year."

"Oh, don't be so pessimistic. I have a feeling that our little spirit girl will bring us luck. I am tempted to register her adoption when we next go to the village regardless of your misgivings. Now tell me about the re-work."

"It's going really well. I took out the gem and melted down the gold setting but I kept the chain. It's very fine work and it would have been a shame to change it because it somehow fits with the fragility of our visitor. The gem looked as though it had been melted, but, of course that would have required an enormous temperature, a temperature higher than the melting point of gold so it must have been melted before it was mounted. I smoothed the gem as best I could but it is extremely hard and, as I said, it had been melted and so I couldn't cleave it into any classical cut. Therefore I left the gem as it was and thought about a setting. I was sitting by the forge, trying to decide on the best shape when I heard the cry of a firedab somewhere in the forest and the idea came to me. Only dragon fire could have melted the gem like that so it would be appropriate if the gem was once the property of a great dragon. I went out and found one of the firedabs and I brought it back for supper but I used its claws as a model. I've started on the setting. It's going to have three claws to hold the gem and the claws are bonded to a ball to hold them together. I'll make the claws in yellow gold and the ball in red so that there is an echo of the dragon-fire both above and below the setting. I'll re-mount it on the chain. Here, look at this sketch."

Norri drew a piece of paper from his pocket and spread it on the table. Dagmar looked at it and then brought over a lamp to see it better.

"That is good, I can see it in my mind's eye already. It will be an excellent piece," Dagmar said.

The little spirit girl stirred in the cot, she was awake and she'd been listening but she made no noise.

Dagmar cooked the firedab for supper and kept a little of the broth for the girl but, by then, she was asleep so Dagmar saved it for the morning.

Over the next few weeks the spirit girl appeared to become a little stronger and she started to take small morsels of soft food. Norri had gone to the Kraftmoot and had entered the necklace into the re-work competition. Since he didn't know its original creator other than it must have been one of the spirit people he had to submit a sketch of the original necklace (countersigned by his friend Skarn as being a true copy) to the judges and give a solemn oath that the re-work of the gem and its setting was all his. Norri was well known as an honest maker and so the judges accepted his oath. He won second place for originality and first place for workmanship. Coming away from the moot in a fine mood he hurried back to Dagmar and the spirit girl. Dagmar had berated him for forgetting to register the spirit girl as being adopted but he was in such a good mood that he hadn't minded the journey back down to the village to fill out the necessary paperwork. By the time he arrived back with the certificate Dagmar had forgiven him.

It was a week or so later that the spirit girl made her first intelligible sound or rather sounds. Dagmar had noticed that the girl seemed to thrive when her cot was nearest the hearth and she had pulled it as close as she dared. The spirit girl was now strong enough to sit up unaided and she was staring at Dagmar with eyes filled with curiosity. She said "Duhgma" and held up a small hand and pointed to Dagmar. Dagmar was delighted but she was even more delighted when the girl said her second word; "Nohrhee?" in what Dagmar though was a definite questioning tone. Dagmar nodded and said, "Norri is hunting for supper," and then she mimed raising something to her lips and making a smacking sound. To her amazement the spirit girl didn't laugh in delight as a small child may have done. Instead she mimicked Dagmar, "ting upper."

Dagmar sat in thought until Norri came home. The spirit girl was sleeping again and Dagmar told him of the girl's first words. Then, after he'd expressed his own delight, she said to her husband, "I'm not sure that the girl is actually a child. She seems too serious. And it was as if she was, well, analysing what I said, trying to understand."

Norri nodded, "It's true. I've noticed that she doesn't act like a child. She always makes a clamour before she needs to pee or shit and that's not how a baby would behave. Perhaps you are right. We can only wait and see what happens."

"I know," Dagmar said, "We need to giver her a proper name and see how quickly she learns it. I think we should call her Brannhår.

Norri nodded his head slowly in agreement; it was a good name.

******

Einar paused and pretended to take a drink. He'd managed the first ten verses without anyone throwing anything or walking out in disgust. The audience were starting to fidget though, starting to gossip and losing concentration. He'd pick up the pace and leave out a few of the less interesting stanzas. Clearing his throat loudly, the audience quietened.

Ch 2: From Strength to Strength

A month later Dagmar was sure that Brannhår wasn't a child. She began to think that the wasted limbs were something that needed attention. Therefore she began to help and encouraged the girl to move about. It was clear that she was weak and she wasn't fluent but she could talk now. Dagmar smiled to herself when she thought of this. Brannhår could talk but mostly she asked questions. She wanted to know everything and had spent most of her waking hours pointing at things and saying 'what?'. Dagmar would say the name and the girl would learn the word by repeating it until Dagmar nodded her approval. That wasn't the end of it though; she'd then ask what, why or how until she understood what the thing was, how it was used or why it was as it was.

Dagmar worried that Brannhår was still too weak to get about unaided even though she was getting stronger and she seemed to be hungry all of the time. She talked it over with her husband, "I don't know what to do," she said, "I thought we might make her something to help her stand by herself. I could make her a cage for her body with extensions for her legs; something that would let her move but, at the same time, something that would support her frame so that she could rest without straining her muscles. I can make the frame from willow but I need you to make some hinges and stays from iron to let it bend and to keep it strong."

Norri liked the idea and the pair of them started to sketch what the contraption would look like on a piece of slate. It was inevitable that this would attract Brannhår's attention. Dagmar showed the sketches to the girl and Norri was astonished when the girl seemed enthusiastic and pointed to the sketch asking the inevitable questions; what, why and how.

The problem with the brace was that, despite Norri and Dagmar's best efforts, they couldn't make it light enough for Brannhår to move by herself. Brannhår quickly grasped which levers and locks to operate to let her stand in comfort, however the girl was still too weak to move without assistance from Norri or Dagmar.

It was one of the fine days between storms when Brannhår first asked Dagmar about the lake. Dagmar had explained that the lake provided food in the form of fish and browth but it seemed that the girl was asking about something else. Dagmar was puzzled; it was clear that Brannhår wanted something from the lake but she couldn't fathom what. Brannhår had tried to explain but her vocabulary was still limited. At first Dagmar thought that the girl must have remembered something of her origin and wanted to go back to the water spirits but, after a long question and answer session, she realised that it wasn't what Brannhår meant. When Dagmar had asked the girl, point blank, if she wanted to be carried down to the lake the girl shook her head. Instead the girl had pointed to a bowl that lay at Dagmar's feet and said, "put water." Dagmar filled the bowl with water but when she offered it to Brannhår to drink the girl pointed to the ground. Frowning, Dagmar put the bowl down. When she turned back to the girl she saw that Brannhår had pulled a small piece of the willow from her frame. Brannhår inexpertly threw the willow towards the bowl. It missed but Dagmar had understood her intention. She retrieved the small piece of wood and dropped it into the bowl. Brannhår seemed to get excited then and kept saying "Wood on water, what word?" Dagmar said, "Yes the wood floats on the water."

Brannhår seized on the word 'floats' and said "Brannhår floats water. Brannhår move."

Dagmar realised what the girl meant, Brannhår was too weak to move on land but, with the water supporting most of her weight, she might be able to move unaided in the water.

Dagmar grinned, why hadn't she thought of this before? She said, "Yes Brannhår can float in water. You will be able to move on your own. But we don't have to go down to the lake, it would be too dangerous what with all the fish, snakes and fiskur. However, there is a hollow just downstream where the water collects. It is just big enough for you to float in."

Brannhår looked at her, she could only understand one word in ten but Dagmar looked pleased so she nodded vigorously.

Dagmar and Norri carried the girl down to the pond but they were uncertain how to introduce Brannhår into the water. Brannhår kept saying 'no cage' which meant she wanted free of the wicker brace However, Dagmar thought that although her body would be supported by the water it was going to be difficult to move the girl's limbs. They managed to get her into the water and, to their surprise Brannhår started to swim by herself. Drying the child an hour later Dagmar asked, "How did you learn how to swim. Did you swim when you were with the álfur?"

Brannhår looked puzzled, "Not know álfur."

Dagmar explained, "The álfur are the water spirits, you know, the people you were with before we found you."

Brannhår said, "Not with people before. Not with anyone before. Not remember anything from before: only lightning."

******

Over the next year Brannhår grew stronger and learned. The daily swimming in the quiet pool had strengthened her body so that she could now get around unaided although she still looked too thin to be a dwarf. Her capacity to express herself had expanded beyond all expectation and she seemed to soak up words like a sponge. Dagmar had ceased to worry about her frailty once Brannhår had insisted that she could find her own way down to the pool. Still, Dagmar thought, the girl was a puzzle; she looked about ten years old but she acted and spoke like a grown-up. She cheerfully helped around the cave and she had learned to gather the browth and other food from the forest. She'd learned to fish but her weak limbs still struggled.

However Dagmar was even more impressed by the girl's solutions to her own problems. She'd persuaded Dagmar to make her a kind of sled with a single barrel-like wheel. Brannhår could drag this across level ground and along shallow gradients. This often meant that the girl had to go the long way around but Brannhår never complained. Brannhår had modified the sled herself. She fitted it with a brake that prevented it rolling away and she had rigged several poles, hooks and pulleys on it. She threaded thin ropes through these and used them to take the strain when she fished. Even fiskur were no match for the girl's ingenuity.

It wasn't the only example: There was a spot near to the cave where the path up became too steep for the cart no matter how Brannhår zig-zagged to minimise the gradient. Brannhår had asked Dagmar to rig a set of pulleys over the cave entrance and had attached a large rock to a rope that ran over them. The rock acted as a counterweight and the girl could manage the last steep stretch on her own.

Brannhår seemed cheerful but never more so than when she was permitted to observe Norri in his workshop. The workshop was in a cave a little way down the slope towards the lake. It was an exclusive place; even Dagmar wasn't allowed to come and go there at will. However, Brannhår could often be found sitting under the little overhang of rock near the entrance in the hope that Norri would have something to teach her.

Norri, for his part, liked the fact that his daughter took an interest in his work and he'd often pause when he came to a part where he could teach Brannhår something of the art. On one particular occasion he was in his workshop and he'd let Brannhår in to shelter from a Ryrjunarstormur. She'd sat watching him in silence while the lightning and thunder raged overhead and the rain lashed down.

Norri was expounding on the finer points of filing; which edge of the file to use and which stroke made the cut and which smoothed, when Brannhår asked a question that stopped him in his tracks. "How does the lightning know which path it should take to the ground?"

He'd never thought about it. Lightning fell from the sky and it was just luck where it landed. He told Brannhår so.

"But that isn't true, the lightning will seek out a tree if it can find one, and usually a tree on top of a hill," she frowned, "but not always, sometimes the lightning stays in the sky or it will ignore a tree and hit a rock or the ground itself."

Norri smiled, he had to admit that, now that he thought of it, she was right. "Well, little one, I have to agree with you but I have never studied the subject and I don't know why it strikes in one place rather than another. You will have to ask your teachers when you go to school."

He shook his head, had it already come to this? He and Dagmar had had their daughter for only a year and it was clear she was growing. They couldn't put off sending her to the school much longer especially as she was obviously so curious about the world. When they'd found her she'd seemed like a baby, now, after a year with them, her body seemed to have aged to a child's and her mind was even older.

Brannhår though didn't seem too excited about the prospect of school. "But father, I want to stay here and learn the ways of the forge with you."

He gave a small laugh of regret and said, "Ah, little one I would like nothing better but I am only a mountain dwarf. I am ignorant of so many things about the world. It is a long time since your mother and I went on the Menntunleit, so many things have changed. If you go to school you will meet teachers who can answer your questions much better than I can," then he brightened, "and your mother and I will always be here when you come home."

Brannhår smiled at him and flung her arms around him, "My home is in your hearts and I will never be away whilst I am there." Norri looked away so that she couldn't see how much that statement had touched him.

Brannhår seemed to notice though and fell silent as she listened to the rain thundering down. Then she seemed to rally and said, "Father, you know the rock that I use to counterbalance my cart. Well sometimes it is too heavy and sometimes it is not heavy enough. Water doesn't weigh as much as rock but if I tied a big fiskur skin to a smaller rock I could fill it with water or let it out to make it heavier or lighter whenever I needed. Will you help me with the design?" It wasn't much but it was enough to distract Norri from his thoughts. He pulled out a slate and a chalk and began to sketch: somehow Norri knew that his daughter's Menntunleit would be epic.

******

A fortnight later Dagmar called to Brannhår to come in out of the storm only to find that she wasn't in the shelter at the cave entrance de-husking browth where she was supposed to be; she was nowhere to be seen. Thinking that something might have happened to her, she found Norri and they both set off to look for their daughter. They went to the pool but she wasn't there and so they split up; Norri went downhill towards the lake and Dagmar climbed further up the mountain.

Dagmar came over a small ridge that surrounded a relatively flat meadow. The rain was pelting down but Dagmar could see something moving about a hundred paces away. She went over to investigate and found her daughter driving some long poles into the soft ground. The poles were braced with thin ropes tied to pegs.

"Brannhår what on earth are you doing. Being up here in a Byrjunarstormur is dangerous. You need to get under some shelter. Come on, I know a shallow cave just near here. We can wait until the height of the storm has passed."

Brannhår smiled at her mother, "Oh, it's only rain. The lightning isn't above us yet. We've plenty of time. Here, help me get this in," she pointed to the long pole, "I'll hold it up whilst you hammer the pegs in further. This is the last one. Once we're done I'll come with you to the cave and we can watch."

Dagmar started to protest but she could see that her daughter was determined. She decided not to argue; that way they would be out of the storm quicker.

When they were both standing under the meagre shelter Dagmar asked, "What are you doing? What are the poles?" Dagmar noticed that the air had become quite still, the howling wind had died and a peculiar calm had settled over the meadow.

"Oh mother, it's a surprise. Just wait and you will see. The lightning is nearly overh..." The last word was drowned out by the loudest sound Dagmar had ever heard. A bolt of lightning had descended from the sky and it had hit one of the poles about sixty paces away. She was dazzled and closed her eyes but it made no difference, the blue image of the bolt was clearly visible on the back of her eyelids. Brannhår shrieked with delight. "I knew it, I knew it," she said over and over again then, "Here comes another."

This time Dagmar was prepared, she covered her ears and shut her eyes as tight as they would go. Sure enough this explosion was louder and more brilliant than the previous one. Brannhår was laughing and, although Dagmar couldn't see it, nearly dancing with excitement. Dagmar started to open her eyes but Brannhår shrieked, "And another" and she closed them again; just in time. The third explosion felt like the earth had split itself open and then there was silence. The silence was so deep that Dagmar thought that she'd gone deaf. But then the wind picked up again and began to howl.

Dagmar looked around, Brannhår wasn't beside her any more she was scurrying across the field over to some blackened patches in the dirt. There were several of the poles still standing and Brannhår rushed from one to the next. Dagmar called out to her to come back but Brannhår shouted that it was safe to come out, "The lightning has passed over us. Don't be afraid."

Dagmar gingerly crossed to her daughter. She'd been nearly scared out of her skin and she was in no mood to take excuses, "Young lady, you will come away from here immediately. Your father will be frantic, he went down to the lake. We thought you might have had an accident." Dagmar was so shaken she took Brannhår's arm and pulled the girl down the hill.

When they arrived back at the cave Norri was back, "I couldn't find any sign of her at the lake and I came back here to get a sled and come up to try to find you. I can see that I wouldn't have needed a sled; you look fine daughter, if a little wet."

Brannhår was clearly still excited about something and she said, "Father, I know why lightning strikes in some places and not in others."

Dagmar wasn't to be sidetracked though, "You, young lady, are grounded. I'll see to it that you have enough chores to keep you busy for the rest of the month. You are never, I repeat never, to go off on your own like that again."

Brannhår's face fell, her mother's words had just penetrated the glow of her excitement. She said, "A whole month, oh no." However the prospect of a month's chores was quickly dispelled by her father's question, "You were up there, on the top, when the lightning struck?"

"Yes father, I know why the lightning hits some trees and not others. It prefers the spiky ones and especially iron-oak."

Dagmar could see that she wouldn't get any sense out of the pair of them as Brannhår explained her experiment they both began to swap theories and began sketching things on the slate. She shook her head in dismay and went to get them all some dry clothing.

Later, when Brannhår had gone to bed and she was alone with Norri, Dagmar said, "I am worried about Brannhår."

Norri replied, "I know what you mean, that stunt with the lightning was dangerous but she didn't seem to be worried. Still, it was a good piece of work and it just proves that she may have the body of a little girl but her mind is much more developed."

"No, I know that, what worries me is something that she said when we were on the hill. She seemed to know where the storm was and when the lightning would be overhead and when it had passed. It was as if she could feel it. I think she may be sensitive."

Norri was silent for a while, then he said, "Well I'm not going to report my own daughter. It might just be that she is part álfur. But she's becoming more Dwarf with every day. She might just grow out of it."

"I don't know, I've a feeling she won't. Oh Norri I won't have them take her and turn them into one of them. She's much too fragile."

"Well, if we say nothing she won't be examined officially until she enters school. She's still small and we can say she's younger than she is. It will give us time, maybe a year or two. Meanwhile I will find out for myself how sensitive she is. If I can, I will try to explain to her what it means. She is bright and, as you say, her mind is much more developed than her body. She may be able to understand the implications and then she must choose for herself."

"Oh, Norri there must be some other way. You know what the justicers are like. Every few years they perform a gathering looking for children who are fey. They take them away and persuade and indoctrinate them in their ways and the next thing that we will know is that she's become one of them. I would hate that, our little girl forced to serve the temple and spout dogma every day."

"It might not come to that," Norri said, "We still have time to teach her what she needs to know."

"I just hope you are right," Dagmar replied.

******

Einar paused again and listened for a few seconds. He'd put in those controversial stanzas about the justicers and he crossed his fingers hoping that there weren't any zealots in the audience. The generalised muttering seemed genial and he caught the phrase 'so the thing with the lightning is true'. Good, they were picking up the story. He'd got one difficult bit past them; "Better press on whilst I'm winning," he thought.

Ch 3: The Fey and the Baar

Norri began to take Brannhår with him when he went in search of materials for his projects. Sometimes he needed metal and at others he needed wood or skins. Each time he came across a new material he would explain to Brannhår what the material's properties and usefulness was. She soaked the information up like a sponge and soon she started to see where something was before Norri spotted it. Spotting mineral deposits was her speciality. On one occasion they needed copper because Norri had wanted to make bronze. Norri would have missed the green patina of verdigris because it was out of sight down a narrow moss-covered crevice in the rock. After they'd dug it out Norri had asked, "How did you see that? It was well hidden."

"Oh father, you must know. Copper twists the lightning patterns more than other metals except silver and gold," Brannhår answered.

"What do you mean, lightning patterns?" Norri asked.

"You know father, the patterns that lightning makes in the air and in the water and in the ground." Brannhår replied.

"I am sorry daughter, but I can see no patterns. Can you describe them to me?" Norri asked.

"But surely, everyone can see lightning patterns. How can you tell when a storm is coming otherwise?" Brannhår asked.

"I can tell that a storm is coming by the look of the sky and the smell in the wind. I can't see the lightning before it strikes." Norri said, "But that is ordinary. What you tell me about lightning patterns seems to be something different. Can you show me?"

"I don't know how to father, I just feel the patterns. I thought everyone can feel them." Brannhår said.

"No, my daughter I think that these lightning patterns are something only you can see. Your mother told me that you could tell where the lightning was the time you went out in the Byrjunarstormur. Is that what you mean by the patterns?"

"Sort of father, but the lightning in the sky is different to the lightning patterns in the rocks. The lightning in the sky moves but the patterns in the rocks just spin."

"Then I think that you have a wonderful gift, little one, but it is a gift that may put you in danger."

"Oh don't worry father I won't be chasing lightning again. Mother was really scared and I don't like it when she's scared."

Norri laughed, "No, I didn't mean that sort of danger. You see, there are some dwarves that have special talents like the álfur; like yours that let you see lightning patterns. Other people will try to take these dwarves from their homes so that they can use the talents for their own purposes. I know that you are young and know little of how the world is, but trust me on this. If others found out that you can find metal when it is underground then you would be taken away from us and you would be forced to find metal for them."

"But I would tell them that I didn't want to leave you and mother. I would tell them that I wouldn't find any metal for them."

"Ah, little one, these people would not give you the choice. They would hurt you until you did what they wanted."

"I would hurt them back, I don't want to leave you and mother." Brannhår said tearfully.

"And we don't want you to leave us, at least until you are ready. So you see, little one, you mustn't tell others that you can see the lightning patterns. We must keep it a secret between you, me and your mother."

"I won't tell anyone father," Brannhår promised.

"Now, let's see if you can find us some tin." Norri said.

"Oh father, you know that tin doesn't live in the ground as metal but I do know where there are some crystals. They're not far from my swimming pool. Can I watch you smelt it?"

Norri considered. Smelting and forming metals was a dangerous process and so far he'd not let Brannhår help him because smelting required strength and she still wasn't very strong. However, he considered that it may be time for her to watch him. Just to see how it was done. "I think it might be time but you have to promise me that you'll stay well out of the way. I don't want you to get hurt."

"I'll be good father, I promise."

It was getting dark by the time Brannhår and Norri returned to the cave and Dagmar had supper waiting. Norri told Brannhår that it was too late to start the forge and they would have to begin first thing the next morning. Brannhår started to protest but then she stifled a yawn. "Get some sleep, we will start fresh in the morning," Norri said.

When Norri awoke the next day it was early and he thought that he would go up to the forge before he had breakfast so that he could start warming it up for the day's work. As he rounded the turn in the path that brought the forge into view he saw Brannhår sat on a rock beside the forge door.

"You're up early," he said.

"I wanted to see it all, I want to know how you light the forge," the girl said.

"Well I'm sorry to disappoint you, there's really very little to see," he said as he unbolted the door.

Inside the forge it was dark except for a small flame that hovered in the air above a metal pipe coming out of the rock at the back of the cave. Norri went over to it and lowered a mantle onto it. As the flame heated the mantle it began to emit a soft white light and the dark of the cave was dispelled. Brannhår could see that there was a solid iron-oak bench at one side. Above the bench were racks of tools hanging from pegs and loops hung on the cave wall. At the other side of the cave was what looked like a large rock capped with an iron plate. Emerging from the plate were a series of tubes that had valves on them. The tubes disappeared into the bottom of a large stone hearth that was filled with rocks. By the side of the hearth there were a series of anvils and a stack of wooden boxes. Piled behind these was a large mound of sand.

Norri went over to the light and took something from a shelf next to it. Brannhår could see that it was a waxed taper. Lighting the taper from the flame he went over to the pipes. He turned the valve on one of them and waited. A faint smell of sulphur filled her nose and the dwarf applied the taper to the top of the rocks in the hearth. There was a soft pop and Brannhår could see small flames dancing between the rocks. He turned to her and said, "Since we will be smelting tin and copper today we will need two crucibles, I keep them in here so that they do not get damp." He went over to a cupboard that was beside the bench, opened it and took out two large stone pots that showed the marks of being heated in a flame. Norri made a depression in the flaming rocks with a long iron rod and then he settled the crucibles into it. He turned to Brannhår. "Well, that's how you light a forge. It will take an hour or so to get nice and hot and then we will open the other pipes to make it even hotter. You must be careful that you don't put too much heat into the forge when it is warming up otherwise any water that has dripped onto the rocks might turn to steam inside them and make them explode."

Brannhår was looking at him, taking everything in. He could see her mouthing the words as if she could remember them better that way, "Heat slowly or they'll explode."

"Now, let's go and have some breakfast. The hearth will be fine on its own for an hour or so," Norri said. He removed the mantle from the small flame and the light dimmed but didn't extinguish altogether; there was still the dim orange glow that was starting to appear around the rocks in the hearth.

When they returned an hour or so later the dim glow had brightened considerably and had suffused most of the rock. Norri nodded with satisfaction. He spooned the tin ore into the crucible a little at a time until it was about two thirds full. Then he went over to the valves on the pipes, he opened one all the way and then watched the rocks in the hearth. When the light coming from them became more yellow than orange he closed down the valves. He turned to Brannhår and said, "We need to roast the ore for a few hours to drive off impurities so we can leave that crucible alone for a while. Now for the copper. Since this is mostly metal rather than ore this doesn't need as much roasting. He broke up the copper that they'd found the previous day with a hammer and fed this into the second crucible. Well, we need to leave them now for a few hours. That's the thing about smelting, it's a slow process, it can't be rushed otherwise the metal will turn out bad. The next stage is to add the charcoal to the tin ore and raise the temperature." He glanced at Brannhår to see if she was listening and saw that she was staring directly into the glowing rocks in the hearth. She seemed to be fascinated by the sight. Norri said, "Don't get too close, the heat will burn you without you realising." He saw that the girl hadn't heard him and she was moving closer to the hearth. He also noticed that the flames that danced around the red hot rocks looked peculiar. Brannhår was moving her hands in a complex cats cradle pattern and he could see that the flames were following her movements. He watched as the flames built themselves into the shape of an animal, something that looked sleek and deadly, and the animal seemed to prowl around the hearth in response to his daughter's will. He wondered whether he should try to break the spell that she was under. It was clear that it was a spell of her own making but this might make his interfering with it worse. He decided that he should just watch. Perhaps five minutes later Brannhår shook herself out of her trance. She saw her father staring at her and asked. "What happened, father?"

Norri shook himself and said, "You were moulding the fire with your thoughts. So it isn't just lightning patterns that you can see. What you just did just tells me that keeping your skills secret from the world is even more important. But we can't just pretend that your skills don't exist. You must practice them until you gain enough skill to master them completely. Only then will you have the control necessary to prevent others from discovering them by accident. We will start practising the day after tomorrow when we have made the bronze and I have cast the piece for my work."

Although mountain dwarves are mostly self sufficient there were some things that were needed to make life comfortable that couldn't be obtained by hunting or foraging in the wilderness. This meant trading with other dwarves. Cloth was one of these items and it could be obtained from the dwarf village.

Norri had decided that it was time that he introduced Brannhår to the rest of dwarf civilisation and so he proposed that she accompany him into Leifbær; the nearest dwarf village. Norri had taught Brannhår to keep quiet when strangers were about and the result was that, after they left the village, Brannhår had stored up enough questions and observations about civilisation to keep a sage occupied for a lifetime. She asked them one by one on their journey home. Norri could answer most of them. Why some people did what others told them to even if they weren't family? What was money, how did it work? How so many people could live in one place and not run out of things to hunt and gather? Why had someone carved lines over all the doors?

The last question threw Norri. Of course, Brannhår couldn't read. Living as they did there was little need for reading writing or arithmetic. He'd never even thought about it but he could see that she would need to learn. He made a mental note to include reading in her curriculum. She'd also need an understanding of numbers if she was to learn about money. It would be difficult to teach her those skills whilst they were outdoors. Since they always seemed to be outdoors when he and Brannhår were together Norri decided that those particular skills should be taught by Dagmar.

He expected that Brannhår would follow in his footsteps and be content with only the basics but he was wrong. Brannhår discovered the world of numbers and she never looked back. She'd always known that some things were bigger or more numerous than others but now she could relate how much bigger in a logical fashion. It was something of an epiphany; for weeks after her first lessons from Dagmar, she could be seen counting and measuring all sorts of things. Norri treated her enthusiasm as a phase, a thing that would pass.

She didn't seem as excited by reading and writing. She learned as she always learned things; as if her mind had always known how to do them and she just needed reminding. It took her a month to learn the shapes and sounds of the words then it was as if she'd always known them. There was no need for practice and repetition. He wondered what the teachers at the school would make of her?

Winter came and Brannhår spent a lot of time in the forge. She was learning quickly but she just didn't have the strength to wield the large hammers so Norri asked her whether she would like a set of tools of her own. "Oh yes father, that would be wonderful," and Norri could see her looking around the room as if he had a secret stash of Brannhår sized tools in one of the cupboards.

"Good, now every dwarf needs his or her own tools and the best tools are the ones you make for yourself. So lets start with the basics; I'll show you how to make a knife."

Norri saw the girl's face fall, she said, "But if I have to make all my own tools then it will be ages before I can help you properly."

"Oh, you will be helping me but you will also be learning. When the snows fall we only have to go outside to gather food and fuel for the cooking fires. You will have plenty of time to make a fine set of tools. Now a knife is basically a thin piece of plate set into a handle and sharpened along one edge. Can you tell me why we only sharpen one edge?"

She thought for a moment, then said, "So that when you have to cut something tough you can press down on the back of the blade and not cut your hand."

Norri beamed, "Precisely, now some knives have both edges sharpened. Can you think of a reason…"

And so the winter passed. When the darkest days were over, Norri Dagmar and Brannhår ventured out to replenish their supplies. They had been cooped up in the cave for a fortnight by a blizzard and they emerged on a fine sunny day to find that the last howling gale had been too much for their storehouse. There was a gaping hole where the roof should have been. Some of the enterprising local wildlife had taken advantage and had made off with a deer carcass and much of the dried meat.

Norri surveyed the damage. "Dagmar and I will go and gather more food but I'm afraid that you will have to stay and fix the roof. You should be able to manage if you use some long branches as levers and you are careful and prop things as you go. I'm sure that you can do it."

Brannhår nodded. If Norri could bring down some game then they would need somewhere to store it safely. The damage didn't look too bad. She started to say as much to Norri but he was speaking, "Here's the key to the forge, you know how to use the fire in case you need to straighten anything that has bent. You have my permission to use my tools but be careful. Your mother and I will try to be back before dark but, if we're not, then leave the storeroom and get inside. We'll make our own way back and if it gets too late then we'll climb a tree and wait for morning."

Brannhår said, "Yes father but you and mother be careful. I would rather have you safe than a full belly."

Norri chuckled but Dagmar said, "Yes my darling, and we would rather have you than a brand new storeroom. So heed you father and don't take any chances; make sure you're inside before dark. We're not the only ones who are hungry after a long winter."

Brannhår spent the morning clearing away debris. One of the support beams had become dislodged from its socket in the rock and had fallen. The crossbeams and roof bearers lying on it had followed. The wooden shingles had come loose and some needed to be replaced but others would be fine for a temporary fix if they could be turned and re-laid. The main beam itself was reasonably intact however the socket in the rock had crumbled and would have to be chiselled square again. Then she'd have to make a packing piece so that the roof beam rested at its original height.

24

Chiselling the socket was hard work and Brannhår needed frequent rests to ease her straining muscles. She was using one of Norri's chisels but couldn't manage Norri's massive mallet so she was using her smaller prospecting hammer instead. She was quite proud of the hammer; it had an ash shaft with a wrought iron head. The head was a rounded hammer on one end but the other end featured a flattened taper; part chisel and part spike. It was similar to Norri's own but his was much heavier.

Brannhår had just paused after finishing a cut when she became aware of two things. The first was a massive thunderhead gathering in the sky above her and the second was that she was not alone. Someone, or something, was making plumes of white condensation emerge from a mound of boulders over to her left. The mouth appeared first, followed by a head four times the size of Brannhår's. The snout on the beast was sniffing the air and Brannhår became aware that she too could smell something. The sun had defrosted some of the remnants of the meat left behind by the nocturnal raiders. Its smell had attracted the baar that was now eyeing her up.

The baar was a young one and had probably awakened early from its hibernation. Baars were omnivores but they were big enough to dine on whatever they chose to. The ugly head rested on a thick neck and a massive chest. Long arms ended in paddle-like hands with three large claws. Its body tapered to a waist then widened again at the hips to massive thighs each thicker than the large stump that held Norri's anvil. The body and head were counterbalanced by a long flat muscular tail that ended in two vertical spikes. The powerful, multi-jointed, legs were tensed to spring.

Brannhår knew that the creature's small brain was trying to decide if the smell that had attracted it was coming from her. She moved slowly to one side so that the roof beam was between her and the baar. Her small hammer would be no use against the baar but she might be able to reach one of the steel staves that she'd been using as a lever. The creature appeared to make up its mind.

It leapt and Brannhår moved as quickly as she could under the beam and out the other side. The creature landed clumsily on the beam which promptly toppled away pivoting on the pile of shingles beneath it. As the bulk of the beam fell, its bottom end rose straight into the baar's exposed stomach. The baar bellowed its hurt to the sky and turned. Brannhår pulled the stave upright, braced one end into the earth and pointed the other end towards the enraged creature. Her only hope was that the creature would impale itself on the steel.

The baar charged and its flailing arms caught the stave and pushed it to one side. Brannhår stumbled and the baar's grasping claws snatched at thin air just above her head. She rolled and found herself under a small rock overhang. The baar lunged but it misjudged the depth of the overhang and the claws on one hand caught in a crevice. It spent a few seconds pulling itself free then it turned its back on her. The muscular tail swept around below the level of the shelf and Brannhår was thrown out of her shelter. She was out in the open and the creature's head turned towards her.

The jaws opened and she saw the glistening fangs approaching; instinctively she used her hammer. Time seemed to slow and she became aware that, somewhere nearby, a bolt of lightning had descended from a dark cloud above. She felt the lightning patterns try to twist the hammer but she wouldn't let them. Instead she used them to push the hammer forward. The hammer gained a massive amount of kinetic energy in an instant. Rather than bouncing off the baar's thick skull, the chisel-spike slammed through it and into the baar's brain. Maddened, the clawed hands tried to pull out this latest torment; but it was just reaction. The baar was already dead; it just hadn't realised it yet.

Brannhår took a few moments to recover and assure herself that she was still alive. Then the pain in her leg hit. It was trapped beneath the massive form of the baar and was being pressed onto the steel stave. Brannhår gritted her teeth and reached for another stave. Using this to lever the baar off her relieved some of the pain but it was another half hour before she felt like moving.

When Norri and Dagmar returned the sun was just setting. They saw that there had been some work done on the storeroom but there was still no roof. Their daughter was shaping the spacer for the socket in the rock. She was using a small adze but the shavings from the wooden block were flying quickly. Then they saw the baar.

Brannhår turned to Norri, "I'm sorry father but I couldn't get my hammer out. I had to use your adze to shape this block and it's taken ages. Then she seemed to fold into herself. Dagmar rushed over to her daughter, caught her up and carried her indoors. When they examined her they saw the massive bruise on her ribs with the white spots still showing where the baar's tail had impacted and the livid purple and red slice on her thigh where the stave had dug into the skin. Mercifully Brannhår was unconscious and Dagmar made a healing poultice and stewed some willow tea for when her daughter awoke. Dagmar was glad that there didn't appear to be any broken bones but she knew the pain would be bad.

By the time they had Brannhår settled it was too late to do anything about the baar or the storeroom so the dwarf couple retired to bed. They wondered what could have happened to their daughter: Even a fully grown dwarf in his prime would have been hard pressed to kill a baar single handed and he would have had to be armoured and been wielding a good weapon. The small hammer embedded in the beast's skull looked too little a thing to have killed it but they couldn't deny the evidence. There was one consolation, the meat that had been taken from the storeroom had been replenished; they'd be eating baar for weeks to come.

Brannhår slept for the whole of the next day and late into the day after. When she awoke, she asked Norri to carry her to the forge. Puzzled, he agreed and lifted her into the jury-rigged cot beside the hearth. Then he stood back to watch. Her eyes were unfocussed again and he could see the flames dancing to her bidding. Her face, that had been a mask of pain when he carried her in, had relaxed into a vague smile. A shiver ran down his spine and it had nothing to do with the freezing weather outside. His daughter was indeed fey, he just hoped he could hide the fact until she could fend for herself. He considered; maybe he should allow her to go to school and meet others. With luck she would gain some insights into dealing with other people by him registering her in one of the junior streams. The last gathering in the village had been a few years ago, with any luck the justicers wouldn't come sniffing around and discover her talents for at least a couple of years.

******

Einar could hear the approval from the audience. The tale of the baar had captured their imagination. They obviously wanted more of the same but he was determined to do the poem justice. After all, it was the history of a real person and real people didn't go around killing monsters every day. Then he smiled to himself; well maybe a few more monsters... the gods knew that the girl had had more than her fair share of battles.

Ch 4: Friends, New and Old

School started in summer and during the spring Brannhår kept to the training regime that Norri had prescribed. It had grown her muscles and thickened her bones. She'd not been idle in her other duties either. The storeroom had been repaired and Brannhår had discovered how the forge was fuelled. The cave housing the forge had a natural gas vent that had been capped and the pipes leading from the cap ran under the rocks in the hearth. It was a simple matter of opening the correct number of pipes to supply a variable amount of heat for a range of metalworking jobs from annealing to smelting. Using her senses Brannhår had detected a similar vent not too far from the home cave. She had fabricated a pipe, as Norri had taught her, and had devised a valve system to feed the gas into the cave. Dagmar could now selectively heat a large slab of ironstone along its back wall. This served as a heater in winter and as a cooker all year round. It meant that the wood they collected could be used for other things.

Norri had insisted that the baar's skull was mounted on the wall just above Brannhår's bed. They still hadn't managed to get Brannhår's hammer out of it, but Norri had helped Brannhår to make a replacement. She didn't tell him that the relic still gave her nightmares.

The weeks flew by and soon it was time for Brannhår's first day at school. The journey to the village took nearly two hours but Brannhår was adamant that she'd just get up early and travel to the school each day and back again at night; she didn't want to stay in the school dormitory.

Dagmar was pleased that their daughter wanted to come home each day and that her daughter's commute would also make it less likely that her fey powers would be revealed. On days when the thunderclouds gathered Dagmar had seen Brannhår practising with her hammer. When she thought nobody was watching she would raise it above her head and start its downward swing. Then, suddenly, it would seemed to speed up unnaturally of its own accord. It would hit whatever Brannhår was aiming at and shatter or cleave it with the power of a mighty blow; one that even the strongest of their friends could not have delivered. Invariably the action would be accompanied a few seconds later by a clap of thunder. Dagmar quickly came to the conclusion that Brannhår's fey powers were involved but when she mentioned it to Norri he said that she was merely using the energy from the lightning.

He told Dagmar that Brannhår had explained it to him. She didn't make the hammer move fast by magic she directed the power of the lightning into it. Brannhår had shown it to him one day in the summer when they had been up on the mountain. She had put an ordinary length of iron into a twisted tangle of roots from an iron-oak then she'd fixed a long branch from the same iron-oak to point up into the air. They had both watched and inevitably one of the bolts from the afternoon storm had hit the branch and he'd seen the iron bar leap into the air of its own accord. It had taken a while to come back down again. He said that he'd tried the trick himself one day when Brannhår had gone swimming and it had worked for him as well.

Dagmar had reserved judgement, perhaps it was just the lightning but Brannhår had been controlling the hammer and there hadn't been a piece of iron-oak in sight. People wouldn't discriminate, if what Brannhår did looked like magic then they would think that it was magic. She was thankful that Brannhår never used the trick when she was being observed; perhaps she'd learned something at least. Still Dagmar reminded the girl that she should never mention lightning to anyone except her and Norri.

On the first day of summer Brannhår arrived at school early, it was just as well because Dagmar had insisted on accompanying her. "Really," she thought, "What would the other pupils think if she had to be brought into the village by her mother. She had killed a baar. It was as if she couldn't be trusted to make the journey to the village on her own."

However, others turned up in dribs and drabs and she saw that most of them were accompanied by parents. One huge boy not only had his parents but several others in tow. She learned later that he was the son of the mayor of the village and the others had been the mayor's servants.

Soon a large female dwarf came out of the wooden school building nestling against the cliff-side and bellowed at them. The pupils obediently trooped inside and the various parents left to resume their duties.

The large woman told them to sit and said, "I'm going to call out your names. I want each of you to reply by repeating your name and saying 'here' ".

As each pupil answered the woman looked down at a slate and made a mark. When she called Brannhår's name Brannhår had answered but the squeak that emerged from her throat was feeble; nothing like what her voice really sounded like. Brannhår swallowed hard and said her name again. This time it came out better. When the large boy said his name it was loud and confident; "Brognar Ironfist Leifsson, son of the mayor, here." All the other pupils seemed to have no trouble with the roll call except one. She was a very tall girl with long golden hair but her voice was as soft as a whisper, "Bril Hildasdóttir here." The final 'here' was almost inaudible.

The roll call seemed to take forever. Then the teacher made them all stand, one at a time, and asked them tell the others what they enjoyed doing most. The ones before Brannhår said things like playing or hunting; one even said eating. Then it came Brannhår's turn. She stood and she could feel everyone's eyes on her. She had never felt anything like it; it was more frightening than when Dagmar was angry with her; it was more frightening than the baar. Finally she found her voice, "Learning things from my father," she said. She heard a few of the pupils whisper things some even gave a single laugh. The teacher however stifled the comments by saying, "Finally I will have someone in my class who wants to learn. Well-said, Brannhår. What have you learnt so far?"

31

Brannhår was on firmer ground now, "I have learned of ores and metals and how to smelt them. I have learned how to make tools," she held up her small hammer proudly. Then she caught herself; she'd been about to say that she'd learned about lightning but she remembered Dagmar's words in time and kept quiet.

The teacher nodded her approval and moved on to Bril. Bril said she loved to draw. The teacher asked her to show the class what she could do and the tall girl looked nervously around like a small animal seeking a way to escape and shook her head. The teacher saw and said, "Perhaps you could draw Brannhår's hammer." She motioned to Brannhår to give her hammer to the girl. Brannhår handed it over and Bril put it down on one of the desks and took up a slate. Her face became a mask of concentration as her hand flew swiftly across the surface. It only took a few seconds and the teacher came over to Bril and took the slate from her. She smiled broadly and held it up showing it to the class. The image was perfect even though there were only a few lines. Even Brannhår recognised that it was her hammer and no other.

Predictably Brognar liked hunting and fighting and wrestling. Finally the teacher had asked every pupil and she nodded approval. "You are all different, you all have your individual talents. I count no talent to be greater than any other in my class. I am not here to teach you talents. It is my job to teach you about other things that you need to know about this world. Tell me, who knows the name of the king of Svartalfheim?"

Brannhår looked around at her classmates; up to that moment she hadn't even considered that Svartalfheim would have a king. She was glad to see that hers wasn't the only frown of puzzlement. A few had raised their hands and the teacher pointed at Brognar.

He lowered his hand and looked around the room with a smug grin on his face, "Haramir is the current king of Svartalfheim."

The teacher smiled and said, "That is correct, Brognar. Now can you tell me what a king does?"

Brognar's grin faded, "He rules Svartalfheim."

The teacher smiled again, "And can you tell us how he does this ruling? I mean, after he's had his breakfast in a morning and he sets of to work, how does he do the ruling part. What does ruing involve?"

Brognar tried his best, "He tells people what to do and they have to do it."

"So, when did he last tell you to do something?" the teacher asked.

Brognar looked puzzled, "I've never met him," he said.

"So Haramir has never, in fact, ruled you?" the teacher asked.

Brognar rallied, "No, it doesn't work like that. Haramir tells someone what he wants, then they tell others, then they tell others until we get told." He nodded in satisfaction.

The teacher clapped her hands, "Let's play a game called 'telling others'. It's played like this. I will whisper something to Alis here. She must whisper it to the next person," she pointed to a boy, Hrolf, sat near to Alis, "but she isn't allowed just to say what I say, she must say it in her own way. Then Hrolf must do the same to the next person and so on until everyone in the class has spoken. Does everyone understand?" she waited but nobody said anything, "Good, now let's start."

The whisper travelled around the class and it finally passed to the last person who happened to be Brognar.

The teacher asked Brognar to stand up and say what he'd heard. "Lots of birds got killed," he said.

The teacher smiled, "Good, Brognar. Now what I said to Alis was, 'a legion of hawk warriors entered the battlefield at Gildenheim and many were killed'. Now you can all see that 'lots of birds got killed' is not the same. Just telling someone something is not good enough if they have to tell others and they, in turn, tell others. Believe me, when something is important, like telling someone to do something, then just saying it is not enough. To tell lots of people the same thing without mistakes we need something better than speech. We need writing. So my first task is to teach you all to write, and, as writing is no use without reading, I will be teaching you to read as well. Now, I believe that you deserve some time to get to know each other, you can stay here or you can go outside but I will ask you not to go down into the village. I will call you when it is time to come back so don't stray too far."

As if someone had removed some unseen net that had been holding them there, they all stood. Half of them moved towards the door and for some reason Brannhår and Bril found themselves together. Brannhår wasn't used to making small-talk so she just stood there looking around at the others. Bril, on the other hand, clearly wanted to talk. It seemed that Bril knew everyone in the class and she assumed that Brannhår would be interested in who they were. Brannhår was willing to let Bril's words just wash over her and then a loud male voice said something that caught her attention.

"Well, as if it isn't the girl with no father, or should I say, the girl with many fathers. How about showing me some of your mother's tricks."

Bril became silent and Brannhår saw that her face had become pale and her eyes were tearful. Brannhår turned and saw the speaker; it was Brognar. "Why do you say that Bril has no father? Everyone has a father and a mother. Even fiskur have a father and a mother, even trees have fathers and mothers," she said.

"You must be as stupid as her," Brognar said, "She doesn't have a father because nobody knows who her father was."

"I don't see what difference that makes," Brannhår said, "I do not know who my real father was, nor, for that matter who my real mother was. I was found by Norri and Dagmar and they have cared for me and they have adopted me. What does it matter that they did not give me birth? They are my father and mother and I am their daughter."

"Well, well, well, miss goody two shoes. Now I know you're not real. She comes to school and tries to get into teacher's favour by pretending that she is desperate to learn and showing off her pathetic little hammer. You can keep your pathetic little friend,

34

maybe she'll teach you the whoring trade. Now there's a good talent for a uteligger like you to learn."

Brannhår knew an insult when she heard one and her hand went down to draw her hammer. Then she remembered that she'd promised Norri and Dagmar that she wouldn't draw attention to herself. She kept calm and said, "If I'm so low born then why are you bothering to talk to me. What's the matter, won't your high born friends talk to you or have they finally realised where the smell is coming from."

Brognar had seen Brannhår reach for the hammer and had heard her taunt. He turned puce, "You..." He was interrupted by the sound of the teacher calling them back. "This isn't over, uteligger," he said in a low voice.

When they returned to the classroom Bril sat down next to Brannhår and said, "Thank you for defending me but you shouldn't have. He is the mayor's son and his father is very powerful. He can make trouble for your parents, he already makes my mother's life hell."

Brannhår didn't answer and the rest of the day was spent in learning basic letter shapes and sounds. Brannhår already knew these and so she didn't pay too much attention. She kept hearing Brognar's taunting voice. She knew she shouldn't pay him any attention but somehow she couldn't help feeling angry.

Things settled down on subsequent days. There were several pupils that had already learned the basics of reading and writing and Brannhår was one of these. The teacher assigned these pupils to teach the others who knew less. She said that it would serve two purposes; those who knew nothing would learn and those who knew their letters would gain a better understanding from trying to teach what they knew to their classmates. Brannhår accepted the duty without complaint but others didn't. Perhaps it was because her 'pupil' was Bril and she had grown to like the shy girl. Bril had no trouble copying the letters but she had difficulty when combining them into groups to make words. She would say 'b-i-r-d makes bird but it doesn't because it doesn't look anything like a bird' and shake her head.

Brannhår thought that she would never make progress with Bril until she hit upon an idea. "I know the letters don't look like a bird but how would you draw a bird using only the shapes of the letters, would it look something like this?

Bril gave a laugh of delight, "Oh you are funny Brannhår. Yes I could draw a bird with the letters." She took the slate and made a much better attempt.

The letters were subtly curved and Brannhår agreed that she'd done a much better job than she had, "See, the letters do make a bird after all."

There was no stopping Bril then, once she got the idea that the letters didn't have to stay the exact same shape she learned quickly. Of course Brannhår couldn't make every word a picture but she soon realised that she didn't need to. Bril's natural talents took over and soon she was staring to read without drawing, "All you have to do is look at the word and let your mind rearrange it into the picture."

Brannhår hadn't a clue what her friend meant but she mentally shrugged her shoulders; it had worked hadn't it. If Bril was better at it than she was then it didn't matter; Brannhår already knew how to read.

Brannhår was unused to getting regular breaks from chores so having breaks between lessons was a novelty. She spent the breaks with Bril and soon they were swapping histories. Bril and her mother had always lived in the village. Bril's mother did all sorts of menial work to put food on their table. She took in laundry, she chopped firewood, she mended clothes and she fed animals.

Brannhår was amazed and fascinated. She'd never needed money at home; anything that couldn't be made or foraged was unnecessary but she could understand that most people in the village used money all the time. She thought that it must be because there were so many people crammed into one place. Brannhår discovered that one of the reasons Brognar's father was mayor was that he had more money than anyone else. He had a knack of making a profit from a transaction and the more he traded the richer he became. For some reason Brognar's mother hated Bril's mother. Bril didn't know why but something had happened in the past and it had involved Brognar's father.

At first, Brannhår couldn't understand what had gone on but somewhere deep in her other memory, the memory that she thought belonged to another place, she knew what could happen between young men and young women. She looked at her new friend in this new light and she almost kicked herself. The resemblance was fleeting but Brognar and Bril did look something alike. It was something about the line of the ears and the look in their eyes. In fact Bril and Brognar had identically coloured eyes. She'd never noticed it before but now it was obvious. She filed the observation in that other memory; it wouldn't be right to say it out loud.

Bril and Brannhår had avoided Brognar during breaks and in lessons but that didn't mean that Brannhår had missed the fact that, since her encounter with him, he had started wearing a great war-hammer at his belt. He strutted around with a group of smaller boys in tow as if he was their leader rather than just their classmate.

Bril could always be counted on to have something to say but Brannhår had used the occasional lull in the gossip to tell Bril of her own history. She told her about her earliest memories, when Norri and Dagmar had found her and how they'd nursed her back to health. Bril had asked about the time before she had been found but Brannhår said she couldn't remember anything; all she had from before was the gem that had been found around her neck. She showed it to Bril and Bril asked if she could be allowed to draw it.

Of course, this wasn't part of school and so Bril said that she would have the midday meal with Brannhår and do the drawing then.

The two friends were sat on a log. Brannhår had shared some dried fiskur with Bril and Bril in turn had shared her brot with Brannhår. The red and gold gem sat on the stump between them and Bril had taken out a piece of smoothed wood and her colouring sticks. Neither of them heard Brognar's approach and so they weren't quick enough to prevent what happened next.

Brognar reached over and snatched up the gem. "Where did you steal this from? It's too good for an uteligger like you."

Brannhår swirled around, "Give that back, it is mine!" she screamed.

"Oh no, if you want this back then you will have to challenge me for it. Those are the rules," Brognar laughed.

"Then I challenge you," Brannhår yelled.

Brognar laughed again, "What! Do you really think you would stand a chance against me; a weak little thing like you."

Brannhår had gone icily calm, "I challenge you Brognar; or are you afraid?"

Brognar looked hesitant for a second and then said, "So be it," he looked around at the others, "You all heard her, she challenged me."

Obviously the other pupils had seen this sort of thing before and they formed a circle around the pair. Brill pulled Brannhår to one side, "Please don't do it, he'll hurt you," she whispered.

Brannhår shook her off gently, "I'm not afraid of him, I've killed a baar."

Bril looked shocked but she could see that her friend was serious.

Brognar and Brannhår faced off inside the circle; Brognar pulled the war-hammer from his belt and Brannhår took out her much smaller working hammer.

They circled each other for a while then Brognar rushed at Brannhår. She ran around him and he bellowed his frustration, "Stand still!"

Brannhår had no intention of standing in the way of that hammer and so, when he whirled it around again, she dodged again. She couldn't keep this up. Her body was weak and she was already tiring a little. She needed to win this but there was no lightning to help this time. Then she saw it: Brognar's war-hammer was made of iron, it had an iron head and a steel shaft. The answer was there. But then what? he'd just get even angrier. She had to choose her moment and it came sooner than she'd expected.

Brognar rushed straight at her again with the big hammer raised over his head. She put all her effort into the jump then her hammer descended down onto the head of Brognar's hammer. It hit just where the shaft had been fitted into the head. She felt the iron-oak shaft of her own hammer absorb the vibration but the steel shaft of Brognar's weapon took the full force and rang. Brannhår knew what Brognar's hand was feeling, she'd felt it herself hundreds of times when she'd mis-hit the anvil. The hammer flew from Brognar's nerveless fingers and he stumbled to the ground and lay clutching his stinging hand.

Brognar was down but Brannhår didn't go in for the kill as the excited circle of onlookers expected. She put her own hammer into her belt and took up Brognar's in one hand. She stretched out the other hand to Brognar to help him up. In a ringing voice she said to the crowd, "I honour Brognar, a valiant warrior, we have fought and the challenge is over. Brognar stumbled on a root and so I was able to prevail but this victory is not mine; the victory belongs to the earth."

Brognar was on his feet. He meekly accepted his hammer back from Brannhår and looked around at the circle of faces. Brognar was big and strong but he wasn't stupid. This tiny girl had bested him but she had said that he had stumbled and had given the victory to the earth. She had given him a way of saving face. He cleared his throat and said, "We have fought and the challenge is over. I praise the skill of my opponent and I give her what is rightfully hers." He handed back the gem, "No dwarf will take this from her again or they will have me, Brognar, to deal with." He held out his hand to Brannhår and she shook it.

He bent close to her and whispered, "That was a good trick. You will have to teach me it sometime."

And so Brognar became their friend. Soon the trio were inseparable and the eagle eyed teacher noticed. She had heard the gossip from her pupils and had deduced what had gone on but she didn't break up the little clique. The three of them complemented each other and whatever task she gave them they would complete it and, more importantly, the rest of the class would emulate them. This class was going to be one of the good ones; it made her job easier.

The formation of the trio wasn't greeted as warmly by their respective parents. Norri and Dagmar had berated Brannhår for making her presence conspicuous by picking a fight with the mayors son. They wanted her to keep a low profile in case her fey talents were noticed. Brognar's mother was livid, "I am mortified: my son, consorting with a vagabond and the spawn of the village whore." However Brognar's father didn't seem too upset and told his wife not to be so melodramatic. Bril's mother was unsure, she had tried to shield her sensitive artistic daughter from the world's reality. Having her name linked with the Mayor's son and a wild child only served to highlight her daughter's difference from other folk. She also realised what the mayor's wife would think and the mayor's wife wasn't one to forget.

The summer continued uneventfully and soon it was time for the annual kraftmoot. This meant that the various contenders tended to relax their normal duties and concentrate on their entries. Over the years the kraftmoot had become more of a village fete. Oh, the few senior makers that lived in the village took it seriously but the rest of the village looked on it as a few days when rules were relaxed and people could have some time to enjoy themselves.

Norri was fully occupied with his latest project. Brannhår had found a small vein of silver and Norri had smelted it and fashioned it into a semblance of one of the larger moons. He planned to mount this into a glassy tree that had been formed in the sand during one of his and Brannhår's experiments with lightning. Norri wanted to win outright this year and Dagmar was always chasing him to do his regular chores. Brannhår knew how important the kraftmoot was to her father and so she did extra chores to help him out. Of course everyone was so busy with kraftmoot that the school had been closed for the duration. This freed Brannhår from her daily trek to and from the village. She missed her friends but they'd all agreed to meet at the moot itself so she spent her commuting time exploring the land around the cave. She was also fascinated by the lightning and she never missed an opportunity to climb to the high peaks when a storm was due.

One day Brannhår had climbed right to the top of the mountain and she was sat under a small rock overhang with her eyes closed so that she could sense the lightning building. This was going to be one hell of a storm. "Hello, Firehair, what are you doing here? Oh, I see you've been exploring the three. Well, never mind, I am going riding the bolts again, are you coming along?"

The words had formed inside her head and some dim recollection made her think that she'd heard something like them before. Instinctively she remembered that she only needed to think the reply. "What do you mean?"

The answer formed itself in her mind again, "Ride the bolts. You know, like we did last Tyr. Come on or we'll miss it, the first one is always the best. Brannhår opened her eyes, she had a fleeting vision of a tall dancing flame and then she felt herself being drawn upwards. She wasn't afraid; somehow this was familiar. In fact hadn't the fire said they'd done it last Tyr so Brannhår gave up trying to make sense of it all. She was now in the clouds and she could sense the huge energies circling around her.

"Here we go," the voice cried and she felt herself pulled down into a particularly dense pattern of lightning. Then something happened that took her breath away. The lightning had become alive. It snaked through the thunderhead and leap to the ground and she leapt with it. As she rode the bolt across the heavens she could sense the fire creature beside her. It was laughing, obviously enjoying the ride as much as she was. She hurtled towards the ground and then there was a tremendous rush as the pattern twisted and distorted. She felt the exhilaration of the bolt as it hit solid ground; it merged with her own exhilaration and that of the creature's.

"Come on, let's go again," the voice shouted in her mind and she felt herself leap skywards again.

All too soon the storm moved on but, by that time, Brannhår was so excited that her heart was racing and her mind told her that she needed to rest. She opened her eyes and she was still hunkered down under the overhang. Sat, or stood, beside her (it was difficult to tell) was the fire creature. Its words appeared in her mind again, "That was fun. It's much better when you let go like that, sometimes you take it all too seriously. Anyway, I have to get home, mother will be waiting. I'll see you soon."

With that, there was a sizzle and a pop and the creature disappeared. The rain was pouring down and Brannhår knew that she should head back home but she didn't want the experience to end just yet. Closing her eyes again she let her mind reach out to the now distant storm. It was somewhere out towards the north west. Her mind was in a turmoil, she was sure that this had been the first time that she'd ridden a bolt of lightning but that other memory assured her that it wasn't. The other memory also supplied a name for the creature. It was a she and she was called Rakkerskap. The other memory also supplied the fact that the pair of them were old friends; they'd known each other for years.

******

The audience was silent, they were expecting more but Einar knew that soon they would get restless and start to fidget. This was a good time to stop and give them a taste of what was to come. One or two of them would sit through the whole saga without a break but the rest needed their action interspersed by comfort breaks.

When the silence had dragged on long enough he held up his hands; "My friends, What followed next in Brannhår's tale is unknown to anyone who wasn't there to witness it personally and I will not take advantage of your credibility by making it up. I suggest that we contemplate what has happened in the story so far and anticipate the story of her Menntunleit over refreshments in the bar. I will accompany you and you may ask me questions about the work. I may or may not give you answers and they may or may not be the truth," he gave a beaming smile to assure them that he was joking and they all laughed politely.

"My friends, the mead awaits, come."

Ch 5: The Best Days of Your Life.

Brannhår enjoyed school, she'd never known that there was so much to learn and everything she learned seemed somehow connected. Her teacher knew everything, of course, and Brannhår wanted it all and she wanted it now. When she discovered mathematics it was as if a whole new world had come into being and when she discovered that it could be applied to the world then she felt as though she was coming home. She explained it to Norri at home in the forge, "You know scissors," she said, "did you know that they cut best when the material is nearest to the spring?"

Norri nodded, he was cutting strips of leather to make bindings for his winter boots. "Well it's all because of levers," Brannhår announced, "You apply pressure on the blades but you have to press harder as you go along each cut." Norri nodded again. "In fact you have to press nearly twice as hard when you reach the end of the cut as at the beginning." Norri swore and licked his finger where he'd caught it in the end of the leather shears, he turned to her and said, "Yes I know about levers and I also know what happens to girls who distract their fathers when they are trying to cut leather with blunt shears." He sighed, "Levers are fine but have you considered that there is more to scissors than just levers. Yes the lever supplies the force but it is the pressure that makes the cut. Pressure is about the shape that the force is applied over. So if you hit a large rock placed on the earth with a hammer then it will only sink in a short way. However, if you apply the same force to the end of a sharpened stick then it sinks in a long way. Same force, different shapes, different effect."

Brannhår nodded, "So how can you measure the pressure and does it depend on what you use to apply it?"

"Oh, I forget. We did learn something of it at school but that was long ago. I do know that a nail will go in further than a hammer and that sharp scissors cut better than blunt ones. That's all I need to know. I leave it up to others to worry about the counting."

"Well, I think that would be an interesting worry. I'm going to ask the teacher in the morning," she changed the subject, "Maybe there will be a message tomorrow. Brognar's father may have heard from the city. Oh father wouldn't it be good if you won there as well."

Norri paused and thought, "What had possessed him to think that, just because he'd won the village kraftmoot, he stood a chance against all those folk in the city. Wasn't he playing a dangerous game with Brannhår's future with his name being known outside the places he knew? Yes, he was, but he had been so pleased with his victory; his sculpture of the silver moon in the glass tree had won first place in all three categories. He hadn't been able to resist when the mayor had insisted he enter it for the kraftmoot in the city. The mayor wouldn't have suggested it if Brognar hadn't been friends with Brannhår so it was really all down to her. In reality, he stood little chance. There were hundreds of entries in the city kraftmoot whereas there'd only been a few dozen in the village one. Nevertheless he still hoped."

Aloud he said, "Yes daughter, maybe there will be news, but that is for tomorrow. Why don't you go and see your mother, I'm sure she will have something for you to do. Leave me to sharpen these scissors and finish off this piece of leather."

The news didn't arrive the next day, or on the one after that but on the third day Brognar came into school and told Brannhår that his father had received a parcel of mail from the city and that one of the letters had the kraftmoot mark on it. Brognar asked Brannhår if she wanted to come back with him after school to see if the letter had been about her father's sculpture. Brannhår had never been to Brognar's home and she was amazed when she got there. Instead of a single cave partitioned by leather curtains this cave was not one but three caves joined together. Brognar explained that one cave was his father's and that it was where he carried out his mayoral duties. Then the second was where they lived, ate and cooked and the third cave was just for sleeping and bathing. At first Brannhår didn't believe him when he said that you could bathe in the third cave but he showed her proudly. A natural spring flowed from a hole in the roof in one corner. The water drained out through another hole in the floor. Brognar showed Brannhår the oily scented leaves from the soapwort plant in a basket tacked to one wall. Brannhår could only look on in wonder at such sophistication. She didn't bathe, she swam every day instead, but she had to admit that she wouldn't mind trying the luxury of bathing without having to walk half a mile to do it.

When they returned to Brognar's father he was looking pleased. He smiled at Brannhår and said, "Your father has been commended for a fine effort in the sculpture class at the city kraftmoot, he won third place. However, I have a sneaking suspicion that he would have got a better placing if Jephsnar's boy hadn't been competing. When Brannhår asked who Jephsnar was, Brognar's father told her that he was the mayor of the city and he spoiled his son. Brannhår thought that the same might be said of the man in front of her but Brognar was her friend and so she thought it best to say nothing.

She hurried home and she was quite out of breath when she gave Norri the news. He didn't seem as pleased as she thought he should have been and she asked him why. "Oh daughter, I am pleased. It is a great achievement to come third against all those city dwellers but it means that I will have to go to the city to receive the award. That means being away for three or four days and I don't want to leave you and your mother alone. There are still baars and other creatures out there."

"Oh father, you must go and receive your award. Mother and I will be fine here whilst you are gone." she smiled and teased him, "After all, I've already defeated one baar so mother and I should be able to handle a few more without any trouble."

He smiled, "Yes daughter I believe you could."

******

Norri arrived in the city. Unlike the village and his own home, the city was only partly underground. The inhabitants lived in houses cut into the walls of a narrow ravine and only the municipal buildings occupied the cave at the end of it. Norri found the sheer

46

cliff sides of the ravine somehow threatening and enclosed. He had arranged to stay at an inn for the two nights that he would be away. Brognar's father had insisted that he would pay for the accommodation as Norri would be doing the village an honour. Norri hadn't argued much as the cost was more than he normally saw in a month. Even though Brognar's father was paying Norri restricted himself to the basics and he was sat drinking a solitary pot of ale in the large common room when he overheard a conversation that disturbed him. Two dwarves were talking at a nearby table. They'd obviously had a few drinks too many and their voices were loud.

"It's not right, those skogs raiding good honest dwarf communities. Killing and maiming children. What's the king doing about it? I'll tell you; nothing. He's too busy pandering to his rich friends and the justicers to bother about us ordinary folks. I say we should raise an army and go and wipe those lizards out once and for all."

The dwarf sat next to him had had a little less to drink. "Lesnir, keep your voice down, you never know who might be listening."

Lesnir was having none of it, "I'll say what I want, what's the world coming to if a dwarf can't express an honest opinion. I'm a maker and I am well known. My furniture is in all the best homes. But what use will my skills be if those savages run riot and burn down our forests and kill all our livestock? Can't you understand, they were killing children and the king is doing nothing."

At that moment the door to the outside opened and a tall hooded dwarf entered. The room went quiet, even the trio of dwarves who had been singing one of the old ballads trailed into silence. Norri tried to make himself inconspicuous and watched.

The stranger said, "Peace be on all here," in a high, menacing voice. The way he said it sent a chill down Norri's spine. The drunk staggered slightly and sat down with a thump. The stranger pulled back the hood. Norri saw the tell-tale tonsure and realised two things, this was a justicer and it was a woman.

"I believe you were saying something about the king," she said to the man in a voice that dripped venom.

The drunk had sobered "I said nothing. I am a loyal dwarf," he said.

"Are you?" the justicer said, "Then you will not object if we raise a toast to the king. However, you know the old saying that a toast made in falsehood leaves a bitter taste in the mouth."

She motioned to one of the serving girls and the girl brought over a tray with four tankards and a jug of ale on it. She filled the tankards from the jug and handed them to two other dwarves seated nearby then she took one for herself and handed the last to the drunk. "Come, we will toast the king together," she said.

The drunk was now shaking but, as the other tankards were raised, his arm moved upwards of its own volition. Norri could see the muscles in the drunk's arm straining against the action. They all drank and suddenly the drunk clutched at his throat. Steam shot from his mouth and blisters appeared on his lips and cheeks. He dropped the tankard and clutched at his throat then collapsed on the floor unmoving.

The justicer said, "It would appear that the old saying is true." She raised her hood and strode towards the door, the onlookers parted and moved as far from her path as they could. The door opened and she was gone.

The drunk's friend rushed over to the fallen man. He knelt and touched him then looked around, "He's dead."

Norri decided that he wouldn't finish his ale, he would go to his room immediately. His thoughts were racing, he'd known that the justicers had become powerful but he'd never dreamed that they could kill someone for just speaking his mind. However, what surprised him even more was that nobody had tried to help the man, nobody had objected.

The next day Norri collected his award but left immediately after the presentation. He didn't stay around for the celebration, there were too many hooded figures in the audience.

He told Dagmar all about the incident when he got home. They thought that Brannhår was asleep but she had listened. She knew about killing for food and she knew about fighting to defend oneself but killing someone because of what they thought wasn't right. An echo of that other memory agreed with her.

Life settled down and the autumn came and went. School didn't continue during the winter months, children had to do their bit to keep their families fed and warm. Dagmar and Norri were experts at this and, since Brannhår's modification to the cave heating, they could concentrate on gathering food and Brannhår had more time for her own interests. She had become fascinated by the difference between force and pressure and she was determined to quantify the relationship.

Her innovation with the heating system had been adapted by Norri and a secondary pipe now supplied gas to a series of hollow pumice tubes held in a steel frame. The pumice was heated by the gas and gave off a white light.

This meant that Brannhår could spend the hours after dark drawing and calculating on her slate. Many hours were spent patiently performing experiments and making measurements and eventually she made sense of it all. She wondered how the knowledge might come in useful but it didn't concern her unduly; in later years she would coin the famous saying "knowledge will find its purpose when the time is ripe".

The winter passed uneventfully and, as spring approached, Brannhår spent much of her time outdoors. She refined her senses by deliberately seeking out unusual mineral deposits and studying all the various creatures that inhabited the high slopes. Whilst she studied she linked her knowledge together. She couldn't butcher a rabbit or fiskur without relating the positions of bones muscles and tendons to her knowledge of levers. She couldn't watch a snowmink tobogganing across deep drifts without relating it to her new found knowledge of pressure. She couldn't sense the solid patterns in the rocks without relating them to the shifting patterns of lightning in the clouds. This did not detract from her appreciation of the wonders around her, it enhanced them.

School started again and, after they had all settled back in, the teacher took Brannhår to one side. "I was very impressed by the progress you have made over winter and I want to share something with you. I have a library. A library is a collection of writings about many things. Now that you can read I think that you will appreciate what others have written. I can show you them at the midday break if you like."

At the meal break, Brannhår accompanied the teacher to her cave. It was small, because the teacher lived alone, but it was much neater than Brannhår's own home. The teacher showed Brannhår a wooden cupboard set against one wall. When she opened it Brannhår could see several scrolls and some objects that looked like square logs. The teacher took one of these out and put it on a table. "This is called a book and it's from the city."

Brannhår could see that the log was, in fact, a stack of thin yellow sheets, like skins, but very thin. She could read words on the sheets, hundreds and hundreds of them and they were about metals. Many of the words were unfamiliar but she concentrated and slowly they made sense.

"Now you can see why I started teaching you to read as soon as you started school. Reading opens up much more knowledge than I could ever give you by speaking and, because it is written, the knowledge does not get coloured by the telling."

Brannhår was hardly listening. The more she stared at the text the more it fascinated her. It was about copper and it gave names for ores and told how to smelt them and there were lots of numbers. Her other memory told her that she'd seen books before, but not just a handful like here, there was a memory of a vast cave that was crammed with them. Stacked on shelves from floor to ceiling they made up a vast collection of knowledge. She'd read lots of books, some were even on the subject of lightning. Her mind reeled at the thought and she felt dizzy. She closed her eyes trying to see the words in her mind but the memory faded and was gone. When she opened her eyes again her teacher was stood over her with a concerned expression on her face. "I'm sorry, I should know better than deprive a child of her midday meal. You appear to have fainted."

"Oh no, teacher, I am used to eating at all times. When I am foraging I sometimes miss two or three meals. No, I saw books, I remember books from the other place, the place before here."

The teacher frowned, "What do you mean child?"

Brannhår decided that she could trust the teacher, "You know that I am adopted?" The teacher nodded, "Norri and Dagmar found me in the spring four summers ago. I was weak and I was near death. They took me in and cared for me. I could not remember and I still can't remember where I was or what happened to me before they found me. My life seems to have started with them. However, although I cannot remember my own self, I sometimes recollect things and facts that I must have known from before. They are like your books, the memories are there but they need a prod to unlock them. The memories that come are glimpses of things I've seen or, I now realise, that I have read about. That was why I became lost. I remembered being in a cave full of books but that cave was bigger than a mountain. There were tens of thousands of books, maybe more, and I knew that I had read hundreds of them. I cannot remember what knowledge they imparted to me only that I read them."

The frown had deepened on the teacher's brow. What the girl had told her was impossible. She had been to the great library in the capital city on Griprey and it held maybe two thousand books. There wasn't any library on Svartalfheim that was as big as the child had described. The child couldn't have seen what she claimed. Yet she believed the child. She had been a teacher too long not to know when somebody was lying to her. There was only one explanation that she could think of; the child had the imagination of a bard. Yes, the master storytellers could dream worlds that had never existed. The child had seized the fact of her small collection of books and extrapolated it into fantasy.

For the next few days things went back to normal in the classroom but when the teacher was about to leave for the night she found that Brannhår hadn't left with the others. "May I look at the books again?" she asked, "I have told my parents that will I be home later than usual."

The teacher frowned; this was a very peculiar child. You had to force knowledge into most children's heads. She smiled at the thought; giving children knowledge was what the village elders paid her to do. It would make a refreshing change to have someone who was eager to learn

A year later she hadn't changed her mind. Brannhår had devoured all of her books. Sometimes Brannhår had stayed behind after school and sometimes she had taken books home and had returned them in immaculate condition. On one occasion Brannhår had returned a book whose binding had been in bad state only to find that Brannhår had repaired it as good as new. The child seemed to be able to turn her hand to anything. It was partly for this reason that the teacher had decided to enter her current class into the local kraftmoot.

She'd talked to the village elders and had got them to agree that they should have a special section for children. It was a struggle because a few of them realised that, although the children might not have as much skill or experience as them, they had the wit to see that children often had better imaginations. She had been unexpectedly helped by Jorell, a dwarf recently returned from the capital on Griprey, who seemed keen to reinforce old Dwarven values. He had generously volunteered to judge the children's entries and agreed that they could work in groups to make up for the lack of particular skills.

The teacher knew that the class would need a lot of time to create their entries because they would only be able to work on them during school hours. Therefore she'd already secretly broached the idea to the pupils. Not every pupil seemed keen and she let those just work on their lessons as normal. Needless to say Brannhår and her two friends were the keenest. She thought that, if the three of them teamed up, they would give the adults a run for their money. As soon as the official decision to proceed was made the class were told that they could now discuss the idea with their parents.

The teacher was amazed, every break-time she could see pupils gathered together in small groups eagerly discussing their projects. One of the conditions of the contest was that the entrants should supply their own materials and she had been proud of the way that Brognar, the mayor's son, had browbeaten his father into persuading merchants and others in the community to donate materials for the school as a whole. However this didn't deter some from going out to find materials of their own. Brannhår had arrived one day towing her cart behind her, it was full of bits and pieces of metal and leather that Norri had given her. She'd taken what she needed for her project and had given the rest to the others. Brognar had snatched up some of the longer pieces immediately.

She supervised construction of course; you couldn't let even dwarf children loose with some of the more dangerous tools like furnaces and lathes. Thankfully there were only minor cuts, burns and grazes to be dealt with and the whole construction period went reasonably smoothly. However, being a teacher, she had added an extra aspect to the projects. To encourage writing and reasoning she asked every group to document what they had done and the reasons why they had done it. For most of the groups this was the hardest part.

Finally the kraftmoot came around and she organised that each group of children would take their projects to the centre of the village. The atmosphere at the moot was usually festive however, this year, the presence of the children, and their parents, made it even more so. Jorell patiently visited each project and listened whilst the children talked. He would think for a while and stroke his long beard then he would ask questions before finally congratulating the children on their efforts.

Surprisingly Brannhår and her two friends had decided to enter the moot individually. Brognar had made a fine dagger with a keen blade and a hilt decorated with an intricate scroll pattern burned into the leather. Bril had entered a drawing of a small squirrel done in fine ink on a stretched goatskin mounted in a wooden frame. For all that it was just a few delicate lines on a neutral background the squirrel looked alive and ready to scurry away into the undergrowth. Brannhår had entered a peculiar device that appeared to be a banded box with a lever and a small cup arrangement mounted on it. The box was decorated with a snowflake and beautiful scroll patterns burned into the wood.

Brannhår wouldn't say what it was. One side could be removed to reveal a peculiar construction inside consisting of a complex series of levers and bladders and tubes. These ended just under the cup in a metal cylinder covered in goose-down with a copper rod protruding from its top.

The teacher was intrigued; she waited patiently while Jorell examined Brognar's dagger and used it to slice a piece of fiskur skin then asked Brognar how he had managed to create such a sharp weapon. Brognar explained how he'd forged the steel and he told Jorell that Brannhår had suggested that he use curved stones set at an angle to create the edge. Jorell had nodded and asked about the decoration and Brognar had told him that the design was his but that Bril had helped with the fine work showing him where to start each curve.

Jorell moved on to Bril. He gazed at the drawing for a long time and then said, "It is amazing child, I could swear it is about to leap out and run away. How did you get such fine lines and how did you manage to get the goatskin so smooth?" Bril replied that her friend Brannhår had crafted a small bladder of ink attached to a fine hollow needle that ended in a hollow whisker taken from a feather. She added that her friend Brognar had made the frame and had stretched the skin across it for her then he'd scraped it smooth with his dagger. Jorell had nodded, stroked his beard and moved on.

"And what do we have here?" Jorell asked Brannhår.

"Sir, I have a device that makes cold." She took a small flask of water from her pocket and placed a few drops into the cup. Then she pumped the lever for a while; the device made a whistling noise. Jorell watched patiently and after a minute or two the water disappeared and small crystals of ice formed in the cup.

"Amazing," Jorell declared, "How did you make it do that?"

"Well sir, I noticed that, when you want to cool hot soup, you can make it cool faster if you blow on it. The reason is not the blowing but that you move the steam from above the soup leaving space for new steam to form. My device uses bladders and a pump and part of the water to do the same thing."

"And nobody helped you with this?" Jorell asked.

"Oh yes sir. My friend Brognar made the metal cylinder that traps the cold and the fixings for the box. My friend Bril suggested the goose-down to keep the cold in and she drew the snowflake."

"But whose idea was it to make the cooling device in the first place?" Jorell asked.

"Well I suppose that the idea came from the writings of Master Grenblatt in the book 'Air in Nature' where he observed that lakes freeze from the outside edges inwards." Brannhår explained.

"And you took Grenblatt's observations and created this device?" Jorell asked.

"Yes sir" Brannhår answered.

"Well, I will say it again young lady; what you have achieved is amazing," Jorell said.

The kraftmoot went on for another day and then the time came for the judging. The pupils were all excited and they found it difficult to sit through all the speeches about the adult's projects but finally it was their turn.

Jorell climbed to the stage and took out his slate. He appeared to consult it and then said, "I now have the honour of pronouncing the winners of the children's section. We will get to this in a few moments however I would like to say a few words first.

This is the first time we have allowed children to compete in the kraftmoot and I can tell you that what I have seen makes me proud that I supported this innovation. Without exception every child that took part should be praised for their work. As adults and elders we often forget that what inspired us to become makers was the imagination that we had in childhood. I have seen more fresh ideas from these children in the past two days than I have seen from much older and more experienced adults in the big kraftmoot in the city. Some of the ideas are fanciful and would take better craftsmanship than exists anywhere on Svartalfheim to make them a reality but this didn't stop the children from trying. However, since I am the judge, I must pick the ones that I think are most worthy of merit.

Therefore I would like the following children to join me on the stage. Hagar Hagarson, Hilda Gerhasdóttir, Brognar Leifsson, Bril Hildasdóttir, Brannhår Dagmarsdóttir."

There was a short pause as the named individuals made their way to the stage. When they were stood next to Jorell he said,

"Hagar Hagarson, I judge your group the best in leather-work for your fine saddle." There was applause from the audience and Hagar's parents applauded the loudest.

"Hilda Gerhasdóttir, I judge your group the best in needle-work for the beautiful tunic you made." There was applause from the audience and Hilda's parents applauded the loudest.

And last I come to the winning group. However the members of this group each created an item that is worthy of mention. Brognar Leifsson I judge you individually best in metalwork for this magnificent dagger," This time the applause was much louder and Brognar's father could be heard above it all shouting 'My son, my son'.

When the applause subsided a little Jorell went on, "Bril Hildasdóttir, I judge you individually best in art for your magnificent drawing of the squirrel." The applause swelled again and crested at a higher point than before.

"And last, Brannhår Dagmarsdóttir I judge you individually best in creativity for making a snowflake in summer."

The applause swelled and went on for quite a long time before it began to subside. Jorell held up his hands and the audience quietened.

"Yes, yes, these three are a group of talented individuals, however when I interviewed them about their projects I judged them also to be talented dwarves. Why you might ask? ...I'll tell you... Whilst each of them is a superb craftsman in their own right, none of them took more credit for their achievements than was their due and each acknowledged the other's assistance in achieving their goals. This shows the true spirit of the group and it aligns perfectly with the true spirit that is the ultimate aspiration of Dwarf-kind. I ask you to raise your voices again in praise of these future masters of kraft, true friends and fine dwarves."

The applause became frantic and, from their vantage point on stage, the trio could see the glee on everyone's faces. Only Brannhår noticed the sharp look that Brognar's mother gave when she saw her husband enthusiastically hugging Bril's mother in front of the whole village.

The following week at school was an anticlimax. Inevitably the three friends suffered sarcastic remarks for a few days about them being 'true dwarves' but these subsided after a while because none of the three would rise to the baiting. There was only one incident when an older boy tried to steal Bril's drawing pen but Brognar stepped in, his face a mask of divine retribution and the boy apologised and gave Bril her pen back.

Time flowed and years passed. Brannhår corresponded with Jorell who was a font of knowledge about technical matters. He could often be seen deep in conversation with her, the pair of them sketching ideas and scribbling numbers on their slates. It was Jorell who first told Brannhår about the new steam engines that had been developed in the cities to pump out underground workings. He also taught her how people were trying to adapt the same engines to power ships. Brannhår was vaguely aware that she'd known about these things from before but it was as if she had forgotten it until he'd brought the subject up. It was part of that other memory.

Brannhår didn't neglect her parents though and she learned everything that her father and mother could teach her. In particular she worked at the forge using skill and dexterity to make up for her lack of innate strength, until the time that Norri declared her to be 'as good as some masters at fine work'. This was high praise indeed.

When she wasn't at school, at Jorell's, reading any and every book she could get her hands on, or in the forge, she did what the other children did; met with her friends, gossiped, got into scrapes and generally had a good time. She also had a fourth friend, the mysterious old/new friend known as Rakkerskap. Rakkerskap never seemed to want to play with Brognar or Bril and, strangely, Brognar and Bril never expressed any interest in meeting Rakkerskap. Of course Brannhår found it difficult to describe some of Rakkerskap's games to the other two without the explanation seeming too fantastic to be real; like riding lightning or travelling to different worlds that were here but in a slightly different direction than the others were used to. Also Rakkerskap never seemed to be around when the other two were there. Brannhår suspected that they thought that Rakkerskap wasn't real and that she'd just made the mysterious creature up straight out of her imagination. However, they humoured her fancy because she was their friend.

However childhood doesn't last forever. The three friends knew that shortly their lives would change. It was almost time for them to face the Menntunleit.

Norri had explained the process to Brannhår:

"When a young dwarf is ready to move from being a child into the adult world they traditionally test their skills in a task of individual survival. In theory, the dwarf goes out into the wilderness and they have to survive on their own for a period. They are only allowed to take with them a set of clothes appropriate to the season, a flint and steel to make fire and a leather skin to provide protection from the elements. They can to choose two extra implements to make their task a little easier and they are also required to take along a scrying crystal.

This crystal is operated by the justicers and monitored by the elders of the child's village. It allows the child to contact help during any emergency and also to give periodic reports on their status. Failure of a child to report in automatically sets in motion a search and rescue. Mostly the child remains in the general area where they live and they camp out for a few days. Sometimes they find food but often they go hungry and subsist by eating raw browth tuber and drinking water until the Menntunleit is over."

Ch 6: Menntunleit

Einar watched from the wings as the audience filtered slowly back in. He was trying to judge their mood from overheard snatches of conversation. However, all he learned was that the mead had tasted a bit watery; he'd have to have a word with the caterers but he was due on in a few seconds. He grabbed the stage manager and issued some instructions, "Tell Agnar on the bar that if he's watering down the mead there's going to be hell to pay." Business over, Einar strode out to a polite measure of applause.

"Know this, all who are gathered here that the years between Brannhår's youth and her adulthood are shrouded in mystery. There are few that will tell tales and so we must rejoin our story at the trial of life that all dwarves must pass through; the Menntunleit. The audience quietened and he began.

Brannhår stepped ashore from the longship and waited as men threw down her meagre belongings. She had chosen to spend her Menntunleit on Skogrey an island to the south. This was slightly unusual because it was a long way from her own home on Valdirey but her sponsors, who now included some of the best minds in Svartalfheim, had browbeaten their richer friends into coming up with the money for her passage. The Valdirey justicers hadn't been happy and one, in particular, was very unhappy. Brannhår's choice had meant that a justicer had had to travel to the island with her to monitor her progress. The justicer was not in a good mood, he was a poor sailor and he was sat on the dockside, with his head in his hands, waiting for his own possessions to be unloaded.

When he finally raised his head the longship was pulling away from the wharf and he saw a group of men coming down the hill towards the dock. The person in the lead was a fellow justicer; he could tell from the robes. There were others who danced attendance on the figure but he also saw that there was one dwarf at the back of the group that looked out of place. The group approached and he saw the lone dwarf split off from the rest and circle around to where the girl was seated. Then the justicer in the main group was in front of him and she was saying something and he lost interest in the girl.

"Justicer Harald, welcome to Skogrey. My name is Justicer Ulagrth, I will get the servants to take your things up to the temple later but, for the present, allow me to invite you to refresh yourself at the meeting house just at the top of the beach."

The woman, Ulagrth, looked around, "I take it that the pest of a girl that requested this Menntunleit is that creature over there. I would send a servant over to her but I see that Lars has beat us to it. Well, never mind, if he wants to look after her then who am I to argue?"

Harald was still feeling a little queasy and nothing was further from his mind than food. Nevertheless, at least the earth had stopped wobbling under his feet so he thought he might manage to climb up to the building if only to get out of the glare from the water. He nodded and stood and the group moved off up the beach.

Brannhår looked at the stranger who had greeted her. He'd introduced himself as Lars and she could see that he was a smith. His arms were gnarled and blackened with the iron dust from the forge and his hands were covered in tiny burn scars. He'd told her that he'd known Norri in their younger days but that he'd not seen his old friend for many years. He shouldered her pack, even though Brannhår insisted that she could manage, and they set off in a different direction to the other group. An hour later they arrived at Lars's shack that was built into an overhang between the walls of a narrow gorge. His forge was built into the walls of the gorge and it was in a considerably better state of repair than the shack.

When they were settled, Lars offered Brannhår some broth and he sat opposite her, "Well, child. Whatever made you request Skogrey for your Menntunleit? Surely there are better places on Valdirey, they'd be nearer your home and your family."

"Sir," Brannhår began but Lars interrupted.

"Call me Lars or smith, I need no other name or title. Sir makes me feel ancient and I'm not in my grave just yet."

Brannhår nodded, "Smith, I have come to this island precisely because it is not my home. I could have made my Menntunleit nearer home but I felt that I knew so much about my own home that I would learn more and it would be a greater challenge if I went to a place that was totally unfamiliar."

The smith nodded, "A laudable ambition but to be completely new you would have to go to the southern continent of Suðurúrgangur. Skogrey may not be Valdirey but there is still browth in the water and it is still infested with fiskur."

"Ah, but, on Valdirey we don't have skogs or many álfur." Brannhår replied.

"You want to steer clear of skogs. They are not the sort of folk who welcome strangers. As for álfurs, they are rare things even here. I've never met one in the wild," Lars said.

Brannhår decided not to tell the smith about Rakkerskap. Not that she was an álfur. As far as Brannhår could tell, the fire spirit was something else altogether. Still, she wanted Lars's approval of her choice and so she said, "It will still be exciting to explore a new place. At home I know where to go for things, here I will have to discover."

Lars smiled and shook his head, "I wish I was fifty years younger and I had a tenth of your enthusiasm. Then I'd have joined you and we could have explored together. As it is, I am only allowed to give you shelter for the night. Tomorrow you must enter Menntunleit proper and you'll be on your own. Now, I suggest that we have an early night and make an early start tomorrow. I'm sure that the justicers will have all sorts of things arranged to waste your time. If you arrive early they might not be prepared and they will have to cut corners; that will at least save you sitting through one or two boring sermons."

The next day they both set off just after dawn which meant that they arrived at the temple before breakfast was over. Lars parked Brannhår at a seat in the refectory and told her to 'stock up' as she might have a long wait until her next meal. He went to seek out the officials and tell them that he had Brannhår with him.

Brannhår helped herself to slices of toasted brot smothered in honey and found that she wasn't the only youngster there. There were a trio of apprentice justicers sat together: curious, she went over to their table.

"May I join you," she asked.

A scrawny blond-haired boy looked her up and down and then said, "Are you here to join the temple? You look too old. What powers do you have?"

"I have no powers," Brannhår lied.

"Oh, a savage then," the boy answered, "I might have guessed. You're the one that has all the elders in a tizz. Anyone would think that you were related to the king. So are you?"

Brannhår frowned, "Am I what?"

"Related to the king stupid," the boy said.

"No, I'm the daughter of a maker. We have a small cave and forge on Valdirey."

"Ah, so you **are** a savage then," the boy said, "then the answer is NO, you cannot join us. Go and eat your swill with the other commoners." He raised his eyebrows and smiled a smug smile at his companions; they sniggered.

Brannhår went back to her original table and sat down. She didn't like the boy's rudeness or the way that he seemed to hold court over his cronies. She concentrated on her food and waited for Lars. He arrived with another man wearing the tell-tale robe of a justicer. Brannhår noticed that it wasn't justicer Harald and it wasn't only because he had a broad smile on his face. She looked across at the other table where the apprentices sat and noticed that they had their heads together talking. Suddenly there were laughs and collective expressions of glee. Obviously they thought the situation funny.

The justicer with Lars didn't seem to notice. He was a fat man with ruddy cheeks and a genial expression on his face and he introduced himself in a breathless sing-song voice, "Hello, you're Brannhår, I'm Brother Kerian. Welcome to Skogrey. I've been speaking to Lars here and we've made all the arrangements... Oh, is that toast going spare... would you mind if?" he nodded at the plate of toast that stood in the centre of the table.

Brannhår waved her hand, "I assumed it was for anyone."

Brother Kerian pounced on the pile and came back with two pieces, one in each hand. He offered one to Lars who took it and thanked him. Then he stuffed the other in his mouth. If Brannhår thought that this would stop his talking she was quickly proved wrong. It was almost as if the priest had two separate throats, one for eating, the other for talking. "I've arranged for your knapsack to be transported to the temple. Apparently the rules say that you have to start from there. Lars and I have made sure that you have all the necessary items plus the string and the water bottle that you requested as your specials. I'm going to be on the team that monitors you. I've drawn the night shift but I'll be around most of the time except when I'm down at the mission," he saw her puzzled frown, "I can see you're puzzled. I run a mission that looks after people who have been injured in accidents or who are old and can't manage too well any more. Sister Alicia, bless her, does what she can but she's not as young as she was and so I find that it takes up quite a lot of my time. I belong to a sect of the justicers called the Oatsmen, we believe that justice should be tempered by mercy and that all life is due respect. I'm afraid our sect is not that popular with my fellows but it's what you believe that counts, isn't it?"

Brannhår was trying to take it all in but she decided just to agree, "Yes sir," she said.

The sing song voice started up again "Oh, I'm not a sir, just call me Kerian, or brother. Lars will accompany you to the temple but I'm afraid I must be off; got to be there before you arrive, don't you know. Now, is there anything I can do for you before I go?"

"No, thank you brother. I am glad that you will be on watch." Brannhår said.

The fat man jumped as though he'd just remembered something, "Silly me, I nearly forgot," he paused and fished in his pocket and drew out a necklace made from some dull grey metal that had a sparkling crystal attached to a ring on its end. "This is your locator, it tells us where you are at all times but it will also allow you to speak with us if you need to. All you need to do is hold on to it and speak. Someone will be listening and will answer. You can use it anytime even if all you want is to talk. There's many a youngster who just needs a boost in confidence to get them through. I think that's all, I must be off. Justicer Ulagrth gets really irritable if people are late."

He bustled off and Brannhår turned to Lars, "Brother Kerian is about the only one of them I'd trust. He seems to genuinely care for those he tends," he said, "But he is right, we'd best be off."

He led Brannhår through a series of corridors and out across a courtyard. Several people were waiting on a raised dais in one corner. They were surrounded by small clusters of family groups most with one or two youngsters and a set of parents. Brannhår and Lars joined them. While they waited for one or two stragglers Brannhår looked around. Most of the youngsters looked to be about her age or maybe slightly older. Then the audience quietened and Justicer Ulagrth stepped forward. "Friends, we are gathered to launch our children into the next of life's voyages. Menntunleit is not just another ceremony or another life test. It is the gateway through which we all pass to move us to the adult world."

He gestured and the youngsters all moved to one side, Brannhår moved with them, then he turned to address them "Over the next few days you will be on your own, you will have to gather your own food, make your own comfort and have only yourself for companionship. For some it is a time of individual reflection and contemplation on the fact that ultimately we are all alone. However it is also a time of learning when we discover what we can do with our own resources."

He then turned to address the parents, "It is my duty to oversee the Menntunleit and to ensure the safety of all involved. Rest assured that myself and my colleagues will be there to support your children. We will be transporting them to their various drop-off locations and will collect them at the end of their Menntunleit. Of course, if they need to come away sooner then we will be there to help."

He turned back to the youngsters, "Will you now follow Brother Kerian to the wagons. Each of you will find their packs already loaded on their wagon. Good luck to you and I hope that your Menntunleit is a successful one."

That appeared to be that and Brannhår went with the group following Brother Kerian. Her pack was at the bottom of a pile on the lead wagon so she climbed aboard. The caravan set off and gradually, over the day, other wagons fell behind and by the end of the afternoon there was only the one that she was on. They had started with six of them aboard but now they were down to three. The countryside had changed from the rolling dunes of the coastal region to the wooded foothills of some low mountains. The smygl pulling the wagon plodded on up the shallow slope, gradually climbing higher and higher.

Brannhår looked at her two companions, one was large like her friend Brognar and the other quite ordinary but they were silent and obviously engrossed in their own thoughts. The wagon dropped them off near to a stand of iron-oak and, while they unloaded their packs, Brannhår took the opportunity to stretch her legs. She hadn't gone far when she chanced across a fallen tree that had been blasted by lightning. She pulled several broken stems from it and examined them. One of them would suit her purposes exactly, it was about a the length of her forearm and it had a twin branch about a hand-span long at its tip. There were several larger branches and she took them back to the wagon. The boys were about to set off when she returned and she offered the spare branches to them. One of them looked down his nose at the gift but the other accepted with a muttered word of thanks. The waggoner was impatient to be off and he scowled and shouted to Brannhår to get on board. She climbed on the wagon and, as it set off, she looked behind to see the two boys set off in opposite directions. Soon a curve in the track hid them from sight and she looked ahead. She had chosen her destination by consulting some maps of Skogrey in her teacher's library. She'd wanted a place where she could feel comfortable for the first night and so she had looked for a spot that seemed to be like home. It wasn't far from where the wagon had dropped the boys off and so she reckoned that she had maybe an hour of so of daylight before she needed to make camp.

She was sheltering from a light rain when she felt the crystal stone hung around her neck tingle. A voice sounded out of thin air; it was brother Kerian, "I'm just checking that everything is well. I will try and check with you at about this time every evening but, of course if you need help than you can just call at anytime. Is everything well?"

She didn't know how the device worked so she just spoke back as if she was next to brother Kerian, "I am fine, I've made camp and I will sleep shortly. Thank you for checking."

"You're welcome, Sleep well." The tingling in the stone ceased and Brannhår assumed that he'd gone.

She did sleep well despite her first night being interrupted by unfamiliar sounds as the local wildlife investigated the newcomer. The experience went both-ways. When she awoke at sunrise on the next day she knew that there were a pack of ground martens in the neighbourhood and there'd been something larger that had frightened them away. She'd also heard the familiar sounds of tree frogs and fledermaus in their competition to be first to decimate the insect population.

She rose and packed her meagre equipment away then, as she had no food for breakfast, she set off. The landscape looked little different to that at home and so she followed a small brook upstream until she came across a pond. There was some browth tuber in the shallows but a writhing just below the surface told her that there were snakes. She picked up several rocks and threw them expertly. The writhing turned to a frantic threshing of the water which subsided after a while. Gathering some tuber before the snakes returned she filled her water bottle then stowed it in her pack. Next she needed to explore; she left the brook and set off in the direction of something metallic that her senses had detected. The metal was hardly worth the name, it was a thin vein of iron ore crossing the surface of a large boulder. She couldn't see where the boulder had come from; there were no cliffs or steep slopes nearby and so she reasoned that it would be fruitless to try to search out any parent vein.

Just after the sun had reached its zenith she encountered a larger pond. The shallows contained more browth but it was a different variety to that she'd gathered earlier. There were no signs of snakes but she detected several fiskur swimming amongst the tuber's fronds. She took the string from her pack and tied a few stones into the corners of her waterproof cover. When she was satisfied with her handiwork she tried her remaining length of string to the centre of the construction.

With a practised movement she spun the fish trap though the air and out over the browth. She then pulled the middle string slowly and carefully up. A few of the fiskur managed to escape but a couple were entangled in the covering. Brannhår made short work of them with a rock. She scraped the meat from their skeletons with a small sharp rock and tied the skins across her pack so that they would dry out as she walked.

That evening she made camp early and lit a fire using a dry-looking wood that she was unfamiliar with. She took the fiskur meat and browth out of her pack and laid it on a flat rock that she'd positioned at one side of the fire. Soon she had a good, hot, meal to enjoy and, as she ate, she looked at the heavens. The stars were the familiar ones that she knew from home but they were a little higher in the sky. Her gaze returned to her surroundings and she noticed that the hill to the west was still outlined by the last rays of the twilight. However, the silhouette didn't look right; it was too regular and she fancied it looked a little like one of the pictures that she'd seen in a book; a building that wasn't part of the rock. She had her goal for the next day. When brother Kerian checked in a little while later she didn't mention the building and afterwards she settled down to sleep.

Ch 7: The Hammer of the Gods

The next day she set off. As she walked she gathered some of the tough brambles that grew everywhere. You could strip off the thorns by using a forked stick and the iron-oak stick she'd found on the way up was ideal. She wove the neutered bramble stems into a rough open basket. Her makeshift fish trap had done well enough but it meant that her shelter had been damp. As she climbed higher, the nights would get colder and sleeping under a damp cover was not recommended. It was late afternoon when she reached the peculiar formation. It consisted of huge blocks of stone that had tumbled from somewhere higher but she couldn't see where from. Then she realised; the blocks hadn't tumbled from above they'd tumbled off each other. She was indeed looking at the ruins of some ancient building but apart from a scattering of animal bones it looked deserted. Camping a short distance away in case whatever had eaten from the bones was still around, she spent some time lashing a kidney-shaped rock to her forked iron-oak stick to make a primitive hammer.

Brother Kerian's call was later than she'd expected that evening: the sun had gone down and it had been full dark for over an hour. He apologised and told her that one of her fellow candidates had had an accident and fallen. They had had to organise a rescue and that's why his call was late. Brannhår assured him that she was all right and said that she was going to get some sleep. She didn't say anything about the building and she slept the sleep of a hunter; one ear alert and hearing every sound. However, nothing came near enough to disturb her.

The next day she breakfasted on the last of the food in her pack and then took her improvised hammer and the basket she'd woven down to a pond that she could see a little way off. She moulded the basket into a fish trap and set it in the shallows; holding it fast in the outlet of the pond by hammering in a few crossed poles taken from the scrubby undergrowth. With any luck she'd be able to replenish her food supply in the afternoon without too much effort.

Then she climbed back to the building. As she neared it she again detected metal but this time it wasn't the fuzzy sensation of ore, this was the sharp tone of worked metal.

The sensation was coming from the rear of the structure where a tumble of stones were piled against the bank. She searched around for a lever of some sort and found a long stout willow branch. It bent alarmingly when she tried to move the first rock but as the compacted earth around it fell away the branch held and the stone moved; she let it roll a little way down the slope. The rest of the stones didn't present any trouble and a half hour later she had excavated a channel through the rubble. As she'd worked she began to realise that the stones were covering a small opening in the rock. She widened the hole until it was large enough for her to scrabble through to the cave behind.

The cave was pitch black but she reckoned that nothing too large and dangerous would still living in there because it had been well sealed. Anything smaller, such as snakes, would have fled while she excavated. She used her flint to set fire to some dry grass and then poked a stick from an oil-vine into it until it caught fire. The flame was reddish and smoky but it would be sufficient to give her some light. She entered the cave.

As her eyes adjusted from the bright sunlight outside she began to make out shapes. The skeleton was slumped at the base of the far wall, it's knees were raised to its ribcage and the skull rested against the wall. She could see that the metal she'd sensed was the armour that it had been wearing. The skull revealed the probable cause of death. A thin, sharpened, iron-oak wand was protruding from one eye socket. She looked around the rest of the cave but it appeared to be empty.

Norri had warned her about disturbing the dead. Tradition had it that, when a dwarf died his or her spirit had several choices. It could move on to one of the warrior realms or afterlives or it could haunt its burial place. Some ghosts just moaned and made noises but others became Draugr; malevolent zombie wizards who hated anything living.

Brannhår had been taught what to do. If the spirit was a Draugr she was to run and not return, if it was just a ghost, she had to be polite when addressing it and leave it in peace. This skeleton appeared to be neither Draugr nor ghost and so she assumed that the ancient warrior had left for his own afterlife. This was fortunate as the warrior would have no further use for his armour. Nevertheless she remembered Norri's advice about being polite.

"Oh noble warrior, I am sorry to disturb your rest but I have need of a part of your armour to help me with my Menntunleit. I intend to use it to make a hammer. I will always respect its origins and its original owner. I trust that you will grant my request as you appear to have no need of armour in your present being."

She waited, not quite knowing what to expect, but nothing happened. After a couple of minutes she reasoned that she had been correct: the ancient warrior no longer had any interest in the armour and so she could use it in her plan.

She examined the armour; it's leather straps were mostly gone and the breastplate fell away at her first touch. It disturbed the delicate balance of the rest of the tower of bones and the whole thing disintegrated into a pile of fragments. The skull rolled to one side and revealed that it had once worn a helmet. Scraggly strands of dessicated hair were entangled in what remained of the leather skullcap and its mail covering. The breastplate was too large and cumbersome for her purposes but the mail covering and the double ridge-plates on either sides of the helmet would suit just fine. Her oil-vine light was nearly spent so she tugged the helmet from the skull and crawled back outside.

Back in the bright daylight her trophies didn't look as good as they'd done in the cave. Inevitably water had seeped in over time and a good half of the mail was rust. The ridge plates were better, the rust only covered their surface and, because they had been worked, it looked like a few blows with a hammer would turn them into something useful.

She set to work; gathering clay from around a small spring that emerged from the fallen blocks, she fashioned it into a rough bowl. Then she was distracted by the sound of a commotion coming from the pool below. She ran down and was amazed to see that a large fiskur, one of the ones with a squat body and long neck had decided to take advantage of the ready meal that had been caught in her basket trap. Its head had become stuck in the trap and it had pulled the woven contraption free from its anchors. It was honking in rage at the encumbrance and was thrashing around. The rows of needle-like teeth in its jaws were trying to chew through the weave but the fibrous stems of the briar merely jammed between the teeth fastening the creature even tighter into its woody hood.

Brannhår knew that, if the beast managed to shake the hood free, it would become even more dangerous; there was nothing for it. Approaching the thrashing creature from behind she hit the base of its long neck with her hammer. Immediately the long neck slumped to the ground and the thrashing ceased. The creature was dead but she didn't take any chances and gave the neck a couple of extra blows with the hammer until it severed from the body. The bulbous body was about an arms-length long and half that in diameter. She looked on the bright side: she might have lost her fish trap but she had enough meat here for many days, especially if she could dry it. The creature was too large for her to drag back up to the ruins so she went back to retrieve her equipment and finds and brought them down to the pond. A few hours later, using one of the ridge plates as a scraper and her hammer as a maul she had butchered the reptile into useful pieces. She climbed a tree and hung the strips of flesh and skin to dry. The scent would attract predators but the meat would be safe in the thin branches from the larger ones.

She extricated the head from the entangling basket and examined it. It was half the length of her forearm and it tapered from a smooth rounded dome at the back to a narrower, conical muzzle at the front. Its eyes looked directly forwards from hooded pits above the muzzle. The jaws were lined with a triple rows of razor sharp teeth. Despite its size it was quite light. It might make a good trophy but Brannhår had other ideas. She found a nest of ants and put the head and neck at its base. Within seconds it looked as if it had come alive again as the ants accepted their free meal.

She did no more exploring that day but she went further up the mountain to seek out a stand of iron-oak and then onwards to find a place where lightning was likely to strike. The storms called Byrjunarstormur always carried lightning and she'd observed that the dark thunderheads nearly always congregated on the lee side of mountain peaks. She found the clearing, it had been blasted by quite a few bolts in its time and there was little vegetation left. She smiled to herself; she had what she needed and so she returned to her camp to feast on roasted fiskur and the ubiquitous browth. When Brother Kerian called sometime later she told him that she had caught a fiskur and had eaten well. She still hadn't mentioned the ruins nor did she tell him of the dead man's skeleton that she'd found. She'd save that tale until she was less tired.

There was a heavy feeling in the air when she awoke the next day. Today would bring the Byrjunarstormur. She had a lot to do. Her meat store had fared reasonably well. Insects had feasted on the strips of skin and fledermaus had feasted on the insects. The larger portions of meat had shrivelled somewhat but they were still edible. The ants had finished their work and had moved on to more juicy fare: the skull of the fiskur was white and pristine in the morning sun. Picking the skull up she saw that the spherical end-cap would make a fine crucible for her experiment. The eye sockets and other apertures would also come in handy as handles and anchoring points. The clay that she'd excavated had become less mushy and it would hold everything together nicely.

Keeping an eye on the weather she set off. As the morning became afternoon she looked down at what she'd constructed. The fiskur skull was now shrouded in a ball of clay. The inside of the skull contained all the mesh and most of the rusty parts of the mail helmet. One of the ridge plates had been slotted between the two bones that tapered to the front of the muzzle. Protruding from the base of the ball was a thick stem of iron-oak. It had been inserted into the hole in the skull where the beast's vertebrae had emerged.

74

Two, thinner, iron-oak stems emerged from the eye sockets and these were held in place by more clay.

 She looked around for a likely spot and took her construct over to it and poked the thick iron-oak neck into the ground. She then proceeded to build a cage of iron-oak stems around the whole thing. She had to judge it right; too thick a covering would divert most of the lightning's energy: too thin and the lightning would blast the whole thing apart. When she was satisfied she retreated to the shelter of the slope and waited. She closed her eyes and could feel the storm building above her.

She was almost lost to the world when she felt the first bolt strike. It had hit somewhere further up the slope but the storm was just flexing its muscles. The next stroke hit home. As she followed its path down she could feel that it was headed towards her experiment. It hit and she had a fleeting vision of the fiskur skull outlined in actinic light just before the wave of sound hit her. After the electric tension in the air dwindled she hurried over to her experiment. The outer covering of iron-oak stems had been scattered to the four winds and the curious clay ball had split and fractured into a dozen pieces but her eyes were fixed on the object beneath. The skull looked like a demon from hell. It was glowing white hot except where the black iron-oak plugs emerged from the eye sockets. Small arcs still danced across their surface making them look like some living thing. There wasn't a moment to lose. She emptied the cape full of coarse sand that she'd gathered right over the glowing mound and then she ran around the clearing stabbing iron-oak branches willy-nilly into the ground. Just in time she crested the rim of the clearing as she felt the tension building again and she pelted for cover from the torrential downfall that came next.

It was another hour before the storm moved on. It left behind a bright blue sky and a steaming tangle of vegetation. Brannhår went to retrieve her experiment. She had her fingers and toes crossed as she scraped away the covering of sand. Underneath, and still too hot to touch, she could see that the skull had cooled to a shiny metallic grey-orange. It made pinging noises as various flakes of scaly sand and clay broke from the surface. It was probably cold enough now to quench so she hurried down to the pond and filled her water bottle then ran back. There was a hiss as the water hit the surface but this quietened after a few seconds. She continued to pour water over the heap until it ran out.

The surface of the skull evaporated most of the water within twenty seconds but Brannhår couldn't wait any longer. She poked the lump with a stick until it rolled free of the detritus and then she examined it with all her senses. She'd wanted the skull to act as a crucible to contain the molten metal from the mail helmet but she saw that that hadn't happened. Instead the bone had fused itself with the metal and created a glassy-looking replica of the skull itself. When it had cooled enough she set about cleaning it up using her remaining steel side plate to lever off clinging bits of fused clay The iron-oak stems plugging the eye sockets fell out. The layer of sodden charcoal had given way leaving two gaping holes. The thick iron-oak pillar plugging the neck had also suffered. Its surface had mostly burned away and when she managed to extricate it from the skull she saw that it left behind a peculiar ridged hole lined with bright metal.

An hour later she stopped her cleaning and looked at what had been revealed. In front of her, in the fading light, was the metal and bone head of some new, strange type of fiskur. It had no eyes or skin but the prominent rows of teeth were still visible along the jawline and it had acquired a sharp ridge along its muzzle that ended in a turned up spike. It felt lighter than it looked, just as the original skull had, but Brannhår examined it with her other senses. It wasn't quite metal and it wasn't quite bone. There were hollow tubes running through the metal matrix that were filled with fibres of some sort of ceramic. The whole outside surface was a mottled layer of very hard oxide cemented together by a matrix of metal filaments. The filaments mingled with the ceramic fibres in the layers below until the core became a three dimensional matrix of metal-covered bone.

It was better than she could ever have wished for. Here was a tool worthy of any dwarf. She couldn't wait until the next day when she could seek out yet another piece of iron-oak for the shaft.

She cleaned herself up and then realised how hungry she was; she'd not eaten or drunk anything since her hurried breakfast. She gathered up her trophy and set off for her camp.

Ch 8: The Ancient Battle for the Planet

That evening, when Brother Kerian called to check on her she couldn't contain herself any longer. She told him of the ruins that she'd discovered and about the skeleton then she proudly announced that she'd managed to make herself a tool from the remains of the man's armour. The Oatsman seemed very impressed nonetheless. Some of the other candidates had started to tire of their wilderness life and had requested that they be allowed to return home. He asked whether she had had enough but Brannhår told him a firm no: she was quite happy as she was. Kerian said that he understood but warned her that she shouldn't stay out too long as there was a limit to the length of time that Justicer Ulagrth would be prepared to send out transport to collect her. She assured him that she was fine and then signed off. Despite the excitement of the day she fell asleep quickly but she was awakened in the middle of the night by a drip that had developed in the centre of her waterproof canopy. Moving the canopy and re-folding it didn't seem to help. The drip persisted and seemed to find the crack between her collar and neck irresistible. She didn't sleep well after that.

A dull overcast sky heralded the next morning. It wasn't raining but the clouds looked threatening. Brannhår gathered all her things together. There was quite a collection and so she decided to take just what she needed to explore. She filled her pack with the semi dried meat, her waterproof cover, her water bottle and the string and firelighter. The steel ridge plate that she'd hammered and sharpened into a serviceable knife went in as well but not before she'd slit some of the fiskur skin into strips and braided it into a thin rope. She threaded this through the eye sockets of her hammerhead and slung it over one shoulder. Choosing a single pole from her collection of iron-oak she set it aside as a staff. The rest of the dried meat, the fiskur skin and bone, the iron-oak wands and the other finds that she'd made went back into the small cave where the skeleton was. Then she set off heading west. She made good progress that day, the next and the one after. The only event that interrupted her wanderings was when she stumbled across a small patch of her favourite plant; the iron-oak. She thought that the gods must have been watching because the second branch she picked up was relatively young, it was supple and it was an ideal length for a hammer shaft. She whittled the root end into a series of circles extending up the stem with her makeshift knife. Then she hammered the shaft onto the head. It was a tight fit but she made sure that the joint was firm by binding some of the braided leather around it.

The landscape had changed and was now lower and covered with trees. Small escarpments protruded here and there following old fault lines in the bedrock. Brannhår had been observing the local flora and fauna; there were fewer clumps of iron-oak here and there were frequent trails cutting through the woods. Once or twice she saw groups of elgrott with their huge incisors ambling along them.

In mid afternoon she heard the sound of shrieking accompanied by savage growling. It was coming from the base of a cliff that rose vertically out of the forest floor. She clambered up the cliff face and walked along the top. In less than a hundred paces she saw the origin of the commotion. Four small humanoid shapes were shrieking and gesticulating with short iron-oak spears at something within a cleft in the rock base. She went closer. A large she-wolf was standing at bay pacing back and forth across the entrance to the cleft. She saw the wolf glance backwards at a movement behind her. Brannhår heard the wolf give a bark of warning and the cub retreated back into the cleft.

Brannhår looked down at the leathery skins, the three fingered hands and the long snake-like prehensile tails of the wolf's tormentors. These were skogs and they were obviously hunting the wolf and her cubs. Then Brannhår noticed a movement on a ledge just below her. A fifth skog had climbed the rock and had circled behind the wolf. It raised its spindly arm to throw.

Brannhår didn't stop to think. She launched herself down upon the creature. The pair of them tumbled down the slope coming to rest at its foot. Both of them scrambled to their feet and the skog scampered off to join its troupe. Brannhår slid her hammer from her back and she glanced across at the wolf. The look in the wolf's eyes told her everything. This was a fight to the death, it was a re-enactment of the ancient battle that had raged on Svartalfheim since the dawn of time: mammal against reptile; warm blood against cold.

Without warning the troupe attacked, spears jabbed and were met by claws and hammer. Brannhår put everything she had into her blows to make them count. The tip of her hammer sank deep into one of the reptilian skulls. She felt a pain in her side where an iron-oak spear had penetrated her clothing but she ignored it. One of the skogs flew past about eight feet in the air. Its body had caught the full force of the side swipe from the wolf's powerful paws. Brannhår didn't see what happened to it because she was occupied with another of the reptilians. This one was cleverer than its fellows and was keeping just outside the range of her hammer. However, she was within range of its spear tip. As it jabbed forwards she swiped it aside with one hand and stepped forward. Her hammer descended and there was one less reptile to deal with. Suddenly she heard a shrill scream and a crunching sound. All went silent for a second and Brannhår looked around. The fourth skog fell from the wolf's jaws and the remaining one broke from the fray and ran off into the forest jabbering gobbledegook at the top of its voice.

Brannhår noticed that her leg was hurting and something just below the edge of her jerkin was stinging like blazes. She looked across at her ally. The she wolf was in bad shape. Numerous cuts covered her head and one ear was almost hanging off. Several spear shafts emerged from her body and her breathing was laboured. Brannhår stared into the she-wolf's eyes and she heard a short huff of gratitude before the light in them faded forever.

Brannhår needed to move on but the pain in her leg was bad. She removed her jerkin and tore a strip off her undershirt. Retrieving her pack she used some string to bind the strip into place over the gash in her leg. She found her staff and, using it as a crutch, she stood and hobbled over to the cleft in the rock. There were two still forms there. Both of the cubs had spears protruding from their hides. Then a whimper made her turn around. A third cub crept out from below an overhang in the bank. It was small and furry. It crossed to its siblings and sniffed them. Then it went to its mother and licked her face. When the she wolf didn't respond it tried again. Then, after a third try, it sank down to lie beside the great head.

Brannhår scooped the pup up in one arm, "I'm sorry, little one but she's gone. It's just you and me now and we'd better get going before the one that escaped returns with some of its friends."

 They moved along the base of the escarpment until it became a gentle slope and they climbed away from the battleground seeking a space where they could spend the night and recover. When Brother Kerian called that night she didn't tell him what had occurred but he seemed distracted. He told her that Sister Ulagrth had declared the official Menntunleit over. It had been nearly a fortnight since they'd set off. All of the other candidates except two had returned safely. One girl had been bitten by something venomous but had managed to contact the town using the scrying crystal. She had been found and she was being brought back to be cared for in the Oatsman's infirmary. The other missing person was one of the boys that Brannhår had spent the last part of her cart journey with. He'd been out of contact for two days. They had traced his scrying crystal to a location quite near to the place where he'd been dropped off but, despite a search, he hadn't been found yet.

Brother Kerian then hesitated and said, "I'm afraid that Justicer Ulagrth has declared an end to the monitoring. She wants no more resources wasted on this venture and has declared that you and the missing boy must make your own way back here or perish. I protested but her word carries much too much weight with the council and I was overruled. I'm afraid I disobeyed her a little and kept your scrying crystal back when she demanded their return. I gave her an old crystal that barely functions any more instead. I had a word with Lars though and, if we don't hear from you regularly he says he will come and find you."

Brannhår thanked the Oatsman but she was too tired to speak further and, by the time he said goodbye, she was falling asleep. She felt the warm bundle of fur nestle into her side just below the sore spot; it relieved some of the pain.

There as something wet in her ear and she snapped awake. It was full day and the sun was high in the sky. It appeared that her body had overruled her interior clock and had extended her slumber to almost midday. She groaned as she sat upright and her groan was answered by a series of sharp yips. Then her face was washed by a rough but very wet tongue. "Fine, fine, I'm awake. Just let me take things at my own pace for a while." Her mind did a quick inventory of her body. She had been injured in the leg and just below her ribcage but the pain wasn't as bad as it had been the day before. Her mouth was dry and she was hungry. She reached for her pack and pulled out the last of the semi-dried fiskur and her water bottle. She split the meat between herself and the pup. It snatched the strip she offered and ran away a dozen or so paces before it settled down to eat. It had obviously had to grab its share and run to a safe place to eat in its former pack. Brannhår smiled at its antics. Soon it was back for more but she shook her head, "Sorry, I've run out. We're going to have to replenish our stocks before we feast again." She drank some water and dribbled some more into her palm for the puppy to lap.

That evening they came across a small lake. It had a good crop of browth growing in the shallows and Brannhår caught some small fiskur. In fact she didn't so much catch them as they jumped into her hands. The puppy darted into the water and snapped at them. It made so much commotion that the fish-lizards literally jumped right into her hands. That evening the pair of them feasted on fresh roast meat again. Brannhår decided that her new companion should have a name. For some reason the word Mistle came into her head and that was it. From then on the puppy was called Mistle.

Brannhår rested the next day, they made camp by the side of the lake and Mistle did her duty and literally scared up dinner again. The day after, Brannhår decided that she'd come far enough and should think about returning back to civilisation. She wanted to retrace her route but she felt more comfortable in the mountains so she skirted the forest escarpments until the ground was rising again.

She was crossing a low range of hills at the base of what must have been a dormant volcano when she saw a strange sight about half-way up its slopes. Her wounds had almost recovered and scabbed over and Mistle had acclimatised to her new life: she no longer fled to safety to eat her food. Of course, this might have been because Brannhår had taken to tossing her the odd scrap from her own meals. The puppy wasn't a fan of browth but mixed in with a little meat it went down well all the same.

The interesting thing that she'd seen was a tree, a tree that was twice as high as any other. Moreover it was iron-oak. She'd never seen iron-oak growing so tall and so she went to investigate. Just before she reached it she felt the tension in the air that heralded lightning. This made her even more puzzled because the tree was a prime candidate for being blasted. She'd just reached the clearing that held the tree and she climbed to a vantage point atop a small boulder. Mistle was bounding around and she felt her playfully nip at her ankle. Then she nipped harder and Brannhår overbalanced and fell. An instant before she reached the ground the air split in two and the lightning struck. There was the clap and, as the echoes died away, there was the sound of ten thousand angry soprano bees hurtling through the air around her.

Everything went silent for a second until the creaking and crashing started. As Brannhår raised her head from the soil she saw a tree just behind her fold gently at its middle and topple to the ground. A leafy branch floated down beside her and she noticed, before Mistle grabbed it and tried to worry it to death, that its stem had been sliced through cleanly as if with a very sharp knife.

 She pushed herself upright and looked around. Her gaze travelled in a circle and she saw that almost all of the foliage up to a height of about ten feet had been shredded by some unknown agent. The sole exception was the iron-oak. It had been blasted to nothing. She circled the boulder and saw that the side facing towards the iron-oak was hatched with fresh gouges. A similar fate had befallen the ground nearby, it had been slashed into long open grooves by something. Brannhår dug into the end of one of the grooves and found a small spear-shaped seed. She recognised it as an iron-oak seed. What she didn't realise at the time was that she'd been one of the first people to witness the end of the natural reproductive cycle of the iron-oak and survive to tell the tale.

A voice sounded behind her, "Bloody hell, It was a good thing that I saw you duck. I managed to get behind a thick trunk just in time."

She looked up and saw a boy. Mistle was tensed with her back arched. She was staring directly at the youth and she was growling deep in her little throat. The boy didn't seem to notice.

"I didn't duck, I fell. Mistle pulled my foot from under me and so technically she saved both our lives."

"In that case," the boy turned to the puppy and said, "Thank you, little wolf. Karol Tynarsson owes you a great debt." Mistle hunkered down still making rumbling sounds in her throat but Karol crouched down and extended his closed fist to the pup. The pup's nose investigated it then licked tentatively. When the boy opened the fist it contained a few grains of powder which the pup lapped up eagerly. Hostilities between boy and dog had obviously been resolved. Karol then looked up at Brannhår.

"I'm Karol Tynarsson," he said, "I've been following your trail for a couple of days but I only caught you up this afternoon. I've no idea where I am. I thought the Menntunleit might be over but since you're here it clearly isn't. Don't you remember me, we came out here on the cart together, you gave me this." He held up an iron-oak pole.

Brannhår vaguely remembered the boy. "You must be the one Brother Kerian told me about. How is it that you haven't been using your scrying crystal?"

The boy looked shamefaced, "I was crossing a stream and a large fiskur chased me. I dropped the crystal and ran. When I returned after the fiskur had gone I couldn't find it. I decided that I'd be OK without it for a few days and so I moved on."

He was looking at her, "You've hurt yourself, haven't you?"

"Not exactly, it was a skog spear," she said.

"I should have known. So it was you who killed the reptiles."

"I had help from her mother," Brannhår replied pointing at Mistle.

"I should have guessed. I ran across the troupe of skogs last week and they have hunted me ever since. I survived by hiding in caves and barricading myself in. But a couple of days ago the troupe that were outside my cave suddenly left. I waited a while and then I decided that I'd better move on before they came back. I was coming this way when I ran into one of them again. It was running as though the devil himself was after it and it didn't stop to bother me. Since it was obviously frightened of something and it was running in one direction I decided that I'd better be wary. I came across a clearing in front of a crevice in the escarpment and found four dead skogs and three dead wolves. I could see that two of the skogs had tangled with the big wolf because of the bite and claw marks but the other two had smashed skulls. I couldn't see how a wolf could have smashed those skulls and so I thought that someone or something else must have been in the battle. From the look of the blood on that hammer that you have across your back I take it that you were the someone. That was pretty amazing, what you did."

"Look, no offence but you just don't seem the type to go this far into the wilderness just to prove you are a good dwarf. Why on earth didn't you stay nearer the coast?"

"Because I was a fool. I'm a herbalist by training and I thought that if I went deep into the wild I might discover a new herb or plant. All I did was get lost, lose my contact with civilisation and spend the week being frightened out of my wits. Err… you don't happen to have any food on you do you? I've been living on leaves for a week and I'm pretty sick of them."

Brannhår laughed for the first time since she'd come to this island. This boy was from the town, he had survived in the wild by sheer luck. She opened her pack and handed him some meat.

"Thanks," he said around a mouthful of roast fiskur. He stooped and shared the bounty with Mistle.

Brannhår said, "Menntunleit has been officially over for days but Justicer Ulagrth has refused permission for anyone to come and collect us. I'm making my way back overland. We can go together if you like."

He nodded but continued chewing. Mistle had suddenly become interested in the boy; she was sniffing around his ankles for any dropped scraps. Brannhår smiled at the puppy and reached to pull the scrying crystal out from under her shirt. "I'll have to let Brother Kerian know that you've been found but I'm afraid we'll still have to make it back by ourselves." She strode away to the lee of a rock and sat down heavily. She closed her eyes and said, "Brother Kerian, if you can hear this I have to tell you that Karol, the boy who was missing has turned up. He is with me here and I'm going to make my way back to the town with him. We're both fine so we don't need rescuing." She listened for a while and when nobody answered she put the crystal away. She'd try again later. As she rose her leg spasmed and she stumbled.

Karol rushed over to her. "Your wounds are bothering you. If you let me, I might be able to give you something to help them heal."

She nodded and pulled down her trousers. The boy became stony faced and then he stared directly at the gash in her leg. The wound was open and it was showing some sign of infection. It hadn't progressed to a stage beyond his skills but he needed several herbs.

He told Brannhår that he had to search for some herbs and that she should stay here until he returned. She pulled her trousers back up and said, "It will be quicker if I come with you."

"No," he said, "You shouldn't open that wound any wider. I won't be long, I promise."

She nodded, "If you say so, but I've another cut here," she lifted her tunic and shirt to show him.

He bent to examine it again and then he straightened. "It's actually slightly better than the one in your leg. The same herbs will help."

He turned his back strode a few paces towards a copse of trees and then looked around. Brannhår noticed and said, "I'll call out every few minutes so that you can find your way back."

"Oh that's a relief, I'm afraid one set of trees looks much the same as the others to me. I won't be long." He turned and strode off into the low scrub.

Brannhår called every couple of minutes and it was half an hour before he returned. "Now I need a fire and a bowl to stew these," he said.

Brannhår gathered some wood and lit the fire, "I'm afraid that I haven't a bowl but we can make do with this rock. It's impermeable and it's got a small dish-shaped hollow in it. I'll set it to warm. It took a while until the water in the hollow began to steam and then Karol added some leaves, then some other leaves and stirred the mixture with a small piece of stick. After a few minutes he declared that the mixture was ready.

Brannhår pulled up her tunic and shirt and was about to rip off another piece for a bandage when Karol stopped her, "Allow me," he said.

His under-shirt was considerably cleaner than Brannhår's and he tore off two strips and soaked them in the solution. Then he gathered up a handful of the steaming mixture into a fold in the cloth and gently pressed it against the wound in Brannhår's side. He wound the rest of the bandage around her waist and did the same with her leg but here he wound the bandage around three or four times before he tied it off.

Brannhår said, "That feels better already. Now we eat and I'll try Brother Kerian again."

She reached the monk and heard his voice emerge from the crystal, he sounded out of breath, "Oh I've just come from the infirmary. There's been another casualty, one of the boys was rushing to meet the wagon to bring him home and he fell and broke his leg. Thank you for calling, I was just about to call you to explain why I was late."

Brannhår told the Oatsman about meeting Karol and she admitted that he'd treated a couple of wounds she'd sustained on her travels. She didn't give him any details but she reassured him that they were coming back to town together and that it might take some time but that they would be fine. The Oatsman apologised again for not being able to pick them up but said he'd listen out for any communication from her the next evening.

They ate and talked for a while and then it was time to sleep. Karol had also lost his waterproof cover and Brannhår said that he could share hers. Mistle crawled under the cover as well and curled up next to her injured side. The warmth from the furry beast was comforting.

The next day they set off early. Brannhår had told Karol about the ruins that she'd discovered and she wanted to visit them again. Karol wasn't too keen but, when she pointed out that it was on the way back to the town, he relented. The weather held and the trio made good progress with Mistle running ahead pouncing on things and then returning offering whatever she'd picked up to them. Brannhår noticed that the puppy quickly learned that Karol greeted these spurious gifts enthusiastically and rewarded the pup with tidbits whereas she never rewarded it.

They reached the peak on the second day and Karol agreed that the diversion had been worth it. He marvelled at the state of preservation of the skull saying that it was very old. He pointed out the cause of death but Brannhår told him that she'd already come to the same conclusion.

"And you didn't know these ruins were here before you came?" he asked.

"No, I've never been to Skogrey before, how could I know?"

"Then you must have the luck of the devil to find the ruins and be able to recover that knife and your hammer."

"I made them," Brannhår insisted.

"Oh yes, you made a superb war-hammer without a forge or tools or any smithing help. No, why don't you admit it? You found them here with the dead dwarf. Don't worry, nobody is going to take them away. You found them, the dwarf obviously doesn't object, so they're yours."

Brannhår fumed and started to argue but then she remembered what Norri had told her. "The justicers will find out about your powers and they will take you away from us." She snapped her mouth shut and gritted her teeth. Maybe she should just let Karol's explanation stand. After all it was more believable that she'd found the hammer than that she'd used lightning and her intrinsic powers to fashion it from scratch.

"OK, I found it," she said, "just like Mistle."

"Oh yes, you saved her life and she saved ours, she's now our responsibility. Don't worry, from what you've shown me and from what I've seen nobody will question your rights. I'm just glad that I found you otherwise I don't know what would have happened to me."

When the trio walked into the town two days later, Brannhår's leg was almost healed and Karol looked resplendent in the ancient dwarf's breastplate and he was looking forward to meeting his friends and relating his adventures. He was right, Brannhår had had enough adventures to be the talking point for a year and he didn't mind too much because everyone thought he'd been in on the adventures with her.

Of course the justicers objected, they said that she'd not qualified because she'd had help. However she, Lars, Karol and Brother

Kerian testified that the justicers themselves had declared an end to the menntunleit before the pair had met. Mistle was further proof, if any were needed, that she was telling the truth about her other adventures.

When Brannhår sailed away from Skogrey a few weeks later she left behind the beginnings of a legend. She left the island behind but she took her hammer and the memories of her four new friends. Lars the smith, Brother Kerian the Oatsman, Karol the soon-to-be herbalist and Mistle the wolf.

******

Not everyone was happy. In the dim light of a room deep in the Temple on Skogrey Two people were talking.

"She must have cheated. Nobody just comes across a temple of the ancients by accident. She must have known about it before she came here," Justicer Ulagrth said to her companion.

"Or been told about it," said Justicer Harald. For a man who had supposedly been ill for a fortnight Harald looked to be in suspiciously good health.

"Then she may have just been a pawn in some other's game. But who?"

"Well she has no lack of sponsors in the makers, perhaps one of Jorell's cronies or even Jorell himself?"

"No, not Jorell. He is a spent force but you may be right about his followers. There are several in the capital that might be involved. But I can't see what they hoped to achieve. One small girl undergoing Menntunleit is hardly going to further their cause."

"Perhaps it wasn't about her at all," Harald said, "There was that hammer."

"Yes. The youngling Karol told me that at first she claimed that she had made it by herself but then changed her tune when he pointed out that she had no forge or tools. Thereafter she claimed that she found it in the ruins."

"Of course there are ways of shaping steel without fire and hammers," Harald reminded the senior justicer.

"Hah! You mean magic. That's impossible. Even I would find it a major task and it would take weeks of effort to shape ore into metal and I am considered quite skilled in the magic arts. No, the girl couldn't possibly have made it. It must have been an artefact that was buried with the dwarf in the ruins."

"That's another thing. How on earth did she find that cave? Even if someone had known the location of the ruins surely they couldn't have known about the cave. If they had, then why wasn't the hammer plundered before? I examined it; it appears to be like some of the axes drawn in ancient writings but it looks new. The breastplate and the rest of the armour that was recovered definitely showed signs of decay and the skeleton must have lain undisturbed since it died. As soon as the air got to it it started to crumble."

"The girl has certainly left many questions behind. Too many for my liking," Ulagrth said, "We must investigate. When was the last time she was tested for magic?" When was the last gathering in her village?

"I don't know," Harald replied, "I will check up as soon as I get back to Valdirey."

"Yes. Keep me informed. It seems too great a coincidence that she chose Skogrey for Menntunleit especially after what she supposedly discovered. Perhaps word of our work here has leaked out. Whatever the reason we must keep our wits about us."

Intermission

"And so my friends, Brannhår became known to the world outside her native Valdirey. It is from such small beginnings that great tales are made but I have kept you too long seated in this hall listening to me droning on. If we are to continue this tale together then we must adjourn until the morrow for I am in need my creature comforts," Einar patted his belly which, on cue, gave a loud gurgle.
"Therefore, I will greet you all in the morning to continue the tale of Brannhår in Niðavellir."

Einar relaxed, bowed and made his way off stage. Even he had to admit that and the next few years of Brannhår's life were mostly shrouded in mystery. Little was known about the time between her return from Menntunleit until her meteoric rise to wealth and fame from her discoveries concerning electricity and her adventures with the ancients. He was certain that there was much still to discover about those years but, from his point of view that would be another story. What he had to do now was to pick up the story a few years later and hope that his audience wouldn't be too inquisitive about the intervening period.

Einar listened as the audience filed out; there didn't seem to be too many arguments. It was probably a good sign.

Ch 9: Back Home

Brannhår came home triumphant. She was now an adult but Norri was still worried. Her very success posed a danger. He said as much to Dagmar. After Menntunleit, Brannhår would theoretically have to make her own way in the world. While she'd been a child they'd been able to provide some protection but now she was an adult close protection was no longer an option. Of course they wouldn't abandon her and they both agreed that she could still live with them as long as she wished.

Norri's fears were realised only a few weeks after her return. A delegation of justicers arrived in the village to perform a gathering. There hadn't been a gathering for ten years and the villagers had never pointed out the omission to the authorities. The gathering party consisted of three justicers and Norri recognised one them as the woman who had casually killed the man in the tavern on his visit to the city years earlier. Her companions seemed to fear her and they never contradicted her in anything. Ostensibly they had come to test the children for signs of magic as there had been no testing for several years. This was due to some new administrative rule that stated that villages with fewer than a hundred people did not justify the effort of a frequent examination.

Adulthood did not excuse anyone from the 'gathering' but it was unusual for the justicers to call an adult forwards. The process of testing for magic was simple: since most magic manifested under stress each child was taken into a room on their own and blindfolded. One of the justicers created a spell to induce fear and the others would watch to see how the child's magic aura reacted. The greater the aura's reaction the more likely the child was to have magic. If a proclivity towards magic was detected then more tests were performed and if real power was detected then the child would be taken back to the temple in the city to be indoctrinated into the justicer hierarchy. For adults the process was similar however the fear was replaced by actual pain and, if magic was detected, the individual was arrested and taken away. Magic outside the justicer system was not permitted, adult practitioners were automatically outlaws.

Examinations were to take place in the schoolhouse and the school had been closed for the duration. Inevitably they called Brannhår for examination. She could have fled but she knew that the justices would only take their anger out on her parents or her friends. On the first day of testing she arrived at the school early. She was taken into a room and the chief justicer produced a small brazier. It was lit and a needle was placed in it until it became red hot. As the needle approached Brannhår's exposed skin she flinched and when it was applied to her hand she tried to move away as anyone might have done. The justices watched and said nothing. After a few seconds the brand was withdrawn and she was told to go outside and wait. She had tried to control her reactions, she'd often received minor burns when working in the forge but the needle had hurt. The temptation to use her knowledge of fire to cool the needle was great but she resisted it because she was sure that doing that would be a certain give away. Nevertheless she had been using her power to sense the flame and the metal in the brazier and the needle's composition so she couldn't be sure she'd not unwittingly revealed her nature. She went outside and waited.

Inside the room a heated discussion was taking place. "What do you mean, she has no aura. Everyone has an aura even animals have aura's. How can she have none?" the chief justicer demanded.

"Well there was a sort of aura but it was so narrow that it was almost all inside her," one of the other justicers said.

"Yes, but did it react?"

"Only about as much as an ordinary dwarf would have reacted. There was certainly no overt magic there. I couldn't even get a clear reading of her life magic. It was tangled, as though she was old and young at the same time. I've never seen that in anyone before. One thing is clear she doesn't have any of the kind of magic we'd be interested in."

"I don't understand," the chief justicer said, "why would the council be so interested in her if she is just a commoner?"

"She is supposed to be a skilled maker even though she is young," her colleague replied, "and we know that the makers are trouble. She's a friend of Jorell and the council have had their eye on him for some time. Perhaps that's why they made us test her."

"Yes perhaps you're right. A pain-in-the-butt maker; but not magic. Go out and tell her that she can go. Now bring in the first child."

The justicer came out, "You can go. You have no magic but be warned, the temple has noted your tendency to cause trouble and we don't like people who cause trouble."

Brannhår couldn't understand, she'd been certain that they'd discover her powers but it appeared that they hadn't. She wasn't going to question her reprieve but she didn't immediately leave for home. Outside the schoolhouse there was a long line of younger children forming. Most were accompanied by one or both parents. Without exception all the adults looked worried. One by one the children went into the schoolhouse. Then, after a few minutes, the child would emerge, to the evident relief of its parents. After six or so children had been examined there was a longer period and no seventh child emerged. A few minutes later one of the justicers appeared and crossed over to where two people were anxiously waiting. Brannhår wasn't close enough to hear what had been said but the woman's reaction didn't need words. She screamed and flew at the justicer. The woman seemed to bounce off him and she was flung across the street landing heavily in the dirt. Her husband looked as if he would challenge the justicer but he hesitated, he ran to his wife and helped her up. She was weeping and the anger seemed to have been knocked out of her. They turned and, supporting each other, they limped off in the direction of the mayor's house.

Brannhår was angry also, she'd not quite believed it when Norri had been so worried that her powers would be revealed. However she could see that he'd been right. If only there was something that

95

she could do. No other child would be taken today. She felt in the sky and there was the tingle of lightning and another presence that she'd not seen in a while. It spoke inside her head. "Why are you so sad? Come on; let's ride the lightning."

"I can't Rakkerskap, I can't leave these children." she thought.

"Oh, I see. But why don't you just make the magic go away?" the fire spirit said in her head.

"And how am I supposed to do that?" she thought sarcastically.

"You should know, you taught me; remember?" And now one of the old memories appeared in her mind. It was one of those that only came when she was reminded. Sometime, in another place, she'd been able to control magic. She had used it to protect her friends and to heal some people who were having nightmares. The way of it came back to her, a small part of her had always had this power it was separate from her but joined to her in a most intimate way. Walking over to the wall of the schoolhouse she went around the back. There was a small room behind the classroom where her teacher worked whilst the children were outside taking a break. Taking care not to make a sound, Brannhår entered and crept over to the door to the main classroom. She could hear voices inside.

"That's one more for our numbers." Brannhår recognised the voice; it belonged to the chief justicer.

"Indeed," agreed a second voice, "there are always a few in these wild villages. I really don't know why the parents make such a fuss. I was brought to the temple when I was five and I have learned so much since then."

"Get the next one," the chief ordered, "I want to be away by evening. I hate having to sleep in a cave."

Brannhår heard the door open and the assistant justicer said, "We are here to see if you are clever enough to join the justicers. Not everyone can. It's a really special thing to be. So I am going to ask you to sit at this table and I'm going to put this cloth around your eyes. Just relax."

Brannhår heard the justicer start to chant and she felt a chill run down her spine. She could feel the fear growing but she'd felt fear before and she knew how to control it. She reached out and nullified the magic around the child.

A few seconds later she hear a justicer's voice say, "No, this one doesn't have any magic, I can't sense anything."

"Very well," the chief justicer said, "Send this one out and bring in the next.

Several hours later Brannhår was stiff from crouching at the classroom door but she shrugged off the soreness. The justicers had examined all the children and hadn't been able to find any magic in any of them. They left sooner than they anticipated taking the unfortunate magical child with them. The examination had almost been a complete waste of time. No wonder they hardly ever tested the small villages. There wasn't enough magical potential in these isolated communities. In a larger town they might expect to recruit maybe three or four magical children but there'd only been the one. The young woman that they'd been told to test had also turned out to be non magical; the chief knew that her superiors wouldn't be pleased about that either.

Brannhår was also frustrated, if she'd only known about the power to nullify magic before then maybe she could have saved that sole child. There was nothing that she could do about it now and trying to steal the child back would be foolish in the extreme. She consoled herself with the fact that she would be ready next time justicers came to examine her village for magic.

Needless to say, her efforts with the justicers meant that she'd missed Jorell completely and so she went home. When she arrived Dagmar rushed to her and hugged her. Brannhår was a little puzzled but then all became clear as Dagmar said, "Oh we were so worried when you didn't come home. We thought that the justicers had arrested you. It was all I could do to stop Norri going to the village and trying to rescue you. I'm glad you are safe but you should have let us know."

Norri came in and just came over and hugged her. "So you managed to hide your magic then?"

"Not really father; when they tested me they couldn't find any magic. And that was before Rakkerskap reminded me that I can control magic."

"What do you mean you can control magic?" Norri asked.

Brannhår spent the next half hour telling her parents about meeting the fire spirit and how she'd remembered that in her other memory she knew how to negate magic. She told them about the child who had been taken and then she told them how she'd sneaked back into the schoolhouse to make sure no other children were found.

Dagmar seemed to approve of her actions and she told her so. Then she went off to make something to eat. Norri sat thinking for a long time. "On the whole what you did was good, but I'm slightly worried that, in the long run you might have made things worse for those children who you saved. If some of them do have magic and, if there is another ten year gap until the next tests then if they are tested again they could be arrested and imprisoned or worse. The Justiciary doesn't tolerate magic users that it doesn't control."

Brannhår smiled and said, "Don't worry father, I'll just negate the magic again if they come back."

"And what if they come back when you're not here? You are an adult now and, although we would like to have you stay Dagmar and I know that you are too good a dwarf to spend your life in these backwoods. You will become a master maker and to do that you will have to travel and learn from others. You need to find out what you are capable of and you need to make the most of it while you can. You will have to make up your own mind where you go, you have corresponded with many people and I'm sure that some of them would welcome you as an apprentice."

Brannhår hadn't realised, but her father was right. She wanted to learn, to explore and to be independent. Even she had to admit that she'd learned and explored everything that the village had to offer.

She'd never given what happened next much thought before; maybe it was time that she did.

She wanted to speak to Jorell, he would give her advice so the next day she went back to the village. The elderly maker greeted her and invited her in to his home for some light beer. She accepted even though she didn't usually like alcohol. She needn't have worried, Jorell's light beer was so weak it was only slightly more intoxicating than water. However it tasted good with a nutty malted flavour. Once she was settled she asked Jorell what she should do about her future.

"My dear, it's not really my place to say. You should really make your own decisions. However I will give you some advice. Going away from home seems like an adventure and it is easy to get carried away with the freedom. I know because when I first left home I spent too much of my time with my friends just having a good time. Oh, I wasn't so bad that I completely messed things up but I did find that I missed quite a few opportunities. I'd had quite a sheltered upbringing in a small village much like this one and the city was overwhelming. You see, when you are on your own, nobody tells you what to do and so you tend to do the easiest thing rather than the right thing. So, I think that what I am trying to say is that you should make sure that you don't make the same mistakes that I did."

"But Master Jorell, you are a great person, you have accomplished many things. Surely you've overcome any shortcomings of your early years."

"Yes you could say that. But I was lucky. I became ill and I couldn't go carousing with my friends. I spent a lot of time just laid up in my bed and it gave me time to think. I realised what I'd missed and so I moved to another town to take up a new task. The task involved many makers with different talents and it was exciting to be involved. My new colleagues became my new family and I began to learn again. After that, I never stopped learning and I never will. So you see, if I hadn't been lucky enough to fall ill I would never have learned to love learning and that's what made me who I am today. It would have been so easy to carry on doing the easy thing and enjoying myself but I wouldn't be the person that I am now."

"So what you are saying is that I shouldn't go to the city, I should go somewhere else to learn."

"Oh no, not at all, my dear. The city is no better or worse than anywhere else. What I am saying is that you shouldn't always just take the easiest path, you should think about what you are deep in your soul and follow that even if it isn't that easy."

"But how will I know what to do? Can nobody tell me?"

"I'm sorry Brannhår, no one can. If you choose a path and it is the wrong one then once you realise it turn away and choose another. You cannot go through life without making mistakes. What you must do is realise when you make a mistake and learn from it. It is difficult but it is how life works."

She didn't make her decision straight away, she talked it over again with her friends and her teacher and then her parents. They all said different things but they boiled down to the plain fact that she had to make the choice herself. Finally she went to her father.

Her father had told her that he had a friend who was getting on in years but that, in his day, he had been the cleverest man that Norri had known. The man lived in a small town near to the capital on Griprey and her father had said that his friend would welcome her and give her a place to stay in return for Brannhår helping with the household chores.

Her mother had approved of her choice but she was concerned that Brannhår would be so far away: if anything happened, she couldn't help. Both her parents were aware of what she'd done when the justicers had visited the village and they thought that it would be taking a chance being near to the main base of the justicers. Brannhår assured them that she would avoid the wizards

Ch 10: An Inconvenient Child

His eminence Lord Skald of the Justiciary seethed with anger but he let none of his emotion reach his face. He said, "The Justiciary is most displeased with the tale that you have just told me, most displeased indeed."

"Yes, your eminence," the terrified monk who had told the tale whispered.

"It was fortunate that you came to me. Now how could this have happened? Were the groups not separated?"

"The groups are generally kept separate during waking hours and they have separate dormitories as you know," the monk hesitated, "but we do not have the facilities or the staff to enforce the rule absolutely."

"Obviously, but such things are not the result of a momentary encounter, they require time."

"Yes your eminence, however we did discover it in time. The supervising sister became suspicious when the child was seen to be suffering from nausea on several occasions in the mornings. She confronted the girl and the girl admitted it."

Lord Skald couldn't contain the rage any longer, he thumped the table and the monk nearly jumped out of his skin. "And then the stupid woman just let the child go without restraining her?"

"I'm afraid that she did, your eminence, she is not the brightest of creatures. She has been disciplined."

"And where is the girl now?"

The monk cowered, "She is gone, your eminence."

Lord Skald gestured with his hand and the monk's head twisted as if it had been struck a heavy blow. "Get out of my sight and send for Kalten"

"Yes your eminence," the monk said and he scurried away.

It took half an hour for the tracker to arrive and, by that time Lord Skald had had time to think.

"You wished to see me, your eminence," Kalten said.

Lord Skald regarded the man. He was tall and thin but his skin was like old leather and he exuded an air of toughness. His speciality was finding things that were lost and making sure that they stayed lost.

"Kalten, I require your services on a delicate matter. It would appear that one of the novices, a girl named Racka , has managed to get herself with child and she has fled. You will find her and find out who impregnated her. Unfortunately we cannot just banish her to Aldredsfarne or some other wilderness outpost because her parents happen to be very generous supporters of the Temple and in return they like to see their daughter around the place. So I'm afraid that, after she's found, she will have to have an accident. You will appreciate that no bodily remains can be found lest the pregnancy be discovered. However, there must be sufficient evidence that will identify her. I will leave it to you to arrange matters. Oh, and it might be an idea for you to disappear for a while afterwards. I wouldn't want any of the other members of the council asking awkward questions."

"I understand your eminence. I will be discrete as ever."

"Good, then I will leave the details up to you."

"Yes, Lord Skald," Kalten said and he left the room.

Lord Skald summoned his assistant, Blade. There were a few postings to Aldredsfarne that he had to arrange. The monk would need a thick pair of socks and a good winter coat where he was going.

Kalten had found Racka easily, there were enough traces of her in the novices quarters and his talent zeroed in on her without any trouble. She'd managed to get quite a distance from the capital but she'd made the mistake of sticking to the roads. Then it seemed like she'd realised that this would make her vulnerable and had set off across country. It didn't matter to Kalten, in fact it probably made his task easier. There were fewer potential witnesses in open country and what he had to do would take a while. First he'd have to persuade her to go with him until they reached a sizeable lake near to the road. This would save him the job of lugging her body to a suitable spot. Then he'd kill her and cut out the child she was carrying. He'd dispose of the child in the lake. There'd be no telltale tiny skeleton to give evidence of her condition, just as Lord Skald had ordered.

Then he'd gather her knapsack and any identifiable jewellery that she was wearing and wait. It wouldn't take long for the amphibious scavenger lizards to make a meal of her remains leaving only bones and any remaining rags of clothing. Inevitably some traveller would need water and seek out the lake. With any luck they'd find the remains and report it at the next town. He'd be well away by that time and the girl would just be the unfortunate victim of the fiskur.

******

Brannhår wanted to take her time entering this new phase of her life. By taking the a fishing boat to the small village of Beltafiirn on the southern coast of Griprey and travelling overland to the capital she could conserve her meagre funds for any unexpected expenses. She'd been on the road for three days and she'd noticed a few differences between her home island and this one. Griprey was warmer and she found that she could trek without wearing her normal over-jacket. The landscape was also different. There were fewer hills and rock escarpments and many more varieties of plant life. This meant that there were also fewer caves, a fact that displeased her because she was used the security of caves.

She was just wondering whether she should alter her route slightly when she heard the scream. It cut off abruptly and, at first, she thought that it must be some unfortunate creature that had become the dinner for another. However, the scream didn't sound right and she decided that it would be prudent to investigate: when travelling

103

in unfamiliar territory it was always good to know the location of any large predators.

She set off in the general direction of the sound. As she came closer to the source of the cry she pushed her pack into the lower branches of a tree and took out her hammer. Fixing her current location in her mind she set off cautiously through the undergrowth. There were voices coming from just below her on a narrow path that wound through the wood. One of them was high pitched and was obviously in distress. The other was lower and more menacing.

"It's your own fault for running. In this undergrowth you were bound to trip. You should have known that they would send someone after you girl. The Justiciary can't be seen to allow anyone to break the rules even someone with a talent like yours. You need to come back with me now."

"I can't go back. You don't understand. They will take the baby," Racka said.

"Oh, I understand all too well. Now why don't you tell me what happened while we walk. There's a small lake just over there and we can wash that cut."

Something told Brannhår that the situation wasn't as simple as it appeared and so she just kept silent and followed. The man, who was dressed in a hunting outfit accompanied the girl along the path but he kept looking around as if he suspected that he was being followed. He said to the girl, "My name is Kalten and my talent is finding things, I found you. You are a novice aren't you?"

"Yes," the girl replied.

"It's a shame, however did you get yourself into this mess ?" Kalten asked.

"I don't know, really. I can't remember," she replied.

Kalten laughed, "He can't be that bad at it."

"No," the girl insisted, "I really can't remember anything my memories are missing for about a week."

They'd arrived at the lake and the girl went to the water's edge. "Careful, there are some large fiskur lower down the bank," Kalten said.

The girl stooped and dipped the hem of her robe into the water then retreated and sat on the bank cleaning the wound. Kalten circled behind her and took a length of strap out of his pocket. With a practised motion he looped the strap around the girl's throat and tightened it. The girl struggled for a few seconds and then fell limp. Brannhår could see that she was still breathing. The man took more straps from his own knapsack and trussed the girl's hands behind her then he forced a wad of cloth between her lips and tied it in place with another strap. Racka seemed to be recovering and her eyes opened wide in fear.

Kalten stood over her, "You really are a fool. Didn't they teach you anything? Boys who have mental powers always try it on with easy marks like you. Never mind, this time I'm going to make sure you feel everything and believe me you'll remember it for the rest of your life." The girl struggled but Kalten pulled up her robes and grinned. I might as well take some payment in advance," Kalten said, dropping his trousers. A few minutes later he pulled out of her. The girl was in shock but Kalten hadn't finished. He drew a dagger and made a swift slash across the mound of her belly. She screamed against the gag as the blood welled, but no sound escaped.

He stood up and looked at his handiwork, "By the time the lizards have finished with you there will be just enough evidence left to convince whoever finds you that this is just some tragic accident." Then he gave a chilling laugh.

The laugh was cut short. He felt the tap on the back of his head and he slumped over the girl's thrashing body.

The girl suddenly went limp and Brannhår saw that she'd fainted. She pulled Kalten off and rolled the man down to the water's edge. Then she stripped off his tunic and smashed his feet with her hammer. The pain woke him. She said, "I heard what you said, you were planning to leave that girl for the fiskur. Well the plans have changed. You may, if your gods are feeling generous, survive. Otherwise they'll find remains and her clothes and belongings just like you wanted. However I can see that the fiskur have already scented the blood and so I have to go now."

Without looking back, Brannhår climbed the bank back up to the unconscious girl. There were some screams and a few unpleasant noises that sounded like bones being crunched before everything became silent again. Apparently the man's gods weren't in a generous mood.

A few hours later a roaring fire was keeping most things except the mosquitoes at a safe distance. Brannhår reflected on another difference between Griprey and her home: the reptiles were bigger. She had retrieved her pack and had dressed the girl's wounds as best she could but the girl's forehead was burning hot: the knife had been poisoned. She kept raving about someone called sister Amelia but Brannhår didn't have a clue who she meant.

On the second day the fever was worse and the girl's body was racked with convulsions. Brannhår steeled herself and took the pathetic remains of what had been inside the girls belly down to the shore of another small lake. It was better that way, if she'd buried it some creature might have dug it up and it might have been discovered. Then questions might have been asked and, for the girls sake, Brannhår wanted to avoid questions.

The girl awoke on the third day. The wound across the girl's belly looked nasty and Brannhår wished that she had paid more attention to her mother's lessons on herb lore. Despite being packed with a poultice made from hyssop and crushed honey ants and the frequent bathing that Brannhår supplied, the wound felt hot to the touch and it oozed a yellowish fluid. There was nothing more that Brannhår could do and she decided that she would have to get the girl to someone who could help. She rigged up a travois from some branches and what remained of the assassin's leather pack and bound the girl onto it with the straps to keep her from falling off.

After half a day Brannhår concealed the travois in a cluster of rocks and returned to the bank. She carefully removed all trace of what had happened on the bank. Retrieving a few fragments of bone and rotten flesh from what was left of the assassin she stuffed them into the girls blood-stained robes. The girls scrip and notebook were left beside the remains of the fire. When they were found nature would have added the finishing touches to her deception.

Returning to the rocks where she'd concealed the girl, Brannhår started the long trek to her destination. By the third day Brannhår was tired from the effort of dragging the sledge and she began to have dark thoughts: It would have been simpler if the girl had died and she hadn't become involved.

However, Brannhår couldn't bring herself to just leave the girl and let nature take it's course even if the girl was a justicer. On the fourth day the girl opened her eyes and this time, when she spoke, she seemed to make sense; "Water?" Brannhår called a halt to that days journey and gradually the girl recovered enough to understand what had happened. Brannhår started to tell her what she'd witnessed but the girl shook her head. "I know what happened. I remember the leather straps that Kalten used to tie me up and the knife he used to kill my child that you buried back there. You saved me and cared for me but I can't understand why they wanted me dead."

Brannhår was puzzled but she could answer one of the girls questions, "They probably wanted you dead so that you couldn't reveal the identity of the child's father." At this the girl burst into tears and shut her eyes tight against the world, obviously Brannhår's words had brought back the horror. "I'm sorry but there was nothing I could do. The infection and the trauma of what the assassin did were too much," she said.

After half an hour the girls sobs stopped and she became silent. She didn't speak for the rest of the day or for most of the next. Brannhår ignored her and continued to pull the injured girl along like some sack of browth that needed hauling back to the village.

Finally the girl seemed to have come to some resolution. "I can't go back" she said.

"No, you can't go back," Brannhår said, "I would advise you to flee as far away as you can but you cannot do that with such wounds. I will try to take you somewhere where you can be helped."

"But the healers will see my talent and they will tell the temple. They will drag me back or they will kill me." the girl said fearfully.

"I know a way to conceal your magic," Brannhår said, "and I will not take you to temple healers. The maker that I am going to see will know what to do. Until then you should rest." The girl went silent and, after a few minutes, she appeared to fall asleep. Brannhår gritted her teeth and set off again.

Ch 11: The Old Man of Griprey

It took three more days during which Brannhår learned that the girl's name was Racka and that her parents were rich and that they lived on Lungrey. When they came in sight of the town of Longbarrow, Brannhår hid the girl again and walked the final mile into the town alone. The girl was awake and Brannhår had left her food and water so she should be safe. She was now able to move about on her own but her wounds still troubled her, "Try to rest as much as possible; it will help the healing," she said.

Norri had warned her that her destination would be different to the towns she knew. Griprey was further south and had a warmer climate and so Dwarf communities did not use cave networks as extensively as they had at home. However, Brannhår had seen buildings before and so it wasn't a complete surprise that the town appeared to grow out of the flat ground rather than out of a hill or cliff face. As she approached she saw several people in robes standing by the main gates. They were stopping anyone who entered the town. Brannhår walked up to them and a middle aged man approached her. He scowled at her and said, "Who are you and why are you here?"

"I am Brannhår Dagmarsdóttir and I am visiting an old friend of my father's. Now, in return for that information I would ask you the same questions; who are you and why are you here?"

"Don't be insolent. I am a justicer and I don't need to tell you anything."

Brannhår held her temper and said, "I have told you who I am and why I am here, if you do not wish to answer those same questions then I will be on my way."

"Not so fast, girl. I have not finished," the justicer said.

Brannhår experienced a sensation like a cold chill of fear passing through her body and she found that something inside her reacted to it. The fear stopped abruptly. It was the same reaction that she'd experienced in the school when she'd suppressed the magic there. The man had tried to use magic on her and her instincts had nullified it. However she did not react, she needed to know what was going on and the best way to find out was to let the man believe that he'd frightened her. "Please, don't harm me," she said.

The man looked pleased with himself, "Now you will tell me what you have seen on the road. Have you seen any young women, we are looking for a woman with blonde hair who would be travelling in the direction of the coast."

Brannhår saw that the man had been joined by a woman dressed in the same coloured robes. She said, "I have met nobody travelling on the road to the coast ever since I left Beltafiirn over a week ago." She noticed that the woman gave the man a small nod.

"And why has it taken you so long to travel from Beltafiirn?" the man asked.

Again Brannhår felt the hint of fear generated by the man's voice and again her power suppressed it. She swung her hammer from where it rested on her back and held it out, then said, "I was in no hurry to get here and I spent some days hunting; I enjoy hunting."

The man looked at the hammer, its head showed unmistakeable signs of bloodstains from recent kills. He glanced at the woman who gave a small nod again. "Get on your way, girl. I will be keeping an eye on you."

Brannhår nodded and walked through the gate. It was all she could do not to swing the hammer into his thick skull but the impulse quickly passed. The Justiciary had clearly not given up the search for Racka and, just as clearly, they hadn't yet found the remains of the assassin. Whatever power she had that allowed her to negate magic had surfaced again and had protected her from its influence; it was a warning from inside herself that she needed to be careful.

It took her an hour of talking to people to find out where Master Magnusson lived and another half hour to find the place. The house was free standing and didn't appear to be connected to any cave. It was made of wattle and it had clearly seen better days. The roof had holes that must certainly have leaked when it rained and the panels that made up the door had become loose and one looked to be held on by only a single nail. This house was not well maintained.

She went up to the door and rapped on what looked to be the most solid panel. When there was no answer she tentatively pushed at the door. It swung inwards on squealing hinges revealing a dark interior. She entered, calling out, "Torin Magnusson, I am Brannhår, the daughter of your friend Norri. I am here to stay with you."

There was no reply but Brannhår could sense that the house wasn't empty of life. There was something buzzing over in one corner of the room. Brannhår unsheathed her hammer and stepped forward towards the sound. Then she smiled and sheathed the hammer again. Slumped in a chair beside a fire that had been allowed to burn itself out was an old man. His snores ripped the air apart like two men sawing at an ironoak tree. Was this who she'd come to see? Asleep, he didn't seem that formidable, his tunic was worn and patched and the laces were knotted in a couple of places where they'd snapped and been tied together again. The waistband of his britches was strained to its limit trying to reign in the man's beer belly and the mismatched pair of hose beneath them were holed in places and darned in others.

Brannhår gave a loud cough and then, when nothing happened, she went to sit on the front step and think. She had to get the girl some help. It was unlikely that help would go to her and so Brannhår would have to bring the girl into the town right under the nose of the justicers. She could hide the girl's magic but she couldn't hide the girl's wounds or the girl herself. The only option that Brannhår could see was to go back to the girl and persuade her to keep herself hidden until her wounds could be concealed. As the justicers were monitoring the gate onto the southern road, Brannhår thought that she should find a hiding place for the girl to the North of the town. Some local knowledge would be useful; maybe her erstwhile mentor would have some ideas when he woke up.

As if the thought had summoned him, the door behind Brannhår suddenly burst open and the old man came running out. He didn't see Brannhår sat on the step and, in his hurry, he fell over her and went sprawling into the dust of the street. He picked himself up and spun around glaring at Brannhår. "What the *&**! are you doing hiding there?" he demanded.

"I wasn't hiding I was waiting for you to wake up," Brannhår replied.

"I nearly corpsed myself and I think I broke my toe. What have you got in that backpack? Steel bars?"

"No. Just my hammer," Brannhår replied.

"Well, whatever it is it nearly broke my toe. Now, who are you and what do you want? You're not from the town council are you? If you are you can *&**%$ off and tell them that the answer is still no!"

"No, I am not from the council. I am Brannhår Dagmarsdóttir and I have come with a message from my father, Norri Thorvaldson for his friend Torin Magnusson."

"You're Norri's girl? I would never have guessed. You don't favour either your father or your mother."

"No sir, I was adopted by them when I was an infant." He scratched his head and then said, "Show me your hammer." Brannhår removed her hammer from its sheath and handed it to the old man. He held it in his hands and examined it carefully. Finally he said, "Good work: your father has taught you well. Your own, I can see, and an interesting motif but I'd have added a band here to stop vibrations," and he handed it back.

"Thank you, Master Magnusson," Brannhår said. She was unaccountably pleased that he'd recognised that the hammer was her own work.

He waved his hand and nodded, "What day is it?" he asked.

"Err... Mani, I think." Brannhår replied.

The old man nodded again, "I've been out for two days then. No wonder I'm thirsty." He hobbled over to a barrel raised onto a high shelf and took a wooden cup from a ledge below it. Brannhår could see that the barrel had a spigot which the old man twisted. A stream of liquid splashed into the cup and he drank it down in two gulps. "That's better," he said, "I expected you a week ago, well no matter. Come with me and I'll show you where you'll be staying." With that the man went across to the door and left. Brannhår hurried after him.

As they walked down the street Brannhår said, "I thought I'd be staying with you."

"What, no, you don't want to stay with me. You'll be better off at the widow's place; she's used to women. It's just along here. And, I am Torin or, if you want to be formal, Master Magnusson: it's all the same to me. Now, I will call you Girl, is that acceptable?" When Brannhår said nothing he continued, "Of course I'll call you that even if you do object and I'll call you other things if I want to. So that's settled. Ah here we are."

The house where they'd stopped looked like the one they'd just left except that it had clearly been better maintained. They climbed onto the front step and Torin rapped loudly on the door. A high pitched voice came from inside, "Go away," it shouted.

"Widow Oggnar, it is Torin Magnusson. I've brought the girl I told you about," Torin shouted back.

"Well, come in then. I'm busy."

Torin pushed at the door and it opened onto a single large room filled with steam. A round woman stood beside a huge shallow barrel that was filled with steaming purple-coloured water. She was hauling a large hank of twisted fibres out of it with her bare hands. Her arms were purple to beyond her elbows but above that point they turned to a more natural shade of skin. Her hair hung in lank coils around her face; the result of the steamy atmosphere, and she didn't look up as they entered. Over in one corner of the room was another tub sat on a table under a complicated machine consisting of gears, rollers, springs, helical jacks and a huge windlass.

"There's no wind so you can help by providing some muscle power as you are clearly with us today," the woman said.

Torin moved across to the machine and positioned himself at the windlass. Brannhår moved with him examining the machine to guess its purpose.

The woman swung the dripping skein across to the maw of a huge pair of rollers, "Pull it in just till it bites, then stop. I need to arrange it before you squeeze it," the woman ordered. Torin inched the windless around and then halted. The woman spread the fibres out until she was satisfied then she said, "haul away old man, at least you're good for something."

Torin grimaced and began to turn the wheel again, there was obviously a lot of inertia in the system. As the wheel speeded up the effort became less and he had breath to talk. "I'm asking you to give this girl somewhere to stay. I'm not used to females but I've agreed to supervise her and give her the use of my workshops but she obviously can't live in my place. It's too small."

"Whatever you say Torin," the woman replied and she turned to Brannhår.

Brannhår had never seen anyone who had such a variegated face. Dye had splashed onto it over the years and it was covered in spots in every colour of the rainbow. It made her features difficult to see because the eye kept trying to make patterns from the dots and splotches. "My name is Widow Oggnar and I dye fabrics for anyone who pays me. I'll give you room but I won't ask you to work at the trade in return. Dyeing is hard work and Torin tells me that you have the makings of a maker so I don't want to be held responsible for creating the first of Torin's pupils with a purple face. You'll pay me for your food if you eat with us or you can provide your own or you can hunt for us to help out. I have a spare bed now that my Anna is married but I normally lock up at nightfall so, if your out after dark you'll need to make other arrangements. Is that all clear?"

"Yes Widow Oggnar," Brannhår replied. Torin had stopped pushing the wheel but it kept turning on its own. The fibres were now almost all the way through the rollers and the purple liquid that had been expelled from them had collected in the tub. Widow Oggnar took a bucket and turned a tap on the base of the tub. When the purple liquid had drained into the bucket she went over and tipped it back into the steaming barrel. The widow returned to the huge mangle and nodded in satisfaction. The skein of fibres had completed its journey through the rollers and had emerged as a much stiffer but very much drier product. It was a pleasing shade of purple.

"I'll show you to your bed," the widow said and she went through a door and Brannhår followed. They climbed some stairs; these were a novelty as far as Brannhår was concerned but she didn't make any comment. Opening a door that led off a short corridor at the top of the stairs Brannhår saw a room that just contained four beds. A room with a single purpose; another novelty. Three of the beds were rumpled but the fourth was flat and neat. "This is your bed," the widow said pointing at the unruffled one. "Stow your pack underneath it, it will be quite safe," the widow said. Brannhår did so but she took her hammer in its sheath out and swung it across her back. She descended the stairs and found Torin examining the vat of purple liquid; he'd stuck a finger into the vat and was just raising it to his lips. The widow screamed "Noooo" at him and he looked up startled. "You old fool, don't you know that the dye is poisonous." Torin turned his face towards them. Brannhår could see that its expression had changed and it stared back at them dully. "Oh no," the widow said sadly, he's gone again."

"What do you mean?" Brannhår asked.

"Didn't anyone warn you?" the widow asked.

"About what?" Brannhår replied.

"His mind wanders. One minute he is as astute as he ever was and the next it seems that there's nobody home. He doesn't actually become uncontrolled like some poor things in his condition: it's more that his mind has escaped his body and is off somewhere else and has temporarily disconnected itself from his body. When he's like this it's best just to get him home and let him sleep it off. He'll wake up in a couple of hours or days and be together again. Sometimes he's lucid for days and sometimes its only for hours. It's one of the reasons that he asked me to take you in."

Brannhår understood, but inside she was wondering why she had come to this place far away from home just to learn from a man who was only occasionally in this world.

******

Brannhår and the widow took the old man back to his house and the widow made him lie down in the bed. He was asleep within minutes. Brannhår asked whether she should stay with him in case he awoke but the widow said, "Oh no. You needn't do that. He'll be out of it at least until morning. You're new here so, if I were you, I'd do some exploring; get to know the town. If you're to be studying with Torin you could always have a look at his workshops. Just look, mind you; he has all sorts of experiments rigged up and he might not appreciate you disturbing any of them. Anyway, I've work to do so I'll leave you and see you this evening; if you get lost just ask for widow Oggnar's place, everyone knows where I live."

The widow left and Brannhår wondered what she should do. The girl was still in the camp outside town but Brannhår thought that she'd be fine for a few hours so she thought she might do as the widow had suggested and explore. Since the widow had mentioned workshops she decided to try those first. When she went out of the rear door of the house she saw that there was a sort of open area surrounded by several sheds like the food store that they had outside the cave back home on Valdirey. She tried the door to the first one: it opened up onto one massive room. It was much larger than the food store at home and it was cluttered with all kinds of things. Some appeared to be items in the process of construction, others were finished machines of some kind. There were two long benches; one was littered with glassware and odd tools and had a large earthenware tub at one end that was full of water. The other bench was more familiar; it was equipped as a silversmith's forge. There were the tools, in neat racks, and the hearth that looked to be fired by charcoal but which was cold and anvils of various sizes. It even had a small lathe. A tall set of shelves against one wall held a dozen books and numerous stacks of paper. Brannhår examined them and saw that most of them were drawings and sketches; presumably of the old man's ideas. However one stack was different. This consisted of maps, most were rough and hand-drawn but a few looked like works of art and had obviously taken the artist months or even years of effort.

Brannhår wondered what would be in the other sheds and so she went to look. One was stacked to its roof with materials. There was timber, she counted at least four varieties and there were strips and coils of metals. There were sheets of leather and cloth and parchment and, stacked against one wall a series of sheets of glass protected by thick sheets of felt. Another shed was obviously used as a store; but, judging by the layers of dust and the cobwebs, it was only used infrequently. She saw chipped crockery, broken picture frames and stacks of surplus furniture. There were ladders and something that looked like a winch. This shed wasn't full by any means and she saw that there was a bed propped up against the rear wall. It needed re-roping but it looked serviceable.

She wondered whether she dared move the girl into this place. Perhaps she could hide here until she recovered. In the first shed there'd been a pile of maps and one was of the town and so she went back to find it. When she examined it, she could roughly identify where she'd left the girl and she could see that the spot wasn't ideal. It was away from the main road but it was almost on top of a hunting trail. There was nothing for it; she'd have to bring the girl into the town and try to keep her concealed in the shed.

When she got back to the widow's house the widow was up to her elbows in purple dye again. "I thought that I would earn my keep and bring something back for your larder but I'm afraid I won't be back tonight before sunset. I'll be fine camping out; I'm used to being outdoors."

"Well, I wouldn't say no to some fresh game if you can manage to get some but there's not much about these days. That's one of the problems being so near to the capital. There are too many people to support the old ways of hunting. Nowadays most of our meat comes from farms. It's fine for most folks but my husband was a traditionalist and he used to trap fiskur for the table at least once a month."

Brannhår nodded, "I'll be back tomorrow, or maybe the next day. Can you tell Torin where I've gone."

"Of course, but his mind will probably still be away by the time you return. It seems that it stays away longer and longer these days. I'm afraid that soon it will never come back. It's a shame, he was a great maker in his day."

Brannhår nodded again and said farewell then she hurried off to collect her pack.

It was almost dark when Brannhår found Racka. She had managed to fend for herself and she was in quite a cheerful mood. The girl was unsure whether hiding in the town was such a good idea but Brannhår explained that it would probably be the last place that the justicers would look.

Racka needed to stop frequently. However, there was a clear sky and bright aurora and Brannhår used the time whilst the girl was resting to hunt. Game was scarce but the unwary Brockviken was too intent on its own prey to notice Brannhår's thrown hammer until it was too late. The beast was very scrawny and Brannhår didn't think that it would make much of a meal but it would give her an excuse for her nocturnal wanderings.

They reached the town about an hour before dawn and they carefully picked their way through the streets to Torin's house.

Over the next couple of days, whilst Torin's mind was still sleeping, Brannhår set to work cleaning and repairing the neglect that the house had suffered. She found all the tools and materials in his sheds and she was just repairing the roof when she heard a commotion coming from the direction of the southern gate.

Brannhår climbed down and went to see what the fuss was about. As she approached the rear of the crowd she held back. There was something that involved magic just ahead. Several people were talking to each other and Brannhår listened in.

"The poor thing, it must have been terrible. Eaten by the fiskur and only a few scraps of clothing left." one woman said.

"And so near the road. I've always said that we should have more patrols. Just think, if the justicers hadn't found her then it might have been years until we found out what happened." a second woman answered.

"What I can't understand is why they went looking for her in the first place." the first woman said.

"I asked one of the justicers and he said that she was a bad sort. She'd attacked a healer and stolen the healer's crystal."

"Well then, she got what she deserved: but still, to be eaten by fiskur. I've often said that we should get a hunting party together and go and hunt all the fiskur down. Then we'd be safer." the second woman said.

Brannhår moved away, the conversation had started to circle around and she didn't want to hear any more. Personally she thought that even the fiskur had their place in the great scheme of things and, if you left them alone, then they generally weren't that dangerous. She moved forward through the crowd and saw that there were three justicers stood around the back of a cart examining something. It just looked like a bundle of rags.

One of the justicers was waving a crystal pendant above the bundle and she overheard him say, "I can't really tell. The traces are very faint but I'm getting two types of blood. The majority is human and female but there's some different types as well. Either she wasn't alone when she died or the she managed to damage the fiskur."

"Yes, that's right. There could have been someone else involved," another of the justicers said.

The third justicer, the one who had tried to frighten Brannhår had been briefed by his superiors that there was to be no suspicion that the girl had met with anything other than an accident. He interrupted, "It doesn't matter, there's not enough left to tell exactly what happened. The case is closed and we will return to the capital tomorrow. I suggest we leave this mess for the townspeople to clear up. I need a drink."

The trio turned and walked away. As there wasn't any prospect of further action the crowd followed suit. Soon there were only a couple of children left staring at the bloody bundle. Brannhår felt some relief, there'd been too little of the assassin left to identify, and then she remembered. The assassin had been dragged away by the fiskur; there should have been no other blood left behind on the girl's clothes. Perhaps the second type of blood had been from the unborn child. Maybe that was why the third justicer had wanted to close the case down quickly. When she arrived back at Torin's house she found the old man sat at the table in the main room."I want to know why there's an injured girl in my storage shed. I don't remember her being there two days ago before you came."

"I'm sorry Master Torin but please let me explain."

It took a while but finally the old man sat back in his chair. "So you brought me trouble even before you arrived. Well, by rights I should turn you both over to the justicers but I'm not going to. First because what you did seems to be just in itself and second because I have never really forgiven them for taking away my little brother when he was eight. So, for the moment, I'll help you keep the girl a secret. However she does present a small logistical problem. I could pass her off as another pupil but that would be stretching the truth too far. Perhaps she could be a distant relative who has come to look after me in my dotage."

"That sounds like an excellent idea," Brannhår replied.

"Yes, I can still have good ideas, I'm not altogether senile yet. However the other problem she creates is one of finance. It would be too much to ask the Widow Oggnar to feed yet another waif and so we will have to generate some income to feed the three of us. How good a smith are you? Ever done any fine work? It doesn't matter, there's always pots and pans in need of mending. Think you could do that or is it beneath you?"

"Oh I am not averse to work and it would make me feel better to pay my own way. I'm sure that I can repair pots and pans if you think it will help."

"Good, I would have expected no less from Norri's daughter. I suggest we leave things for today. You should go back to the widow's tonight and not say anything. We'll sort things out in the morning."

"But what if your mind wanders?" Brannhår asked.

"Oh most of the time it only starts to wander if I get bored. I have a feeling, with you around, that life is going to become much more interesting."

Brannhår arrived back the next day to find that nobody was around. Both Torin and Racka were missing and she began to worry that the justicers had found the girl and had arrested her and the Master maker. There was little that she could do without more information and so she went back to the widow's house. The widow was outside in the yard mixing up an evil smelling liquid in a large vat. She had no idea where Torin was. The widow was helpful though, "Occasionally, when he is in one of his good phases Torin sometimes goes to the inn at the North gate, you could try there"

When she arrived at the inn she found Torin seated outside at a table; he was sipping a hot bru. He beamed at her when he saw her and said in a loud voice, "Ah Brannhår, I was hoping you'd come and find me. I am waiting for the morning coach from the capital."

Brannhår was perplexed because she had no idea what was going on. She nodded and replied, "Master Torin, I'm glad I found you. I appear to have misplaced the item we discussed last night."

"Oh what am I to do with you girl? I leave you alone for a few hours and you lose one of my cherished maps. As penance you can carry my niece's luggage when she arrives." Torin said loudly.

Brannhår couldn't make out why the man was speaking so loudly, he was almost shouting but he'd mentioned his 'niece' and he obviously had a plan.

Ch 12: Lord Skald

Lord Skald was pleased with the report from the group at Longbarrow. It had taken the devil's own time for the body to be found but it was better that it had been found by a traveller rather than his own agents. Still the matter was now successfully resolved. The girl and her child were gone and her incompetent supervisors had been posted away. He was now the only person left in the capital that knew the full history of the girl's transgression. As he'd ordered, Kalten had made himself scarce. He'd not been seen in the capital for several weeks. All that remained was to report his success to the other Lords.

He summoned his aide, "There is a council meeting tomorrow. Prepare my robes and my mitre. I will not require you to accompany me."

The next day Lord Skald filed into the meeting chamber along with his fellow Lords of the Justiciary. The chamber followed ancient dwarven practice; it was in a cave deep underground. The temperature was a constant four degrees but the lord's robes were designed for comfort and none of them noticed the cold. Apart from the lack of windows the room bore little resemblance to a traditional cave. The walls and ceiling were decorated in the classical style showing friezes of ancient battles and scenes from history and the opulent furniture and fixtures glowed gold in the light from hundreds of lamps.

 After the usual tedious preliminaries and apologies from the lords who couldn't attend they settled down to business. Lord Valdur began the proceedings with a long financial report on the income from the subject temples. Six items later Skald was passed the speaker's gong and stood to open the debate on the status of the maker rebellion.

"My Lords I am glad to report that we have broken the power of the maker rebellion, the likes of Jorrel have fled and their supporters are in disarray. My men are eliminating the rank and file and are making sure that the leaders are apprehended or neutralised in other ways. However the Justiciary must continue to show a firm hand. Therefore my men will continue to root out remaining pockets of rebels and we will continue sanctions against those already identified."

There were murmurs of approval from around the table but then Lord Hadrur spoke up, "But the makers only want equality, not power. Jorell and the others are old men and will not survive long. They argue that justice must be tempered with mercy and understanding. That's why their message is so popular with the lower orders. If we demonstrated a similar flexibility we might not be so unpopular."

"We are not engaging in a popularity contest. The rebellion has been dealt with and the populace have learned that we will not be crossed. However our victory is only temporary, we must consider the causes of the rebellion and deal with those.

The rebellion is not the main threat from the makers. We all know that there are too many advancements from the makers that are supplanting our magic. This is a direct challenge to our authority but it is one that cannot be resolved by force."

Lord Froal interrupted, "They are too bloody clever for their own good. Each tiny weakening of the power of magic from their infernal devices chips away at our control."

"That's true," Lord Sandrey interjected, "Why, I received a report from Kirastuun only the other day. Some clever maker has created a system of sending messages using mirrors that reflect sunlight from mountaintop to mountaintop. It is in direct competition to our system of magical communication by crystal and it needs no participation from a justicer to make it work. It is a good thing that it only operates during daylight. At least we should be grateful for that.".

"Yes, but it's only a matter of time until some other clever bastard works out how to do it in the dark and then there'll be no stopping them," Lord Froal said.

"Gentlemen," Lord Skald banged the gong to override the growing hubbub, "let's have a little order and get back to the business in hand. The maker disturbances are just the tip of the iceberg. We need to show that we are the supreme authority on Svartalfheim

We must be seen to be the defenders of morality and proper order. What we need to do now is to change tactics. Clearly making is deeply entrenched in society and trying to imprison or intimidate every practitioner is impossible. However we can divert their energies away from new things and encourage them to adopt traditional arts. We need to make invention unpopular or, even better, suspect.

My lords I propose that we take the following approach. First we need to discover what inventions are planned before they become realised. Then we can make a judgement whether to suppress it before it becomes widely known. To this end I intend to set up a system of registration of invention. We will encourage makers to participate by telling them that the system will ensure that whoever thought of the idea in the first place has a claim on its application. We will tell them that this will give them protection against others claiming their work."

"The maker code of honour already forbids falsely claiming someone else's work as your own. So I can't see how prior registration helps us." Lord Hadrur said.

"Ah but it does," Skald continued, "Makers tend to be absorbed in their own worlds and they keep details of their work to themselves until they are ready to reveal it to the world. If we reinforce this behaviour by insisting that they can't get the protection that registration will give them if they reveal details before they register. Therefore we will gain first knowledge of any developments and we can suppress those that threaten our magic quietly by claiming that it has been registered previously or we demonstrate that it is too dangerous to use safely. We reinforce this by publishing those inventions that are patently absurd and subjecting their makers to ridicule and scorn. This will then encourage the rest of the populace to think of this type of maker as mad or dangerous."

"But, if we suppress all technical invention, how will dwarf society advance?" Lord Hadrur asked.

"Ah, my measures will still allow society to advance. However, the advances will be at our pace. Discoveries will be steered into the right channels; channels that we will control." Lord Skald answered. Several groups had started talking between themselves but he let them continue for a few minutes before tapping the gong to gain their attention.

"The registration process by itself will not be enough. We might not realise the implications of an idea before it is too late. We need to throttle the current fashion for technology and reduce the number of makers involved. However, I have a strategy that will change that fashion.

Maker dwarves are like the rest of us; they need an income and if the income from pure invention isn't forthcoming they will turn to other sources. Therefore, in parallel with establishing control of technical invention, I propose that we secretly fund new categories at Kraftmoot to encourage makers to channel their creativity into artistic endeavours. New prizes for jewellery, painting, music, crafts or even poetry will divert their ideas into harmless avenues. The prizes will be funded from our supporters and they will be generous."

There were general murmurs of approval from around the table. As they'd arranged before the meeting, Lord Sandrey stood and Skald nodded to acknowledge him. "I think that I speak for the rest of us when I say that I approve of Lord Skald's proposals. I would, however, ask when we might expect these measures to be put in place?"

Skald smiled, "I am glad that Lord Sandrey has raised this important point and I am happy to report that my office has completed the necessary preparations for the registration. I have also donated a considerable sum from my own reserves to start the ball rolling with the new prizes for the Kraftmoot. I would encourage other members of this council to follow my lead and to recruit more financial support from amongst their friends."

As Skald sat down there was a smattering of applause. A clerk appeared at his shoulder and took up the gong. Another clerk consulted a list and signalled the first one to put it down again. The action signalled the end of one item and the beginning of the next.

Skald stood again, "My lords, I can now report that the matter of the pregnant novice has been dealt with."

"I can't see why we needed to make such a great fuss over such a commonplace occurrence. Surely we could have just banished the girl or sent her back to her family in disgrace," Lord Hadrur said.

Skald frowned, "We all know that we cannot allow sexual relations between novices, or anyone in the Justiciary for that matter. It is our canon rule."

"But surely it's against nature, they may be nascent wizards but they are just teenagers after all. It's not natural for them to be celibate when they are undergoing the hormonal changes of puberty. I'm sure that, a few decades ago we used to turn a blind eye to such happenings and then banish the culprits. It seems harsh that they must be executed along with their offspring." Hadrur replied.

"We are not talking about ancient history. The morals of our society have undergone a reformation since those dissolute times. We no longer indulge such practices. The rules are the rules and they will be enforced to the letter of our laws." Skald raged, "There are enough dissenters amongst the masters; we can do without them in our own ranks and if we cannot control our own then how can we hope to control the rest of the populace?"

Every other person around the table tried to look away. Skald's face was red and his eyes were protruding. They knew that the meeting was at an end and there would be no more discussion.

Ch 13: A New Arrival

The coach from the city came through the gate right on time and it drew up at the inn. It was immediately surrounded by a crowd of children who circled around it playing some game. The driver of the coach shouted and shook his fist at them for upsetting his team of smygl and so nobody noticed the passengers disembarking. Brannhår ignored the children, she was following Torin's gaze. She saw the girl come from behind the coach and mingle with the passengers. The girl was lugging a large bag. Torin jumped up and rushed over to her; Brannhår followed. "Torunn, my dear niece. It is so good to see you again" Torin said at the top of his voice as he embraced her." He turned to Brannhår, "Brannhår, may I present my niece Torunn Jonaldsdóttir, Brannhår Dagmarsdóttir meet Torunn, my niece."

Brannhår had finally worked out what was going on. The wily old man had arranged everything. He had probably even arranged the children's antics as a distraction. His 'niece' had appeared when the coach had arrived and she'd been with the passengers who disembarked. There were a dozen witnesses who would swear that she'd just arrived from the capital and another dozen who had seen Torin claim her as his niece. Therefore she was Torin's niece from the capital and nobody would connect her to the justicer fugitive whose remains had been found to the south. Brannhår cheerfully shouldered Torunn's bag, it was incredibly light but she managed to act as though it was full of clothes. They set off back to Torin's house.

Life settled down in the town and people became used to the new arrangements. Torin's mind still wandered but not as often and not for as long. Torunn became well again and began to look after the household for Torin. Brannhår began to take on small jobs as a smith and people quickly recognised her skill and brought all sorts of things for her to repair. It didn't keep her too busy and she would spend a lot of her time going through Torin's sheds learning from Torin's vast store of eclectic interests. She had also persuaded the Master maker to teach her silversmithing. Norri had taught her all the traditional methods but Torin's skills were legendary and he wasn't afraid to try new things. "After all, if we never try anything new we never learn anything and that's the secret, Brannhår, Never stop learning."

Of course there were times when the old man's mind was elsewhere. Brannhår and Torunn had spent the evening exploring objects in Torin's collection. They came across a small figurine carved from stone.

"I wonder where Uncle Torin got it from?" Torunn asked, "We'll have to ask him when he wakes up."

They did, Torin told them that he hadn't a clue where he'd acquired the figurine. He said that he'd often picked things up in markets when he'd travelled through the isles in his youth. He'd often thought of cataloguing all the bits and pieces that he'd collected but he'd never seemed to have the time. Now, when he had the time, he couldn't remember where everything had come from.

Brannhår thought that it was a shame to see the old man's memories fading but he told her that it really wasn't a burden at all. "When you get to my age I think that the mind starts to clear out all the old junk that it's accumulated. It leaves room for new knowledge.

Torunn nodded and began to wander away. She was humming to herself and then she began to sing. Brannhår had never heard her sing before and she said, "You've got a lovely voice, sing some more."

Torin hadn't heard the girl singing before but he was slightly alarmed, the girl's voice was good but it was too good she was small but the sound that she emitted was too big for her frame.

"Tell me Torunn, did you always have such a deep voice?"

"Oh no, the sisters at the Temple taught me how to use my magic to sing. They do it all the time but they said that I had a real talent for it."

"Yes, little one, you are correct and it reminds me that I need to warn you of something. When you and Brannhår are plotting together you should always be on the lookout for anyone who might be listening. There are plenty of people in this town who would jump at the chance of turning you both in to the justicers for the reward."

"What reward?" Brannhår asked.

"Don't you know that there's a standing reward posted by the Justiciary for information leading to the capture of renegade magic users. Last I heard it was a hundred gold crowns." Torin replied.

"But that's enough to set someone up for life," Brannhår said.

"Yes, girl. It is. So you both best be careful," Torin replied.

It was sometime later that Brannhår realised what the old man had said. He had included her. Did he know or guess about her power?

Brannhår had gained quite a reputation as a mender and her lessons on silversmithing were progressing nicely but she chafed at living in the town. It didn't feel right somehow. She took to escaping into the small hilly country to the south when time permitted. She preferred to be alone. Torunn was a puzzle. She had spent half her life as the spoiled daughter of a rich merchant and the rest of it being taught the ways of the justicers. Even though they'd plotted her death and killed her unborn child she still acted like one of them. The girl occasionally ordered Brannhår about and she would skimp on chores. Privately Brannhår thought that she wasn't too bright especially as she spent much of her free time with the widow's youngest daughter who was boy-mad. During one of her silversmithing lessons she broached the subject with Torin. "I forget sometimes that you are Norri's daughter, he would certainly have disapproved of Torunn's behaviour. When he last wrote to me he told me that you seemed old for your years and now I know you I think so too. Have you never wanted to go off with some boy and do silly romantic things?"

Brannhår considered, "Not really, I have male friends at home but I was never drawn to any of them. Perhaps it's because I think that exploring new ideas is more interesting."

Torin nodded, "As I said, an old head on young shoulders. Never mind, I'm glad that you came. Now tell me why does drawing wire fascinate you so? We have enough in our stock drawer to decorate the town meeting hall in filigree."

"Master, wire has other uses besides decoration, may I show you?"

"Of course,"Torin replied.

Brannhår cleared a space on the bench and then went to her personal store and took out a peculiar metal jar. Torin looked at it curiously. It wasn't solid, it consisted of two very thin metal cups one inside the other. The thin space between them was filled with pitch. She then took some silver wire from the store and twisted one strand of it around a tab on the inner cup and another strand around a tab on the outer cup. She let the end of the second strand fall to the floor. Next she attached the strand from the inner cup to a silver plate held in a wooden clamp.

Torin said, "It doesn't look very decorative.

"No master it's not meant to be. Now you know that you can produce small sparks of lightning by rubbing a piece of amber with fur?"

"Yes, even a young apprentice knows that. I used to have such fun making sparks in my parent's cave. Some were even bright enough to light up the walls."

"Well Master, I think I have derived a way of capturing the lightning and storing it for later." Brannhår demonstrated charging her device with a large piece of amber and some fur from a ferret. She pointed her finger at the charged plate and a fat spark jumped from the plate to her fingernail.

"It seems like magic," Torin observed.

"No Master it's not magic because it works for anyone. It even worked for Torunn when I persuaded her to try it."

"And what was her reaction?" Torin asked.

"She told me that I was wicked because I'd not told her that it hurts when the spark jumps."

Torin smiled, "As I might have expected. I can see that it's clever but it seems of little practical use."

Brannhår said, "But it does have a use Master. I used lightning to make my hammer. Just think, if we could store lightning, we could release it at will to melt metals and do all sorts of other things."

"You've told me how you say you melted the metal for your hammer but I never quite believed you. You also said that you showed Norri how to gather lightning. Do you think you could show me?"

"Of course Master. It would mean a journey to the highlands."

"I think that the prospect is exciting enough to keep me awake for a few days, let's plan. Torunn can stay behind to mind the shop."

Ch 14: The Lightning Tree

It took several days to plan their trip. Despite Torin's protestations the excitement of the trip didn't keep him awake and Brannhår privately wondered how she would manage if her mentor had an attack whilst they were away. She was pondering the problem when the solution arrived in the mail. The letter had been forwarded from her home but she didn't recognise the writing.

She opened it curiously and had a pleasant surprise. It was from her friend Karol who had accompanied her in the last days of her Menntunleit.

Dear Brannhår

I hope you are well and are enjoying life as an adult. I received word from a mutual friend that you are now on Griprey. What a coincidence! I myself am staying with friends of my parents in the capital as I am studying under the renowned herbalist, Master Kuhlfefer.

I occasionally get time off from my studies to go out into the countryside to gather herbs and ingredients and I was wondering if I could visit you. I know that Mistle would love to see you again, she gets quite fractious living near the city even though the house where I am staying is actually a good distance from it. Please let us come to visit you.

I can probably arrange to be away from my studies for a few days. It would be good if we could be together in the wilderness again as we were in Skogrey. Please write back soon and please say yes to my visit.

Your friend forever

Karol.

Brannhår re-read the letter and realised that, with everything that had happened since, she had pushed her memories of Menntunleit to the back of her mind. Now they came flooding back and she realised that she too would like to see the boy and the puppy again. She smiled, she was sure that Karol wanted to spend time with her alone and he'd included the part about the wolf-puppy becoming fractious as a subtle blackmail. However, she could see how a visit from an old friend who might be amenable to spending a few days in the highlands with her might help her out.

Karol had included a return address and so she immediately went in search of some writing materials to frame her reply.

Dear Karol

Your letter was a surprise but a very welcome one. Of course I would welcome a visit from you here in Longbarrow. However, I might be able to go one better and arrange that we could re-create our time in the wilderness together. My mentor has expressed a wish to learn what I know of lightning and we are planning a trip into the highlands.

I must admit that, although Master Torin is a man who finds all knowledge fascinating, he is elderly and having someone more my age along for company would please me greatly... and Mistle of course, I would dearly love to see how she's grown. She must be almost an adult by now and I wonder if she'll remember me.

Write back soon and we can make plans.

Your friend

Brannhår

Less than ten days later the coach from the city arrived bearing Karol and Mistle. Brannhår was waiting and smiled as she saw that Karol had had to ride outside because the adolescent she wolf that accompanied him would have caused difficulties with the other, more gentrified, passengers. When Karol alighted he stood there awkwardly for a few seconds. Brannhår surprised herself by rushing over to him to hug him. Mistle was wary at first but when Brannhår offered her the back of her hand to sniff the wolf's reticence melted away and Brannhår was almost bowled over by the wolf's excited greeting.

As they walked back to Torin's house Brannhår told Karol how she'd decided to come to Longbarrow to study with Torin. She didn't mention her run-in with the justicer assassin or how she'd rescued Torunn. Karol was nice and she felt that she could trust him but she wasn't ready to admit that she had a distinct aversion to justicers and their antics.

Karol told her how he'd come to Griprey and how his knowledge of herbs had blossomed whilst studying with Master Kuhlfefer. When they arrived at Torin's house he was amazed to discover that Torin and Kuhlfefer had know each other for years and that he was welcomed like a long lost son.

The trio spent a long evening making plans and none of them noticed when Torunn slipped away to go to visit her friend, the widow's youngest daughter, Elsa. Neither did anyone notice that Torunn hadn't returned when they all boarded the hired cart early the next morning. This was mainly because Mistle had been overjoyed that they were clearly going on an adventure and were taking her along. She bounded around yelping at imagined phantoms and it was a while before she settled and allowed herself to be tethered in the back of the cart ready for the journey.

The cart made good time along the main road to the south and they were well past the fishing village of Beltafiirn before the light was gone. They made camp and, after supper, they sat around the campfire talking, or rather Torin talked and the others listened. Torin was an amazing fount of knowledge. The aurora was dim and you could see the stars. He pointed out stars and told them their names and their stories: the stars were other suns and that some of them had planets like Svartalfheim. Soon even Torin fell silent, lost in the wonder of contemplation and, when the air started to get chilly, they all settled down to sleep. Mistle, of course, wasn't interested in cosmology and so she took herself off into the woods to hunt.

The next day everyone was awake early and keen to get on. They turned the cart north and encountered some rougher terrain that made the going slower. Brannhår wasn't discouraged because she

135

could see distant hills looming on the horizon and where there were hills, sooner or later there would be lightning. Karol kept up a running commentary about the various plants that they passed on the way. Torin listened politely at first but Brannhår could see that his mind was elsewhere. This was what she'd feared; Torin's mind wandered if he wasn't interested in a subject. Karol didn't seem to notice until the old man swayed in his seat and nearly toppled from the cart. Brannhår caught him just in time and there was a brief pause whilst she and Karol transferred Torin to the back of the cart where he could 'take a nap'.

Karol was secretly pleased. With the master maker out of the way he had Brannhår all to himself. She, however seemed more interested in throwing sticks for Mistle to retrieve. He decided that he would be on safe ground if he reminisced about their time together on Skogrey. "I'll never forget how you saved my life when that ironoak tree was hit by lightning. If it wasn't for you I wouldn't be here now."

Brannhår looked at him, "Technically it wasn't me it was Mistle. She instinctively sensed the danger and pulled me over. If she hadn't I'd have been shredded as well. It was something though, wasn't it. Torin tells me that nobody had ever witnessed the propagation cycle of an ironoak before and lived to tell the tale."

Karol nodded enthusiastically, "Yes, I know. It was one of the things that helped me get a position with Master Kuhlfefer. I wrote about it for the journal of herbalism and he read the article. As he already knew my parents he wrote to them and I was invited to Griprey. I'd been hoping to visit the capital because I'd learned from Brother Kerian that you'd moved to Griprey as well and I thought it would be good to see you again. I even kept a seed from the ironoak as a souvenir. It's quite amazing. It's not like most plant seeds it has a peculiar structure." He fished in his pocket and brought out a large, arrow shaped, black lump and handed it to Brannhår. "It's very unusual, most seeds have a hard shell and a soft interior. The shell protects the actual part that grows into a new tree and the soft part provides the food to start it growing. That one is very heavy and seems to be hard all the way through. The one that I dissected blunted and corroded my best scalpel in a few minutes. Little sparks kept flying out where I cut."

Brannhår had only been paying a polite attention up to that point but Karol's remark triggered a thought. She looked at the seed with her other senses and what she saw nearly made her fall off the wagon just like Torin. The seed glittered with tiny sparks of the same energy that made up the lightning. Could it be that the ironoak had evolved a way to harness the lightning for its own purposes. Clearly there were other ways to propagate seeds but this plant had chosen to use the celestial bolts to its advantage. Perhaps it didn't just use the explosive effect, maybe it stored some of the blast to start new life in its seeds. Brannhår stared at the seed for such a long time that Karol grew concerned. "I know you'll think I'm silly but I imagined that the seed had saved some of the lightning..." his words trailed of uncertainly.

Brannhår turned and grasped his hand, "No! No! It's not silly at all. Don't you see what you discovered. The ironoak uses the lightning as the energy to start its new life. Karol, you're amazing. Don't you realise what this means. The ironoak has solved the problem of storing lightning. It's something I've been working on for some time. Let's see..." She stood up on the cart seat and gazed around at the countryside. "I can't see any ironoak around here, let's move on and tell me as soon as you see some."

Karol was puzzled, "But I thought that we were going to the hills to find lightning?"

"Oh we can do that any day. What we need now is to examine an ironoak closely. You can help. With your knowledge of plants you can probably discover more. This is exciting."

They carried on at a steady pace keeping a lookout for any sign of ironoak. However, anyone knows that the harder that you look for something the more difficult it is to find and so the ironoak was nowhere to be found. It wasn't until just before sunset that they spied the distinctive outline of one of the trees, by then it was too dark to do any real study and so they camped near to its base. Karol insisted that they didn't camp right under it because he wasn't prepared to risk a lightning strike. Brannhår could have told him that there wouldn't be any lightning around for days but, although she liked the lad, she wasn't ready to share secrets just yet. Mistle provided dinner, she brought back a young elgrott that she'd caught. They roasted it and sat together under the aurora again: Torin was still fast asleep in the cart.

The next day they breakfasted on the remains of the elgrott then climbed up to the ironoak. It had always puzzled Brannhår why the ironoak seemed to insist on growing in exposed areas on the tops of hills; it hadn't made sense for the tree to invite being blasted by lightning. Now it did, the tree needed lightning. As she approached the tree she reached out with her senses and wondered why she'd never noticed before that the tree was seething with a soft electricity. It differed from the spinning electricity that she sensed in metals, this electricity seemed to move up and down the tree's limbs. Brannhår wondered why she could sense this electricity when there was no lightning for miles around. Surely the tree couldn't still be storing the energy from its most recent encounter with lightning. For one thing the tree was in full leaf which meant that it hadn't been blasted for many months. She sat on the ground staring at the tree for so long that Karol grew concerned, "You've been staring at it for an hour, shouldn't we be gathering samples or taking measurements or at least sketching parts?"

"Oh, I wish you could see it like I can, it's beautiful."

"I don't know how you can say that. It looks too dull to me. There is no colour, even the leaves look like old metal and, as for the twisted stems, they look like an old man's arm with all his veins standing out."

Brannhår looked at the tree again, "I can see what you mean but the veins, as you call them are just that. They are carrying the energy down from the leaves to the roots. The leaves are dull because they are drinking in the sunlight and letting none go to waste. Oh Karol, this tree is a wonder. You're going to be the most famous herbalist on the planet when you write this up in your journal."

"What do you mean? You're teasing me aren't you?" he laughed," most famous herbalist on the planet."

"The first thing we need to do is look at the leaves." she said.

"I'm sure botany is very interesting but aren't we supposed to be in the mountains?" a third voice asked.

"Master Torin, you're awake!" Brannhår exclaimed.

"Obviously," the old man replied, "now why are we sat under an unremarkable tree in a wood that is clearly in the foothills. Shouldn't we be higher up by now?"

"Oh Master Torin, we don't need to go any higher. This tree holds the secrets of lightning if only we can unlock them."

"I don't know why but I am curious. Tell me more."

By the time Brannhår had explained her observations and theories to Torin and then again to Karol and then discussed and argued it was mid day. The sun was hot and Mistle, the most practical member of the party, insisted that it was time for some play. Brannhår laughed at her antics and they rolled and tumbled together on the ground.

Torin looked on amused, "You wouldn't think that that dusty creature playing with a wolf has one of the best minds I've come across in years."

"No Master Torin, you wouldn't," Karol nodded in agreement, "Master Torin, can you understand what she's saying about energy currents and conductors and all the other stuff. I'm totally confused?"

"Like I said, lad, she is very bright. She sees things clearly and is always struggling to understand how everything works. And there's something about the way she thinks. It's as if she knows things already and only needs to be reminded of them. Tell me, what do you know about her?"

Karol frowned, "To tell you the truth, I don't know that much. We met by accident during Menntunleit and we were together for most of a week. She showed me the ruins that she discovered and she told me how she made her axe, she saved my life and I healed some of her wounds. Other than that, I know very little."

"Well, her father, Norri is an old friend of mine but he's not her biological father. Her parents found her half drowned in a lake near their home. She was tiny, only the size of a baby, and at first, Norri thought that she was some sort of álfur water sprite. However, he soon changed his mind as she grew. He told me that he'd been mistaken when he'd associated her with water he now believes that she seems to have an affinity with fire. So, you tell me lad, is she a dwarf or something else? She's been tested by the justicers and she's not magical but, all the same, there is something otherworldly about her. I've tried asking her but she considers herself as normal as you and me. One thing is for sure, she's clever and she's more curious than a barrel full of skogs."

"Yes I'd agree. Now why is she so excited by this tree? I can appreciate that it doesn't seem to work like other trees but surely it's still just a tree."

"Oh, it's not the tree in itself that fascinates her, it's what the tree represents. Surely you can see that storing the energy of lightning could be useful for all sorts of things. She's been experimenting on storing lightning energy for a long time. If the tree has already developed a way of storing the energy then maybe we can adapt it to store energy for us. Then we can use it to power other things. She's excited by the prospect, I'm excited by the prospect and, if you have any sense of wonder then you should be excited by the prospect. It's not going to be easy extracting the secrets from the tree but between the three of us we should be able to make a good start. Jump on the bandwagon lad before it passes you by, it's the best prospect for fame and fortune that I've ever come across."

"If you say so Master Torin," Karol replied.

They were interrupted by Brannhår who had come back dusty, sweaty but with a huge grin on her face, "I hate to tell you this," she said, "but I'm starving."

They spent three more days just studying the tree and they returned home with more questions than answers. However, they'd loaded up the cart with enough samples of the branches, bark, leaves and roots to continue their research for months. One thing was certain, they'd be back. The lightning tree hadn't revealed all its secrets in the few short days that they'd been there.

******

Brannhår was walking down a street in a strange city but she wasn't afraid because part of her mind was telling her that what she saw was normal. The other part of her mind was counting impossible things. There were too many people and they were all giants but they were ignoring her. The street was lined with shops and whilst one part of her mind ignored the displays another studied them intensely. They had huge sheets of glass between the people and the goods; that in itself was amazing. She'd seen sheets of glass but never any that were so big and so clear. The curious thing was that someone had stuck paper onto the glass in a diamond pattern. The part of her mind that found all this normal told the curious part that this was also normal.

She turned off the street and started to climb up some steps. At the top of the steps there were doors, these too were glazed and covered in the paper strips. However all thoughts of the strips vanished immediately as she saw her reflection. No wonder the giants were ignoring her, she was a giant herself. Her reflection matched the part of her mind that found all this normal. It climbed some other steps and went down a long corridor to a door. The door opened and she saw that she was in a vast workshop. There were half a dozen giants already in the workshop but they also ignored her. She marched across the room and sat down at one of the workbenches. There were fine tools scattered across it and pieces of strange wire covered in a peculiar, hard, waxy substance. One of the other giants had come across to her. He spoke "Hello Ann come

141

and see this." The giant part of her mind was a little irritated at the giant's suggestion but the curious part, which she was beginning to think of as her real mind, was intrigued. She followed the giant man.

"Lo, the amazing disappearing iron bar trick," he said, and he pointed to an iron bar that was resting inside a cylindrical coil of the wax covered wire. One end of the wire was connected to a large cylinder and the unreal part of her mind recognised it as a device for storing lightning energy. The giant held the other end in his hand. "Now, watch. Don't look away or you'll miss it," the giant said. She stared at the bar and, out of the corner of her eye, she saw him touch the end of the wire to the lightning device. She must have blinked because the iron bar wasn't in the wire coil any longer. The giant reached out his hand and caught it as it fell from somewhere high over their heads. The giant looked inordinately pleased with himself and he said "Tra-la!"

Then she felt her knees go weak and she was falling. She had visions of the iron bar jumping into the air of its own accord and she remembered another time when some iron had moved like that. She'd been small and she'd been left to mend the food store at home and a Baar had attacked. She'd killed it by hitting it in the head with her small hammer. Somehow the two events were linked. She'd almost forgotten that lightning had been involved on that occasion as well. The lightning from the storm had propelled the hammer head into the baar just as the tame lightning in that strange workshop had propelled the iron bar into the air.

This connection was important and she strained to tell herself to remember it but the dream was fading and she could hear Karol's voice echoing in her ears, "Come on, sleepy head. Breakfast is ready and we need to get on our way if we're going to get back to Longbarrow before dark.

Brannhår was distracted all the way home, she couldn't get the vague snatches of dream out of her head. It was important but she couldn't understand why. She was slightly annoyed; her giant dream self had watched the events and had understood what was happening and her real self hadn't. It was unfair. And then she realised that she must have understood what happened at some level... hadn't she used it when she'd defeated the baar? So she calmed herself. The idea wasn't gone, it was there hiding in the back of her mind. All that she had to do was let it come out of its hiding place. The gentle rocking of the cart they'd hired quickly lulled her to sleep. Having lurid nightmares was all well and good but they always left her tired.

******

The trio had spent more time than they'd intended on their trip and Karol's return to the capitol was overdue. It seemed to Brannhår that they'd only been back for a few hours and already it was time for him to leave. What made it worse was that Torin had taken him aside to have what he called 'a private talk' and Karol had come back subdued and not at all like the cheerful boy that she'd grown fond of. Perhaps if she'd been privy to their conversation she might have understood but she didn't discover what they'd said until much later.

Torin grabbed Karol's shoulder, "Just a minute lad, I want a word with you in private. Come into my storeroom, we won't be disturbed there."

Karol had followed the old man and, when invited, he sat down puzzled.

Torin cleared his throat noisily and said, "You know I like you lad and I can see that Brannhår likes you as well. Now I'm not so old that I've forgotten what it was like to be young. I like Brannhår but I have a responsibility towards her that goes further than mere liking. You know she is the daughter of my old friend Norri," Karol nodded, "well I promised him that I'd look after her whilst she was here with me. In fact I've grown to like her so much that I consider her to be like my own daughter. I can see that you feel more than just friendship for Brannhår and I want to get some facts straight. Understand that she is quite naive when it comes to men. She has spent most of her life amongst simple country folk and isn't used to the sort of society that treats flirting as a sport. I promise you that, if you ever hurt her in any way, physically or mentally, I will come after you and, although I may be an old man, I still have enough influence to make your life very uncomfortable in many ways. Do you understand what I am saying?"

"Yes Master Torin, I understand. You're right, I do have feelings for Brannhår and I'm also sure that she doesn't feel the same towards me... yet. However, I will persevere and I will try to win her affections. Rest assured that I would never dream of harming her in any way, you have my word."

"Good, then that's understood. As long as you keep your word you're welcome to come back here and visit. Let's say no more of this and get back. I'm sure that Brannhår will want to talk to you before you leave."

Ch 15: Running Away to the Circus.

Karol left for his home in the city and suddenly the adventure was over. Brannhår had a few misgivings. On the one hand his departure seemed so abrupt she felt somehow left behind. However, on the other hand she was eager to examine the samples that they'd brought back from the ironoak to see what she could discover. Besides she wanted to explore what she remembered of the dream. Torin was as eager as she was to start the investigation and so she went to find him.

As she walked along the street to the dye-works she saw Torin hurrying towards her. He looked red in the face and he was clearly annoyed about something. The first words he said to her were, "Damn the girl, she's got about as much common sense as that plank of wood. I told her not to do anything that might attract attention and she goes and does this."

Brannhår held up her hand to stop the old man in his tracks, "Master Torin, calm down and tell me the whole story. First, who is 'the girl', do you mean Torunn?"

"Of course I mean Torunn. You know how we've done everything to hide her from the Justiciary and now the silly girl has played right into their hands."

Brannhår was alarmed, she'd told Torin about her rescue of the girl but hadn't told him about the justicer assassin and how she'd dealt with him. She didn't want to attract any attention from the justicers either. She said, "What has she done?"

"Apparently, whilst we were away, she and the widow's youngest decided that life here was too dull and they wanted more excitement. They ran away and left a note for the widow explaining that they were going to the city to make their fortune by singing ballads in the theatre. The widow was distraught and she made a fuss and went to the justicers. Luckily nobody knows Torunn's history other than us so, just now, the justicers think that she's just a runaway. However, imagine what they will do if the ninny lets slip who she really is. We'll be arrested for harbouring her and it's likely we'll all end up dead. There's nothing we can do. We will have to leave, I know a few people that will hide us until the fuss dies down."

Brannhår shook her head, "If she's not completely stupid then she knows that someone is bound to come looking for her. She'll not want to be arrested or brought back here with the widow's daughter and so, if we're lucky, we might be able to find her before the justicers do."

Torin looked relieved, "You're right, we might have a chance," he paused, "I'm sorry Brannhår"

"Why are you sorry? It's not you that ran away."

"No, but I know that you were looking forward to investigating the ironoak. I was as well. We'll just have to postpone it until after we find Torunn and we'd better find her quickly. If the justicers get involved we won't be investigating anything for a while."

"Then we'd better get started," she said.

They caught the afternoon coach headed towards the city. It occurred to Brannhår that she was following on right behind Karol and she chuckled to herself that he would be very surprised to see her so soon after they'd parted if they met up.

When they arrived it was nearly dusk however Torin seemed to know where he was going and soon they were outside an inn called 'The Mallet'. When they entered the main room was only half full. Brannhår thought that it looked run down and most of the people were sat in secluded alcoves or were huddled around dimly lit tables. Torin strode across to the bar and nodded to the bartender. They exchanged a few words and the bartender disappeared into a back room. When he emerged seconds later he was followed by a small woman. She was dressed in layers and layers of scarves each held in place by jewelled clasps and glittering chains and she had a pair of lenses half covering her eyes. She peered at her visitors over the half lenses and then a scowl appeared on her face, "Torin, you old bastard! Get out! You're always trouble."

"I seem to remember that I wasn't the only one who was trouble. Hello Krin, you're as beautiful as ever."

The woman turned her gaze on Brannhår, "Watch him like a hawk, dearie. He'll charm the pants off you and then leave you without another word. I wouldn't trust him as far as I could throw him when I first met him and he looks to have put on a few stones since then."

Brannhår supposed that the woman was joking, she didn't seriously think that Brannhår would be involved with a man old enough to be her father did she?

Torin laughed, "Now you leave her alone Krin. This is Brannhår, my friend and student. She is Norri's daughter"

Krin looked at Brannhår again, "I can't see the resemblance but it is a few years since I've seen Norri. How is your father, dearie?"

"Lady Krin, he was fine when I left Valdirey but I haven't heard from him or my mother for a few months. I imagine that they are getting ready to go back into the mountains for winter."

"Well I'm glad to see that he, at least, has well mannered offspring. I am pleased to meet you, Norri's daughter," the woman turned back to Torin, "I suppose you'll be wanting somewhere to stay, you old rogue?"

"If it pleases you, dearest Krin," Torin replied.

"Well, I suppose I do have a couple of rooms to spare. Mind you it will cost you extra if you don't share."

Torin chuckled, "I'm afraid that we couldn't do that; Brannhår snores terribly"

Brannhår frowned at him but saw that he was joking and the frown turned into a grin. "I don't snore; it's you that keeps the street awake at night Master Torin."

Torin laughed again and they followed Krin up a flight of stairs to their rooms. When they'd dumped their bags Torin said that he was going back down to have a word with Krin. Brannhår had seen the easy comradeship that her mentor had with the woman and she decided that she would only be in the way if she went with him. So she told him that she wanted to have an early night and said that she'd see him in the morning.

At breakfast the next day she waited for Torin and, when he appeared, she could tell that he'd had a few drinks on the previous evening. "That woman can still drink me under the table," he said holding his head in his hands.

"Yes, Master Torin, I can see that."

"Still it was worth it. Krin told me about a few places to start our enquiries. Apparently youngsters coming to the city seeking their fortunes on the stage is nothing new. There are a few, well-established, gathering places for them and Krin suggested that we start there. However, first I've got to have a drink to clear my head," he gestured towards the pot of herbs brewing on a small spirit burner in the centre of the table, "Pour me some will you."

Half an hour later Torin declared that he was fit to face the world and the pair left the inn. They walked for about half a mile until they reached the first of the venues that Krin had suggested. Brannhår had never been in the city itself and she couldn't help feeling uncomfortable with so many people about. She wasn't used to such crowds. Torin, however, acted as if he was a native and he threaded his way through the thronging masses with evident skill.

The first venue didn't seem that impressive to Brannhår. It was a small open space sandwiched between the back of a tall building and a low spread of wooden huts. Various stone benches were scattered about and Brannhår could see that some of them had pairs or trios of teenagers sat on them. Nearly all of the teenagers had musical instruments and she watched as first one group, then another started to play. What she hadn't seen was that there was a set of benches that were hiding in the shadows of the large building. Each of the groups seemed to be directing their performances towards the shadows. Brannhår listened to the groups until one particular duet began to play. They were a young woman and a young man, he played a bass stringed instrument and she played a dainty, high-pitched silver flute. Unexpectedly the combination sounded quite beautiful and at the end of their performance a bell rang out. Immediate looks of disappointment appeared on the faces of quite a few of the youngsters as, out of the shadows, a wizened old man tottered towards the players. The old man was supported by a much younger man who was obviously his assistant. The pair approached the duet and exchanged a few inaudible words. The girl clapped her hands in glee and the boy's face became a wide grin. Even Brannhår could tell that they had been chosen for something. Torin, however was indifferent. "This isn't the place, all these teenagers are musicians. We're looking for singers. Let's get on to the next venue."

******

Justicer Grimm gazed at the crowd in the well lit space in the centre of the amphitheatre. He felt uncomfortable and it wasn't just because it had begun to rain outside and he'd forgotten his waterproofs. This crowd bothered him because he knew he didn't belong. The crowd had also noticed the officer and they'd had the same reaction; here was an outsider, someone who didn't belong.

Grimm shrugged, he shouldn't be here looking for some runaway teenager who probably didn't want to be found. He didn't deserve this assignment and he seethed inside because he knew full-well why his superiors had given it to him. It was punishment. The murder case that he'd investigated a couple of months ago had had repercussions. There'd been nothing wrong with his investigations and that the culprit he'd arrested had been the person who'd committed the crime. However, the culprit was well connected with the higher rungs of society and several senior justicers. They had grown uncomfortable at the implication that they too had criminals amongst their ranks.

He squared his shoulders and strode forward. The knots of gaily clothed youngsters parted before him and he approached the dais on which sat several older men and women in more expensive but equally outrageous dress.

"May I help you officer?" The words came from a round red-faced middle-aged man who was wearing more jewellery than some of the whores that Grimm knew from the seedier parts of the city. Grimm's keen eyes stared at one of the rings on the man's pudgy fingers, they might look like a whore's fakes but Grimm could tell that this one was real. It was probably worth more than Grimm earned in six months.

"Damn it," Grimm thought, "I definitely don't belong here."

What troubled the detective wasn't just the man's effete manner, it was the fact that he was obviously a creative. He belonged to the artistic fraternity, as did the hordes of youngsters gathered around him. Grimm was uncomfortable with creatives, he prided himself in being practical and down to earth. He didn't have fancies, he didn't do things on a whim, he wouldn't be seen dead in what this rich toad was wearing and he would have been willing to bathe in pig swill before he'd wear perfume. The man positively stank of flowers.

Nevertheless the man was obviously rich and he must have some influence with this crowd. Grimm swallowed his instinctive reactions and said, "Yes Sir. You may be able to assist me with my current inquiry. I am looking for two minors who have left their home in Longbarrow to seek their fortune in the city. Their mother is anxious and she has some influence with the authorities there. She has asked the Justiciary to try to find them and return them home and I have been assigned to the task."

"Yes, officer," the man said in a high-pitched voice that grated on Grimm's senses, "Sadly, such runaways are all too common. They believe that the streets of the city are paved with gold and that all they have to do to gain fame and fortune is to be noticed. Unfortunately, as we both know, life is cruel and they often fall foul of unscrupulous people and, dare I say it, the criminal elements of society. I'm afraid that all that I can do is to ask my dear friends here whether they have noticed any such strangers amongst us but I am not hopeful. There are so many and they come and go like the wind."

Grimm gritted his teeth and forced a smile, "I would be grateful if you would do that sir. Perhaps you could send word to me if you hear anything. I will be in the area for the next few days."

The fat man chuckled nervously, "And obviously people will be able to find you. You don't exactly blend in, do you Officer …?"

"Grimm, Sir,"

The man grinned, as if he found Grimm's name funny. "Yes, I guessed that it would be something like that. Well, I must be getting on. I will let you know if I hear of any new arrivals."

Grimm turned and made his way back into the shadows.

******

It took Brannhår and Torin another hour to find the next venue. This was in a large shed that backed on to the main cliff face in the North of the city. As they entered heads swivelled to inspect them and then, just as quickly attention returned to the stage at one end of the shed. Stood on the stage was a young man clad in armour but Brannhår could see that there was something wrong with the way that he was standing and gesticulating. She knew how much armour like that should weigh and the boy didn't look that strong. Then she looked again with her metal-finding senses. What appeared to be thick metal was just a very thin layer of foil covering a thick woollen jerkin. The plates covering his legs were also fake. Brannhår asked one of the audience what was going on but she was shushed immediately. She turned her attention back to the stage. The young man was reciting poetry emphasising each word with dramatic movements of his hands.

Torin leaned over and whispered, "It looks like we've come in during a saga. It will be hours before we'll be able to speak to anyone, Let's go." They crept out amidst the glares coming from the rest of the audience.

******

Grimm missed their departure by only a few minutes and he received just as many glares from the audience as he entered. He ignored them and strode across to the one man who hadn't glared or even looked up. The man was sat at a table silently counting piles of coins. Grimm cleared his throat and said, "I am Detective Grimm of the Justiciary. Can you direct me to whoever is in charge here."

Several of the audience had turned around to protest at Grimm's interruption but they quickly turned back and held their tongues as they heard him announce himself. The justicers were well known for their lack of a sense of propriety. The man at the table looked up and quickly swept the neat piles of coins into a sack which then disappeared under the table.

The man at the table smiled, "What can I do for you officer?"

Grimm explained again about the teenage runaways and the man frowned. "This is a serious professional establishment. What makes you think that we would know anything about children. I'm sure that we have better things to do than to take any notice of what the lunatic fringe do." He waved his hands at the audience. "Officer, you won't find your runaways here. You'll have to go elsewhere, I can't help you." He pulled out a satchel and began putting bags of coin into it. "Now, I'm afraid we need to get on with the show. Our audience don't appreciate being interrupted and the last thing I need at the moment is more distraction… if you'll excuse me."

Grimm snarled inwardly at the man's attitude. He considered doing something about it but he was conscious that some of his fellow justicers were too quick to take offence and wreak their own retribution. The last thing he needed was more grief from his bosses over public relations. Besides, his particular skills weren't along those lines. His curses were no more effective than anyone else's. Still, the man could have been more helpful and so he clenched his fists and let a small growl escape.

The man started and he let a bag of coins fall. Quick as a flash, Grimm's hand shot out and caught it before it hit the floor. That was his talent; he had lightning fast reactions. It came in handy in fights and other dangerous situations, but was pretty useless when performing higher magics. Grimm replaced the bag on the table.

The man's attitude seemed to abruptly change. His eyes now showed fear as if he'd realised how rude his responses had been. "Excuse me Officer but, as you can see, my clientele are very demanding. I apologise. I will, of course, give you any assistance that I can. Please call on me if you need anything."

The man was now visibly trembling and Grimm felt uncomfortable. He had a job to do but he didn't need to frighten people into obeying him. He was a detective, his job was to solve crimes and catch criminals: not to terrify people out of their skins. He couldn't help it if he was bigger than almost everyone that he met. His father had always joked that he was sure that Grimm had been swapped for a baar cub in the cradle. Grimm muttered something and turned to leave but he couldn't help noticing that the man at the table appeared to be visibly relieved.

Ch 16: Lost Girls and Boy Scouts

Brannhår and Torin arrived at their next destination but Brannhår though that they must have taken a wrong turn on the way. They were at one end of a dark alleyway sandwiched between a cliff face and a huge building that blotted out the light. There was a cluster of young men at the other end of the alley. All of them were surrounding a giant of a man who stood in their centre. Clearly something was going on and Torin tugged on Brannhår's sleeve to catch her attention, "Don't go near that lot. The big one in the middle looks like a justicer and we don't want to attract attention."

They were just turning to leave when a woman rushed up to them, "Please, you have to help, they're going to kill him."

******

Grimm tried to concentrate on the two youths in front of him but he was acutely aware that there were three others behind his back. Whichever way he twisted there was always someone behind him. He needed a good wall or something solid at his back, then he might stand a chance. It was typical, he always started off with the best of intentions but they always seemed to backfire and land him in trouble. He had been going down an alley behind the opera, the great theatre that backed onto the cliffs of old town when he'd seen the woman. She'd been surrounded by the gang and they started pulling at her rich clothing. They'd been shouting, demanding money and he'd seen the terrified look on her face.

As the gang saw him approach, one of the gang pulled out a knife and Grimm had waded in. The woman had run away and he'd been left to face the youths. They didn't seem to care that he was wearing the robes of a justicer in fact he heard one of them shout, "Kill this one. It will make one less of the bastards."

One of the others shouted, "But it's a capper, Hrolf."

The first youth snarled, "Yes and now he knows my name, all the more reason to make sure that he can't talk. There's five of us and

154

only one of him. If he'd had powers that could stop us he'd have used them by now. Get him!"

Grimm had felt the blade coming and he'd reacted to intercept it. Instead of entering his chest the blade had stuck in the back of his hand. It hurt like blazes and the hand now dangled uselessly by his side. His senses detected another blade coming from behind and he whirled. The pain from his injured hand slowed him down so that, instead of dodging the blow, he felt the knife sink into his back. The gang moved in for the kill and Grimm knew he was done for.

Then one of the gang staggered, his eyes appeared to cross and he fell to the ground. The other gang members whirled to face the new enemy but, too late, a second one was already falling, felled by a mighty blow. Grimm couldn't believe his eyes, his rescuer was tiny, and a girl, and she was wielding a war-hammer, but he didn't stop to ask questions. He swept his useless hand around in a savage backhand arc and there was a sickening crunch as it hit home and another of his tormentors fell. It was now two on two but Grimm could see other people in the background running up to see what the fuss was all about. He noticed, in passing, that one of them was the woman who'd been the gang's intended victim. Hrolf and the other gang member took one look and fled.

Grimm staggered, the world was spinning and he heard someone say, "No, don't pull it out, it's stopping the bleeding." Then mercifully, the world went black.

******

The woman who'd asked for Torin's help looked down at the four unconscious bodies. She turned to him and said, "You there, help me. Forget them, let the other cappers sweep them up. Come on, we'll take him to my place. It's not far"

Torin looked at the woman, she was obviously one of the upper classes and she was obviously used to giving orders. He started to tell her that he had other priorities but Brannhår replied, "Of course, which way?" Torin gave up, it seemed that his attempts to avoid any involvement with the justicers had run aground. He took

155

the injured man's arm and Brannhår took the other. Between them they managed to haul him to his feet.

The woman was now shouting at two labourers who were passing, "You there, a gold crown apiece if you carry this man to my house." One look at the woman's rich clothes and they rushed to help. They took the weight off Torin and Brannhår and hoisted the big justicer up. "This way, and hurry. That wound is starting to open up again," the woman said.

Relieved of their burden Torin tugged at Brannhår's sleeve and nodded down the road. Brannhår understood and they both turned to go, "Oh no, don't go. The least I can do is reward you for your help."

"No need, lady," Torin replied.

"Well if you won't accept a reward, please let me extend the hospitality of my house to you." When Torin shook his head she said again, "Please Master Torin, I insist."

Torin frowned, he was pretty sure that he would have remembered meeting the woman but he couldn't place her. How did she know his name?

As if she'd read his thoughts she smiled and said, "You won't remember me but I attended one of your classes on identifying gems at the guildhall. My name is Silfuryn Jarasdottir."

Torin searched his memory, he vaguely remembered teaching the class and a beautiful young girl showing him a huge emerald ring wanting to know how she could be sure that the gem was genuine. However, he couldn't place the name, Jarasdottir. That was it, the girl had had a different name, he remembered now.

He smiled, "Ah yes, how could I not remember you, Lady Risavinur." The name alone placed her in one of the higher echelons of society and suddenly he was intrigued. What business would a rich heiress have in such a dismal location? "I would be honoured to accept your hospitality."

"Then let us go before this poor man bleeds to death."

They followed the woman down the passageway. However at the end, instead of turning back into the city, she went through an impressive archway that was cut into the sheer cliff face. The archway was, in fact, a short tunnel that opened out into the largest cavern that Brannhår had ever seen. Instead of bare rock, ornately carved facades covered every wall. The facades all had metal doors and Lady Risavinur crossed to one that looked richer than most of the others. She thumped her fist on it in a peculiar rhythm and the huge double doors swung aside. "In here," she said to the labourers.

As the doors opened an ancient dwarf rushed up. He'd emerged from a side room off a well lit corridor that disappeared into the distance.

"Ah Alfsen, we have an injured man. These fellows will carry him to the kitchen. Put him on the table and send for a healer. Quickly man!"

The man Alfsen nodded, "Yes mistress. Are you unharmed? Shall I send for your maids?"

"I'm fine Alfsen, just a little dishevelled. Take care of the justicer, I'll be along presently, Oh, and Alfsen, give the two fellows who carried him in a gold crown each and thank them for their trouble."

"Yes mistress. At once mistress, and I shall inform Helgathyn that we have visitors," he nodded at Torin and Brannhår.

"Thank you Alfsen, we will be in the drawing room." The woman went to a door at one side of the corridor and pushed it open. She gestured to Torin, "Please Master Torin, miss, go in and make yourselves at home. I just need to clean up a little. I will join you presently." She stripped off the thin gloves that she'd been wearing, tucked them into her belt, and hurried away.

Torin and Brannhår went into the room. Surprisingly it was brightly lit. A single panel in the ceiling glowed with daylight even though it must have been a hundred feet below the surface. Torin saw Brannhår staring, "It's daylight piped down to the room through a series of mirrors set inside an inactive fumarole," he explained.

Brannhår just stared and nodded. Torin looked around the room. As he'd expected, it was richly furnished and it had a plush couch as well as a series of comfortable looking armchairs. He crossed to one of them and sat. Then he bounced a little as if he was testing the upholstery, "Excellent workmanship, probably over a hundred years old. Not many dwarves can afford this quality these days."

Brannhår's attention was diverted from her contemplation of the lighting, "Sorry Master Torin, I was wondering how they managed to get the mirrors into the fumarole."

"That panel above is deceptive. I'll bet the space behind it is much bigger than it looks. It's not a natural fumarole. They'll have tunnelled along the original fumarole's path and widened it to accommodate the mirrors. There'll be some mechanism on the surface above that gathers the light and directs it down here. This place is ancient, it was probably owned by one of the first dwarf families to settle on Svartalfheim. Of course they will have modernised it over time."

Brannhår frowned, "But where are we Master Torin?"

Torin smiled, "This is the old city, the original Holastan. The capital wasn't always above ground; originally it was all in one massive cave. All the dwarves that migrated from the first world lived here at one time. Over the thousands of years since then, their descendants moved out and colonised other places but this was where it started. Did you never wonder why the capital city was in such an illogical location. It doesn't have a harbour, It's not particularly rich in minerals, they have to import food and water from miles around. No, the capital is here because this was where it all started."

Just at that moment the door opened and Lady Risavinur came in. She was considerably less dusty and she'd changed into an even more ornate gown than she'd been wearing in the street. She looked at them then shook her head, "Oh, where are my manners, please forgive me, I should have offered you somewhere to refresh yourselves."

"It does not matter, Lady, my companion and I are used to taking things as they are," Torin said.

Lady Risavinur grinned at Torin then she turned her attention to Brannhår, "And who do we have here Master Torin, a veritable warrior I'll be bound. That is a very impressive hammer, young lady."

Brannhår looked up, tongue tied.

Torin said, "My Lady Risavinur, may I present my student and companion, Brannhår Dagmarsdóttir. She is assisting me with an errand that we have here in the city."

The lady nodded still staring at the hammer, "Tell me, my dear, where on earth did you find such a magnificent weapon?"

Brannhår found her voice, she was on firmer ground now, "Lady, my hammer is not a weapon, it is a tool and I did not find it I made it."

The Lady's face grinned even wider, "I might have known. Even Master Torin's apprentices create works that would be master's pieces for any other dwarf. May I see it?"

Brannhår handed over the hammer. The aristocrat took it and Brannhår thought that she saw the aristocrat's delicate hands shake. She examined it carefully for a very long time, then she hefted it once or twice and swung it over her shoulder and back. "Surprisingly light but superbly balanced. Tell me my dear how did you manage to shape it into the likeness of a fiskur," she paused, "Ah, that would be a trade secret, I shouldn't have asked."

Brannhår shook her head, "Not at all, Lady, It resembles a fiskur skull because I used a fiskur skull as a crucible when I cast the head."

Lady Risavinur smiled, "I have no doubt that you did. Tell me, how much will you take for it?"

"With respect Lady, this hammer is not for sale, it is my own hammer. However I would be glad to make one like it for you," Brannhår answered.

"Well said, young dwarf. I agree I wouldn't part with such a superb piece if it were mine. I will consider taking you up on your offer though."

There was a knock on the door and the ancient fellow called Alfsen came in, "My Lady, the healer has arrived and has done what he could for the officer. He says that the officer will remain unconscious for at least a day and he must now rest until the salves do their work. I have taken the liberty of having the officer transferred to one of the spare rooms."

******

Grimm surfaced from the black pit and immediately wished that he hadn't. His back was a mass of pain and his hand and arm felt as if they were on fire. The agony doubled when he moved so he decided to keep still. His mind felt fuzzy but he tried to make sense of his situation. He remembered fighting and pain and, for some reason, he remembered a fiskur attacking one of his tormentors. Now, he was lying face down on a bed. It was a very clean bed, totally unlike the one in his quarters in the barracks. The room was unfamiliar but it was brightly lit so he reasoned that someone had put him there deliberately. They had also summoned a healer; it explained the fuzzy feeling in his head and the numb sensation in his intact arm. The healer had given him drugs to counteract the pain, if the numbness in his intact hand was anything to judge by, his injuries must be quite bad to feel so much pain even through the drugs. He could hear people moving about but he was alone in the room and this wasn't the justicer barracks. At least someone was taking care of him, they hadn't left him to die out there in the street. Then he realised what was wrong, he could smell perfume, in his book perfume always spelled trouble. He gave up fighting the drugs and slipped back into unconsciousness.

******

Meanwhile, in the drawing room, another of the lady's servants had appeared with refreshments. Brannhår politely refused the wine but wolfed down half a dozen sandwiches and three of the delicious sweet cakes. Torin had accepted wine but had only picked at the sweet cakes and sandwiches. Lady Risavinur hadn't eaten anything but she was nursing a huge glass of wine that was already half empty. "Tell me Master Torin, what is this errand that brings you to the city? I might be able to help."

"Oh, it's nothing Lady. Just a personal matter concerning my niece."

Lady Risavinur drained her glass with one gulp, "Well, if your sure I can't help." The old dwarf Alfsen came in holding a silver tray. There was an envelope on it and the lady picked it up and opened it. She read the enclosed note, frowned and crumpled it up. Then she stood, "My apologies, I'm afraid I must leave you. My dear friend Lady Krump is hosting a charity event and I promised her that I would attend. Please remain and finish your refreshment. Alfsen will see you out when you are ready to leave." She crossed to the door and was gone.

✦✦✦✦✦✦

The great metal door clanged shut behind them and Torin walked quickly away, Brannhår had to run to catch up.

"Master Torin, did you think that she meant it when she said that she wanted a hammer like mine?"

Torin looked to be deep in thought, "What? Oh yes, probably. You could charge her a fortune for it and she'd not bat an eyelid. What did you make of her Brannhår?"

Brannhår frowned, "She was clearly someone who was used to giving orders but she seemed to do it in a kindly way. The only thing I can't understand is why someone who seems to have lots of people to do things for her would be in a dark passageway alone. I'd have expected her to have guards with her."

"You're right, a rich woman going into an area like that without guards is almost asking for trouble. She must have had a very good reason to risk such a dangerous act."

"Or she wanted to meet with the youths for some reason. Maybe she would have been fine if the justicer hadn't shown up. Maybe he triggered the trouble."

"But why did they attack her?" Torin asked.

"Perhaps, when they saw the justicer, they thought that she'd betrayed them. That would be a good reason to attack."

Torin shook his head, "I think that we're letting our imaginations run away with us. The simplest explanation would be that she got lost, wandered into a place where she shouldn't have been and got attacked. The justicer saw and reacted and got injured."

"Yes, Master Torin; as you say sometimes the simplest explanation is the correct one. However we still need to find Torunn."

"Yes, we still need to find her before the justicers do. It's too late to continue the search this evening. We'll have to start again tomorrow."

Over dinner that evening Krin told them who Lady Risavinur was, "She's probably the richest woman in the Holastan. Of course she is descended directly from one of the founders but her family wasn't one of those that traded on their pedigree. Her great great grandfather owned and operated several mines and her great grandfather was one of the first to log trees to make paper. He took a group of young dwarves over to Vatersey and set up a colony of foresters. They founded Vatnarheim and there's more than ten thousand living there now and thousands more in the forests. Nearly all of them are involved with logging or paper making and the Lady more or less runs the lot. Now you might expect that someone with all that wealth and power would be arrogant but the Lady seems to be an exception. I've never heard anything bad said about her. Lady Risavinur seems to treat her workers fairly and she's always giving to one charity or another. I've heard she is a bit of a recluse and isn't too involved in the social scene. She tends to keep herself to herself and seldom attends any of the grand functions.

The gossip is that she's had lots of offers of marriage from men but she's never shown much interest. The only man that she takes any notice of is her butler, Alfsen and there's no romance there. He's almost twice her age and he used to be her grandfather's butler. People say that he and the old man raised her after her parents were killed and so he's more like a father to her than her servant."

Torin said, "I agree, she didn't seem to be the usual aristocrat. Most of them would have let the justicer die but she took him to her home and sent for the healers."

He turned to Brannhår, "If she's that rich then maybe we could pick up a commission or two. It would be worth taking a little time off from ironoak: we could use a new roof on the workshop. What do you say, girl? Fancy making a bit of bespoke jewellery?"

Brannhår shook her head, "I suspect the commission wouldn't involve jewellery. The way she handled my hammer I suspect that she might want something more practical."

Ch 17: Last of Her Line.

A few hours later, Silfuryn, the Lady Risavinur, was seated in her office. Alfsen was standing in front of her giving his report.

"I followed them back to the inn where they are staying. It seems that Master Torin knows the proprietor Krin well. I bought a few drinks for the regulars and it would appear that the Master and the girl arrived yesterday evening. One of my informants said that he overheard them asking Krin about some runaway girls. He told me that they claimed that one of the girls was Torin's niece."

Silfuryn frowned and pursed her lips., "Mmm, I wonder if they are searching for the same girls that we are? Oh, if only I'd been quicker, this whole business would have been settled and we could have been on with more important matters. Damn Lady Krump, if she'd not interfered I could have intercepted them before Cyten got his hooks into them. He disappeared so fast that I'm sure he must have seen my interest. He's always been suspicious when I've taken an interest in new talent," she paused for a moment and then said, "Now what about our friend in mother's old room?"

"He appears to be just what he is, a justicer assigned to the cappers. It seems, from the reports from my contacts in the amphitheatre, that he was asking questions about runaway girls at each of the venues where they might have been seen and that's why he happened to be coming along the alley behind the opera. It was to have been his next port of call. He saw you with the youths and assumed that you were being attacked."

Silfuryn shook her head in exasperation, "And he tried to play the hero by coming to my defence. He wasn't to know that I would have been fine. I had my armour on and as you know, I can take care of myself. Not that I would have needed to resort to force, Hrolf had been drinking and he wanted more money. I would have paid and he would have told me what I needed to know and then I'd have been out of there. I've dealt with his kind before, violence brings too much attention, they've learned to be discrete and accept what they're given."

"Yes mistress but the officer wasn't to know that," the ancient retainer said.

"You're right as ever Alfsen but it does leave me with a problem. Really, I examined him after our other guests departed, I don't know what the Justiciary is doing nowadays. The man only has the slightest of talents. He's hardly a wizard at all. My grandfather would never have recruited him, well, at least not to the magical arm of the department."

"Quite, Mistress. However, sadly you grandfather is no longer with us."

"Go on say it, Alfsen, and I'm the last of our line."

The ancient dwarf said nothing and his face looked sad but Silfuryn didn't notice. His mistress was distracted and he knew that she had withdrawn inside herself to think. He quietly left her to her own thoughts.

Alfsen was right, Silfuryn's mind was chasing itself in circles, Three days ago she had been bored and had been contemplating a return to one of the country estates. Then she'd been dragged along by Isola Krump to some charity auditions that were taking place at the opera. Most of the singers were nondescript and she'd almost been falling asleep then she'd heard a peculiar tone coming from a couple on the stage. She'd sprung alert, someone was using magic to modulate their voice. She'd looked at the singer and she'd seen something familiar about the child.

By the time she'd made her way backstage, the child was being led away by Cyten the theatrical agent. The old bastard could smell an opportunity to make money a mile away. Of course he'd not realised that the child had been using magic and had just thought that he'd discovered a new talent. Silfuryn had detected the magic because it was one of her talents. The child was too old, either she'd been missed in the justicers trawl for magical talent or she'd run away from one of their indoctrination camps. Either way the child would be in trouble if anyone else noticed her talent.

However, when she'd looked at the girl she'd had a shock. She recognised her. The girl was the spitting image of the wife of one of the board members of one of her companies. She vaguely remembered that the couple had had a daughter who had entered justicer training through the normal channels. Silfuryn had assumed that the girl would be lost in the system but she'd heard that a terrible accident had befallen the girl and she'd been killed. The couple, who lived on Lungrey had been bereft and she'd not seen the man at the past few meetings.

What she'd seen at the opera was impossible. Young girls didn't magically come back to life so her 'death' must have been staged by the Justiciary for some other reason and she'd somehow escaped and had run away. Silfuryn desperately wanted to find out why the child's death had been staged.

Unfortunately, just as she was about to catch up with Cyten, Isola Krump had arrived and had started to make a fuss. Whilst Silfuryn had been disentangling herself from the woman's panicked clutches she'd lost sight of her quarry. She'd spent the past two days trying to find out where Cyten was keeping the girl. He wouldn't have made the connection with the justicers yet but it was only a matter of time until someone else recognised the girl. Silfuryn had a nasty feeling that such a revelation would not bode well for the girl and that she might well be destined to meet with another 'accident'.

She reached for a glass and absent-mindedly filled it with the rich red wine that was her only vice. There was something rotten in the Justiciary system and she wanted to root it out. It had all started when she'd been a girl.

******

"But why can't I play with the village children?"

"Because I say you can't", her mother replied, "Besides you won't be here for long. We've arranged that you will go and stay with

166

your Grandfather for a while. Your Grandfather lives in the country far away from Holastan, you will make new friends there."

"But I don't want to go to the country Mama. I like it here with you."

"I'm afraid that that is impossible. Your father has his work in the city and I have my own work. We wouldn't be able to look after you properly. You'll like it with your Grandfather, he's like you."

Silfuryn hadn't fully understood what she'd meant until years later. Like most parents her mother and father had dreaded losing their daughter to the temple. They weren't the only couple that had seen the way that the justicers had twisted the minds of their recruits away from any allegiance to their family and towards an allegiance to the Justiciary. They had detected her talents early and they were rich, very rich. Her mother's father, her Grandfather had been born in better times, times when a magical child's recruitment to the temple had been less certain and much more flexible. Her Grandfather had magic and it had matured outside the strictures of the Justiciary and he had dedicated his life to curbing the efforts of the zealots who had taken over the temple hierarchy. Silfuryn remembered him as a really powerful wizard who had taught her many things but his greatest lesson to her was how to hide her magical talents from others, especially from members of the Justiciary.

She had had quite a lonely childhood, her parents rarely visited before they were killed and the promised new friends never appeared. She had tutors that taught her about the world but only after she'd become adept at hiding her talents. And she had her Grandfather who had taught her how to use and train her talents so that she could use them discretely and not be discovered. It was probably a good thing that her Grandfather had died many years ago. He would have been horrified to learn that the situation had deteriorated even further from the state it was in when he had been a young man. Nowadays an adult wizard who wasn't a justicer was automatically considered a renegade and was hunted down and killed. Silfuryn had survived so long only because she'd been taught to hide well and because she was the heiress to a vast fortune and commercial empire. She helped the concealment by associating with airheads like Isola Krump and pretending to be one of them. However, she'd inherited her Grandfather's crusade against the fanaticism of the current Lords of the Justiciary and she devoted much of her time to clandestine investigations into the true state of affairs at the summit of the dwarven hierarchy.

She smiled to herself and took another drink. She wasn't her Grandfather, she didn't have his power either in the political sense or the magical one. Her powers were limited; she could sense things about objects. It was almost like she could see their past. She had to be holding them or touching the object for the sense to work. That was why she often wore gloves. There was nothing more distracting than shaking hands with someone and seeing that they would rather be doing something else than meeting you. She also had her Grandfathers ability to make herself insubstantial or look like someone else. That had been why she hadn't been afraid of Hrolf. If he'd attacked her she could have slipped through his fingers, literally. Of course she would have had to do it without him detecting her talent but her Grandfather and Alfsen had spent many years teaching her how to hide her skills. She sometimes envied her Grandfather, he had had the talent to become insubstantial as well but his ability was much greater. He had been able to move his whole body to the side just by willing it. When she'd been a young girl she'd played tag with him for hours and she never managed to catch him and she remembered the sense of frustration that it engendered. However, she'd made up for her lack of magic by training her body to become an efficient fighting machine. Her exercise regime would have daunted even the capper's elite forces and her acrobatic abilities could have earned her a place in any circus.

Thinking about her talents brought her recent encounters to the front of her mind and, in particular, the memory of that girl: Torin's companion. The girl's name was Brannhår, it described her perfectly. Not only did she have hair that was the colour of fire but the second that Silfuryn had touched that hammer she'd seen that the girl was a powerful fey. The paradox was that the girl wasn't magical in the traditional sense. In fact Silfuryn had the impression that, if anything, the girl was the opposite of magic, if such a thing could exist. The hammer was a testament to the girl's power and Silfuryn wondered if the girl had meant it when she'd said that she could create a similar axe. Silfuryn wanted a weapon like that and she wondered how much she would have to pay. Weapons like that weren't cheap, but whatever the price, Silfuryn would pay it.

She wondered if Torin was aware of the girl's power. Surely he must be, and that meant that he was also aware of his niece's magical talent. They were searching for the wayward teenager just as she was. That thought reminded her that there was another who was searching for the teenager. The justicer who was lying at death's door in her mother's old room at this very moment.

The images of the new actors in her life flitted across her vision. There were so many new faces that Silfuryn wasn't sure how to proceed. Well, her Grandfather had always told her that it was no use making plans without knowing all the facts so she'd better find out what she could. She rang the bell for Alfsen. Alfsen was her last link with her Grandfather and she counted him more as a friend and substitute father than an employee. He was loyal to a fault and he knew her so well that he could anticipate her needs without being told.

Alfsen appeared within a minute and she saw that he'd brought another glass of wine, "You rang, Mistress."

"Yes Alfsen, I want you to make some discrete enquiries about today's guests. I have a feeling that the matter with the teenage runaways is going to become more complicated before it gets resolved. I need to know where I stand. Could you open dossiers on the man in mother's room and Master Torin and his companion; Brannhår Dagmarsdóttir."

"As you say Mistress,"Alfsen nodded, "If you won't mind me saying, I think you need to get some rest. Word will have spread that we have the justicer and his superiors are bound to send someone around to check on him. You will need to have all your wits about you if you are to appear as an innocent bystander."

******

The light pipe in her ceiling was just showing a faint grey when Silfuryn awoke the next morning. She rolled over in the bed and she heard a soft knock on her door. The door opened and Helgathyn, the cook, came in carrying a tray laden with porridge, smoked fiskur and a steaming mug of bru, "Your breakfast Mistress"

Silfuryn sat up and yawned whilst the cook expertly arranged the meal on the side table. Alfsen gave a discrete knock on the still-open door and Silfuryn said, "What have you got for me?"

Alfsen came into the room carrying a large slate covered in tiny writing. "We know a little more mistress, the name of the officer in the guest room is Detective Grimm. As I surmised, my informants say that we should expect a visit from his superiors within an hour or two. The news of his attempted rescue of a Princess of the Nobility has already become the talk of the streets. Oh, and it would appear that there were eight attackers, the five that we know of and three others generated by wagging tongues. Also your attackers appear to have aged. They were, and I quote, 'big burly toughs armed with clubs, knives and pistol bows'. The word on the street is that the officer is at death's door."

Silfuryn laughed, "I'm not sure about the Princess of the Nobility bit but the rest of it is just as outrageous as I expected. Any advice on how I should play the interview with the detective's superiors?"

"I would suggest that imitating your friend Lady Krump might be a good starting point,"Alfsen said.

"Yes, my thoughts were running along the same lines. Now what do we know of the Detective himself?"

Alfsen consulted his slate, "Detective Grimm is thirty five years old, he has been with the justicers since he was ten and his tutors and contemporaries say that he is known for his dependability, if not his intellect. The word is that he is honest and he really does try to find wrongdoers and bring them to justice. Unusually, he doesn't seem to abuse his Justiciary powers. In fact he is seen as something of a liberal by his superiors and, as such, they keep a close watch on him. As you might expect, he adheres strictly to the rules of the temple and I can find no evidence of any dalliance even though he spent several years patrolling in the red-light districts of town. In short, mistress he is what your grandfather would have called 'a solid man'."

"And what about Brannhår, Torin's companion?"

Alfsen looked taken aback, "Don't you wish to know about Master Torin first, Mistress?"

"No, I knew Torin years ago and I have kept abreast of his life and work since. He doesn't seem to have changed much."

"Then you will know that he is not well, Mistress"

It was Silfuryn's turn to look shocked, "Not well?"

"It would appear that Master Torin's mind has deteriorated somewhat over the past few years. He suffers from periodic bouts of mental incapacity and spends most of the time when incapacitated in a semi-coma or asleep."

"I didn't know that. What a shame, he was one of the most intelligent dwarves that I have ever met. Is that the reason he now has a companion? Is she his nurse?"

Alfsen shook his head, "It would appear not, he refuses professional help and he insists that his 'lapses' are just because he is bored."

Silfuryn nodded and took a sip of the bru then grimaced, "Why can't I have wine with breakfast?"

"Because Mistress you have expressly forbidden me, on pain of death, to supply alcohol in any form before the evening."

"Damn...then I rescind the order, I could do with a decent drink." Silfuryn pouted.

Alfsen's face grew stoic, "Mistress, if you remember, you have forbidden me to listen to any instructions that would countermand your original order. I believe the phrase you used was, 'don't you ever let me get into that habit again even if I threaten to kill myself and everyone else in the vicinity'. Mistress. I can, however, get cook to bring you a slice of honey brot which may make the infusion more palatable."

"Yes, do that, and while you are talking to cook, let me see what else you've found out about the girl, Brannhår." She held out her hand and he handed her the slate.

******

A mile away Brannhår was also having breakfast. Torin wasn't being chatty, perhaps because he'd spent the previous evening drinking with Krin again and so Brannhår was mulling things over in her own mind.

Lady Risavinur was an enigma, she acted the scatterbrain Noble but Brannhår had seen her reaction when she'd held her hammer. Something had happened, the Lady had sensed something, almost as if she had a magical talent. But that couldn't be because she was certainly no justicer. And another thing, why would someone wear body armour and carry a flexible concealed blade in her dress. The woman was a Noble and so she might need to defend herself if attacked; that might explain the blade... but gauntlets and that tunic? Brannhår hadn't been fooled by their silken disguise, they might have looked ephemeral but she had sensed the metal and ironoak filaments woven through them. They were every bit a piece of armour as any steel chain-mail glove or scaled bronze plate. It was as if the woman had expected trouble.

The other thing that bothered Brannhår was that the Lady had run to them asking for help for the justicer. If the lady was magical and she was concealing her magic then why save a justicer? Brannhår's logical mind told her that the Lady should have let the thugs kill him.

Her mind returned to her companion; he was saying something, "How on earth are we going to find Torunn and Elsa now? Yesterday's events will have frightened people in the theatre district and they'll have gone to ground. Plus we now know that the justicers are looking for the runaways as well. We've been careful so far, but if we're to carry on the search we'll have to be even more careful from now on."

"Yes Master Torin"

******

"Since Brannhår Dagmarsdóttir comes from a remote part of Valdirey, available information about the girl is sparse. A similar situation exists for her time before she came to the city although she and Torin have just arrived back from an expedition into the wilds that they took a short time before they arrived here."

Silfuryn became aware that someone else was in her study. A maid had come in to tell her that she had visitors from the Justiciary. She put down the document and checked her appearance in the mirror, then put on her most inane smile and went to greet them.

Her visitors consisted of an old man flanked by two younger officers in armour and a severe looking woman who was looking around the hallway with a scowl on her face. The old man was there for the protocol, You didn't interview a 'Princess of the Nobility' without having one of her peers present. She vaguely recognised him as Lord Pidur. He was nominally a member of the council but he never actually contributed anything. The two constables, one male, the other female were muscle, although why they thought they needed muscle in a routine interview was beyond her. The fourth member of the group terrified Silfuryn the most. She knew the justicer by reputation; a senior enforcer, nominally a capper like the man in her mother's room but one who enjoyed using her power to make others suffer. It was said that the woman killed on a whim and did it with impunity. Her name was Gibra but she was known by all as 'the Gibbet'.

As Silfuryn went across to greet them she deliberately stumbled so that her elaborate coiffure unpinned itself and came apart. She then fussed with it theatrically, looking at herself in a mirror and muttering inane phrases like, 'Oh dear I'll never get another appointment at this short notice'. She used the confusion to study the justicers in the reflection and noticed that the Gibbet was staring at her back with a look of arrogant disgust.

The old man was the first to speak, "Lady Risavinur, we understand that you were attacked by some vagabonds yesterday and for that please let me extend the apologies of the Justiciary that we are unable to police every street in the city."

Silfuryn saw that the Gibbet was giving the old man the same withering look. She fluttered her hands in the air, "Oh I quite understand Lord Pidur. It was my own fault really. I shouldn't have taken that short cut but I was in such a hurry to get home, I was due to meet my dear friend Isola later for one of her charity events and I needed a bath and a change of clothes beforehand."

"You say that you were taking a shortcut, but you never said where you'd come from," the Gibbet interrupted, "Where were you coming from Lady Risavinur?"

Silfuryn simpered, "Oh, I know it was wicked of me but you see I can't resist those new confections that they sell in the market," she turned and smiled brightly directly into the face of the Gibbet, "You know, the ones with the sweet and savoury coating, the ones that resemble," she giggled and waved her hands vaguely in the direction of the two pieces of muscle, "men's parts. They're simply heavenly."

The Gibbet's face turned to stone at the reference.

"Then suddenly I was surrounded by these young men. They grabbed at me and started demanding that I give them money. They were very rude! The next thing I knew was that your officer was there and he was confronting the men. He was so gallant. I'm afraid I panicked and ran but I looked over my shoulder and I could see that the young men had attacked the officer, he was bleeding. I ran to a group of people at the other end of the alley and begged them to help and one of them went to help the officer. I'm not sure what happened next but the young men must have run away because when I went back to the officer I could see that he was gravely injured. I paid two workmen to carry the officer here and then I told Alfsen to send for a healer."

"These bystanders who went to the officer's aid, give me their names," the Gibbet demanded.

Silfuryn nearly lost her temper. This woman needed to be taught a lesson and she felt her hands itching to grab a blade, then she remembered who she was supposed to be. What would Isola say? She wouldn't say anything she'd treat rudeness with arrogance. Silfuryn deliberately turned to Lord Pidur, "Your Lordship, you will know as well as I do how difficult it is to tell some of the lower orders from each other. They were just street people, I didn't ask for their names, it was their duty to help."

Lord Pidur was between a rock and a hard place, his gaze jumped nervously between the two women and then he cleared his throat, he was a Lord after all, "I agree, it doesn't matter who the people were. They were just men of the street. We needn't trouble the lady with any more questions. She has told us what happened."

The Gibbet glared at him but he was technically her superior, she couldn't countermand him in front of witnesses. She ground her teeth and said, "I think that we have all we need."

However, Silfuryn noticed that the Gibbet's eyes had suddenly become glassy. Silfuryn thought, "She's scanning me, It's a good thing that I'm wearing this dress, the gold piping and the ironoak and silver embroidery will confuse the justicer's magical senses. All she'll get is noise."

The Gibbet shook her head as if to clear it and said, "I hope that you have learned that a craving for sweetmeats can be dangerous. From now on I would advise you to keep to the proper routes." She turned her back on Silfuryn and gestured to the two junior officers.

175

Silfuryn noticed the deliberate snub, even the lowest workman knew that to omit her title and patronymic when leaving was a gross social insult. Lord Pidur gasped but covered the comment by pretending to cough.

The Gibbet turned to Alfsen who was stood waiting at the rear, "Take me to Officer Grimm."

"Follow me Madam," he said.

Silfuryn was pleased. They'd accepted her airhead story and now they wanted to confirmation from one of their own. Well, they were going to be out of luck. She'd told Alfsen to make sure that the big capper would be in no state to say anything. She followed the group along to her mother's room at a discrete distance.

Grimm was lying face down on the bed, just as she'd left him an hour earlier. He was breathing shallowly but even to untrained eyes he was clearly unconscious, not just sleeping. Alfsen had done an excellent job, the detective's hand was swathed in bloody bandages and the towel that was over the wound in his back was a mess of congealed blood and the greenish remains of the healer's poultice. Silfuryn steeled herself for the next act. It happened just as she'd foreseen.

All the justicers, even the Gibbet, could see that a) the man was sorely wounded and b) was in no fit state to talk. Alfsen knew his cue and said, "My mistress sent for her own healer, he advised that we keep the officer in this position and not disturb him unnecessarily. I believe that he gave the officer something that would help him sleep so that his wounds would have chance to close themselves."

"He needs to be transferred to the temple, we have healers there," the Gibbet said.

"Oh no. You can't," Silfuryn cried, "the poor man has lost so much blood. Please don't move him. I feel so responsible. He received those wounds defending me. It is my duty as a noblewoman to see that he is looked after until he is well."

"I insist he is transferred to the temple," the Gibbet said and pointed to the two muscular justicers, "Move him."

Even Silfuryn was alarmed at what she witnessed next and she'd known what was going to happen. As the two constables took Grimm's shoulders, the towel on the man's back slid aside and it fell to the floor with a wet squelch. Copious amounts of blood welled up from where it had been resting and an evil stench arose from the wound. The two justicers recoiled in alarm and let Grimm fall back. Even Silfuryn felt a little queasy but she played her part, screamed and appeared to faint away. Alfsen rushed forward to catch her and one of the junior officers grabbed another towel and pressed it over the wound.

Alfsen looked up, "For Hel's sake leave him or he'll bleed to death" the old man exclaimed. The two men looked at their commander for instructions. Out of the corner of her half-closed eye Silfuryn saw that it wasn't Lord Pidur that they looked at but the Gibbet. Silfuryn moaned and started to push herself up. The Gibbet was clearly furious but even she couldn't sanction the death of one of their own in front of witnesses and the other justicers.

She rasped, "Leave him, he's going nowhere. He'll be dead by tomorrow morning, we can collect his corpse then." She turned and headed out of the room. Lord Pidur and the two younger men followed her out without a backward glance.

Twenty minutes later the justicers had gone and Alfsen found his mistress in her study. She was reading the slate that he'd given her earlier. "How is the patient, Alfsen?" she asked.

"He is resting, Mistress. I have re-dressed his wounds with clean bandages and I have cleared up the pigs blood. I must congratulate you, Mistress, the sausage skin split exactly as you predicted and even I was amazed at how much blood and stench of decay there appeared to be. Lord Pidur was clearly trying not to vomit."

"At least Grimm won't have to suffer the attentions of the temple healers. If we can make it appear that he is worse than he actually is then maybe we can give him at least a fighting chance of getting out of here alive."

"Yes Mistress. After all he did save your life."

"Quite, Alfsen."

Silfuryn handed the slate back to her old friend. "I've just read what you found out about Master Torin and Brannhår. It would appear that they've just returned from an expedition to the mountains. They went with one of Kuhlfefer's apprentices and they appear to have discovered something. The apprentice appeared very excited. I think that this affair merits a further conversation with the girl and I have a perfect excuse to get her back here alone. I want you to send out some invitations, my friend, really formal ones that nobody could refuse. Invite them to Hárbru."

Ch 18: An Invitation to Tea

Brannhår looked again at the ornate card that had been brought to their lodgings and given to her personally. She'd not known what to make of it and so she'd taken it to Torin. He'd grinned broadly and had said, "Oh you are moving in high circles now. A formal invitation to Hárbru from a Princess of the Nobility is not something you see everyday. I noticed that she hasn't sent me one so it must mean that she wants to talk to you alone. My guess is that she's after your hammer or wants to hire you to make her one like it. What a Noble like her will do with it is beside the point. This little trip to the capital and our jaunt to the countryside have cost quite a bit and it would be nice if we could get someone like her to replenish our coffers and there's the workshop roof to consider.

My advice would be to hold out for at least two times what she offers you to begin with. The rich are never eager to part with their money, that is usually how they got rich in the first place, but I saw the look on her face when she was examining your hammer. She wants one like it and she'll pay. Now we've a few hours before the Hárbru so we'd better start to get you ready."

"But Master Torin, shouldn't we be searching for Torunn and Elsa."

"Yes, but they will have gone to ground after yesterdays events so we'll need to make some enquiries first. I can do those whilst you keep the Princess sweet. Now I need to talk to Krin, you go to your room and finish those notes on the ironoak. I'll be back soon."

An hour later Torin returned with Krin in tow. She was carrying a bundle in her arms and she dumped it on the bed in Brannhår's room.

She shooed Torin out and turned to Brannhår, "Right, first thing we have to do is get you out of those clothes and into a bath."

"But I swam only two days ago," Brannhår protested.

"Then you'll only need one tub of water instead of two. Come on, the tub is heating in my room. Be a dear and bring that bundle with you."

An hour later Brannhår was stood in Krin's room wrapped in only a large towel. "I don't see why I have to wear that. It's not practical. There are no pockets."

Krin shook her head, "You can't turn up to a formal bru in a muddy old leather tunic and patched trousers. It's formal, you have to be presentable."

"But I've never worn a dress," Brannhår protested, "I don't know how to wear one. I'll be practically naked."

"Nonsense girl, and I won't have any argument. You'll wear this dress and like it. It's not as if you're going to be climbing hills or working in the forge in it. It's only for the bru and that won't last more than an hour or two. Now, lift your arms whilst I get it over your head."

******

Brannhår felt uncomfortable, the dress itched and stray breezes were getting to places where they had no right to be. Torin and Krin had insisted on accompanying her to the gates of the underground city so she couldn't just turn and run. She could feel her hammer bouncing on her back between her shoulder blades. It was funny because she always wore it there and she'd never even been aware of it before. Perhaps it was the new harness. Torin had produced a magnificent belt from somewhere and had added several loops and twists of leather so that her hammer sat in the makeshift sheath. It was good work and she had to admit that it was more in keeping with her outfit but she missed her usual cracked-leather one. She gulped and mounted the steps up to the Princess's ornate double door. As if by magic the doors opened before she touched them and she saw the corridor behind them open up before her.

180

The old man, Alfsen was stood in front of her, "My mistress will be pleased that you could come. Please follow me and I will show you into the dining room." He turned and strode slowly away.

Brannhår ran to catch up but the stupid dress got in the way, she muttered a curse. Alfsen turned and said, "I understand your nervousness, young dwarf. My mistress is very kind and she will understand as well. However, perhaps I could assist you?" he held out a hand. She reached out for it and the old Dwarf gently tugged it until he'd folded her arm under his, "Now slowly, there is no hurry and a young lady shouldn't ever run," then he bent and whispered in her ear, "At least not when she is attending a formal Hárbru" She couldn't help it, she giggled and suddenly she felt better.

As they entered the dining room Brannhår saw that Lady Risavinur was talking to someone who was sat in an armchair in front of her. Brannhår couldn't see who it was because the back of the chair came up almost to head height. She saw that the Lady was dressed in a glittering silk dress that was a beautiful shade of lemon. The Lady was smiling and she gave a short laugh and then she appeared to notice Brannhår. "Ah, my dear, I'm so glad you could come. Follow me, I've a surprise for you."

Brannhår followed the woman and she saw who had been sat in the chair. She felt a burst of pleasure at the sight. It was Karol. He stood up from the chair and smiled at her. Gone were the rough clothes that he'd worn when they had been exploring, he was dressed in a long emerald-green robe and his hair was neat and shining. Suddenly she was glad that Krin had made her wear the dress.

Karol was even more surprised than Brannhår. He'd only ever seen her in her wilderness guise and he couldn't quite reconcile the beautiful vision standing before him with the rough and ready explorer that he'd always known. He couldn't help himself. He stood looking at her with his mouth open.

Silfuryn had noticed the attraction between her two guests but there were proprieties to be observed. "Brannhår Dagmarsdóttir, may I present my new friend Karol Tynarsson but I believe you already know each other. Karol has been telling me of the adventures that you've shared. I must say I envy you both. It must have been a wonderful Menntunleit."

Karol knew what to say, "I am pleased to meet you again Brannhår Dagmarsdóttir. It was so kind of Lady Risavinur to invite me along to Hárbru so that we could meet again."

Brannhår was just staring at him and Silfuryn could see that she needed to break the formal mood, "Ah, I see that you've brought along your hammer. I hadn't realised it's uniqueness until Karol told me how you made it from nothing but old armour and fiskur remains. Did you really use lightning? How exciting! Now come and sit down and you can tell me all about it."

Three hours later Silfuryn was back in her study, she'd changed out of the elegant dress she'd worn earlier and she was now in a much more comfortable robe and she was relaxing in an armchair in front of a roaring fire. Brannhår and the lad Karol had left over an hour ago and she'd been pleased to see that he'd offered to escort her back to her lodgings. He was a pleasant young man and she didn't need magical powers to tell that he was infatuated by the girl. She smiled to herself, he'd offered to escort her but from what she'd learned of Brannhår over the past hours Silfuryn thought that Brannhår would have been the one to defend the couple if anyone tried to assault them.

Silfuryn was intrigued by the girl. During the Hárbru she'd watched Brannhår with all her senses including her magical ones and even so she still had more questions than answers. As she'd suspected Torin's apprentice wasn't like any other that she'd come across. The Master pupil relationship that she'd expected was almost non-existent, in fact she couldn't see any evidence of formality other than a mutual respect for one another's skills and person. At first, the relationship between Brannhår and Karol had seemed more straightforward, he was clearly besotted by the girl and she was attracted to him but the sexual attraction wasn't what you normally expected between youngsters of their age. They didn't gaze longingly into each other's eyes or hold hands, Silfuryn thought that that might be because of her presence and the formality of the Hárbru. However, when the subject of conversation turned to their discoveries about ironoak they had both become vital and animated. In keeping with her normal disguise that she used with people she didn't know well, Silfuryn had pretended to be an airhead and she had insisted that she couldn't understand 'all the technical thingumies' but she'd listened. The pair, and presumably Torin with them had discovered something quite amazing.

Silfuryn and her Grandfather had always known that ironoak had special properties. Her Grandfather had inherited the gloves that she wore when she was going about her investigations into the Justiciary and they contained threads of ironoak running through them. The dress that she'd worn during the visit of the justicers had contained more of the thread and its effect was to generate magical noise so that magical senses became confused. However, Brannhår and Karol had been talking about properties other than magical ones. Their technical affinities, Brannhår's analytical and visionary engineering skills and Karol's knowledge of plants, were a perfect complement to each other and Silfuryn was sure that, if she'd not been present, they would have become engrossed in each other in an entirely different way than mere sex. One thing she'd decided was that she wanted to be part of this new discovery. She conceded that she might not be at the same technical level as the youngsters but they had discovered something that could make them all very rich. The problem was that they were naive and were so lost in the thrill of discovery that they would be exploited mercilessly by some. Silfuryn, although she admitted that her motives weren't absolutely altruistic, thought that she could provide a necessary commercial footing for the new science of 'lightning use' as the youngsters had called it. She would have to give the whole matter a lot of thought.

She sighed, it wasn't as if she had vast amounts of free time, her continuing investigations into what was happening to the Justiciary and magic in general took up a lot of it. Then there were the little things, like the small problem of what to do with the justicer in her mother's room and how to rescue the teenagers from the clutches of Cyten. What she needed was someone that she could talk things over with. Oh, she had Alfsen, he was always dependable, but he neither understood magic nor was he young enough to do field investigations. Her dossiers on Torin and Brannhår said that they were also seeking the teenagers and neither of them was stupid. That meant that they probably knew of the girl Torunn's magical abilities.

Torin was in the same category as Alfsen but Brannhår, she was young, extremely intelligent, good in a fight and was, although not magical, some sort of fey. Might she be distracted from her technical enthusiasms to become a confidant in Silfuryn's greater plans. She made a mental note to make an excuse to get the girl alone to explore that possibility.

Silfuryn grew aware that someone else had just come in. Alfsen gave a small cough to attract her attention and said, "Mistress, the hour is late and there is much to do tomorrow, might I suggest that an early night might benefit us both"

Silfuryn looked at the clock, it was a work of art but it measured the time nonetheless, Alfsen was right, she'd spent the whole evening thinking about what she'd learned during the Hárbru and it was quite late now.

"Yes, Alfsen, as always, your suggestion is welcome. I will get some rest." She rose and went out of the door towards her bedroom. Alfsen reached for the almost full wine glass that sat forgotten on his mistresses desk. He thought that it was a good sign.

******

"She never even asked about the hammer?" Torin asked.

"No she just seemed to be content to let Karol and I talk. You know she pretends to be an airhead but I think that she's really quite intelligent. She pretended that she couldn't understand what we were talking about when Karol was telling me about his dissections of the ironoak leaves but I got the impression that she was taking more in than she let on."

"Probably. You know what we discovered about ironoak might be valuable and her family didn't get to be one of the richest on the planet by ignoring opportunities. I think that you should keep any discussions about ironoak between the three of us for now. By the way, where is Karol staying?"

"At an inn called the Anvil. It's somewhere near to the old city."

Torin nodded, "That's one of the better inns, his parents must be quite wealthy if he can afford to stay there. It seems that we are being dragged into the upper strata of society whether we like it or not.

Now tell me about Karol's dissections, and after breakfast we need to go and seek out whoever does auditions at the opera. Krin says that Torunn and Elsa might be there."

They hadn't left the breakfast table when their plans were put on hold again. There was something of a commotion in the inn's hallway and when Torin and Brannhår looked up from the remains of their meal they saw an elegant form striding across the room with her hand outstretched in greeting.

"Forgive me for interrupting your meal but I felt that I needed to get in touch with you before you went out searching for your friends again," Silfuryn said.

"There is no problem, lady, we have quite finished," Torin said.

"Then let us go out into the square, I have things to tell you that are better said where we are unlikely to be overheard."

"By all means Lady, lead on."

They left the inn and went out into the square. They were followed by four burley men in mail armour who Silfuryn explained were guards employed by her estate. The three of them sat on a bench in the early morning sunshine and Brannhår noticed that the guards arranged themselves around the bench but outside of earshot. The formation meant that other passers-by would have to take a wide detour around the bench. Brannhår found out later that this arrangement wasn't uncommon when the nobility needed privacy.

Silfuryn started the conversation, "I see that you've changed out of your dress, my dear. I agree, dresses aren't very practical for everyday wear but I am afraid that I am expected to keep up standards," She gestured at her full length robes as if in apology.

Brannhår wasn't having any of it, those robes were shot through with metal filaments. They would have stopped most blades or even an arrow. However she didn't comment.

"Yes, Lady, as you say, a dress would be most unsuitable."

Silfuryn looked at one of the guards who gave her a discrete nod, "My man there thinks it is safe to talk," and she turned to Torin.

"Master Torin, I address you because you are the most senior in this enterprise but I acknowledge that my two young friends have made great contributions as well. I couldn't help overhearing the conversation between my young guests yesterday afternoon and I have come to both warn you and to make you an offer.

Even I can see that the discoveries that you have made might alter the way that kraft will progress in the world. However, there are many unscrupulous people who would seek to use your discoveries for their own ends and therein lies danger. Now, I am already a wealthy woman and, believe it or not, I care about dwarf society and I believe that kraft should be shared for the benefit of everyone. However, you may or may not be aware that the Justiciary are bringing in rules regarding developments in kraft. They say it is for the benefit of the individual practitioners; to protect their ideas, but my people have informed me that their motives might have another purpose. That of stifling certain developments and controlling others. What they hope to gain from this I cannot say but I can assure you that it is the case.

I believe that your discoveries will be one of the advances that they will seek to suppress and I want to offer myself as a potential partner in your enterprise. I can offer you a shield. My wealth can deal with the justicers attempts to stifle your developments and that will allow you to concentrate on bringing your discoveries to their practical fulfilment. As evidence that I am not one of those who may try to cheat you, I am willing to give my services free and I am willing to sign the relevant papers that will state that I have no claim on any of your discoveries."

Torin was silent for some time then he said, "Lady Risavinur, I hear what you say and your offer does sound most generous, however, I also have realised that what Brannhår and Karol discovered has potentially far reaching consequences. I must admit that I have no expertise in dealing with the Justiciary but I feel a need to consider the situation more carefully. I am not without friends in the various kraft guilds and I will ask them what they know of the justicer's plans for the kraft. I will discuss what I learn with Brannhår and Karol and I will give you an answer in two days time. Would that be acceptable?"

Silfuryn smiled, "Of course Master Torin, I will await your answer with anticipation. Now, I may be able to help you with your other quest. I believe that you are seeking two girls from your village that have run away to join the opera. I myself have taken an interest in the pair for my own reasons; I am a patron of the opera and I heard the pair sing at our auditions the other day. One of them has a beautiful voice that was magical to hear, and this was spotted by a man who I know is a notorious theatrical agent. He has most likely got them hidden away until he can induce them to join his company. I do know where they are likely to have been taken and I can give you directions. However, I must warn you that the agent, Cyten is in league with criminal elements and therefore rescuing the teenagers may get rough. In addition I believe that it would be wise if we avoided any involvement with the justicers."

Both Torin and Brannhår had noticed the Lady's peculiar phraseology when she'd described Torunn's voice as magical and they had independently guessed that the Lady had discovered Torunn's magic. It was what they had both feared but they were relieved that the Lady didn't want any interference from the justicers.

"What do you propose, Lady?" Torin asked.

"We must be subtle, a direct confrontation would be inadvisable therefore I suggest that, since Brannhår has proven herself to be a warrior, I will include her in a clandestine raid to free the girls. We would then need to hide the girls safely until we could devise a plan to return them to their homes," Silfuryn answered.

Before Torin could say anything Brannhår said, "I agree, I will join your party, Lady."

Silfuryn grinned, "Just don't wear a dress."

Brannhår answered, "I'm afraid I don't have any dresses like yours Lady."

The remark went unnoticed by Torin but Silfuryn's face showed a momentary alarm. She recovered quickly and grinned again, "Then I propose that you, young lady, come to supper at my house at sunset tonight. Don't forget to bring your hammer..."

Ch 19: The Rescue

When Brannhår arrived at Lady Risavinur's home she was shown in immediately. Despite her hint to Brannhår, the lady was wearing a dress. Brannhår could see that it wasn't an ordinary dress because it was threaded with fine ironoak fibres and it looked old fashioned. She was also wearing a pair of gloves. These were the ones that the Lady had been wearing on the day that she'd been attacked and they were heavily laced with both ironoak and steel fibres. It was clear that the Lady would be joining the expedition.

Brannhår supposed that the Lady would be joined by her men later but they seemed to be alone at present. "Your dress, Lady, it's not what it seems, it is like the one that you wore this morning but it is much finer."

"Ah, so you noticed, tell me my dear, how you come to be able to see my armour when others can't?"

"I do not know Lady, I have always been able to detect metal, I used to help my father find metal in the mountains back home."

"And yet you were never recruited by the justicers, how did you avoid the tests?"

"Oh, I didn't Lady. They tested me but said I wasn't magical. I don't know why because my parents were sure that my power wasn't ordinary. They thought that, as a baby I was found floating in a lake and I might be some kind of álfur. But I don't feel like one of the spirit people, I think I am quite normal… well almost. I can tell that you have magic, Lady, how did **you** avoid the testing."

Silfuryn smiled. She'd wanted to hide her true identity from this strange young woman but it was obvious that the girl could see right through her disguise. She decided to trust the girl, she had a feeling that her trust wouldn't be misplaced. "Oh I used money, or rather my Grandfather used our family's money. He was suspicious of the justicers motives even before I was born and since he was magical himself he decided to hide my magic from the world. I am nowhere near as powerful as he was but I am glad that I am not a justicer."

"I am also glad that you aren't a justicer, Lady."

"Now that we know each other a little better, please stop calling me Lady, it makes me feel old. My name is Silfuryn, I would be pleased if you called me that. Although for tonight's little expedition I have decided that we will use different names. Tonight I am 'the Ghost' and you will be my 'spirit'.

Brannhår was confused, "Why do we need names? We are just going to rescue the girls, they will know me even if I use a different name. I assume your guards aren't using obscure names."

"Oh, we won't be using guards, it will be just the two of us and we will be in disguise. I know Cyten and I know he will be using his own people as guards. Some of them are justicers who moonlight as enforcers in his establishments. His public persona as an operatic agent hides a much nastier private one. He controls many gambling establishments and quite a few brothels as well as employing a ring of thieves and assassins who will steal anything or murder anyone for a price. If he finds out who we are then we can expect repercussions. Therefore we will go in disguise. Here, I inherited these from my Grandfather,"

Silfuryn reached down into a bag that was next to her chair and she brought out two elaborate masks. Brannhår examined them with her senses and she saw that they were made from the same materials as Silfuryn's gloves. They had been made to resemble the pictures of álfurs that Brannhår had seen in books. Silfuryn's resembled an aeriel and Brannhår's resembled a lampad.

"We'll wear them and I'm going to give you a bit of extra disguise. Here, try these on." Silfuryn handed Brannhår a pile of oddly shaped objects. Brannhår looked at them and frowned. "They are pieces of sponge and, if you wear them in your tunic and trousers then, it will seem like you are a boy. I'm sorry but two women together might attract too much attention. Besides they will help pad your tunic so, if it comes to a fight you'll be cushioned."

Brannhår frowned, "But what about you, I can see that your dress is tough and it might stop a blade but if they use clubs or hammers you'll get hurt."

"Don't worry about me, As you know I have some magic. I can use that to help protect myself. Now, as a final touch, use this," and she handed Brannhår a hammer. "That weapon of yours is too distinctive, anyone would recognise it. I'm sorry, it's not perfect, but it is the best that I can do at such short notice. Now, if you're ready I would like to get an early start. With any luck we'll have the element of surprise on our side because they won't be expecting anything to happen when there are lots of people about. We'll eat when we get back. I admit that I'm nervous and I don't want to fight on a full stomach. That would be asking for trouble."

"So, you are expecting a fight," Brannhår said.

"Taking anything from Cyten always ends in a fight, I'm just being prepared."

Brannhår nodded, "We should go now."

"Not until we get your disguise right," Silfuryn replied, "You need to adjust that codpiece and those fake muscles in the arms of your tunic are lop sided."

It didn't take the pair long to get to the place where Silfuryn thought that the girls were being held and then they waited and watched for a few minutes to assess what opposition they might encounter. Silfuryn whispered, "From here on I am Ghost and you are Spirit."

Although Brannhår had been in lots of situations where she'd needed to use her wits, intelligence and even her hammer, she'd never actually deliberately sought conflict and she was slightly nervous. Nevertheless she agreed with the facts. They needed to rescue Torunn and Elsa. Brannhår nodded and said, "I'm ready ghost"

******

191

Torunn was getting frightened. It had all seemed like such an adventure when she and Elsa had first set out. When they'd sung at the audition and everyone had been congratulating her she'd thought that, in a couple of days, all their dreams of fame and fortune would come true and they'd be rich and famous. The reality had begun to sink in when she'd discovered that Cyten hadn't taken them off to some luxurious mansion but had brought them to this dingy tavern and had told them that they should stay in their room. He'd even made sure that they wouldn't stray by locking them in. Someone had brought them food but when Torunn had asked when Cyten was coming back the surly man just laughed and left the room. Then, yesterday, two men had come in and they had taken Elsa away. She'd protested and then had fought them but they'd been too strong and now Torunn was alone. This was worse than when she'd been with the justicers. Now she was wondering what would happen to her. She wasn't dreaming of fame and fortune any more, now her only dreams were of escaping from this nightmare.

******

Cyten was seated at a table in the back room of the Ship inn. A man and a woman were stood in front of the table giving their reports. The man was one of Cyten's heavies, he enforced discipline in Cyten's brothels. The woman was a justicer who moonlighted for Cyten in return for pay.

"Well, tell me about our two guests," Cyten said.

The woman spoke first, "The witch is locked in her room upstairs, she doesn't seem to have any powers that would trouble us and she isn't very bright in any case. She's safe enough there until we decide what to do with her. I can only suppose that she's a runaway from the temple but she doesn't seem to be on any of the lists of deserters that I've been given. She might be a recent runaway and not made it to the lists or she might be from some other temple. In either case nobody will be paying any money for her return until she is officially missing and they post the reward for her capture."

"And, if she never appears on the lists?" Cyten asked.

"Then she's worthless, if we turned her in they'd regard her as a renegade who escaped testing and execute her."

"How do you know she isn't a renegade?"

The woman snorted a laugh, "She's no renegade, she hasn't the wit to be one, in any case she is obviously temple taught. I started one of the catechisms and she carried on with it word perfect. No, she'll appear on the lists before long."

"I still can't understand why she thought that she could get away with using her magic to sing," Cyten said.

"As I told you, boss, she's not very bright."

"Well, no matter, if we can't squeeze a reward from the Justiciary for her return then she can always join her friend."

Cyten turned to the man, "What about the other one?"

The man shrugged, "She screamed and shouted as you would expect but a few good slaps soon quietened her down. I gave her to Lisk, she is used to breaking new ones in. I don't think that she's started her on proper clients yet. Lisk knows that virgins fetch more, well at least until the clients realise that they're not virgins. Still she's young and we'll get a good few years use out of her."

Cyten nodded, "Well, at least we should get some use out of both of them. Still, I'm not happy that we can't trace the witch. There was a justicer sniffing about the opera a couple of days ago asking about runaway girls."

The woman said, "Oh yes, Detective Grimm. The boy scout. You don't need to worry about him boss, he got into a fight with five of Hrolf's tearaways; they messed him up good. Word is that he's at death's door and isn't expected to survive. I don't think anyone will be taking over his caseload. He wasn't popular with the seniors either; too honest for his own good."

"Ah rough justice for the justicer then," Cyten said and all three laughed.

193

Silfuryn motioned for Brannhår to retreat from the door where they'd been eavesdropping. When they were concealed in a corridor behind the bar of the tavern Silfuryn whispered, "We should be far enough away that they won't hear us. They've separated the girls. This complicates things. It means that, if we rescue one of them then they will certainly wreak retribution on the other. I don't know where this Lisk's brothel is but I would assume that it isn't in this building. What do you think we should do?"

"From what they said we know that the main body of the justicers aren't looking for Torunn yet and so, if we rescue Torunn, Cyten is unlikely to reveal to the justicers that he was holding her. They would start an investigation into why he kidnapped her rather than reporting her straight away. Cyten might try to come after Torunn but he won't be in any hurry; he will turn on Elsa.

That leaves us with the problem of rescuing Elsa before Cyten can get to her. I am inclined to rescue Torunn but to try to do it quietly so that her disappearance won't be discovered until it's too late. From what the justicer said they aren't expecting any trouble and all they have to do is keep Torunn locked up until she appears on the justicer lists. The problem will be getting Torunn to come quietly. As the woman said, she's not very bright." Brannhår replied.

"What about Elsa?"

"I assume that what the thug said about there being a market for virgins is true. You've disguised me as a man, maybe, if I pretended to be drunk and showed an interest in getting a virgin, especially if I was flashing a lot of money about, then he might be tempted to sell Elsa to me himself. If we could get Torunn safely out of the way beforehand then I could go with the thug and find out where Elsa is."

"That's a good idea, I could follow you when you leave the tavern and we could deal with the thug together," Silfuryn said, "Let's go then."

The tavern was quite busy and there were lots of people coming and going so it wasn't difficult for them to slip upstairs. However, at the top there was a long corridor and all the doors leading off it were closed. Silfuryn whispered, "Which room do you think she's in?"

Brannhår went from door to door then she stopped outside one of them, then she pointed and mouthed "In here; there's someone with magic in here."

Silfuryn nodded and she took a small set of tools from her belt. She bent to the lock and, seconds later, there was a tiny click as the lock opened. Silfuryn eased the door ajar and, keeping low, she slipped inside the room. Brannhår followed.

Torunn was in the bed but she was clearly awake. She had her eyes screwed shut and she was clutching the bedclothes to her chest and whimpering. Silfuryn said, "Don't be afraid we're here to rescue you."

However, Brannhår didn't bother with explanations. Her hammer was in her hand in an instant and she gave Torunn a slight tap on the head. Torunn slumped, unconscious.

Silfuryn said, "Well I suppose that's one way of keeping her quiet, she's not dead is she?"

"Oh no, I often stun my prey first when I'm hunting Elgrott, it's a good way of only taking the ones I'm after. I don't take game if it's too young or pregnant. If you do that you very quickly deplete the herd and there will be none to hunt in the future."

"Right," Silfuryn said, she'd been slightly shocked at her companion's matter of fact explanation of how to hunt. "So let's get her out of here. Any ideas where we should put her?"

Brannhår shook her head. Silfuryn smiled, and picked up Torunn's dress and flung it over her shoulder. "Then grab her legs and help me get her along the corridor."

They carried Torunn along the corridor without meeting anyone and Silfuryn pointed to a door on the left. She put her end of

Torunn down and opened the door with her lockpick again. Inside the room Brannhår saw dozens of small barrels heaped up in neat piles. Silfuryn cleared some barrels out of a dark corner and dragged Torunn behind them. Then she tied and gagged Torunn so that she'd stay put even if she woke, and stacked the barrels back around the girl's body.

As she worked she explained to Brannhår, "We'll leave a trail from Torunn's room to an open window so that when they find that she's escaped they'll think that she's left the inn and they'll start looking for her outside. They'll never think of looking for her in here, it's used as a store for mead whilst it's maturing. I could tell from the smell in the corridor, that this stuff won't be ready to drink for five or six months so nobody is likely to come in here if we leave the room locked. If she wakes up then she won't be able to cry out for help even of she's stupid enough to do so. She's not going anywhere for a while so we can come back for her later. Let's get on with the next part of the plan." She tore a strip of lace from the hem of Torunn's dress and rolled the remains up then tucked it beneath the teenager's head as a pillow.

They left Torunn and locked the room. At the end of the corridor there was a window and Silfuryn opened it wide. As she'd expected there was a fire escape outside it and she began looking for something. "Ah yes," she pointed; there was a rusty nail just beside the sill and she snagged the lace strip on it.

"Right now, my boy, let's get you drunk." Pulling a bottle from somewhere in the folds of her dress she pulled out the stopper. She upended it over the top of Brannhår's tunic and splashed more over the cap covering her hair. Brannhår didn't like the stink but she understood it was necessary. Silfuryn then reached into her pocket and pulled out a lumpy bag that clinked. Brannhår guessed that it was full of gold. "Here, take this, but be careful you don't attract too much attention. You don't want to be attacked by thieves instead of being taken to Elsa. I'll keep myself in the shadows and watch. Shout 'Ghost' if you get into trouble and I'll come to your aid."

Brannhår nodded, "Right, how do I sound?" she deliberately made her voice sound gruff and gravelly.

It didn't entirely make her sound like a man but Silfuryn thought that it would pass, "It will do. Now go down the fire escape and come back in through the front door."

Brannhår did as she said and a few minutes later she staggered through the front door of the inn. She wobbled across to the bar and thumped it, "Ale, I need Ale," she slurred.

The barman looked at her and shrugged, he filled a jug and slid it along to her. She took a huge swig and fumbled with the strings of the money bag. Brannhår looked from side to side theatrically and pulled out a single coin which she flipped in the barman's direction. He palmed it expertly and swept it into the drawer where he kept the cash. When she didn't complain that he'd not given her any change he reckoned that she was too drunk to notice. Brannhår took a few more swigs, spilling quite a bit so that it would be difficult to gauge how much she was actually drinking. She inched along the bar towards a woman who was nursing a glass of wine. "Hello Darlin, fancy a bit of company?" she croaked. The woman turned away and Brannhår said to her back, "Suit yourself, you're too old anyway."

Silfuryn, who was watching from the shadows of the stairs, saw the thug emerge from the back room. He crossed over to the barman and they exchanged a few words, Silfuryn was encouraged when she saw the barman nod in Brannhår's direction and even more encouraged when she saw the thug cross over to Brannhår. Brannhår pretended that she hadn't noticed the man as she stirred the pools of spilled ale with her finger.

"What's the world coming to when a handsome man like you is snubbed by a piece of worthless trash like her." the thug said to Brannhår.

"'s, disgraceful," Brannhår slurred, "Don't matter, she's too old 'nway."

"I know what you mean, I like em young as well."

Brannhår pretended to gaze muzzily at the thug, "s 'right…," she nodded and slapped him on the back. "Barman, a drink for my friend and I'll have another." She fumbled with the purse and a few pieces of gold spilled out.

"Yeah young and you know…" Brannhår said throwing a loose arm about the thug's shoulders as she sloshed more ale onto the counter.

"Yeah, I know what you mean; inexperienced," the thug replied.

"But you see…" Brannhår let her head droop then snapped it up again as if she'd been about to pass out and had caught herself, "can't get… you know… inexperienced ones for love nor money these days." She grabbed the purse and slammed it down on the bar with a solid thud.

"Oh, I'm sure a fine fellow like you would have no trouble, especially if you had the cash," the thug said.

"Plenty of cash, just found a new vein in my mine," Brannhår slurred then hiccuped, "but… hic… still no girl"

The thug grinned; he was going to make himself some money, "I'll bet I can get you the right girl, nice and inexperienced just like you like em. You come with me, I know a place."

Silfuryn watched as the thug half carried Brannhår out of the door. She also saw that he'd waved to the justicer as he left. Silfuryn waited a few seconds and saw that the justicer had started to follow the thug then, she too, slipped out into the night.

The thug led Brannhår through the maze of back alleys and twisting passageways until they came to an open space behind four tall buildings. He grabbed Brannhår by the arms and said "You can drop the act now, girlie. Come on give us a kiss."

Brannhår twisted out of the grip easily and reached for her hammer, the thug reacted quickly and grabbed it before she could swing. He said, "You must be stupid to think I'd fall for a trick like that, I knew as soon as I felt the padding that you weren't what you were pretending to be.

He was so intent on Brannhår that he didn't notice Silfuryn slip behind him, "Put my friend down and pick on someone taller," she whispered into his ear. Silfuryn's blade glinted in the moonlight and he let Brannhår go.

Silfuryn hissed at her companion, "I'll deal with this clown, put your mask back and deal with the other one."

Brannhår saw what she meant, the justicer had emerged from the shadows and was approaching. She was making complex gestures with her hands. Brannhår pulled the mask from her pocket and put it on then turned to face the justicer witch. There was a soft glow forming in the witch's right hand. Fire!

Brannhår saw the swirl of energy as it coalesced. The justicer threw the fireball towards her and its trajectory curved and it whirled by her head. The witch was busy readying another and Brannhår had a moment to glance across to the place where Silfuryn was battling the thug. She saw him throw several heavy blows that seemed to pass right through Silfuryn's body with no effect. "Ghost indeed," she thought then her attention returned to her own opponent.

The justicer was a little unnerved, fireballs were her speciality, how could the first one have missed? She readied the second and hurled it straight at the smaller figure. It stopped in mid air, then it seemed to pulse and it accelerated back towards her. At the last second she moved her head and the fireball just grazed her cheek. It stung like the blazes. She tried to conjure a third but she found that she couldn't. Her magic had deserted her. She reacted quickly and reached for her short sword and it clattered to the cobbles. It was red hot.

Brannhår had reacted instinctively, somewhere in that other memory that was just underneath the surface of her conscious mind she'd knew that, as well as negating magic she could manipulate energy, especially fire. She'd redirected the energy from the dying fireball into the metal that she'd sensed at the justicer's belt.

The justicer was nursing her blistered hand, "Who the hell are you?"

Brannhår looked over the justicer's shoulder, Silfuryn was still battling the thug but the battle was a one sided affair. He'd resorted to his knife in a desperate attempt to hit his opponent but the knife was just as ineffective against Silfuryn's ghost body as his fists had been. The same couldn't be said for Silfuryn's knives They had sliced into the thugs muscles and torso leaving raw gashes that pulsed with gore. The thug was weakening. Brannhår's opponent looked around at her thuggish comrade just as he gave a final gasp and fell to the floor. Silfuryn ignored the body and started to come over.

Suddenly Brannhår knew what to do. "Your friend is dead and if you don't want to go the same way you'll stay where you are and listen to me."

The justicer looked at her but didn't move.

"Detective Grimm was given the mission of finding the two girls that were abducted. We are, let us say, continuing his investigation whilst he is incapacitated. Don't try to do anything stupid. You've seen that our powers are more than a match for anything you might try. Even if you are just one of the lower orders you can sense that you no longer have control of your magic.

You know that the girl in the tavern didn't appear on our list of runaways and there is a good reason for that. She has already been sought out and dealt with. However, we now need to question her accomplice. You will take us to her immediately. Just nod if you understand what I am saying."

The injured justicer nodded. Silfuryn recognised her, she'd been with the Gibbet on their visit to her house. Trusting that the mask was a good enough disguise she now stepped forward and said, "I'll take it from here, Spirit."

Brannhår gave a little bow, "As you will, Ghost."

Silfuryn turned to the justicer, wiped the gore off her knives on her sleeve, and said, "Lead on."

They threaded their way through a few more alleyways until they came to the rear of a ramshackle building. The justicer stopped and said, "She is in there."

Silfuryn took a knife from her robes and casually started to pick her nails, "Well, go in and fetch her out, clod. Just explain that your elders and betters want to talk to her and for them not to expect her to come back.

And don't forget what will happen to you if your seniors, especially the Gibbet, find out about your dealings with Cyten. I saw her only the other day and she didn't seem to be in a very good mood. Then again, she never is. I suppose that we only tolerate her because she's useful."

The justicer paled visibly at the casual mention of the Gibbet. She shivered and said, "I will do as you say, elder."

The justicer returned minutes later with Elsa. The girl was in a sorry state. Brannhår could tell that she'd been abused and the girl hardly looked up.

"Leave her with us and get back to whatever rat hole you normally frequent. We will be watching you from now on," Silfuryn ordered.

The justicer dropped Elsa and fled into the night.

Brannhår tracked the metal of her knife and, when she was a few streets away, she said, "What now Ghost?"

"Let's get this one back to my place and then we'll go back for Torunn."

******

Cyten was not happy; the justicer stood in front of him quailed at the rasp in his voice, "What do you mean, you're not working for me any more, I pay you. You'll do as I say."

"I'm sorry boss but you don't pay me enough when the Ravens get involved."

201

"Ravens?" Cyten asked, "Who the hell are Ravens?"

"Elite justicers, they work in the shadows and take their orders directly from the Lords of the Justiciary. I've heard rumours about them but I never met any before. They never use their ordinary names and they go about masked but, make no mistake, they are very very powerful. One of them turned aside my fireballs and drained all of my magic and didn't even blink."

"The Gibbet has never mentioned any Ravens to me," Cyten protested.

"Oh she wouldn't. They operate in secret and most of them are well above her in rank. Those two last night could have dealt with the Gibbet without turning a hair, I tell you, I could feel them sucking the magic out of me."

Cyten thumped the table, "So I've lost both girls, damn! Where did they take them?"

"I didn't stick around to find out. One of them said that the runaway justicer had been dealt with. She's probably in pieces in some hog trough by now. They wanted to question Lisk's new girl and they took her away."

"Why did they want to question a trainee whore?" Cyten asked.

"I didn't ask and I don't want to know. Her body will probably surface in a few days, found in some midden."

Cyten thought, "Damn! I should have paid more attention when Grimm was nosing around asking questions. I thought it was strange, a detective assigned to some nondescript missing persons case. So the Lords themselves were after the magical one. What had she done to provoke their wrath? Anyway, at least I'm in the clear but I better not take any chances." He squinted at the woman stood in front of him, "This one will have to have an accident. I don't want her blabbing to her bosses."

Aloud he said, "Well it looks like we part company for a while, but don't be a stranger. When all this dies down I may have more work for you."

"Yeah boss, when everything dies down." the justicer replied.

******

Once the girls had been taken to safety, Brannhår and Silfuryn had returned to Silfuryn's home via a hidden entrance. It was concealed by one of the light-gathering units that were placed on top of the illumination fumaroles of her house. They were now seated in the drawing room

"I couldn't believe the look on her face when you told her you knew the Gibbet," Brannhår said, "It was like you slapped her."

"I'd never have thought of it if you hadn't laid the idea in her mind, what made you think of it?" Silfuryn asked.

"It just came to me. I suppose it was thinking about the way you hid Torunn right under their noses. I'd been thinking about how we could save the girls without the justicers continuing the search for them and reasoned that they wouldn't continue the search if they thought that the girls had been found by their own. The woman had been raised in a community of magic users like herself. In fact the only magic users she knew were justicers. You were clearly using magic against them and so we must be justicers."

"You used magic as well," Silfuryn said.

"Not really, what I can do isn't magic; it's the opposite of magic. I can make magic go away. I didn't realise it until about a year ago but then, once I used the talent to prevent children from my village being abducted by the justicers, I knew that I'd always have been able to do it."

"I saw you manipulate those fireballs, you can't tell me that that wasn't magic."

Brannhår shook her head, "I didn't use magic, it's different. All I did was control the energy. I can't make myself intangible or generate fire but I can sense and control energy when it already exists. That's how I detect metals; I can see the spinning energy inside them."

Silfuryn laughed, "I think that you are splitting hairs, my friend. It looks like magic so, as far as I'm concerned, it's magic."

Silfuryn's voice became more serious, "Now that we have solved the problem of the runaways and you've learned more about me I hope that it will persuade you to consider my offer. I am serious. I do think that the justicers will try to suppress your discoveries and I think that my money can prevent that."

"For my part I agree with you but I can't speak for Torin or Karol, they'll have to make their own minds up. However, let me tell you that this evening's work was exciting and it was good to thwart that crook, Cyten's, plans. If you are ever tempted to rescue anyone else again, count me in," Brannhår said.

"Oh, I will, I will," Silfuryn laughed.

Ch 20: Discoveries.

A few days after leaving the city Brannhår and Torin were back home in their village. Brannhår had told Torin about their adventure and he'd agreed that they could probably trust Silfuryn and they'd accepted her offer of help. Karol had joined them on the day before they left the city and he'd agreed as well. Silfuryn had promised that she'd find out about the justicers plans to regulate kraft and that she would prepare some strategies to keep the Justiciary from interfering with their work. Torin was in a fine good humour, not least because he'd returned home with Elsa in tow. The widow had been grateful enough not to ask any questions about how they'd rescued the girl and Elsa herself was still too terrified to talk. Silfuryn had taken charge of Torunn, If Silfuryn had survived so far without being detected as a renegade magic user Brannhår had no worries about her being able to hide the young witch.

After a couple of days some workmen had turned up at Torin's house. They'd been given instructions that they were to convert one of Torin's many sheds into a workspace. They had no idea how to do this but they had been told that Torin would give them instructions. When Torin asked who had hired them they'd replied that the contract had come from a dwarf called Alfsen. Brannhår had pulled Torin aside and explained that this was obviously Silfuryn's doing and that he should set up the workshop to be a secure place where she, Torin and Karol could work on the ironoak. It seemed that Alfsen had also told them that the workshop should be secure and that no expense be spared. Brannhår left Torin running around happily giving orders to the contractors. She noticed that he didn't tend to lapse into his dreamlike world at all these days. Maybe it was, as he'd always claimed, that he only lapsed when he was bored. The excitement of this new endeavour seemed to be enough to keep him awake.

Brannhår herself took advantage of the general turmoil to retreat to her own rooms and to think more about the interactions between lightning and metal. She also wanted to examine the specimens of ironoak with her own special senses. She'd not forgotten her escapade as the 'Spirit' and she remembered that nearly all of the special equipment that Silfuryn had inherited from her grandfather contained ironoak fibres. Therefore, the ancients must have known something about the peculiar properties of the plant. Brannhår wondered why nobody had seen it worthwhile to preserve that knowledge. She'd read many books and corresponded with many Masters of Kraft but none had even hinted at such knowledge. It seemed odd that a plant with such unique properties should be so forgotten. It was as if its absence from the archives of knowledge was deliberate. Torin was too busy with the new workshop to speculate on the matter and so Brannhår decided to write to Karol.

"Dear Karol

I hope that you will be able to persuade Master Kulfefer to allow you some time off from your studies of herbal kraft to come and work on the properties of Ironoak. I look forward to the time when we can work together again. However, I need to ask you a question. Is there anything in the lore of herbkraft that speaks of the qualities of ironoak. I have consulted all the sources that I know of in the lore of metalkraft but I can find very little. This puzzles me because I would have expected that its properties would be well known. I know that we were fortunate to have been diverted on our expedition but I cannot believe that we are the only dwarves who have been curious about the plant's properties,

I look forward to your reply, in the meantime I will try to continue our researches alone,

Your friend

Brannhår"

The crate containing the specimens was still in the centre of the shed next to the main living area and it looked like it hadn't been disturbed. However, when Brannhår opened the lid there was a harsh metallic odour that caught in the back of her throat. She cautiously removed the top layer of cloth that had been put over the specimens and she immediately saw the problem. The host of ironoak leaves that they'd gathered had crumbled to a fine greyish dust and all that remained were the thin skeletons of fibrous material that had held the delicate structure of each leaf together. It was getting dark all of a sudden and the room appeared to be spinning.

They found her a short time later collapsed on the floor next to the crate. Torin carried her to her bed himself but he saw some dead rats over by the skirting and ordered everyone out of the room. It was three days before Brannhår showed signs of recovery. Torin was waiting beside her bed as was Karol. They both looked ashen. The first words that Brannhår said were "Ironoak leaves are poisonous."

Karol spoke, "Yes, we know now. However, you will be glad to know that it isn't exactly the leaves. It is the dust from the dead leaves that is the poison. When Master Torin summoned me and explained what had happened I did some tests. I am familiar with the properties of herbal poisons and I immediately suspected the dust in the crate. I have tested the dust and it does contain very high levels of metal toxin. You were exposed to it for quite a while before you were found. If you'd been less fit you might not have survived. Once I identified the metal I was able to create an agent to remove the metal from your body and it would appear that the agent is effective. I've told Master Torin that we will need facilities in the new workshop where we can study the leaves safely. My preliminary tests indicate that, whilst they are alive and part of a living ironoak the toxic metal is bound and it is not directly poisonous. It is only when the leaf decays that the residual dust becomes harmful. I tested my theories on some rats and confirmed the observations.

Brannhår smiled, "Ah, my friend Karol, you think and you evaluate and you draw conclusions from facts. That's one reason why you are so dear to me. Thank you for saving my life."

Karol blushed, "Oh, you've saved my life often enough. I'm glad that I could help."

There was an awkward moment between them which lasted only a second before it was broken by Torin who had come in to find Brannhår awake. "Ah, you're awake. Close call there but you look all right. How do you feel? "

"A bit tired and my throat is raw and I feel that I could drink gallons, but otherwise I'm fine."

"That's good, I've been trying to keep on top of the plans for the new workshop but frankly I'm working in the dark. I'm not sure what we will need to study this new subject; it's too different from the sort of things that I'm used to."

"Yes Master Torin, I understand but I'm afraid that I can't help much. That's the problem, we won't know what we need until we need it. We should start with just the ordinary basics, we'll need tools and materials and places to make things and I'm sure that we will need facilities to make wire. Also we now know that we'll need a place where we can test out anything that's potentially dangerous but other than that I'm afraid we will just have to adapt as we go along."

"Can I suggest that, as we are dealing with things on a small scale that we might install lenses and good lighting. Something along the lines of the light tubes that Lady Risavinur uses in her home," Karol added.

"Good idea, but we might need something more powerful than lenses. Do you have any ideas?" Brannhår asked.

"I have heard that a dwarf over in Anglesheim has invented a device that can magnify objects smaller than the naked eye can see. It's called a sjálitla. They're very expensive though."

"Silfuryn said to spare no expense, let's get one."

******

Brannhår looked up and raised her visor when Karol walked into the workshop. He noticed the deep frown on her forehead and the look of annoyance on her face.

"What's the matter?" he asked.

"Oh, I'm not getting very far with my investigations into the ironoak. The samples we brought back are fine as far as they go but I think that there is more to be discovered. For one thing, I can see the structure of the dead leaf skeletons when I examine them under the sjálitla and I think I can work out how they interconnect with the leaf tissue but, since the leaf tissue has all decayed I can't work out what part the leaf plays in the tree's metabolism. You explained about leaves in ordinary plants and that they are used to gather sunlight which is used to generate food to keep the plant growing but it doesn't seem to be like that in the ironoak. As far as I can see the ironoak leaves do not have enough of the small channels that supply water and nutrients that other types of leaves use. It's as if they just collect the energy from the sunlight itself.

The same thing goes for the branches and other parts of the tree. Their structure is similar to other trees up to a point but there appears to be a secondary structure alongside the plant structure that serves another purpose."

"So, do you know what the other purpose is?"

"No, that's just it. The secondary system seems to be totally inactive. The only thing that I've surmised is that it contains channels that can direct the lightning energy. I tested the branches with my own generated lightning that I store in my metal and glass jars and they channel and direct it just as if they were made of metal. However, they are unlike any metal that I know, their properties appear to be more like charcoal than anything else."

"Well, does ordinary charcoal channel lightning energy?"

"Yes but nowhere near as efficiently as ironwood stems. I have been trying to isolate the parts of the ironwood that channel the energy but every time I try to dissect the fibres they are so fragile that they are almost impossible to remove intact."

"But fresh ironwood stems are anything but fragile, they whip about in the wind and bend rather than break. There must be something in the fresh stems that allows the flexure. Maybe it's the part that constitutes the living part of the plant?"

"Yes, you're right, I'm wasting my time trying to study these dead specimens what I need to do is to study some live plants. Thank you Karol, you've given me a new avenue to explore. Fancy a trip to the hills to retrieve some ironoak saplings?"

"I'd never say no to any invitation to go camping with you. It's always an adventure."

Then that's settled, tomorrow we plan and the day after we'll set out. I think that we'll make better time if only the two of us go. Master Torin won't mind, he seems to be preoccupied with some project for Silfuryn."

******

"Yes, Lady, however it just isn't possible to make lodestones that powerful. I agree that, in theory, you should be able to divert the path of any steel object, be it blade hammer or kettle, whist it is in flight but the lodestone required would be the size of a hill," Torin explained for the twentieth time, "Therefore the idea is impossible."

"But, don't you see Torin. It will confuse them and keep them busy chasing their tails whilst Brannhår and Karol get on with the real work."

The conversation was like many that they'd held in the intervening weeks since Torin had agreed to allow Silfuryn to represent himself, Brannhår and Karol in their dealings with the Justiciary.

"I can't see why we can't just register our proper ideas with them, then we'll be protected against others copying them," Torin said.

"I agree that, in an ideal world, that's what should happen. However this is the Justiciary we're dealing with here. They don't give a fig about what happens with the kraft. All they want to do is to control it, and that's why they've brought in all these 'registration of ideas' rules. We need to register a project that is sufficiently mystical that it will attract their attention but which would never work in practice. Moving things without touching them sounds just the thing."

"Fine, but I think that it's a waste of time." Torin grumbled.

"It's not if it distracts the Justiciary away from the ironoak studies. I don't want them finding out what we're really working on."

"How are we going to know? It's not as if we can just come out and ask them." Torin asked.

Silfuryn smiled, "But that's just what I can do. You remember the detective that came to my rescue and was injured?"

"Yes, Officer Grey, wasn't it?"

"No, his name is Grimm and ever since we stopped him being dragged away to suffer the tender mercies of the Justiciary he keeps making excuses to come around to the house. He says that he is just making sure that I'm not suffering any after effects of the attack but I think he has other motives. He chats away when we are together and he tells me all about the goings on at the Justiciary."

Torin nodded, "Just you be careful, he could be using you to find out what we're up to."

"Oh, I don't know..." Silfuryn replied.

******

An hour later Silfuryn was over the other side of the city on a rooftop overlooking a commonplace but respectable hotel. The people that she had arranged to meet would normally have stayed in their own place which was in an upmarket neighbourhood just outside the city limits. It was a measure of their desperation that they'd agreed to meet her at all. The couple were anxiously pacing in their room and they seemed to be alone. Giving her surroundings one last, quick scan she lowered herself onto the balcony. Making herself insubstantial, she slid through the locked window. Her movements were so silent that it was a second or two before the couple realised that she was there. The woman gave a little scream.

"Do not be alarmed, I am alone and I mean you no harm." Silfuryn said through her mask.

The woman asked nervously, "You sent the letter? It said that you have news of my daughter."

"I did," Silfuryn replied, "You have been told that your daughter met with a tragic accident. Well that isn't quite true. She is alive."

The woman gasped and the man stiffened. "Where is she? Can I see her?" the woman asked.

"She is safe but you cannot see her yet."

The man was less affected or maybe it was just bravado in front of his wife, "So you have her, how much will it cost to get her back?" he said.

Silfuryn was offended, did he think that she was a kidnapper, that she wanted a ransom? She knew that such things happened and so she ignored the insult, calmed herself and said, "I don't want any ransom. I didn't kidnap your daughter but she is in grave danger. You need to be told the whole story, then you must decide what to do."

The man looked at her but said nothing, the woman looked fearful and held her fist against her mouth as if to stifle a scream.

"Your know that your daughter was a trainee justicer in the temple but she made a terrible mistake. She let herself be seduced by one of the other students. The situation is more common than you might imagine. Such liaisons are absolutely forbidden these days and so it was decided that your daughter must disappear. In the normal course of events she would have been banished to a remote convent. Unfortunately your daughter is headstrong and she escaped and fled. An agent was dispatched to find her and kill her."

The woman cried out and buried her face in the man's chest.

"Fortunately a friend of mine happened to foil the assassin and she was rescued but she was gravely wounded in the encounter. However, she is young and healthy and after several months she had recovered and was hiding in the town of Longbarrow having assumed the identity of a niece of Master Torin Magnusson. Master Torin himself could not acknowledge her rescue as it would have landed him in trouble with the Justiciary. All would have been well but, because she is young and foolish she decided to return to the city and use her musical talents to create a more exiting life for herself. Again her foolishness landed her in bad company and this time it was myself who came to her rescue. I took her to a place where I could keep her safe until things in the temple quietened down. It is now time to return her to you. Believe me when I tell you that your wealth alone will not shield her from pursuit by the Justiciary. Currently they believe that she is dead but another foolish act on her part could expose the deceit and I doubt if she, or you, will survive their wrath a second time.

She is currently in hiding but that is not enough. You must get her back to Lungrey and hide her there. She cannot travel openly as your daughter. I will give her a suitable disguise and you will pretend that she is a new servant recruited for your estate and you will reinforce this deception by ignoring her as you would any servant. Once she is back on Lungrey you must make her disappear from society altogether. Since I do not know any details of your household I cannot give you any advice on how you should achieve this. Know only this, all your lives, yours and your daughters will be forfeit if she is discovered. Lungrey is sufficiently remote from the capital that, with luck and time she may be able to live out the rest of her life there. One thing you must promise is that you will never allow her to display her magic; not even in private. The Justiciary has many agents and they are dogged in their pursuit of any who stray from their fold. Do you understand what I am saying?"

The man thrust his chin forward, "What you are telling me is that my daughter can never be my daughter again. She must live like a fugitive."

"No, your daughter will always be your daughter and it is your duty as her father to keep her safe. Yes she will have to remain hidden and you cannot openly acknowledge her as your own child but, with time, she will change and grow and even the Justiciary will forget. In five or ten years you might even be able to welcome her back into your household as a distant cousin. However, none of this will be possible if she is discovered again so you are correct, she is a fugitive."

"And why are you doing this for us? I am a powerful man and I am unused to strangers giving me things without asking for payment?"

Silfuryn shook her head, "I am called the Ghost and my story is also one of hiding my magic away from the world. I understand what it is like to be unable to be what I am; to be forced to become an outcast and be made a fugitive from the Justiciary by a mere accident of birth. What has been taken from me can never be replaced so, you see, no matter how rich you are you cannot give me the reward I seek. Keep your daughter safe on Lungrey and that will be reward enough for me. Someone will be in touch with you to make the arrangements."

Silfuryn altered her mental balance and took three steps backwards through the window and out onto the balcony. The thin, almost invisible, rope that she'd left dangling from the roof was there and she climbed up it and into the night. She perched on the opposite roof and watched. It was a long time before she saw the couple leave the hotel and she followed them, observing from the many hiding places available on the rooftops of the city. As far as she could tell they weren't followed. Once they were gone she found one of her favourite places in amongst the gargoyles and she watched the aurora deep in thought.

It hadn't been as straightforward as she'd explained to the couple. In the first place, no sooner had the child been rescued than she reverted to type. She refused to hide, claiming that her father would protect her. When she'd been told that her friend, the widow's daughter, had been sold as a whore and abused and she'd nearly ended up the same, the girl had refused to see sense. In the end Alfsen had had to sedate her to keep her quiet. They had moved her to a remote cottage on one of Silfuryn's estates and had recruited a formidable, mute-guard from a women's lunatic asylum to keep her confined. The guard was reliable and would be paid well for her trouble. So far the girl, who's true name was Racka, had sullenly accepted her fate. Silfuryn had never visited the child, the fewer people that were involved the better. Still she supposed that it would be good to rid herself of the annoyance and get back to her own problems. With any luck the child would be gone in a few days and she would then be her parent's problem.

No doubt they loved her but the father was capable and probably ruthless. A person didn't get wealthy enough to own his own ocean going Fljúgbátr without having some intelligence and determination. The mother might be more problematic but she would probably do what her husband told her. Silfuryn wondered whether the family would succeed in the deception, the odds were maybe fifty-fifty. Silfuryn made a mental note to check whether any of her people might be exposed if the Justiciary caught the parents. She and Alfsen had been careful but it would be sensible to check. Unfortunately the girl herself knew of Torin's involvement so she had better keep an ear out for anyone enquiring about Torin's niece as well.

******

Brannhår shouted up to Karol, "Hold that mirror still, will you, I need to get this right!"

"Yes mistress," Karol replied mockingly.

"No need to be facetious, I am not your mistress," Brannhår replied.

"If only," Karol said to himself.

"What did you say? I can't hear you down in this hole."

"Oh nothing, I was merely commenting on the time that all this is taking," Karol said in a louder voice.

"We have to get this one right. I've got to get the whole plant and it would appear that these nodules on the root system are vital. If you could see them with my senses you'd see how much lightning is stored there. I've nearly exposed them all now and it should be just a matter of hauling the plant out on the winch. Now, if I could have a bit more light..."

For the tenth time in the past hour Karol readjusted the angle of the mirror. He was trying to reflect the sunlight down into the hole that they had exposed around the roots of the ironoak. The hole was quite deep and Brannhår was anxious to get the whole plant out this time. Their previous attempts on the days before had ended in failure. They had extracted the above-ground branches stems and leaves and a large quantity of roots but the plant, once out of its hole, had died remarkably quickly. Investigating, they found a system of deep nodules which were buried beneath the roots. That morning they had started excavating a fresh plant with high hopes that they would finally get a live plant out of the ground. Their ultimate aim was to take a live plant back to the workshop for further study.

The ironoak was considerably more complex than the usual herbs and flowers that he collected as part of his profession. Herbs and flowers were easy and most of them didn't lose their properties after being extracted from the ground. His thoughts were interrupted by a curse from down the hole.

"Damn, there's something else under the nodules. It looks like a tuber with its roots growing upwards. The roots connect to all the nodules. I think that it might be an even deeper part of the system."

"Oh no!" Karol exclaimed, "It's already after noon and we don't have much time."

"Then stop talking and shine that light down here," Brannhår shouted.

They'd made it. It had taken another three hours and they'd finally got the whole plant into the massive container that they'd prepared. They were just in time. The storm swept in and there was no way that they could have carried on. They were now both sat in the entrance to a small cave under an outcrop of rock watching the lightning play in the clouds.

"I've ridden one of those bolts," Brannhår said.

"Yes, I've often imagined what it would be like as well." Karol replied only half listening.

"No, I didn't imagine it, I've really done it with my friend Rakkerskap."

"I used to have imaginary friends as well," Karol said placatingly.

"No, I mean it. Rakkerskap isn't imaginary she's real!"

Karol was about to say something about her imagination but he found he couldn't. He stared at the column of fire that had just materialised out of thin air just in front of them.

Brannhår grinned, she was pleased. Rakkerskap didn't normally manifest herself when other people were around. She was glad that the eighth-dimensional fire spirit had decided to trust Karol enough to let herself be seen by him. Brannhår said, "Let me introduce you; Rakkerskap, this is my friend Karol. Karol, this is my friend Rakkerskap."

Words appeared right inside Karol's mind, he could hear them but he was pretty sure that they'd not come from his ears, "I am pleased to meet you Karol, Firehair has often shown me your form within her thoughts. Would you like to come and play?"

Karol was stunned, he didn't know what to do. Brannhår saw his consternation and said, "You just need to think your words, she gets confused if you say them out loud. She says it's like trying to listen to someone with an echo."

Karol tried, "HELLO RAKKERSKAP< PLEASED TO MEET YOU<."

The tinkling voice came back inside his head, "No need to shout, I can hear you well enough."

"SORRY...err... sorry," Karol thought.

"So would you like to come and play? Firehair will have to lend you her power but, between us, I think we could manage it!" Rakkerskap thought.

"Yes I would," Karol answered quickly.

Brannhår smiled and took his hand, "Hang on," she said, "It's scary the first time you do it."

Karol wasn't sure what had happened then, he might have imagined it but it seemed to be too real to be just a daydream. Suddenly he was up amongst the clouds and he could see the tiny twists and swirls of lightning before it was born. Brannhår was there with him and there was another presence; the fire spirit Rakkerskap. Then Rakkerskap must have seen something and he and Brannhår had been pulled forward at a dizzying speed. Something condensed and the next thing he was hurtling towards the ground at a terrifying velocity. They struck and it was all over in a flash, quite literally. He heard Rakkerskap cry, "Come on, let's go again" and he seemed to fall down a deep black hole in the sky.

When he came to, Brannhår was sat holding his hand and she was looking down at him with a worried look on her face, "I'm sorry," she said, "Rakkerskap told me that I must have lost concentration when we struck. I'm afraid I let go of my connection with you and you didn't have enough of the right power to carry on on your own. Rakkerskap has had to go."

Karol sat up and tightened his grip, "Oh no, don't be sorry. It was wonderful. I wouldn't have missed it for the world. Oh, you are marvellous, I was right there, you were sharing your mind with me. I'm sorry I ever doubted you. You can ride the lightning and you loved me enough to take me along. I love you too."

"That's good," she said, "Now we have to get some work done before we go to bed."

Karol came down to earth with a thump. Yes, there was work to do, however her words had been full of promise.

The next day Karol and Brannhår continued their work harvesting the live ironoak, For Karol it was a dream come true, he was with Brannhår and they were sharing much more that the physical work. They were a couple; almost one being and he was the happiest herbalist in the world. He didn't even mind when she shouted at him to keep the mirror steady. In the evening they sat beside the fire just content to be together. Karol asked "Rakkerskap is an álfur; a lampad?"

"I think she's a bit more complicated than that. She claims to be the daughter of a fire giant and a human hero. I don't know why but I believe her. Somewhere in my head I have a memory of once visiting them in Muspellheim but I couldn't have could I?" Brannhår replied.

"I don't know; perhaps it was in a previous life. Certainly Muspellheim doesn't exist any more, well, at least not in this universe. In any case it's thousands of years since our ancestors came to Svartalfheim so if you visited Muspellheim it must have been in some lifetime long past. You are a mystery, my love, and I am not going to worry about things past which I can't change."

The work was fascinating though. They'd managed to get two iron-oaks out of the ground and, so far, they seemed to be surviving. What they had to do now was to get them back to the workshop where, with any luck, the large glass sided tank would be waiting. When they'd realised that, to study the ironoak properly, they needed to see what was going on underground they'd asked Silfuryn to have something made to Brannhår's design. She'd told them that she owned several workshops that and one of them specialised in large welded constructions and it wouldn't take them long to knock up a tank with glass sides.

Karol would secretly have liked to spend more time on the expedition but he reluctantly agreed that it was more important to get their specimens back alive. When they returned to Longbarrow they were pleased to find that a huge crate had been delivered during their absence but nobody had unpacked it. It was going to take some shifting.

Ch 21: The Foreign Legion

Officer Stein Grimm of the justicers closed his eyes and tried to get back to sleep. He was normally unaware of the sounds of snoring and other nocturnal noises that his fellow officers made but, since his return to barracks, he'd had difficulty sleeping through the night. He looked at the skylight which was the only source of light and he could see the swirl of the aurora. It was nearly dawn anyway and so he decided that he might as well get up and go out on patrol. It was one advantage of his convalescence; nobody bothered with him and he pretty much made his own hours. He'd been given light duties and a post as an administrator because his injuries had laid waste to his massive frame. His colleagues made fun of him, saying that he'd received special treatment, calling him the darling of the upper classes because he'd spent so much time in the Holastan. However Grimm knew that he wasn't going to let himself waste away at some desk job. He was a Detective and his primary aim was his need to bring justice to those who took the lives of others.

He showered and dressed quickly and he was out on the street within twenty minutes. Breakfast would have to wait, if he was to get back to fitness he needed to use this quiet time to exercise. He set off running. His mind left his body on automatic and wandered through his past.

******

He had been ten years old, not old enough to be an adult but too old to cling to childish ways. He and his family had lived in one of the poorer districts and their lives had been hard. However, there had been some times when life had seemed happy. These were mostly associated with his mother. She had been a strong woman who had a gentle soul. He remembered that his happiest moments had been when she read stories to him. They had always been tales about the times when dwarves had first come to Svartalfheim and his developing mind had been filled with great sagas that chronicled the wars between the newcomers and the indigenous inhabitants who were always depicted as giant reptilian monsters. The heroes

220

were always true dwarves meting out true justice against evil-doers and the villains were always shadowy creatures that inhabited the dark places of the world. The tales often involved other creatures that had followed the first settlers from the ancient worlds; trolls, lorelei, arials and lampur. He didn't enjoy those as much but he tolerated them because his mother had loved them more than the tales of battle.

There was one memory that stuck out in his mind: it was the start of everything.

"Come, my little rock, come and listen to your baby brother while I read to you about Grombard the hero," his mother said. She'd held out her arms and gathered him to her so that his ear was pressed against the swelling in her stomach that she'd told him was his baby brother growing inside her. He'd felt her warmth and her softness and he'd heard a faint rapid thumping that she told him was his brother's heartbeat. That had been a good time but it soon came to an end.

Not long after there was a day when all the adults had become excited and he'd been shunted to one side as various female relatives came and went. He'd been confused and hadn't really known what was happening. Then suddenly it was all over and his mother was gone. His father, a weak man in any case, went to pieces and started drinking. More often than not he was drunk and he'd beat Stein as if it was Stein's fault that his wife had died. Stein resented the beatings; he knew who had killed his mother. It had been his brother, his brother had casually killed their mother and then, to add insult to injury, had died as well.

Over the next couple of years his father had sought revenge on the world by whipping Stein until his back was raw. Stein had become used to the nightly abuse and he bore it stoically until, one night, something snapped. He'd always been big for his age and he lashed out. His father had been sent flying backwards through the broken window to land two floors below, down in the street. People had come and Stein had been taken away. He didn't know what would have happened if one of the justicers hadn't seen a glimmer of magic in him.

They tested him again. He'd been tested before, but that had been in the happier times and no magic had been found. The justicers who tested him told him that this new-found magic had been brought out by his father's abuse and that was why it wasn't very strong. One of them, a bully, had found the phenomenon of the emergence of magic curious and, in a spirit of enquiry, he'd continued the whippings to see if the magic would grow more. It didn't. The bully had given up after a year.

Stein's magic was as weak as ever but his year in the barracks had established his physical prowess. He was inducted into Barr house and that had been that; not ideal, but at least nobody tried to beat him any more.

It was inevitable that, when the time came, he was transferred to the enforcer arm of the justicers as a grunt recruit. His superiors used his mass as a portable human shield for a few years until he had got involved in his first murder case. The officer commanding him had told him to chase a suspect and apprehend him. Stein had done as he'd been told and had brought back the miscreant after four days. The prisoner had protested to anyone who would listen that Stein had followed him on foot to Beltafiirn at the other end of the coast road and had made him walk back without stopping. The prisoner had been protesting that his feet would never recover when the Gibbet had arrived in the barracks. She proved him right, his feet never did recover. Gibbet had appointed herself judge, jury and executioner to save the courts time: she killed him on the spot.

Stein had been commended for his dogged persistence and he'd been promoted to investigator. From then on he'd always been the man chosen to chase wrongdoers whenever they fled the city bounds. He'd therefore spent a lot of time alone in the countryside and living off the land. It had gained him the reputation and nickname of 'the boy scout' who never let a murderer go free.

Several years later he'd made detective and his reputation had hardened. Everyone knew he hated murderers but none knew the reason why. In Stein's eyes, all murderers were like his unborn brother but, unlike his brother, Stein vowed that they would all face justice.

Then fate had intervened again. He'd been making routine enquiries and had surprised some robbers attacking a woman. He'd intervened and had been injured. The woman had brought him back to her home in the old part of the city and he'd been there for many weeks until his injuries had healed.

He only remembered brief snatches of the first few days. At first there had only been fleeting memories. They always seemed to be accompanied by pain.

******

"How is he?" a woman's voice had asked from somewhere in the blackness.

"As well as can be expected, Lady. His wounds are severe and it is a wonder that he isn't already dead. The manhandling by the Gibbet's men didn't help. I'm afraid that not all of the blood that emerged when she ripped away the dressing was fake. The healer has examined the wounds and he joked to me that, if the knife in his back or the blade in his front had been a little deeper then we would have been able to see right through him." This other voice had been male and it had given him the impression that it had seen wounds like his own before…

"Poor man, he's burning up. Can't we do anything about the fever?" It was the woman's voice and it sounded anxious.

Again the man's reply seemed detached, "In this case the fever is welcome. It is burning off the infection. One or other of the blades that cut him must have been dirty and the wounds have become contaminated. We have applied maggots but they can only deal with the surface decay. His own body must deal with the poisons within his blood…

A different female voice, "I'm astonished he's still alive. His body is consuming itself trying to counteract everything that is attacking it. He must have lost nearly a stone since he was first brought here. Even if he survives it will be a long recovery..."

"I'm glad that our efforts seem to be winning. Those wounds are starting to look less inflamed and I can see new tissue forming in places. He'll have more scars to add to his collection. I feel sorry for him. That back of his is almost all scars. What on earth could he have been doing to get so many scars?"

"I'm not certain, Lady. I do know that parts of the justicer code hark back to the old dwarf clans. It would seem that youngsters are still segregated into social groups or 'houses' when they are in training. Some of the training is martial and I believe that the more extreme instructors encourage internecine warfare between the houses. The officer's natural build would make him a natural warrior and, as we know from history, it is the natural warriors that always end up in the thick of any battle. Still, even allowing for his time in the temple, he looks to have had more than his own fair share of trauma..."

Then, after what seemed like weeks, the pain had seemed to ease and there had been long periods of blissful sleep and semi-consciousness. He vaguely remembered people cleaning his wounds and changing his dressings. Amongst them was a woman and he'd grown to know her gentle touch. They were the first gentle contacts he'd had with another person since his mother had been alive.

As the periods of consciousness became more lucid he realised that the woman wasn't a maid or a servant. The Lady of the house had been caring for him herself. He secretly watched her through slitted eyelids and he realised that her concern for him was genuine.

******

When he got back to the barracks he had worked up quite a sweat and he'd gone down to the showers to get cool. He'd been the only

224

one in the male side of the ablution block and he was wallowing in the cool stream as it fell from the perforated bucket that served as a shower head. The water had run out and suddenly there was silence. He hadn't meant to eavesdrop but two women were talking on the other side of the thin wall and he couldn't help it.

"It was terrible, you could hardly see her features. It made me sick and I'm used to horrific sights in the mortuary."

"What happened?

"They said that she'd been run over by a cart but there were no wheel marks. It looked to me like she'd been in a fight with ten giants."

"Well, you know the company that she kept. We all do it, working a bit on the side, but that Cyten is an evil one. She must have done something to upset him."

"Yes, but nobody will do anything about it."

"Why not?"

"The rumour is that she was in trouble with the Gibbet as well. Apparently she'd been shooting her mouth off about how she'd been there when the Gibbet had foul mouthed one of the aristos and got away with it."

"Really, when was this?"

"Oh, a couple of months ago. Remember that Princess who was attacked and got rescued by the boy scout. It was in the news. Apparently the Gibbet went to the Holastan to bring the boy scout back here and when she found out that she couldn't get him she insulted the aristo who had taken him in. Apparently Lord Pidur mentioned the incident to Lord Skald and he hauled the Gibbet in and gave her a formal reprimand."

"But I can't see how that ties in."

"Look the Gibbet is mad at her and Cyten wants her dead and they both know each other. It doesn't take a genius to work out what happened."

"You can't mean that the Gibbet..."

"Shush! I never said that. Now don't you dare tell anyone about this conversation. I wouldn't want either of us to become the Gibbet's latest punching bag."

Grimm waited until he heard the women leave and then he let out his breath. He hadn't realised that he'd been holding it in. He'd never liked Officer Gibra and he'd certainly heard some tales about her maverick behaviour but to beat a fellow officer to death? He couldn't believe it but he remembered someone in his dreams saying that the Gibbet had snatched off his dressings when he'd been injured.

Maybe what the woman from the mortuary had said was true. Grimm knew that it didn't matter who the dead woman had upset, she had been murdered and it was his job to catch murderers. He would make some enquiries.

One of the women had mentioned Cyten and Grimm knew Cyten by reputation. Outwardly he was a theatrical agent, but it didn't take him long to discover that Cyten had fingers in all sorts of criminal pies. He decided to go and see the man.

He found Cyten in the opera house and watched from a dark aisle as the agent ponced up and down the side of the stage extolling the talents of one of his protégés. Grimm could smell the cloying perfume on the set of flowered robes he was wearing at ten paces. He waited patiently until there was a lull in the action and then he strode forward, "Agent Cyten isn't it? I wonder if you could spare some time to answer a few questions."

Cyten had looked around at the sound of Grimm's voice from the semi-dark and had scowled but when the large justicer stepped onto the stage he dropped back into his foppish character. "Ah officer, so good to see you again. Did you ever find your runaways?"

Grimm cleared his throat, "I am sorry to say that I didn't find them but I remembered your generous offered to help and it seems that you might be able to shed some light on another matter. I am investigating the death of one of my colleagues. She was supposedly involved in an accident with a cart however the curious thing is that there don't appear to be any wheel marks on her body. We are trying to trace her movements just before the accident and we believe that she was seen coming out of the Ship inn that morning where I believe you have offices."

Cyten's eyes narrowed but he covered the reaction by waving a floral handkerchief in front of his face, "It's true that I have an office at the Ship but I can't remember seeing any officer of the Justiciary there."

"Really, sir? Then my sources must be mistaken. They told me that she was seen talking to you and accepting a package from you."

Cyten shifted uncomfortably, "Oh yes officer, now you mention it I did see an officer that day. One of our clients had had a little too much to drink and had left without his money pouch. I gave it to the officer and she told me that she'd try to locate the poor man. Really, I'd quite forgotten about the incident until you reminded me. I do have many business interests and I don't always remember every little detail. I'm afraid I don't recall anything else."

Grimm nodded, "Quite, sir. I realise that you are a very busy man. Well, now that we know the direction that she must have taken, I can make further enquiries at other establishments on the route. Thank you for your cooperation."

* * * * * *

"He suspects something, I tell you," Cyten said, "He was looking for those runaways, he even questioned me about them. Then the Ravens raided this place. Now he suspects that I had something to do with her accident."

"Well you did," the Gibbet said.

"I never touched her, I was with ten other people when it happened."

The Gibbet smiled, "I know. Just leave the boy scout to me."

"Another accident?" Cyten asked.

227

"I said that I will deal with it… but it will cost you."

"How much?"

"Double what we agreed last time," she said.

"Double!! That's outrageous!"

"He's much bigger than the girl. That's the price, take it or leave it."

******

Grimm waved the sheet under the nose of his commander, "What's all this? I've been assigned to foot patrol on night watch around the opera district."

"It's a new idea from on high. They think that detectives are losing touch with the rank and file. Rotating duties will give everyone more insight into how their colleagues operate and it will improve public relations or some such."

"It's lunacy," Grimm said.

"I agree, but orders are orders," the commander replied.

Grimm shrugged, it was no use arguing as the commander had said, orders were orders.

Two nights later he was cursing himself for not arguing. He was cold and soaking wet and his boots had developed a leak. The opera house was a dark brooding shape in the gloom and the streets around it were deserted. Even career criminals didn't go out in weather like this. Rounding a corner the biting wind lessened. He was standing between a flight of steps and a pair of statues and they provided a bit of shelter. Something silver flashed at his feet as he shook the surplus rainwater off his cap. He bent down to examine it and that was why the crossbow quarrel flew over his head and shattered against the steps instead of skewering him. Grimm never even heard it. It's whistling flight was drowned out by the clap of thunder from above. Pulling his cloak tighter around his shoulders he moved on. He would find the dead assassin on his next circuit of the building but, by then, his unseen guardian had disappeared.

Silfuryn looked down at the crumpled remains of the assassin. The man had been so intent on his target that he'd not noticed her come up behind him. By the time that he did notice her it was too late. He was frantically trying to grab a handful of the high stone parapet but the crossbow got in the way and he fell.

Silfuryn pulled her cloak around herself and went home.

"Well, my Lady," Alfsen said, "Was the intelligence correct?"

Silfuryn shrugged off her cloak and handed it to the old dwarf, "Yes Alfsen, as always your information was correct. Someone is, or perhaps I should say was, trying to kill our tame detective. I wonder who he's upset now. You might make some enquiries."

"Certainly, my lady. It was fortunate that my people learned of the open contract when it was issued."

"Fortunate indeed Alfsen. It seems that I am doomed to keep saving his life."

"Yes mistress, it would seem so; but look on the bright side. At least it gets you out in the fresh air. You've spent too much time indoors recently."

"That's true, my friend, that's true."

******

Cyten said, "What do you mean: he failed?"

"I mean that whoever took up the contract that I put out on Grimm failed. Apparently he tried to kill Grimm with a crossbow and he missed. They found him and the crossbow at the bottom of one of the towers of the opera house. He must have lost his footing in the storm which only serves him right. Only an amateur would try an assassination at night during a thunderstorm," the Gibbet replied.

"What contract?" Cyten asked, "Why didn't you see to Grimm yourself?"

"Because, idiot. I am good and I am as ruthless as the next person but Grimm is a big man. I would need accomplices to deal with Grimm my way and we can't afford any more people who know about my involvement with you. So I put a price on his head anonymously It will mean that every would-be assassin will be out to get him and I'll not be involved. Someone will get him eventually."

"But if whoever it is comes for the money, surely he'll find out it was you," Cyten said.

The Gibbet smiled, "But there's the beauty of the plan. He'll be told to collect the money from where it's buried outside town. There's nothing to link it back to me."

******

Grimm opened his locker but his lightning reactions threw himself to the floor as he saw the match flare. The explosion blew the door of his locker across the room and smashed the lockers either side of his into the walls The gout of flame set the towels hung over the shower doors on fire and it singed all the hair off Grimm's back. In the uncanny silence that followed Grimm saw someone rush into the locker room and then straight back out again. He wasn't certain but the person had looked like officer Gibra.

******

"That's the third attempt on his life this week," Silfuryn said, "Are you sure that you haven't any ideas who could be behind the attempts."

"Oh, I have many ideas, my Lady. In fact I'm sure that it is Cyten and he's using someone in the Justice department as an accomplice but I can't find any proof that it's him," Alfsen replied. "He was very lucky to escape the second attempt. We didn't see that one coming."

"Yes, but there's something not quite right here. All the attempts are amateurish; Assassination from the opera house roof, the swamp gas in his locker and the snake in his bedding. It's as if someone has set up a contest to see who can kill him in the most obscure way. One thing is for certain, it's not only one person who is trying and sooner or later even a bungling amateur will get something right. We have to do something."

"You are correct, mistress. What we need is to remove the threat by making whoever it is that is upset with the detective forget about him and withdraw the bounty."

"A good suggestion, Alfsen and you've just given me an idea. I'm going to have to go cap in hand to the council but I think that I can pull it off."

******

It wasn't often that the Lady Risavinur turned up to a party but she'd seen fit to turn up to the soiree that his wife had organised. Lord Pidur was pleased. His wife would be bragging about it for weeks. However when she cornered him and hinted that she needed a favour he wasn't so sure.

"You see, Lord Pidur, in my grandfather's day there were a lot fewer people in Vatersey. Now the regional capital has twenty thousand souls and there are another ten thousand who work in the forests and logging camps and mills. In Lord Risavinur's day law and order wasn't a problem, but I'm afraid that now crime is on the rise. I need the help of the Justiciary. Oh I know that you have a small temple there but, to be honest they are stuck in their ways. What I need is someone who can go out there and bring some modern thinking to the whole situation."

Pidur temporised, "I'm not sure what I can do Lady. I am only one person on the council and you will appreciate that any change in the temple on Vatersey would have to be sanctioned by the whole council."

"I realise that Lord Pidur, but I'm not suggesting that you change the whole temple. Just the part that keeps the law. 'Cappers' I believe you call them."

Pidur frowned, "Yes, I believe that commoners call them that. We call them Officers of the Justice."

Silfuryn gave a small laugh, "I'm sure that just a small change in personnel may be enough. The right man in the right place so to speak. Of course I would be willing to fund an extension to the temple proper in the capital. I don't believe that it has been refurbished for some years and all those extra nuns and novices must be getting a little crowded by now."

"It is true that the temple is a little small for such a large population and the council needs its funds for other projects at present. However a direct gift from yourself may be seen by some as trying to influence justicer policy."

"Oh, I'm sure that we could arrange for the funds to be donated anonymously"

"In that case my Lady I will speak to the other members and I'm sure that we can come to some arrangement." He drained his glass and pretended to look around for someone.

"There is one other tiny favour, Lord Pidur." Silfuryn almost whispered in his ear.

Pidur groaned inwardly, "Here it comes," he thought, "She's going to suggest that the personnel change involves one of her giddy socialite relatives." He smiled and said, "Yes Lady Risavinur?"

"I do have a suggestion for who might suit any new senior post that you create," Silfuryn said.

"And who is that?" Pidur asked expecting to hear the name of some aristocrat.

"Some months ago a gallant officer came to my rescue and he was injured defending me. He's quite recovered now but I have made some enquiries. By all accounts he is a good law-man and having been promoted to his present rank through his own diligence I feel that he deserves a reward for his devotion to duty. His name is detective Grimm."

******

"So, what else did she ask for?" Lord Skald asked.

"Nothing," replied Lord Pidur.

"The woman's got more money than sense. It will cost hundreds of thousands to bring the temple on Vatersey up to scratch and all this to get rid of an inconvenient peccadillo. You know the rumour is that he spent weeks after his recovery living in her home and tongues were starting to wag. Still, if she wants to solve her domestic problems that way and it will benefit our coffers, then who am I to stop her. I'll have a word with his commander."

"You don't think that he'll make trouble?" Pidur asked.

"I've heard of the detective. They call him the 'boy scout'. He may be a bit soft in the head but he's loyal to the temple. He'll do as he's told."

Pidur smiled; he might be able to afford that new fljúgbátr after all.

******

"But sir, I am needed here. I can't be expected to go off to the other end of the planet to take up a job that I know nothing about." Grimm protested.

"From what I hear Vatersey is a pretty quiet place. All they do is get drunk and try to hack each other's heads off with axes. You shouldn't have any problem.

In any case you've got no option. Every member of the Justiciary is bound to obey an order from the council; its in the rules. If they have decided that you are going to Vatersey, you're going to Vatersey and that's that."

******

Detective Grimm waited patiently, he always waited patiently because impatience made for mistakes and Stein didn't want to make any mistakes. He closed his eyes and silently rehearsed what he wanted to say. With each rehearsal his words sounded more and more inane. Who did he think he was? This was madness, pure and simple.

Grimm became aware of someone standing in the room, he had the impression that she'd been standing there for some time.

"Lost in your thoughts Officer?" Silfuryn asked.

233

"I'm afraid so, Lady. I was remembering how I first came to this place."

Silfuryn smiled, "I'm surprised that you remember anything, from what I recall you spent most of the time unconscious."

"My apologies, Lady, I did not intend to sound ungrateful. I know now that your actions undoubtedly saved my life and I am in your debt."

Silfuryn shook her head, "You owe me no debt. It was my own action that caused you to become involved."

"Do not say that Lady, it was my duty to become involved. I am an officer of the Justice."

Silfuryn laughed, "Oh I can't abide this formality. Let's be done with it. You tried to help me and suffered for it, then you spent weeks and weeks here whilst we tended you. Surely this all counts for something.

Henceforth, to you, my friend Stein, I am not the Lady Risavinur, I am Silfuryn. I admit I have enquired about your past and I know that you are that rare creature, an honest man. I need friends who are honest men and I want you to be my friend."

"Lady, you could do me no greater honour than to let me become your friend but I have some news."

Silfuryn had been expecting this. She pretended that she didn't know what he was going to say.

"My Lady, I have to leave the city. I have been posted to Vatersey and I don't know how long I will be away. So, grateful as I am for your offer of friendship, I cannot be here to be your friend."

Silfuryn shook her head, "Distance won't stop us being friends. Friends live in each other's hearts even when they are apart. I will write to you and you will write back to me. We can converse with each other and tell each other our news."

She took hold of his hand, "What I am trying to say is that your going away won't make any difference to the esteem that I hold

234

you in, my dear friend. I will miss you and I hope that one day your duties will bring you back."

Silfuryn lapsed into silence. Now that it had come to it, despite everything that had happened, she would miss this dour policeman.

Grimm felt the same and even though he wasn't terribly good at letters he would keep his promise and write to her as often as the post would allow.

She had hugged him and told him that he must keep himself safe and that he should hurry back as soon as his duty was over. She'd then held him close and had planted a kiss on his cheek. His imagination told him that he would never forget the sensation for as long as he lived.

Ch 22: The Whip

Brannhår was returning the cart that they'd hired for their expedition to the stables in the town when she saw someone that she recognised. It was the policeman who'd been injured trying to rescue Silfuryn. She was busy and so she tried to avoid him but he'd seen her talking to the owner of the stables and he had come over.

"Excuse me," Grimm said, "but I didn't ever get a chance to thank you for coming to my aid when those thugs attacked the Lady Risavinur. It was you wasn't it? I couldn't help noticing the hammer, it's quite distinctive."

"Yes, officer. I did intervene but there is no need to thank me. I would have done as much for anyone who was so obviously outnumbered."

"Nevertheless, you have my thanks. I believe that you may have saved my life."

At that moment the stable owner came up to Brannhår, "I'm sorry, my men are out on another job at the moment. I'm not expecting them back today. Whatever you have to shift you'll have to do it on your own."

Grimm saw the look of disappointment on Brannhår's face, "Maybe I can help, I'm quite as fit as I was before the attack and I'm strong. Perhaps you'll allow me to assist you?"

"Really officer, I'm sure we will be able to manage." Brannhår said. She wasn't sure that she wanted contact with any justicers, no matter how polite they seemed.

"Nonsense, it's the least I can do to repay your help. Now what do you need moving?"

"Oh, it isn't here," Brannhår said, "It's back at my workshop."

"Then lead on," Grimm said.

The pair walked back to the workshop and on their way they introduced themselves to each other. When they arrived, Karol had made a start on stripping the wooden container from the tank. Brannhår introduced Grimm, "Karol, this is Detective Grimm of the justicers, he was the fellow who I helped when Silfuryn was attacked. He's here to return the favour by helping us shift the tank," she turned to Grimm, "Karol is my associate, friend and companion."

She went around the other side of the huge crate, "It's bigger than I thought it would be, we're going to have to use some ingenuity to move this. You are a big man Detective but I'm afraid to move this we'll need kraft."

Brannhår disappeared into another part of the workshop and Karol turned to Grimm, "You'll have to excuse my partner. Once she decides to do something she doesn't rest until it's done."

Grimm smiled, "Just like the Lady."

"Ah yes, Lady Risavinur. We became well acquainted with her during our stay in the city. But, of course, you wouldn't have known that. I believe you were gravely ill at the time."

"Yes," Grimm replied, "however I am now well, thanks to the Lady. I owe her much."

"I agree she is a fine woman and she's very astute. In fact she's helping us with our researches here," Karol said.

"Really? And may I enquire the about the nature of the research?"

Karol nodded eagerly, "We're studying the ironoak tree. This tank is so we can see what's happening underground in the root system."

"I wasn't aware that the Lady was interested in plants," Grimm said.

Karol laughed, "She isn't, she's not technical. She's funding us and helping out with the admin. Brannhår is the technical one."

Grimm scratched his head, "If you don't mind me saying so your companion seems to be a little too warlike to be an academic."

"You'd be surprised, Detective. According to Master Magnusson she has one of the best technical minds on the planet."

"It's probably just that she carries that war-hammer," Grimm explained.

Karol nodded, "I know what you mean, but it's primarily a tool not a weapon. She carries it because it's her good-luck charm. I was with her when she made it during her Menntunleit. Or rather I should say that I met her when she saved my life with it."

"So we have something in common, we both owe our lives to your companion," Grimm replied.

Karol gave a nod, "Since we have so much in common Detective, I suggest we dispense with formalities. Call me Karol."

"Agreed, Karol," Grimm said smiling, "My name is Stein."

They both turned as Brannhår re-appeared hauling a mass of ropes pulleys and chains. "Right, start bringing those beams over you two, we'll need quite a few levers."

Grimm froze, he couldn't believe his eyes. Just behind the woman was a wolf. It bounded past her headed straight for them. Grimm went for his dagger but it was too quick, it was past him in a flash. It bowled Karol over knocking him to the floor. Something was wrong; for some reason Karol wasn't screaming, he was laughing. "Hello, girl, did you miss us. I'll bet Torin has been spoiling you rotten while we were away."

Grimm realised his mistake; the wolf wasn't attacking, it was greeting the young man. He sheepishly tried to put the dagger away without anyone noticing. Karol had got up, disentangling himself from the wolf. He was laughing and fussing over the animal. Suddenly the wolf appeared to notice Grimm and she became perfectly still. Her head extended itself forwards and she made short sniffing noises.

Grimm kept still, he was a city man despite his nickname and he'd never seen a wolf outside of a picture. He'd certainly never met one face to face at this close a distance. Karol saw what was happening and knelt down to scratch the wolf between her ears; she pretended not to notice,

"Detective Grimm, let me introduce another member of our fellowship. This is Mistle," the wolf's ears twitched at the sound of her name, "Brannhår saved her life as well. Her mother and brothers had been attacked by a troupe of skogs on Skogrey. Between them Brannhår and Mistle's mother killed most of the troupe but Mistle's mother had been fatally injured so we sort of adopted her," Karol explained.

He turned to the wolf who looked up at him attentively. "Mistle, this is Stein, he's a friend, go on, say hello"

The wolf looked at Grimm. Karol said, "Just stay still. Hold out your hand, palm down and let her sniff it."

Grimm tentatively held out his arm at full length with his hand held palm down. The wolf casually strolled over and gave it a good sniff. Then, for good measure she licked it with the tip of her tongue. Grimm's nerve nearly broke but he steadied himself. Then he relaxed, the wolf had turned away and had gone over to Brannhår to sniff at the pile of lifting equipment. Grimm had passed some sort of test and he was no longer relevant. He still hadn't moved but Karol broke the stasis, "Come on Stein, lend a hand here."

Between the three of them they managed to un-crate the steel and glass tank and manhandle it onto a trolley, "Let's get it outside and into position. If we put the ironoak in there first we'll never move it," Brannhår said. They pushed the tank, still on the trolley, through a set of double doors and out into a small courtyard that was open to the sky. Brannhår chocked the wheels of the trolley and they returned inside.

"We're not finished yet," Brannhår said, "We have to get the ironoak saplings in there now." Grimm followed her out into the street. A large crate was stood there on a second trolley. Grimm could see some branches and leaves protruding from its open top. The crate was sat next to a large pile of black soil. "Let's get some soil in to form a base layer before we do the transfer, there'll be less chance of damaging the roots." She strode back into the workshop and emerged with three shovels. After handing Grimm one and Karol another, the three of them dug into the soil heap and carried a shovelful each back to the courtyard.

Brannhår reached up to one side of the tank and unlatched several clamps. The whole wall of the tank hinged out vertically and she lowered it to form a steep ramp resting on the ground. "Right, we need a layer about a hands-span deep to form a bed." She picked up her shovel full of soil and threw it into the open tank. come on, she said, we need to finish this before dark, from the look of the sky we won't need to water it in because there's a storm due later.

By the end of the afternoon they'd transferred the two ironoak specimens into the tank and filled the space around them with the rest of the soil. The trio stood back and admired their handiwork and, on cue, the first drops of water fell out of the clouds.

"Let's get in and get something to eat. I'm starving," Karol said. They'd washed up and they were sat around the table having a bru when there was a knock on the door. Brannhår went to open it and smiled, "Widow Oggnar, what can I do for you?"

"I saw you were back because Mistle was missing and then, when I came past earlier I could see you were busy so I thought I might bring across one of my pies for your supper as I know what it's like cooking after a long day's graft."

Brannhår thought, "You mean that you saw that we had someone new with us and you couldn't contain your curiosity," however, she said, "That's kind of you Widow Oggnar, please come in."

The widow stepped past Brannhår and looked around. Grimm had taken his uniform jacket off whilst he'd being helping them but it was draped over the back of his chair. The widow Oggnar's eyes spotted it immediately and she hesitated. Brannhår couldn't help herself, "Widow Oggnar, can I introduce Detective Grimm. He is helping us with our experiments but I think you owe him a debt of thanks too."

The widow looked at her curiously. "Detective Grimm's information was instrumental in rescuing Elsa from those villains," she said.

The widow placed the pie on the table, temporarily forgotten. She strode over to Grimm, "Oh officer, how ever can I thank you for rescuing my dear daughter from those fiends in the city. I've never been one for the city justicers but I must say you saved an old woman from a lifetime of grief. Thank you, thank you!" She flung her arms around Grimm's massive shoulders and hugged him.

"Errr... It was nothing, lady. I was merely doing my duty."

"Well, I never did thank you when Master Torin brought Elsa home but I'll make it up to you," and she excused herself and shot out of the door."

"But I never did anything," Grimm protested after she'd gone.

"Don't worry Detective, just play along and we'll tell you the whole story later," Karol said.

"Later?" Grimm asked. Then he realised that the widow had re-appeared. She was clutching a dusty bottle in her hand.

"The finest Raasrey Mead," she said, "please accept it as thanks for what you did for my little girl." She hugged him again and sat down at the table expectantly. Karol reached for the bottle and opened it whilst Brannhår brought drinking mugs from the cupboard.

An hour later they'd consumed all of the pie and half the mead. The widow had made her excuses and left after giving Grimm one final hug. Karol put his mug down and turned to Grimm, "Detective, let me explain. We told the widow that it was the justicers who found her daughter and rescued her from her kidnappers but the plain truth was a little more mundane. You see it was the Lady Risavinur who really saved the child. Her guards found out where they were holding the girl and she bought the girl back off them. She didn't want people to know that she paid the ransom in case other villains got the same idea so she sent her guards to tip off some people that they knew in the Ravens. Of course Master Torin couldn't tell the widow that, we'd never hear the end of it, so he told her that some brave justicers had rescued the girl. Her daughter won't say anything, she's just grateful to be alive."

Grimm nodded. Yes it would be just like his Lady to come to a logical solution like that. It was so typical of her, she was so generous, paying the ransom out of her own pocket. He already thought that she was wonderful and that he couldn't admire her any more than he did but he'd been wrong.

They spent the rest of the evening polishing off the mead. Karol had asked Grimm what had brought the detective to Longbarrow. Grimm considered; he'd enjoyed the company of the two young makers and he'd enjoyed the mead as well so he was in a generous mood.

"I'm just passing through. To tell you the truth I was working on a murder case where it seemed that some corrupt officers were involved when, out of the blue I received some new orders. I've been posted to Vatersey to take charge of a police force in the main city Vatnarheim. I'm travelling on to the port at Beltafiirn where I'll get passage to Valdirey then on to Vatersey."

"That seems odd," Karol said, "Can they do that; just send you across the world at a moment's notice?"

"Justicers have to obey orders and my orders are to go to Vatersey," Grimm replied.

"But what about your home and friends and your work in the city?" Brannhår asked.

Grimm grimaced, "I'm afraid that my superiors never consider things like that. Besides, I have very few friends and I live in the barracks. The only person that I will miss is the Lady."

"Couldn't you just resign," Karol asked, "I'm sure that Silfuryn could find you some work."

Grimm shook his head, "Justicers can't resign, once you've been admitted to the temple it is for life. The temple controls everything

242

about you. It never really bothered me before. I had a job, somewhere to live and I got fed. I don't suppose I ever looked for more."

"But what about your wife or family?" Karol asked.

"We aren't allowed to marry or have children. We are allowed to have friends outside the justicers but not in the way you have Brannhår." Grimm replied.

"So now you've been ordered off to a new life at the other side of the world."

"That's about the size of it," Grimm nodded, "I leave for Beltafiirn on tomorrow's coach."

Karold said, "Well, It leaves after breakfast so we'll have time to bid you farewell before you go."

Brannhår said, "And I hope you'll stop by if you have to break your journey again. We're always pleased to see one of Silfuryn's friends."

Grimm spent the rest of the evening in pleasant company. He didn't mind when the two young people lapsed into technical talk. It was almost soothing just hearing a word that he thought he should understand being used to mean something quite different. In between the technical bits he listened as the pair told tales of their childhood and he marvelled when Brannhår told him the tale of the Baar. He even half believed her however he wasn't concerned whether the tales were true or not, they were good tales and they rivalled the tales that he remembered his mother reading to him when he'd been small.

Later, when he was settled in his bed in one of the spare rooms, Grimm reviewed his day. It had been a good one. He'd got to meet and thank the girl who'd saved his life and he'd discovered that she and her partner were both makers. Funnily he'd found them to be fairly ordinary and he'd grown to like them. They were completely different to the arty types that abounded in the city who always set his teeth on edge with their airs and graces. The couple were down to earth and not at all what he'd imagined the intellectual class to be like. In a way they were like Silfuryn, completely different to what his prejudices had led him to expect. His thoughts turned to Silfuryn. That night he slept soundly. His dreams were filled with visions of 'His Lady'.

******

Brannhår turned over in bed and said, "Are you awake?"

Karol gave a soft groan, "I am now... what's bothering you?"

"I can't help feeling that meeting Grimm this afternoon was more than a chance coincidence. It is almost as if we were meant to meet."

"You and your fancies," Karol said, "Whatever happened to the most brilliant and logical mind on the planet that I fell in love with."

"Ha, if I'd been that brilliant and logical, how did I end up with you?"

He started to reply but Brannhår pulled him to her and all that could be heard then was the creak of the bed ropes.

Grimm awoke the next day and went into the kitchen but there was nobody there. He heard a noise in the workshop so he went in.

"Look out!" someone cried and instinctively he ducked. It was just as well, a fraction of a second later something like a small crossbow bolt buried itself in the wood inches above his head.

"Sorry about that," a familiar voice said. Grimm picked himself off the floor. "Please excuse us, we were just playing with this new toy that Brannhår has made." Karol waved a small squat tube with a bulbous end in front of the detective's nose.

"Look, come over here and we'll show you how it works." Grimm followed the young man across to a bench where Brannhår was bent over examining something through a large magnifying glass. She didn't look up but she said something to her partner, "It's burned out the coil again. Either we'll have to use less charge or we'll have to reinforce the conduction paths."

"Or we could try to control the flow," Karol added. Grimm hadn't the faintest clue what they were talking about. All that he could tell was that they were excited.

"Do we have enough charge for one last go so that we can show the detective?" Karol asked.

Brannhår looked up, "Hello Detective, I didn't see you there," she went on, "We've probably got enough for one more. Then we'll have to put the cells back so that they can charge tomorrow."

"Watch this detective," Karol said and he dragged the policeman over to a bench. All that Grimm could see was another small squat tube with a large bulbous something attached to one end of it. He watched as Karol picked up an ordinary nail and placed it into the tube.

"Don't forget the flight," Brannhår warned and Grimm saw Karol take the nail out and wind a few twists of cloth around its end. Then he put it back.

"Ready detective? Don't blink or you'll miss it."

Grimm watched but all that happened was that there was a sound like a giant bee buzzing for a second and then there was a thump as something hit the wooden door. Grimm looked at the nail, it had been driven half its length into the wood and the piece of cloth dangled from its end like a tiny flag.

"Magic," Grimm said.

"No, Detective, that's the whole point. It's not magic, its kraft and it will work for anyone. Of course, a hammer is much more efficient but that's not the point is it?" Karol replied.

"Err... No?" Grimm replied, thinking of what a mess the nail would have made of his head if he hadn't ducked. Then he brightened, the youngster had a point, his head would have been the same if a hammer had smashed into it.

Karol turned to Brannhår and said, "Why don't I tidy up here and you two go and see what we've got for breakfast."

She turned to Grimm, "Come on Stein, I'm afraid there isn't any mead left but we do have bru."

Grimm followed the young woman back into the kitchen, she was just as excited about what they'd just witnessed as her partner, "I know what you're thinking detective, what you've just seen would make one hell of a weapon."

"I must admit the thought had crossed my mind."

"And that's one of the reasons I like Karol," she said, "he is so caught up in the moment that he sometimes doesn't think ahead. However, I wouldn't worry detective, we're not developing weapons. Believe it or not we're just exploring fundamental principles. In any case, I could make you something very similar from springs and levers that would fire nails just as lethally. It would just be a better version of the pistol bows that some gangs use in the city."

Grimm shook his head. He'd only really known this young woman a day and already he knew why Master Magnusson had said that she had a brilliant mind.

She smiled, "Sit down and grab some brot. I'm glad you're up early. Karol will be a while in the workshop so we can talk."

Grimm helped himself to a chunk of brot and a bru and then sat down.

"I've not had a very good night detective," Brannhår said, "I had the weirdest dream. I was in a place that shone as bright as day even though I knew it was the middle of the night and I was talking to an old man. Except the language we were speaking wasn't Dwarfish and neither I nor the man were dwarves. He seemed to want to tell me something and it was about the future but there was a terrific buzzing noise coming from overhead and then there were the sounds of huge explosions as though a volcano was erupting under our feet. The man started shouting at me and the two words that I understood clearly were Grimm and danger.

Now don't laugh, Detective, I haven't lost my mind and I don't believe in prophecies but that dream scared me. So, if you'll let me I'd like to give you something."

She stood up and went over to a cabinet of drawers. She pulled one open and took out what looked to Grimm to be a short rod about as long as her forearm. She walked back over and handed it to Grimm.

"I was making this for a friend of mine but I can make another. I think that it might come in useful to you in your travels."

Grimm twisted the rod in his hands. The bottom half of the rod consisted of a rounded pommel and handle covered in leather and the top half was also made of leather except that this leather was in thin strips braided together and twisted in a complex weave. At the top of the rod was a disc of metal in the shape of an inverted heart. The metal showed two seams running around its edges but its surface was dull grey and covered in intricate spiral lines. The whole thing looked like a short spear that could be used for stabbing.

Brannhår took it back off him, "Let me demonstrate, Detective," she said.

He saw her push down on a small gem that he'd not noticed in the pommel and the thing appeared to come alive. The leather braid uncoiled into a long whip about as long as three arms-lengths and it was tipped by the heart-shaped metal. Brannhår flicked it and he saw the metal describe a shallow arc and slice through a candle that was stood on the table about eight feet away. The candle wobbled for a second and then it fell onto the tabletop in two pieces. Brannhår released the gem and gave the whip a flick and it was back into its original form; a short leather rod with a dull metal tip.

Brannhår smiled "It takes a bit of practice. The tip," she said tapping the metal piece, "slides apart slightly under the influence of the whiplash to present two, very sharp, cutting edges but when coiled it is relatively harmless. The rod also has a couple of other tricks up its sleeve but I'll let you discover those for yourself. Take it, Detective, use it with honour, and good luck. My dream said that you'd need it."

Grimm looked at the whip. It wouldn't have been his first choice as a weapon but this girl clearly wanted him to take it. He thanked her and slid it into his belt. She was right, the razor sharp edges of the disc were now dull and harmless.

Grimm left Longbarrow an hour later. He didn't know what was going to happen and he didn't know whether he'd ever come back but his day with the young couple had refreshed his spirit like nothing else had since he'd been injured. As the coach drew away from the depot and the gentle rocking soothed his thoughts, he began to drift off.

Some day he'd be back and he'd meet with the youngsters and his beloved lady and the world would be bright and the future glorious.

Ch 23: The Paperchase

Silfuryn was getting nowhere with the people she'd bribed for information about the department for the registration of ideas. Therefore, she'd decided to take a look at the files that the Justiciary were amassing on the huge numbers of the latest maker creations. The files were in one of the above ground wings of the temple and so she'd reasoned that they mustn't be too difficult to get at. What she hadn't reckoned with was the sheer number of documents. The administration of the scheme had become a monster and there was nowhere below ground in the temple that was big enough to house the sheer volume of paper needed. It was ironic; they'd even had to commission a separate paper manufacturing company to supply the scheme's voracious demand; it was one that she owned.

 She also hadn't reckoned with the security precautions, The handful of low level enforcement justicers had been supplemented by wyres. Packs of them roamed the aisles between the shelves of the archive. Silfuryn could easily handle a single wyre but the problem was that they never came singly. Currently there were about ten on her trail and they'd have cornered her already except that she'd taken to high ground. She was running along the tops of the rows and rows of shelves, The reason that the wyres weren't up there with her was that the shelves were so stuffed with paper that there was nowhere stable enough to allow the beasts to climb up after her. However she was running out of places to go. Ahead she could see rows of shelf tops but their lower shelves mustn't have been so stuffed with papers. Already she could see the lithe shapes of wyres climbing up them. She turned and began to run along the shelf. There was a gap between the end of the shelf and the low mezzanine floor that circled the room. She gauged the distance, it was too far for a jump but she had no choice, she started to run faster. At the final instant she launched herself into space and used her power.

She nearly made it, but her reaching hands slid through the floor of the mezzanine level as if it was thin air. Her momentum carried her through the wall and she fell down through the floor of the archive room. She became substantial again in mid air several feet above the floor of the room below. It was some sort of storage room and she landed heavily on a crate. She caught her breath for a moment listening to the sounds of pursuit coming from the room above. People were shouting. Amongst the general hubbub she caught the odd phrase.

"He came this way... He was running across the tops of the shelves and then he jumped... The wyres are going crazy, they're clawing at the walls..." a more distant voice shouted, "I could swear that this was where he must have landed but nobody passed me on the stairs and there's no body or any sign that anyone's been here. You lot concentrate the search on the floor down there."

Silfuryn decided that discretion was the better part of valour; she'd wait in the storeroom until things died down.

The commander of the guard surveyed the pandemonium, "Why the hell would anyone break into here? There's nothing here but papers," he asked his second. "Can't anyone shut those damn wyres up. For Odin's sake somebody round them up and get them out of here." He turned to the trooper stood next to him, "We had all the doors secured as soon as the alarm sounded so nobody got out. Whoever it was might have tried the mezzanine but it doesn't look as if anyone got out that way either. There's only one answer, The intruder must still be here."

"But the wyres, sir, if he was still here they'd be going mad searching." the trooper said.

"Haven't you heard of kattdaun, whoever got in probably sprayed the walls with it. The wyres would have been so keen to get at the stuff they'd have forgotten all about anything else."

"Yes sir, I'll get the men organised and start a row by row search."

"Good, and see if you can spot if anything's missing. Are the master ledgers all still there?"

"It would appear so sir, the cabinet behind the desk appears to be undisturbed."

"Well what the hell was he after?"

"I can't say, sir," the trooper replied.

The commander strode off muttering under his breath, "Idiots, I'm surrounded by idiots."

Silfuryn nodded, maybe this evening's enterprise had been a fiasco but thanks to sheer dumb luck she now knew what she needed to look at the next time she was here. She also gave a silent word of thanks to the commander, "Kattdaun, she'd never thought of that. Karol would know where she could get some. There was a set of overalls and a mop and bucket in a cupboard she put them on and waited. Three hours later she left the building with the rest of the cleaning staff.

Two days later she waited until the building was mostly empty. The archive was locked so she went insubstantial and walked through its double doors. As soon as she'd passed through, she flung the home-made scent bomb as far as she could over the tops of the shelves. The action was quickly followed by the sound of claws scrabbling along polished floors in pursuit of the powerful scent. Walking over to the cupboard she used her lock-picks to open the simple lock. The ledgers were stacked in date order and there were ten shelves each with about eight ledgers on each shelf. She picked up the two of the most most recent ones then went back to the doors and she was soon outside and handing them over to Alfsen.

Alfsen had stationed himself close to one wall of the temple where some ancient architect had decided to install a lamp for the convenience of the night people. He quickly thumbed through the latest ledger. After a while he opened it at a page and held it out to Silfuryn, "It would appear that these ledgers not only catalogue the maker's ideas they also act as a filter for their later perusal. See, the recent entries just have a number, a description and the maker's name and address but nothing in the subsequent columns. Earlier in the ledger," he thumbed back through a dozen pages, "the other columns have been filled in. There's a summary, then a category, then a column that says approved, withheld, impossible or requires more scrutiny and then the assessors name and his signature. This earlier book is filled identically but most of the entries have a coloured line drawn through them and there's an extra column at the end with another signature. It would appear that the impossible ones are scored out in black, the ones allowed are untouched but the 'withheld' and 'needs more scrutiny' ones are scored in red and blue respectively. Of course this is helpful but I'm afraid, mistress, it still leaves us with an impossible task. There are too many entries, even if we only tried to read the ones that are withheld we would need forever. It would take even longer if we tried to copy everything.

"I think you're right Alfsen, this isn't the right approach. Nevertheless we don't have another. Let's persevere. I suggest we concentrate on only the most recent submissions and only those that have all the columns completed. Let's narrow it down further and only look at those that are marked in blue. We needn't copy out the ideas, all we need is a list of who invented them."

Now she knew what to look for she visited the archive again every night for the next four nights. Alfsen had hired two women that he could trust and who worked in one of the guild libraries. Between the four of them they managed to extract a list of over two hundred names and addresses. They'd further streamlined the search and limited the copies to people who lived on Griprey.

Several days later Silfuryn had collated all their data. "It's something to start with but we really need to get one or two complete ledgers but they would be missed and then the Justiciary would become suspicious," she told Brannhår.

Silfuryn was visiting the workshop to check up on the progress of the research and she'd talked her problem over with her friend.

"What you need," Brannhår said, "is a way to take away the ledgers but leave them there at the same time."

"I know but copying them would be impossible and, even if I could bribe one of the scribes then I'd be no further ahead. No scribe could commit that amount of text to memory."

Brannhår nodded, "I didn't mean copying the ledgers, no, I was thinking more along the lines of stealing them but leaving something behind that the justicers would believe were the ledgers."

"I don't understand?" Silfuryn said.

"That room contains an awful lot of paper, if it caught fire and the cupboard containing the ledgers was destroyed then they wouldn't be able to tell whether the ashes were the real ledgers or not."

Silfuryn smiled but her smile quickly faded, "I see what you mean but paper doesn't always burn completely, especially books. There'd be something left."

"I know that but you said you only needed one or two of them, surely you could fake two and pre-burn them so that their contents were unrecognisable then steal those before the place caught fire. Faking the burnt books shouldn't be too difficult but creating the fire without raising any suspicions will need some thought. It would be easier if I could get inside the archive to get a better idea of the layout."

"I think that I might be able to arrange that but how long would you need?"

"As long as you could get me. The solution may not present itself immediately. I'd need a couple of hours."

Silfuryn nodded, "I'll see what I can come up with."

Brannhår and Karol accompanied Silfuryn back to the Holastan. Silfuryn went in search of Alfsen to find out what had happened whilst she'd been away.

"I've been watching the comings and goings into and out of that building," he said, "There's a delivery at around midday, a cart unloads a couple of boxes into the building and collects two from it. As you know mistress any maker with an idea fills out a form and they are sent to the local temple. I assume that the boxes that I saw are the collated forms.

Every morning a group of novices come across from the barracks, they stay there all day and then they are led back to the barracks in the evening. I suspect that these novices are the ones that transfer the information from the application forms into the ledgers and file the original submissions on the shelves."

"How many novices are there?"

"Eight or ten."

That explains why there are ten shelves in the cupboard, one must be assigned to each novice."

"Quite, At the end of each day a courier arrives and he collects another box. I followed him and he goes to the kraft guild. The same courier collects the box from the guild the next morning and returns it to the temple."

"Ah, that's interesting. Obviously the justicers don't feel confident to assess all the ideas themselves. They must be using someone in the kraft guild."

Alfsen nodded and then he sneezed. "I beg your pardon mistress but I seem to have picked up a cold."

Silfuryn said, "Oh don't worry Alfsen, that sneeze has just given me an idea. I need to talk to Karol."

******

Karol said, "It's easy, I know the very thing. If I can get access to the barracks kitchens then I can mimic a harmless epidemic but I can't see how that helps us."

"It means that it won't be the same novices that are assigned to copying the forms. We can sneak Brannhår in as one of them. I can

254

make her up to look younger but she'll have to cooperate and maybe dye her hair."

"Good luck with that, I remember how hard it was to just get her to wear a dress for your Hárbru."

****

Brannhår was uncomfortable, she was an adult, not a child. Brannhår knew she wouldn't get away with it she looked too old to be a schoolgirl but nobody had seemed to notice. She was dressed in the short pleated skirt and the long stockings that all novice female justicers wore and her hair had been coloured black by some brew that Karol had devised. He'd assured her that it would wash out completely but her partner didn't always get his concoctions right. Silfuryn had got her into the morning detachment for the archive by the simple expedient of getting her to join the line queuing outside the novice barracks. There were so many new faces since the outbreak of whatever illness was going around that another one wouldn't be notice. It helped that the novices were expected to maintain a strict silence when they were out of barracks. The woman in instructors robes hardly glanced at the students whilst she was counting them and then they set off

When they arrived and the instructor had led them inside she sat the novices apart from each other assigning them a desk each. A guard opened the cupboard containing the ledgers and handed one to each novice then he returned to the corner of the room and sat down on a chair. Brannhår noticed that he left the cupboard door open. The instructor spoke, "Some of you are new here so pay attention. You are here to help the office of the Justiciary. You are here to work not to engage in idle chit chat. Any inattention or unnecessary communication will be severely punished, and I will be keeping a close watch on you, Gretchen Ironfist." The instructor glared at a girl sat a few desks away from Brannhår. "Next time it won't just be a slap on the legs, you will be up before Sister Viric". Brannhår saw the girl give a little shudder, "Do you understand me girl?" Brannhår saw the girl nod and say "Yes sister Jun."

255

"Now, as I was saying, your task is simple, each of you will take a single application form from the pile over there on that desk," she waved to a desk just under the windows, "You will return to your own desk and you will **carefully** copy the information on each form into a fresh row in your ledger. You are to copy accurately, there are no prizes for the fastest copiers so take your time but get it right. Where you cannot read or are uncertain what the applicant has written you are to bring the form to me and I will tell you what to do. Is that understood?" There was a chorus of 'Yes Sister' from all the novices, Brannhår only just managed to join in in time. "Extra writing implements and ink are available from the cupboard. Work silently and carefully. You will be unfamiliar with some of the terms that the applicants use. This does not matter, just copy what they've written no matter how obscure it is. Now, open your ledgers and commence: and remember, no chatter!"

The instructor then sat at the main desk and watched as the novices took an application form each and returned to their desks.

Brannhår went to get her own form from the table. As she did so she looked around, mentally measuring distances and observing what she could. There was a strong stink of wyre as she approached and she saw three of the creatures curled up in a basket beneath it. They were asleep. Returning to her desk she had a chance to see the rest of the room. It was as Silfuryn had described, rows and rows of shelves stacked with paper stretched into the distance and a mezzanine floor occupied three sides of the upper space. It looked empty except for a few scattered boxes. Dotted around the walls of the mezzanine were large windows letting in copious amounts of sunlight. And this was directed to illuminate the lower parts of the room by large curved mirrors. The ceiling itself was a network of dark, open rafters and beams which supported the timber roof of the building. Brannhår directed her attention to the beams of sunlight that hit the floor. At the moment the light was diffuse reflecting the dull, overcast sky above but when the clouds cleared each pool of light would be dazzling. She started work. It took most of the novices between ten and fifteen minutes to complete transferring the information from one form into their ledger. One of them repeatedly visited the desk where the instructor sat and Brannhår supposed that she wasn't good at reading handwriting. Brannhår kept pace with the others completing six of the forms in an hour. The work was boring, it wasn't as if any of the forms contained much of interest. Most were descriptions of items of kraftwork like jewellery or pottery, some were sketches of simple machines none of which she considered to be worth documenting. The one in front of her, for instance, was a simple device for measuring out equal amounts of flour or some other powder, The powder was pored into a hopper and it descended down a chute into a basin. When the basin was full its weight operated a lever which diverted the chute to the next basin. There were six basins arranged in a carousel and, according to the description, someone took full basins from the carousel and replaced them with empty ones. She never found out why someone would need such a device. Then she got a form that was illegible. There was nothing for it she would have to approach the instructor. She put the form on the desk in front of sister Jun and waited. The sister looked up at her and said, "Well, what's wrong with it?"

Brannhår's voice wavered, "I can't read it." Sister Jun snatched up the paper and looked at it. "It's pure scribble. What is the education system coming to if this is the level of skill of the maker cast." She screwed it into a ball and expertly flipped it into a basket behind her that was already half full of screwed up balls of paper. "Just give it a number and write illegible in the description." Brannhår nodded and turned away, "Wait," the instructor said, "I don't recognise you, what barracks are you from?"

Brannhår had been prepared for this, she'd been told, if anyone asked, to say that she was from a barracks in the poorest district of the city. "Sister Jun, I am from Hyggetort . I was told to join the group assembling at the temple barracks and follow instructions. The instructor sniffed, "We must be low in numbers if we have resorted to recruiting from Hyggetort. Are you sure you can read and write, girl?"

"Yes Sister Jun," Brannhår replied lowering her eyes to the floor.

"Well don't just stand there, get another form and take it back to your desk."

Brannhår nodded and did as she'd said.   Late in the morning another batch of forms arrived and one of the girls was taken off her copying duties to sort them out into neat piles. Brannhår noticed that the room was becoming increasingly warm. The dull sunshine had become a full glare and she saw the guard move around the room opening the windows to let some air in. As he opened one there was a flurry of wings as he disturbed a pigeon. Brannhår smiled, it had given her an idea.

As the day wore on and Brannhår became so hot and bored, she made up ever more elaborate plans to destroy the archive just to pass the time.

Not that she'd need an elaborate plan, the place was a conflagration waiting to happen. There were large quantities of paper in piles dotted here and there. The building itself had been converted from a stables and Brannhår could clearly see that, under the floor matting, there were saltpetre crusts leeching from the flagstones underneath them. Around the mezzanine level someone had mounted a series of oil lamps at intervals and, had added others placed on the furniture on the lower level. There was even a pair perched on the top of the ledger cabinet. The open-wire basket containing the discarded screwed up forms was just waiting for some discarded match. She might ask Silfuryn to add one or two embellishments but even without them any fire would certainly spread quickly and consume the records.

 Eventually the instructor called a halt and the novices filled out of the building. She was surprised to see a grey haired man come up to her dressed in a justicer uniform . He marched straight up to the instructor and said, "This one is one of ours, I'll take her now. Did she give you any trouble?" Sister Jun looked at him and said, "Errr... no, is she usually trouble?" The justicer smiled, you wouldn't believe the things this one gets up to. Come on now." he said to Brannhår and took her roughly by the arm and led her away.

They rounded the corner and the officer couldn't contain himself any longer, he burst out laughing. Brannhår punched him hard. It was a good thing that nobody was looking; a schoolgirl punching a justicer would have attracted notice. Brannhår was half angry and half ready to burst into laughter herself. "What do you mean, the things I get up to? If you weren't an old man..."

Karol pecked her on the cheek, again something that, had it been seen, might have elicited some comment, "What do you think, I think the grey makes me look distinguished?"

"Makes you look ancient, more likely," Brannhår replied, "I take it that this is more of Silfuryn's handiwork. Let's get back to her place and I'll tell you what I found."

The four of them were sat around the kitchen table some time later. Brannhår had finished describing the archive stressing that it was already a major fire hazard.

"Just to be sure I'd like to make it a bit more unstable. The wire basket isn't emptied each day and so I'd like to get a few screwed up papers that have been soaked in saltpetre mixed in there. Also I think that a liberal sprinkling of oil from a leaky lamp down the back of the cupboard might help things along."

"So all that we will need to do is apply a match," Alfsen said.

"No, when they investigate they're sure to look for points of ignition. We can't guarantee that a match would be consumed in the blaze. I have a better idea. I'll need to go out hunting tomorrow..." and she explained the rest of her plan.

The next night Silfuryn set off in her ghost disguise accompanied by Alfsen who carried an assortment of things for her. She passed through the walls of the archive and, having distracted the wyres, placed things around the room. She mixed the saltpetre-soaked paper balls into the wire basket and dribbled lamp oil down the back of the cupboard. She removed two of the earlier ledgers and replaced them with saltpetre-soaked duplicates and then she left the way that she'd come to give her booty to Alfsen. He handed over

Brannhår's trigger, the bundle was chilly and she tucked it into a large pocket in her robe then she crossed the street to a building that overlooked the archive, climbed up to the roof and swung herself across to the roof of the archive building. She passed through the roof as easily as she'd passed through the wall and she deposited the chilly bundle on a wide rafter. She was so stealthy that the wyres didn't even notice.

The following afternoon Silfuryn and Brannhår watched events unfold from the upper floors of the building across the street. They'd been uncertain when things might start to happen but they had been patient. Brannhår was looking out of the window and she said, "Here we go." Silfuryn joined her. There were shouts and screams coming from across the street and already plumes of smoke were emerging from the windows. The first to flee the building were several packs of wyres and they were quickly followed by Sister Jun who herded her novices to safety like some elderly mother hen. Various guards and other inhabitants of the temple could be seen running to and fro and there was general pandemonium. A bucket chain was set up to a nearby fountain but it was clear before the men had got organised that the fire was out of control. There was the occasional explosion as a lamp, its reservoir of oil heated to boiling point, exploded.

Brannhår and Silfuryn stayed around long enough to see the blaze start to die down a little but the ashes were still smouldering the next morning when the sun rose. As they left Silfuryn said, "I hope the firedab got out."

Two days later the guard commander was talking to his lieutenant. They were stood in the pouring rain in amongst the soggy remains of the archive. To add insult to injury the gods had seen fit to organise a downpour every day since the day after the fire and now everywhere was covered in a slippery black ooze.

"Are you sure it was a firedab?" the commander asked.

"Yes sir. The guard confirmed it. It must have flown in through the open window. The wyres saw it first and went berserk. The firedab panicked and started shooting flames everywhere. With all that paper the result was inevitable."

"Well thank the gods nobody was hurt, how much did we lose?"

"Probably about six days worth sir. We have the copies in the guild and there were the daily additions that had been taken for assessment so it wasn't as bad as it might have been. The guild copies were updated a week ago so we lost whatever new entries we've had since then minus the day before yesterdays entries which were being assessed."

As you say lieutenant, it could have been worse. What made it go up so fast?

"It would appear that the archive was built in an old stables and the floor and walls were saturated in nitre, sir."

"Yes, that would explain it lieutenant. There's nothing more we can do here, let's get inside and out of this rain.

******

Silfuryn looked up from the ledger that she was reading, "This is good, I can work out a good list of contacts from this. I can already see areas to exploit. Did you notice that a lot of the entries were sanctioned by Delai and it's obvious even to me that he's been favouring members of his own circle when it comes to approvals. I wonder what some of his rivals would have to say about that?"

"You're not going to tell them are you. I thought the whole idea was to stop the justicers suppressing ideas?"

"Yes, it is, but one way of achieving that is too let the people whose ideas have been suppressed know who has been telling the justicers to suppress them."

"I suppose," Brannhår answered.

Silfuryn chuckled, "I still can't get over what you did. It was a truly classic idea to put the fire lizard on ice to keep it torpid until the heat of the room revived it the next day. Remind me never to get on the bad side of that devious imagination of yours."

"Oh, it wasn't all me. Karol supplied the ice and stopped me accidentally freezing the poor thing to death."

"Whatever... it's funny how even ordinary beat cappers flinch and crap themselves when a shadow flies over their heads these days."

"My Lady," Brannhår, mocked, "what would your grandfather say if he heard you using such common language?"

"He'd probably join in," Silfuryn answered, "Now the next part of our campaign is to find out who is doing the assessments for the temple. It can't only be Guild master Delai; even he couldn't get through a hundred new applications in a day."

"I think it must be journeymen. Apprentices probably wouldn't have the experience and other masters would consider it beneath them. Whoever is doing it they are generally getting it right. Trinkets and skill stuff like precious metal work are getting approved quickly and they are good at spotting the out and out fakes and the ones that go against the laws of nature. Some of those border on magic. Not that they can't be true, just that they wouldn't work for everybody and that's the aim of true kraft; to make things that everyone can use regardless of their magic."

"Then we'll have to investigate, Does the spirit fancy an outing with the ghost tonight. I thought we might try to see what's happening in the kraft guild building after hours."

Brannhår and Silfuryn were sat in Silfuryn's office. Their nocturnal visit to the kraft guild had proved to be pointless. Brannhår had already guessed that Guild-master Delai would be biasing any review of the ideas registration in favour of his own guild and they'd watched from the shadows. The library was dark apart from a long bench at one end that was illuminated by a series of oil lamps. Four young people were sat at the bench absorbed in their work. An older man strode up and down behind them occasionally looking over their shoulders at the papers they were reading and making a comment.

They'd heard the guild-master give his briefing. "Each of you will assess the ideas in your ledgers. If the idea concerns an item of decoration or art then the idea may be approved without further scrutiny and the name recorded in the tax ledger. If the idea concerns kraft then you will determine whether the idea is novel. To do this you will ask yourself whether the device or technique is known to you or is an obvious application of your own level of knowledge. These items will be rejected with the phrase 'known to the art'. Complex or unusual ideas will be dealt with by determining who the registrant is and then look the person up in the guild register. If they are not in the register or have demerits against their names then the idea will be labelled, 'awaiting further consideration'. If they are members in good standing then the registration will be labelled, 'approved subject to guild tax'. You will then make a note of the registrants name and the idea reference in your tax ledger. You will work through all the incomplete registrations in the ledger until they are completed. When you have completed the task you are dismissed and may go."

They'd watched the journeymen start work. Needless to say, being youngsters doing this chore under sufferance, most of the assessments took less than ten seconds and at the end of half an hour the library was deserted.

Ch 24: It's a crazy world but we've got a plan.

Brannhår and Silfuryn were waiting in the drawing room for the arrival of Karol and Torin. Silfuryn had invited everyone to a meeting to discuss what they needed to do next to further their research. It was to be a meeting over dinner and the two friends were discussing the recent happenings over a drink. Silfuryn had her usual glass of wine but Brannhår was drinking a bru.

"I've lost track of everything you've been doing over the past months. Care to bring me up to speed?"

"Of course, you know Karol and I have been working on the ironoak?"

"Yes," Silfuryn said.

Brannhår smiled, "Well we've cracked the problem of how the ironoak stores the energy from the sun. It stores it in nodules connected to its root system."

Silfuryn frowned, "But I thought that the ironoak got its energy from the lightning."

Brannhår shook her head "Oh it does, but a lot of it is wasted, the ironoak can only cope with a small fraction of a major bolt. It diverts the rest into the ground. Most of its energy is derived from its leaves, the same as any other plant. It's not quite the same as other plants because it stores the energy from the sunlight as electrical energy."

"Fine, so how does this help?"

"Now that we know how to store the energy we can use it to do other things. Steam engines use the heat from the steam to move things. I've made an engine that can use the energy from the ironoak nodules to move things. I've got one in my luggage would you like to see it?"

"Of course," Silfuryn answered.

"I'll go and get it," Brannhår said.

When she came back she had a small model cart in her hands. She set it down on the floor and did something to a lever on top of it. Silfuryn gasped as the little cart set off across the floor on its own.

Brannhår explained, "It's a bit like clockwork except you don't wind it you use this," she picked up the cart and turned it over. Underneath was a small black cube. "This is made using the same principles as the ironoak nodule except we've modified it so that it doesn't need to be in the ground. It doesn't last as long as the nodules because it's not living but that isn't too much of a drawback."

Silfuryn was fascinated, "But what happens when you've used up all the energy in the nodule?"

Brannhår laughed, "The cart stops of course. That is until you put the energy back or you replace the nodule."

"How do you put the energy back?" Silfuryn asked.

"You can connect the nodule to others of its kind that are full of energy," Brannhår explained.

"This sounds great but how will it help us?"

"It will benefit all of dwarf-kind more than the semaphore because it will allow us to drive ships without wind and drive carts without smygl and all sorts of other things. Of course, it will make us money even if we don't register the idea of the engine with the justicers."

"How?" Silfuryn asked, intrigued.

At that moment Alfsen appeared in the doorway and gave a discrete cough. "The gentlemen have arrived, mistress. Shall I show them in and tell cook to start serving your meal?"

"Show them in Alfsen but give us a few minutes before we eat," Silfuryn replied.

"Of course, mistress."

Torin and Karol entered the room. Both men shook hands with Silfuryn and Karol kissed Brannhår on the cheek.

"I was just showing Silfuryn the motor," Brannhår said.

"Yes," Silfuryn agreed, "but I can't see how it can make us money if you just give the idea away."

"Are you talking about registering the idea with the Justiciary?" Torin said.

"I thought that you didn't approve Silfuryn. Don't tell me that your enquiries have convinced you otherwise."

Brannhår interrupted, "No we both still think that the idea is a mockery of dwarf principles. Delai is just using the registration scheme to make money for the guild. The tax on ideas that are approved is just daylight robbery."

"There is one interesting thing though," Silfuryn said, "If the justicers are effectively taxing any kraft then the makers aren't going to be too pleased. How will they justify the tax?"

"They will probably say that it's to pay for any action they take against violators," Brannhår said, "Do we have to register ideas?"

"No, not at all but the justicers argue that unregistered ideas don't belong to anyone and anyone can use them."

"So how is that different to the present situation?" Karol asked.

"Well, currently any dwarf worth his salt would declare that the idea wasn't his own so as not to take credit, but he could always declare it as a re-work so, technically you're right, young Karol. It's really no different to the current situation," Torin replied.

"Then why has the Justiciary come up with such a crazy scheme?" Karol asked, puzzled, "Apart from the guilds making money from it I can't see how such a scheme benefits the justicers."

Brannhår was silent, she was thinking. Now that Karol had asked the question out-loud she couldn't see how it benefited the justicers much. Plenty of makers had no qualms over using a well

266

established idea and not acknowledging credit. In the extreme, every time she used a wheel she should have acknowledged some ancient dwarf for inventing it.

"The justicers don't give a fig for who invented what. I originally thought that the scheme is more about controlling developments as a whole but I've been doing some research of my own and I've come to the conclusion that they could have another motive. They could be using the scheme to monitor developments, that way they can use the makers themselves to gather intelligence about any breakthroughs and, by bringing in the scheme they get advance warning about what's coming. My sources tell me that they were really upset about the semaphore. It takes away their monopoly on distant communication. I'll guarantee that if the scheme had been in place before Dyrr came up with the idea they would have done something about it. As it was it took them completely by surprise."

"So the idea that registration gives someone some form of protection is nonsense," Torin said.

"I can't really say it does," Brannhår said, "Certainly any maker unscrupulous enough to copy an idea wouldn't let a little piece of justicer admin stop him. So I think you're right, Silfuryn the justicers must get something out of the scheme; they're not stupid."

"Oh I don't know," Karol said, "Some of their rules are pretty stupid."

"What do you mean?" Torin asked.

"Well, when that capper, Silfuryn's friend Grimm, was staying with us he said that justicers couldn't marry or have families. That is about the most idiotic rule I've ever heard."

The others stared at him so he went on, "Any botanist or biologist knows that plants have to adapt to their environment to succeed. They do that by natural selection. However, a good botanist will go one step further and he will breed desirable characteristics into the next generation and help the whole process along."

Silfuryn said, "Yes, my woodsmen plant saplings from trees that have straight grain. It makes logging easier and improves the quality of the wood. But how does that apply to the justicers?"

"It doesn't. Look, the justicers rely on their magical talents. In fact they go to great lengths to find magical children and then co-opt them into their ranks. So their aim is to increase their magic. We all know that the characteristics of the parents are inherited by their offspring, so why don't the justicers encourage their members to have families within their own organisation?" Karol paused, "But they don't. They do the exact opposite and forbid marriage so magical talents are lost. I'm only glad that the rule is only recent; within the past two generations, otherwise magic would have been bred out of the dwarven people ages ago."

"You're right," Silfuryn said, "I never thought of it that way. I just assumed that the celibacy thing was something to do with religion."

"It does seem strange, especially as they were so upset when Racka got pregnant by another magic user," Brannhår said.

They all went silent, each thinking about what Karol had said.

At length Silfuryn broke the silence, "Let's just agree that the justicer religion is crazy. So what do we do about the ideas registration? Do we encourage makers to ignore it?"

"I think we should although now that the registration is in use some makers might not want to share their ideas with others," Torin said.

"Well, I've got an idea and I don't mind it being used by others," Brannhår said.

"What's that?" Silfuryn asked.

"The motor that drives that little cart that I showed you." Brannhår said.

"But you said that it would change all sorts of things. I may be rich but my family didn't become rich by giving things away. Are you sure you want to do this?""

"Oh yes," said Brannhår, "but we'll still make more money than the rest."

Silfuryn frowned, "I'm sorry, how are you going to do that?"

"You have lots of land don't you?" Brannhår asked.

Silfuryn nodded.

"Well the first thing we do is plant ironoak," Brannhår said.

"Huh?" Silfuryn said.

There was a polite cough, Alfsen had come in silently but he obviously needed to interrupt their conversation.

Silfuryn looked up, "Yes, Alfsen, what is it?"

"Your pardon mistress, but cook says, and I quote, *'If they don't get a move on this dinner is only going to be fit for the wyres'.* Would you mind coming through to the dining room?"

"Of course, Alfsen."

******

They'd discussed it at length and after many hours of argument and theorising and planning they'd agreed on a strategy. Brannhår had pointed out that, once the concept of her electric motor became widespread it would generate a need for a source of electric energy. She had told them that it would be impossible to predict all the uses that her motor concept would be put to and it would be even more impossible to design and make all the possible applications themselves. Since every application of the electric motor used the electric energy it made more sense to become the providers of the energy and that was where Silfuryn's land would give them an advantage over all the other makers who would want to jump on the bandwagon of electric power. They'd agreed to set up a plantation of ironoak to harvest the electrical energy and to provide a source of the storage nodules that would be needed to store it. Karol was confident that the work that they'd already performed studying the ironoak meant that any others that tried to harvest the electrical energy would find it a very difficult task even if they could find someone with Silfuryn's financial resources and who owned enough land of the correct type. They'd agreed that they wouldn't make a firm decision for a few days because each of them had wanted to think over what would be needed to put their plan into action.

The next day Silfuryn's mind hadn't relinquished her own desire to defeat or at least emasculate the Justiciary's plans to control innovations in kraft. Her motives weren't altogether altruistic but she saw no reason why breaking the mental chains that the Justiciary wanted to place on the dwarven craftsmen shouldn't help their own endeavours. She'd already realised the potential of what they'd discussed and she'd seen the sense in allowing free access to some of the technology.

She'd been playing with the small cart that Brannhår had left behind. It had run out of energy; she been idly pushing it around on her desk whilst she was thinking. On one occasion she had just pulled the cart backwards and she'd slipped and let it go. To her surprise it had moved forward of its own accord for a split second. Intrigued she had picked it up and pushed it back again. It moved again.

Brannhår and Karol had stayed the night so she went in search of her friends to see if they could explain the phenomenon.

Brannhår listened to Silfuryn's explanation of what she'd seen and followed her back into her office. Silfuryn had repeated her actions with the cart and Brannhår had been delighted, "Look what you've discovered. You can generate electric energy by driving the motor mechanically. It's the complement of using the electric energy to create mechanical energy. That, my dear friend is an absolutely amazing invention. You should register the idea immediately with our friends at the Justiciary."

"Now, you are teasing me," Silfuryn said.

"No, no, I'm serious," Brannhår said, "It's a real discovery. All right maybe you should think about whether you want to give it to the justicers but it opens up so many new opportunities for us. Don't you see?"

Silfuryn frowned, "Err. I'm not a maker, explain them to me."

"Well, for one thing it gives us a means of recharging the power nodules without having to use others that have been harvested directly from the ironoak. If we use a small steam engine to drive the wheels of the cart backwards we can make it charge the nodule directly. I could probably knock one up in a day or so and power it from your heating system.

Silfuryn your discovery makes you a maker! Welcome to the guild. I'll get Torin and he can make it official!"

Silfuryn was inordinately pleased. She was now a maker, even though she was magical. As Brannhår had pointed out, "There's nothing preventing anyone from becoming a maker. That's what makes kraft so much more powerful than magic. It's open to everyone."

Silfuryn's discovery was praised by everyone and Brannhår insisted on telling Alfsen and the cook all about their mistress's new skills. The cook wasn't impressed, "Tell her to come back when she makes something that will peel brot tubers. Now that would be useful" but Alfsen was almost as pleased as Brannhår. "Her grandfather would have been very proud, as am I." Silfuryn had hugged him when Brannhår told her what he'd said. The old dwarf had pretended to be shocked but Brannhår could see that he was really moved.

They'd agreed that they would hold a second meeting after three days and everyone had things to say and discuss. Silfuryn had said that she was still a little annoyed that the justicers were manipulating the makers with their power but Brannhår had told her not to worry. She had discussed things with Karol and they'd decided that the best way of avoiding the justicer's intervention would not to declare the motor as an invention but publish the research that they'd done on actually working out how to make one. They could start with something everyone knew about; lightning and lodestones, and build from there. A text book wasn't an actual device and so it didn't need registering.

Karol said that he wouldn't be much use at writing and he thought that Brannhår and Torin should be the authors but they'd insisted that he and Silfuryn would be credited as well.

Silfuryn had leapt at the idea and had said, "And I know how you can write the book quickly. Not only do I own paper making factories I also have dozens of copy scribes in them that are used to creating the typefaces for books. You can dictate your thoughts to them and get the ideas down in draft then polish them later into a proper book. It will save heaps of time.

And whilst you are doing the technical parts Karol and I can organise distribution. For maximum impact I propose that he and I make a list of all the makers in the ledgers we acquired who were rebuffed by the justicers and invite them to a party. We can give them copies of the book as gifts. Torin is the most well known of us and so he can give a speech at the party about all the exciting new prospects that are possible. The makers will be so overwhelmed that the applications of electric motor technology will come flooding in and nobody will be able to claim the original idea because all of them will have had the same ideas independently. Oh I like it! I can't wait to see Delai's face It will be the most amazing shade of purple."

In reality, although they all agreed on the plan, when it came to implementing it in practice they all realised that it would be some months before it could be put into action. The book needed writing before they could do anything and, even though Silfuryn's clerks were good, Torin and Brannhår would spend hours discussing every technical argument and statement so that it would be understandable and accurate. Karol and Silfuryn chipped in from time to time and so that meant even more revisions. In addition there were aspects of the science that needed expressing in mathematical form and that took even longer. Silfuryn and Karol had also pointed out that creating an agricultural project on the scale that would be needed would take time and they insisted that this phase of the plan had to be started first.

Ch 25: The Plan Develops

Six months later they were almost ready.

"What do you mean, it isn't quite right, we must have visited twenty sites since we arrived and none of them have been just right," Torin complained.

Karol said, "I'm sorry Master Torin but I agree with Brannhår, you can see how the rain has left runnels all across the field. That means that the field doesn't have sufficient slope to drain quickly. Ironoak needs good drainage especially underground. The storage pods for the sunlight and lightning are very sensitive to correct soil humidity."

Brannhår smiled at her partner, "You're right, of course but I don't think that it will suit because of the hills behind here. They aren't tall enough to promote a good updraught to start the cloud formation for a storm. We need to try higher. Now, let me see the map. I think that Silfuryn's land extends much further north and there looks to be a high ridge a couple of miles that way."

"Oh, just another couple of miles. That makes my job more difficult. It's one thing to harvest the lightning but you've given me the job of getting it to the city. A couple of miles may seem like nothing to you two but, for me, it means more headaches," Torin growled.

Brannhår laughed, "I though that the challenge of this new project was just what you wanted. If I know you, you've already had ten ideas how you can get around the problems. Still, it is getting late, let's just try one more site and then we'll call it a day and set up camp."

They reached the next site after another hour's journey and the sky was getting dark.

"Looks like a storm," Karol remarked, "We'd better keep clear of the ironoak."

"Yes, a storm is building," Brannhår replied looking at the sky, "but we're fine for a while, let's have a look around."

It was Torin who found the cave and he called them across. Once they were inside Brannhår said, "This looks good. We can observe what conditions are like in a proper storm."

No sooner had the words left her mouth than the heavens rumbled and the first bolt of lightning struck. It was followed by a downpour. Mistle had also sensed the storm's approach and knew what was coming. She left the dwarves and curled up in the back of the cave.

"That's strange," Brannhår said to nobody in particular.

"What now?" Torin asked.

"Can you see what's happening to that ironoak over there, it's glowing."

"I can see it," Karol said, "It looks like fire is sprouting from the tips of the branches. Look, it's doing the same from all of the trees around. That stingbush is positively glittering."

"Yes," Brannhår said, but Karol could see that she was lost in some inner vision of her own. He was used to it. When she started thinking it was best just to leave her alone. She got irritated if he asked questions and distracted her. She'd tell him her thoughts presently. He turned to Torin, "Let's start a fire and make a bru. We can camp in the cave for tonight, it looks like the rain drains away from the entrance so we should stay dry."

The old man nodded but he was also lost in thought. Karol shrugged and started unpacking the gear.

He'd just finished heating some stew and the fire was burning merrily when the other two emerged from their own minds. It was uncanny, they started talking as if they were already in the middle of a conversation. "It must be conductive and there must be something directing the energy flow," Brannhår said.

"I thought that as well but did you see the pattern? It moved," the old man replied.

"You're right, it did move. We need to stay an extra day." Brannhår said.

"At least. Especially if we have to take some back," Torin said.

"Oh no," Karol groaned. They'd discovered another plant that was involved in this whole lightning and sunlight thing. That meant another day of trying to excavate another incredibly complex plant and root system.

As Karol had predicted, it took them the whole of the following day to extract a single specimen of the stingbush. Since they hadn't brought the cart up to this high plateau there was no chance that they could get it back to Longbarrow on this trip. Therefore they had part excavated it and had packed the sides of the excavation with a mulch of decaying leaves and twigs so that when they did eventually return to fetch it back to their workshop most of the heavy work would have been done and retrieving the specimen would only take a day or so.

As they worked it was inevitable that Brannhår and Torin would theorise about the purpose of this root fibre or that leaf system. Karol knew that their words made sense to each other but he was constantly at a loss when he listened in. The old man could keep up with Brannhår's constant vocabulary changes but Karol couldn't. The problem was that the pair invented new words for new concepts and thereafter used the word as a verbal shorthand. Karol got confused by the never ending hierarchy of abstraction but Brannhår and Torin chattered away as if they'd used their new synthetic vocabulary since childhood… and he didn't stand a snowflake in a volcano's chance when they started talking numbers.

Karol knew plants and herbs and he could recognise the various parts of them, he even knew what function the parts served in the plant's existence. It was enough for him. However, Brannhår didn't just stop at form and function, she wanted to know the why, how and how much of everything and he still felt like a footnote in this enterprise. He'd realised long ago that Brannhår was a very desirable partner to court. He liked it best when she was just content to be with him and she wasn't re-inventing the world but that was how she was and he loved her for it. He was in on the ground, so to speak, and it was an advantage, but there'd be plenty of offers from other suitors. Brannhår and he weren't married and so she could still choose someone else; he was lucky that she'd currently chosen him and he was going to keep it that way if he had anything to do with it.

So, he helped where he could and she often praised him for his insights, For instance he'd pointed out that the stingbush was peculiar for a stinging plant in that there were no venom sacks associated with the stings. Brannhår had gone silent for over a minute and then she'd hugged and kissed him and then rushed off to examine something on the plant. He hadn't realised the significance of what he'd said until much later. She explained it that night when they were in bed. "Stingbushes sting," she said, "but if they don't use venom then what makes their sting so painful? It started me thinking that maybe it had something to do with the electric energy and then, when you showed me how the stings were all connected to different fibres within the branch it was obvious. The sting is actually a small spark of electricity. Then that made me wonder where the energy for the spark came from because stingbushes sting even when there's no storms. So I looked for something that could generate electric potentials and I found it in those odd gnarly knots that occur every few inches along the twigs. They actually generate a high potential from the low potential electric energy stored in the root nodules. If we could find out how they do that we are much nearer a solution to the transmission of electric power. You are clever, my love, what would I do without you?"

He didn't tell her the thought that momentarily passed through his brain that she would probably do fine without him, he just grabbed her and kissed her. At least there would be no more theory that night.

Silfuryn read the letter; it had come via her fastest fljúgbátr from Vatersey. Even so it had taken over a week to get to her. It was from Officer Grimm and it was in prose.

"Dear Silfuryn,

Let me say again, it is no imposition to keep you abreast of the news from Vatersey and to tell the truth there is not much news to give. Work has started on the rebuilding of the temple here and it is amazing to see how quickly it rises from the bare ground. Although it is supposed to be a secret it is common knowledge that the restoration is being funded by you. I would like to extend the thanks of all the people on Vatersey for your generosity. The healers are now able to cope with all the inevitable accidents and injuries associated with large scale logging.

For my own part I have settled into my duties very well. I am afraid that, like all citizens of the capital, I thought that dwarf cities outside of Holastan were mere shadows of it. I have seen my error; Vatnarheim is larger and more complex that I ever imagined and it has as much need of law as Holastan. My new position makes it difficult to make investigations by myself and I must admit that the variety and complexity of some of them would be beyond the ability of any single justicer. However I find it refreshing that my colleagues here have a similar outlook on law enforcement as I have myself and I am somewhat saddened when I remember the venality, politics and downright corruption that used to characterise some of my fellow justicers in the capital.

It is my great regret that you must cope with that environment every day. I realise that you have your duty to your heritage but Vatersey would be a far better place to have your home. I urge you to consider this seriously and I am sure that you could easily manage your affairs just as well from Vatnarheim.

> *your friend always*
>
> *Stein Grimm.*

Enclosed is the information you requested.

Day Two

Einar Balder strode out in front of the audience, he was pleased to see that there were only a few seats vacant. He gave an inner shrug, it was a characteristic of dwarves that many would be late for their own funerals if that were at all possible. He let the tambour call for silence and he began.

"We rejoin our tale after some years. Brannhår has been developing her ideas concerning the properties of lightning and its uses and she has teamed up in a partnership with her consort Karol, Master Torin and the Lady Risavinur. Thanks to the ideas of her team and, in particular, the wealth of the lady who has seen fit to sponsor her, she is now ready to change our world. Gentle dwarves, changing the world is not an easy task and there were many who opposed her at every turn. However, in the true spirit of dwarf kind she won acclaim for her even handed dealings as I will tell. And there is the great adventure that she undertook with her companions that tells us more about a forgotten part of our own history.

However, to understand that part of the tale, my dear friends I must first tell you of the game:"

"In the days before Dwarves moved to Niðavellir each tribe of dwarves had an army. The armies had been needed because of the constant state of petty warfare everywhere in the nine realms. Dwarves battled men, men battled giants, giants battled gods, in fact any culture that had a separate identity would occasionally war against any other.

In the great diaspora Dwarves chose to migrate to Niðavellir and they brought with them Nine dwarven generals. They came at the head of armies and, for a while, the armies had banded together to conquer the native inhabitants and secure the territory. Then the dwarf population had settled down to peace and the armies had been disbanded.

On the home world the nine had been warriors: each in charge of an army. Their names were; Volinar, Severell, Rahgot Wotar Volksun, Konraak, Otankei, Krokin and Siskevn.

Eventually they grew old and died and, as warriors, they were given their choice of afterlives. It seemed a natural choice for them to go to Valhalla but none of them could stand humans, living or dead, so they chose to become draugr. The nine were powerful sorcerers in their own right and they were undead so they never aged and it was almost impossible to kill them. Hence, to keep themselves amused down the centuries, they had looked for alternative ways to continue their chosen careers.

In the earliest days, the generals continued as before. They controlled armies made up of thousands of people and creatures and they pitted their armies against each other. Inevitably many people perished in the battles. When the casualty rate became unsustainable the generals created the Game. Instead of armies the generals would control a much smaller number of people and the number on each side was fixed at thirty six warriors. However, it soon became clear that using dwarves and deciding contests on survival was wasteful of manpower and too many warriors perished. Hence they invented a different form of combat that wouldn't be as wasteful. It was decided that the warriors would be drawn from the ranks of wizards who could phase their bodies through adjacent physical dimensions to avoid injury. This didn't totally negate casualties amongst the players but it reduced them. None of the generals could decide how they would judge a contest that didn't have casualties and so it was decided that each warrior would have a thousand 'disposable' troops under his or her command. The troops were specially bred insects whose numbers could be quickly replenished.

Wars were re-named 'games', the warriors 'players' and the generals 'managers'. Games were still decided on the number of surviving combatants but these now included the insect troops. Thus a game was over when one side or the other's troops or players became incapacitated or were reduced to very low numbers.

Most games were now decided on the number of troop casualties. As the games evolved, players became more adept at phasing and, because the troops were living creatures they could be affected by the players phase. You might think that this would reduce the troop casualties but it took much more concentration from a player to move both themselves and a thousand other entities through the adjacent dimensions so the players became better and better at phasing.

Thus the game evolved into the form which existed in our tale. Thirty-six player-wizards on each team would battle with conventional weapons and thirty six thousand insectile troops whose numbers gradually fell during a game. A player that lost more than eighty percent of their troops was deemed 'conquered' and took no further part in the game. A fatal or incapacitating injury to a player naturally took them and the whole of their troop allocation out of the game.

Players were allowed to act independently, form alliances or their managers could intervene and take direct control. Each player was fitted with a scrying crystal directly linked into his or her brain. The draugr, being powerful sorcerers, used these crystals to override a player and become directly involved in the action.

Often, to end a game where there was insufficient excitement, managers or players would deliberately choose to part-phase their troops so that their numbers were sacrificed. Even this became competitive requiring fine control of the phasing process to retain just enough troops (and players) alive to win.

Of the nine original managers only six remained at the time of our tale; three had already fallen by the wayside:

Otankei had lost herself in her witchcraft and had disappeared one day never to be seen again.

Krokin had challenged Wotar to a duel and, after most of the north part of his domain had been reduced to rubble, only Wotar had emerged intact. The greasy smear that had been Krokin was soon cleared up.

Siskevn had withdrawn into herself and had declared that she was going to find her way back to Valhalla. The last that had been heard of her was that she was wandering between worlds trying to find a permanent way out of this dimension and that was a millennium ago.

The Generals hadn't been the only ones to arrive in the new world. They'd brought with them their engineers, armourers, supplies officers and a host of others who kept their military campaign running smoothly. Most of the support staff disbanded when the armies were no longer needed, but a cadre of engineers and armourers who could fashion magical technology were stubborn. They'd seen the need for someone to keep things in good repair and so they built mechs; mechanical beings to act as their agents. The mechs had built other, more sophisticated, mechs and, when the game was set up, the new army of mechs had built the stadium, the barracks and all the other accoutrements of the game. Over the years the mechs continued to evolve. The most complex mechs eventually became so sophisticated that, when their creators died, the creators joined with the machines to form the ageless and almost immortal beings known as the golden ones. The golden ones abandoned their dwarven names and adopted the much more efficient forms of single letters.

Of the original twenty six engineer-wizards that had come with the armies only seven remained at Leikvangur. The rest had gone their separate ways and were scattered across the near universe.

The seven remaining golden ones were still performing their allotted tasks after thousands of years but none of the managers had a clue how they did it. The managers didn't have any control over the golden ones but then they didn't seem to need any. The machine-sentients did things for their own reasons. The managers had found it best just to leave them alone.

Initially players were recruited from the general dwarf population and this was the origin of the gathering that recruits children to our own Justiciary. However the process was hit and miss and so the managers decided that it would be more effective to have a captive breeding program to selectively breed dwarves with the magical ability to phase through the dimensions. Those without the ability were considered inferior and were called Botches.

Over the years fewer players came from the general population and the captive players mostly lost the ability to perform other magic. The original purpose of the gathering was redundant, however, the draugr still considered the living as a threat and so they withdrew from the world into the city we now know as Leikvangur."

"So, my friends you now know as much as I do about the Game and therefore I give you the next part of the story of The Tales of Brannhår."

Ch 26: The Party.

"Why wasn't I informed of this before!" Lord Skald railed at his assistant, Blade.

"Eminence, the matter has only just come to our attention. Apparently Guild master Delai considered it as a mere social gathering. He himself was invited to attend but he is not on good terms with Master Torin and so he declined."

"Didn't he notice that nearly every prominent maker whose ideas that we have been suppressing has been invited?" Skald asked.

"No, your eminence, in fact if we hadn't had an informant in the printers we would not have discovered it ourselves."

"Get onto Delai and tell him to make some excuse and say that he is now able to attend. I don't care how he does it I want someone there who can tell me what this is all about."

"Couldn't we just infiltrate the meeting with one of our number? Master Delai is, after all, a maker."

"Idiot! That's the reason that we need him. I know these makers and if the speeches become technical then we need someone who can translate whatever is said into ordinary language. Don't you realise that that is why we had to use his people to evaluate the ideas. Some of them were full of so much gobbledegook that the temple novices couldn't even read them at all."

"Your eminence, are we certain that the gathering is anything more than a social occasion?"

"Look, the Lady Risavinur is sponsoring the event. She normally sponsors arty things along with her idiotic friends. If she is sponsoring a kraft event held by Torin then her advisors must think that she can make money out of it. She didn't get to be as rich as she is by missing opportunities. Besides, you told me yourself that everything about the event is being organised by the Lady's own staff. She hasn't hired anyone from outside her own organisations, even the waiters have been recruited from the paper factory. Something is going on and I am determined to find out what it is."

******

Brannhår re-read the manuscript for the twentieth time. On the surface it all seemed correct but she had a nagging feeling that there was a lot missing. It was annoying, she'd realised, when she thought about it that the dream that she'd had all those months ago about the disappearing iron bar trick had actually been trying to tell her something. She pushed her memory to its limit desperately trying to recall the dream to try to remember what it was.

She'd been herself and not herself at the same time. She'd been in a familiar workshop and she'd seen the giant perform the trick. It had prompted her to try to duplicate the same trick when she'd awoken. It had given her the starting point to develop the idea of the motor.

No, that wasn't it. It wasn't the part about the motor it was something else. What was it? She screwed her eyes shut and stared at the backs of her eyelids trying to remember. The sun was shining at a low angle and the after-image on the backs of her eyelids was a virulent green. Virulent green… something about something green. The workshop walls had been covered in large green slate panels and someone had been writing on them. No, not words but symbols and equations. Her giant self had understood the symbols and what the equations meant. That meant that somewhere inside her own brain she too understood their meaning. The memory gelled all of a sudden. Yes, she could recall what the symbols meant but the mathematical language that they were written in was beyond anything that she knew in her present life.

The dream was a dead end, or was it. She realised that, if the vision had been herself in another life then she must have learned the language at some time in the past and it came to her. The equations were complex but they were based on simpler, more basic equations that were within the reach of her present understanding. That meant that Torin might be able to understand them as well. She had to get hold of her mentor. There was another chapter that they had to write and they had to do it soon.

******

Einar Balder looked around at the assembled crowd. He was clearly uncomfortable. Why on earth had the Lady Risavinur invited him here? He didn't belong. Everywhere he looked there were makers. Admittedly nearly all of them were occupied, as he was, trying to balance large glasses of mead on the small sandwich plates in their hands without the whole lot tumbling to the floor. He was a bard, an artist, a genteel soul, whereas some of these fellows still had blackened hands from the forge. He had just begun to summon up the courage to talk to a group of them who looked a little less hairy than the others when he saw someone coming to his rescue.

"Einar," Silfuryn exclaimed, "so good of you to come. I'm glad you made it. So many of the others made some excuse or another. Well it will serve them right if they miss the best event this season. Now, I have to confess that I have a slight motive for asking you here. As you can see these people are not our usual crowd and I felt that I might enjoy the event more if I had some moral support from my, let us say, more artistic friends."

"Lady Risavinur, it is a pleasure to see you again and I too am a little bewildered by the company. Oh, I know that some of the artisans here can create beautiful things but really, I would have thought that they would at least wash their hands."

Silfuryn looked around and gave a small laugh, "Oh Einar, don't you know it's the iron dust in the metal. It gets into the skin and stains it. They would have to scrub the top layer of their skin off to make any difference in the colour. I like to think of it as a badge of honour; it shows that they have spent many years learning their kraft."

Einar nodded, "I meant no disrespect Lady. I am sure that they are all good fellows. It's just that I have so little in common with them that I feel at a loss."

"Oh, we can't have that. Come with me I want to introduce you to someone," she said and she took him by the arm and led him across the room to a small knot of people. There were two women and two

285

men. One of the men was obviously a maker but the others were in ordinary clothes. Both women were wearing gowns and one man was in a dress robe of emerald green.

"Excuse me dear friends," Silfuryn said, "may I introduce Einar Balder, the famous bard. Einar this is my good friend Brannhår Dagmarsdóttir," one of the women wearing a blue gown nodded to him, "her consort Karol Tynarsson," the man in the green robe nodded, "and two of Brannhår's young friends Brognar Leifsson, and Bril Hildasdóttir." The giant maker and the sylph-like woman in the pale gown tuned and nodded to him. Then he recognised the woman. This was the sensational young artist Bril. He had seen her work in the fine arts galleries. This woman was the one who had captured the lightning bolt descending from a looming black cloud that everyone had said was just like looking at the heart of a storm. He'd seen it and it was a masterpiece. He finally found his tongue and spoke directly to the girl, "I saw the lightning and it nearly stopped my heart."

Silfuryn clapped her hands, "I knew you would have something poetic to add Einar. Now, I'll let you get acquainted. I can see my friend Lady Krump, she appears to be surrounded by blacksmiths, I must go and rescue her."

They watched as she hurried off across the room. Bril turned to Einar and said, "Poet Balder do you think the lady will be all right?"

Einar laughed, "If I know Lady Krump she will be matching those fellows glass for glass and I wouldn't be surprised if she was the only one left standing in half an hour." This was better than he'd thought. He'd expected that a meeting with the maker set would be dull but the evening looked to have some entertainment potential. He turned to the giant who had stepped to Bril's side and had put a proprietorial arm about her. "I take it that you are already acquainted with your companion, may I enquire your profession?"

Brognar smiled, "What else would I be? I am a weapon-smith and Brannhår, Bril and I have known each other since we were children. We all went to school together."

"And from your accent I would guess that that was on Valdirey, am I correct?" Einar asked.

Brognar laughed and clapped him on the back, "Yes, is it so obvious?"

"Gods, the man's arm must be made of iron," Einar thought, but he said "Only a little."

The giant weapon-smith looked around, "I need another drink, this talking is thirsty work, anyone else want one?" Einar said that he'd like another but the rest declined and Brognar wandered off.

Einar turned to the remaining man, "Your face looks familiar, have we met before?"

Karol nodded, "Yes it was at my parent's home, you gave a recital at the wedding of my cousin. As you may have gathered, I too am out of my depth here. I am a herbalist and I am only here because my partner, Brannhår is the guest of honour."

The woman in the blue gown punched her consort on the arm, "Poet Balder, take no notice of my silver tongued consort. He knows full well how much work he himself has put into this project. We wouldn't be here if it weren't for him."

Einar was intrigued. So tonight's event wasn't just a social occasion. Clearly something was going to happen and this young couple were at the heart of it. He had a feeling that he'd better go easy on the mead and he might even try to find a piece of paper to take notes. Who knew whether it might be worth a stanza or two.

A new person joined the group and Einar recognised him straight away, "Master Torin, what a pleasure to see you again."

"Einar, good to see you too. I take it you have your notepad ready, tonight's announcements will be worth documenting. It's not every day that a dwarf changes the world. My friend, Master Brannhår here, has something very interesting to tell us all."

Brannhår had frowned, "Master Torin, thank you for the complement but I am not a master, as you well know."

"You're wrong there girl," Torin reached into his pocket, "I have here the official document from the guild. As of tonight you are promoted to the rank of master. Let me be the first to congratulate you."

Brannhår grabbed the old man and hugged him. Her eyes were full of tears but she was laughing. Karol and Bril joined in the hug. Einar watched them and Brognar walked up with two glasses of mead, "What did I miss?"

Einar said, "Brannhår has just been made a master."

"'bout time," Brognar said around a mouthful of canapé, "she deserves it."

Across the room Einar spotted a man he knew who ran a small news sheet and said, "Excuse me, I'll be back in a moment." and he ran over to him.

"You wouldn't have a spare piece of paper that I could borrow from you, would you... and a pencil?"

The man looked at Einar, "Seven copper to you, Balder and a promise you'll let me publish first."

"Done," Einar said pushing the coins into the man's hand grabbing the paper and pencil and then rushing back to his companions.

He reached them just as he heard the sound of a gong. A general silence filled the room and he heard Alfsen's voice boom out, "Masters, makers and commoners, I would like to invite you to go into the dining area; the formal part of our evening is about to start. Please find your places at the tables, each of you will have a place reserved so there is no need to rush. Waiters will come amongst you to take orders for drinks, order what you will, and if we have it, it will be supplied. Dinner will be served in approximately fifteen minutes. Thank you."

There was a general increase in the volume of the conversations but people started to drift towards the dining area. Einar tagged along with his new acquaintances talking to the weapon-smith and the artist. When they entered the other room Einar started to make his excuses, "I must leave you now and find my table..." Karol shook his head and said, "There's no need to Einar, the Lady Risavinur has arranged it that you will be with us. I believe that we are over here." The young man started to move to a table towards the front of the room near to a raised dais.

"At least I'll be able to hear," Einar thought, "That must have taken some quick arranging, the Lady couldn't have known that he would show up."

He sat down and soon enough there was food. He found that rather than the technical discussions that he might have expected the conversation was mostly about what the four young people had been doing since they'd left Valdirey. Master Torin and the Lady Risavinur were seated on a table nearby with Lady Krump and the Guild master Delai. The only other table nearer the dais was covered in a large sheet which had been thrown over piles of lumpy things on it. Einar knew that something was going to happen, he couldn't get invited to a posh event such as this with free food and drink and not have to pay the price… there would be speeches.

Sure enough, when the meal was over and people were just drinking bru or finishing off their drinks, Alfsen, Lady Risavinur's old retainer strode up to the dais and cleared his throat. It was as if he'd bellowed at the top of his voice. The room fell quiet. Einar made a mental note to ask the man how he managed it. He could use the same trick to get his audiences to shut up before a performance.

"Masters, makers and commoners, Lords, ladies and distinguished guests, I have been given the honour of introducing our distinguished friend, Master Torin who has an announcement to make. He will be accompanied by Master Brannhår who I am honoured to call friend to all dwarf kind."

He bowed to the audience and stepped down. Torin and Brannhår didn't mount the dais they moved to the covered table and, between them, removed the covers. Einar saw that one end was piled high with thin books and the other contained what looked like the entire contents of a maker's workshop.

Torin spoke, "My friends, Since the eyes can understand what is difficult to put into words let us show you something."

It had started with what looked like a magic trick. Torin lifted a large glass jar and two of the waiters appeared beside him holding a tall table. A third waiter pushed over a small trolley containing a wooden chest on it. Torin placed the jar on the table and Brannhår seemed to start fastening things to the top of it.

"Master Brannhår and I, together with our colleagues, Karol Tynarsson and the Lady Risavinur have been exploring lightning." The old master threw one hand into the air and Einar nearly dropped his glass. A bolt of lightning, it couldn't have been anything else, had appeared in the jar but, unlike lightning from the sky, this lightning wasn't over in a flash it was dancing around inside the jar, trapped.

There were shouts of astonishment and gasps of wonder and fear from the audience. Einar was scribbling like mad.

Torin let his hand fall and abruptly the lightning vanished. He shouted over the hubbub, "Be calm my friends," and he waited. The audience quietened and he continued. "What you have just seen isn't magic, it is kraft. You can all learn how to produce lightning and many of the other wonders we will show you this evening. It needs only our usual tools; an ability to understand and of course, a little work.

Most of the credit for this wonder must go to Master Brannhår and I freely admit that, in this subject, she has no equal on this planet. She is also a true dwarf. She has told me, and I agree, that this discovery must be shared freely with all those who will learn and understand and build our society for the betterment of the people. To that end you will all receive, at the end of the evening, a copy of a book," he waved at the pile, "that contains the basics of the theory of what we will show you. You are welcome to use the concepts therein in your own pursuit of the kraft. We ask only that, whether you are apprentice, journeyman or master you acknowledge the discoverer of the original knowledge that you use. Now my friends, let us continue, caged lightning is only the start."

Einar ran out of paper a few minutes later and started using the tablecloth. His two new friends, Bril and Brognar helped him cut it up into manageable pieces.

At the end of the demonstrations Torin announced that they would take questions. The general uproar that followed was only quelled because the lady's Guards had moved through the audience and stationed themselves at the head of each table and the lightning bottle in the centre of the dais had emitted a massive clap of thunder and flame. Everyone was stunned into silence. Torin stood and said, "We will take questions from one person at a time, each table will be allowed to ask questions in turn. I urge you all to behave as makers and if your question is asked by another then listen to the answers so we can avoid needless repetition. I know that it will not be practical to answer every question in detail and I urge you to save anything technical until after each of you has read and understood the book. This is not your only opportunity to ask your question. I and my colleagues will make ourselves available during the next week to clarify anything that we can."

"In deference to his seniority I will invite Guildmaster Delai to ask the first question; Master Delai?"

Silfuryn had been right, the guildmaster's face was puce. She could see the fierce battle that was raging between his anger and his shock. Every eye in the room was focussed on him and you could have heard a pin drop as he rose to his feet.

"This kraft of lightning that you say that you have discovered. Why was the idea not registered with the Guild or the Justiciary before putting on this sideshow?"

Torin smiled, "For the reasons we explained at the start, perhaps you would like to re-state them for the guildmaster, Master Brannhår"

Brannhår rose and she'd changed, she was still wearing her beautiful blue gown but everyone now saw that she was holding her distinctive hammer. Karol told Einar in a whisper that it was her lucky charm.

"Guildmaster Delai, the reason that we have not registered our discoveries with the Justiciary is simple. We do not wish to withhold our discoveries from the people and our fellow makers. We freely give what knowledge we have that is contained in this book to anyone capable of understanding and using it. We ask for no licence, we ask for no payment. Therefore the knowledge does not need protection from either Guild or Council."

There was a general chorus of approval from the gathered makers who had had their ideas suppressed. Delai looked around and said, "I see." he turned and marched out of the room accompanied by several others. As he left he said to the general audience, "You have not heard the last of this young lady."

Einar made it home with his tablecloth and his copy of the book. He had managed to get Brannhår to sign it. It had been the best night ever. And he'd thought that a meeting of makers would be dull.

******

The guests had gone and, around them, various waiters were clearing tables and gathering glasses. Torin, Brannhår, Karol and Silfuryn were all seated at a table that had not yet been cleared,

"How do you think it went?" Brannhår asked.

"It was a triumph, my dear,"Torin said.

"You should have seen the look on Delai's face when you answered his question directly. You could tell that he wanted to challenge you but you are young and that hammer of yours has a fearsome reputation. It would have been no contest." Silfuryn answered.

"But I'm not a warrior, I wasn't challenging him," Brannhår complained.

"No, my love but you can bet he didn't see it that way." Karol said.

"Apart from Delai and a few of his cronies I think everyone enjoyed the evening and I can tell you they all went away thinking. Delai stormed out but there were at least three of his journeymen that stayed to the end. You can guarantee that they'll all be up till dawn preparing reports for him." Torin said.

"They won't be the only ones," Silfuryn added. "I invited several of the broadsheet makers and Einar left with his pockets stuffed with notes."

"But Einar is a poet and bard, what on earth could he find to write about in our demonstration?" Brannhår asked.

"Don't worry my friend, Einar might not be be rushing into print tonight but he was interested and I noticed that he left with a signed copy of the book. He will eventually turn this evening into a piece of his art." Silfuryn said.

"So down to the last practical matters of this evening," Silfuryn said becoming more serious, "I have instructed the guards to take all your demonstration paraphernalia back to my house and store it in one of the vaults. Several of the more enthusiastic guests insisted on paying their way, they didn't have to, of course so I told them to give their donations to Alfsen and he would see that it got to a charity. And that reminds me, I have had an agreement drawn up for the company that will manufacture the energy storage cells and generate the electric energy. Since any company must, by tradition have a representative of the people on its board I propose that we include Alfsen. You all know him and you know that he's trustworthy. We can count on him to inject some common sense into the venture. If you agree then let's call him over and tell him the news."

They all nodded.

Silfuryn looked over into one corner where Alfsen was directing the waiters in their duties. "Alfsen, could you come over here for a moment."

The ancient dwarf strode up and said, "Yes, mistress?"

"Alfsen, you probably know more than me about what's been going on recently and so we have all agreed that you should be included in our venture as a full partner. It will mean that you will be able to curb our excesses without feeling that you have to do what I tell you. You have served me for my whole life and I now want to give you something for that service."

Alfsen's face looked stricken, "Do you wish to dismiss me, mistress?"

"Oh Alfsen, I would never do that. I only want to give you something that will make you independent of me. If you want to keep running my household then you are very welcome. No, I think of you as my family and, as part of the family you should have part of our enterprise."

"I can continue to run the house?" Alfsen asked.

"Of course, in fact I insist you do because I could never find anyone I'd rather entrust it to." Silfuryn said.

Alfsen's face had brightened, "Then might I suggest that we retire to the house. It has been a busy day and I think that tomorrow will be just as busy. You should get some sleep mistress."

******

Nobody slept in the next day and, one by one. they appeared in the kitchen in search of breakfast. Alfsen had roused the cook and the smell of smoked elgrott, eggs, honey and toasted brot filled the room.

The only person missing was Torin but he arrived after a short while with several sheets of paper in his hands.

"The broadsheets have been busy. Everyone has an opinion on last evening's party. Delai has rescinded Brannhår's Master's status in a fit of petty revenge and several of the other sheets got the wrong end of the stick and put all the wonders we showed them down to magic."

Brannhår said, "Oh well, it was nice being a master for a few hours."

Torin shook his head, "There's the fun. He can't rescind the Master's status even if he **is** the head of the guild. The charter states that a Master can only be removed from the lists if he or she has been found to 'profoundly broken the tenets of dwarf philosophy'. You haven't done that and neither have I. In fact, by your statements last night you re-affirmed the tenets and there's no place in the charter that says that you can't be too good a dwarf. Your title is safe my dear and there are probably ninety nine percent of the dwarves that were there last night that would back you up if you wanted to argue with Delai."

Silfuryn said, "I expected something like that from Delai but what did the justicers make of it?"

"They've been very quiet and not said a word. They're probably trying to think of a way to put the electric cat back in the bag but they'll have their work cut out. Most of the independent commentators have interviewed maker friends who were there and the general consensus is that your discoveries are so profound that they needed to be shared with dwarf-kind. That means that the makers can already see tons of applications for the technology. I wonder how the justicers will cope with them after they agreed that you should be given credit for the discovery?" Torin said.

"What do you mean?" Karol asked.

"From what I can gather there are queues of makers outside the temple wanting to register their ideas on how to use electric motors first. It will be very hard to sort them out because I suspect that most of them won't have thought their ideas through and once the justicers accept one then there will be all sorts of ructions if they then proceed to resister the rest as 'already been registered'. Sorting that lot out will be just what they deserve for coming up with the notion in the first place."

"Shouldn't we do something?" Brannhår asked.

"I would let it lie for the moment, miss," Alfsen said from the door, "there are more urgent problems. I don't know if you noticed but people are queueing at the gates of the Holastan asking for an interview with 'the new wizard'. The gate guards have asked us for reinforcements from our guards and they want someone to talk to the crowds to get them to disperse."

"I never expected that," Silfuryn said, "Are people so gullible that they believe we have discovered a new magic."

"I'm afraid so, mistress" Alfsen said.

"How are we going to convince them otherwise?" Karol said, "even I think what we do is magical."

Brannhår closed her eyes for a moment then said, "The only way is to show them. Will you come with me?"

"We will all go," Torin said, "what do you have in mind?"

On the way Brannhår told them what she intended. Karol and Silfuryn looked puzzled but Torin grinned, "That really is magic," he said.

They arrived at the gates of the Holastan and saw a crowd of about seventy people. Silfuryn's guards commandeered a cart and Brannhår climbed up onto it. There was a general outcry but she stood there and gradually the crowd grew quiet. "I am Master Brannhår and I am the person who discovered how to use lightning. She waved her hand towards the sky and the crowd looked up. They could all see the storm gathering overhead.

"I am going to demonstrate that what I've discovered is not magic and I need the aid of one of you. Is there a coppersmith in the gathering?"

"Aye, I'm a coppersmith," said a tall dwarf near to the back.

"Come forward smith so that everyone may see."

The smith made his way to the front and Brannhår nodded "I see you wear the traditional token of the coppersmiths," she shouted to the smith.

"Aye," he said and he held his arm aloft showing that his forearm and upper wrist were covered with a coil of copper wire.

"Now I wish you to make me something from your token. I will pay you for it as is proper. Oh, you are not a wizard are you?"

The man looked perplexed and then offended, "No, I am not, the justicers tested me and didn't find magic."

"Do not be offended I meant no disrespect. I only wanted to show our friends that there is no magic involved. Now, if you will, can you remove your token and stretch it out until it is about an arms length long."

"You will pay?" asked the smith. The crowd laughed, they were getting involved.

"Yes, smith I will pay you the value of your token." There was a little more laughter from the crowd.

"Now, smith, Can you straighten out one end of the coil so that it runs along and touches the other end leaving most of the coil intact."

The smith looked puzzled and the fellow next to him said, "I think she means like this." he demonstrated and the smith followed his instructions.

"Thank you smith. Now to make doubly sure no magic is involved," she looked around and saw that several urchins had gathered to watch the fun. She said, "You lot, pick someone to help me and I will give each of you a coin." There was a general scrabble and finally a boy, bigger than the rest was pushed forward.

She nodded at him, "Boy, are you a wizard?"

Someone in the crowd shouted, "He's no wizard he's just a layabout."

"Now that is unkind, I am sure this fine fellow has a steady job. Don't you young one?"

The lad stuck his chest out, "I deliver brot from the bakery in Temple street."

"So Baker, can you take the coil from the smith and climb up on that wagon there."

"O'course," the boy said and he did so.

"Now, this is important. I want you to wrap your jerkin around your hands and then hold the coil straight out above your head."

He did so and Brannhår shouted, "Now we watch the end of the coil and wait for the storm." There was silence for about fifteen seconds and then a flash of lightning crossed the sky. The whole audience saw the matching spark leap between the ends of the coil. The urchin stared at the coil for a second and then dropped it as if it was red hot. Most of the audience laughed and then some started clapping.

Brannhår help her hands up for silence, she was helped by the rumble of thunder from overhead. "Friends, you have just witnessed this boy and this coppersmith tame lightning. Neither of them used magic and they needed none. The kraft that I have discovered is usable by all; Lords, makers, commoners, even Baker's boys. All that is required is to learn and understand. So I am sorry, there is no new magic just kraft!"

Then there was a split second of silence and the uproar started. Everyone was shouting for more but Brannhår lifted her hands for silence, "There is no more, if you want more then I have showed you how to start. I have written it all down in a book and I gave many of the makers copies last night. Go and learn it for yourselves, ask the makers, ask the smiths, ask the justicers or ask the guild."

Brannhår climbed down from the cart and she was immediately surrounded by Silfuryn's guards who shepherded her back into the Holastan. Everyone ignored the two men and the woman that had come out with her. It was only later that the man who'd put the smith right and the woman who had called the boy a layabout could stop laughing for long enough to join her in a bru.

"But how did you know there'd be a coppersmith?" Torin asked.

"It would have worked with any coil. I was going to use one of my bracelets if there had been nobody in the audience but I saw a few gold, silver and copper smiths as I climbed up and I just thanked the gods. All of them wear tokens it's just that the coppersmiths wear bigger ones" Brannhår replied

"Why did you then get the boy to do the trick, surely you could have used the smith?" Silfuryn asked.

"I wanted to show them that there was definitely no magic involved and I needed a distraction until I was sure that the lightning was building. I had to get it right and I had another delaying tactic prepared in case I'd misjudged the storm but I didn't need it." Brannhår said.

Torin beamed, "Now that, my dear, is proper magic."

Ch 27: Building a Fortune.

In the six months since the announcement, the electrical energy business had mushroomed. The founders had moved into a set of buildings that had been a small hospital before the population of Holastan had grown too big for it. Each of them had their own department and had assumed individual roles. Karol was now bringing on their early farms and he was supervising a host of apprentice herbalists who were learning the care and chemistry that the new electric agriculture required. Torin was wrestling with the technology and logistics required to deliver the energy from the fields and generators to the steadily increasing demand that was being generated by all the new applications for electricity that the makers were coming up with. Brannhår was busy working on ever more efficient ways of generating and storing energy and she spent much of her time in her laboratory muttering to herself. Occasionally she would capture Karol and hold him hostage for a day or two whilst she discussed the intricacies of chemicals, cell membranes, and the mechanisms whereby things grew, reproduced and repaired themselves. Silfuryn spent her time finding and supplying everything that the others needed. She had access to most of the raw materials and labour through her existing commercial empire but, even so, the raw materials needed processing and new staff had to be recruited and trained to do the work. She had the largest staff of all and, if it hadn't been for Alfsen's organisational ability and insight, the sheer size of the social and infrastructure problems would have overwhelmed her. She was working eighteen hours a day and surviving on less sleep than ever.

Finally she sought refuge from the chaos in Brannhår's lab. Her friend looked up from some gadget on the bench which was a mass of glass tubing, wires, bubbling mists and eerie green glows. She smiled, "Hello stranger, you look tired?" she said.

Silfuryn slumped in a chair, "Oh, and I guess that the black circles under your eyes are merely a new fashion in makeup," she replied.

"I know what you mean, there's so much to do. I don't think that I ever thought it would be this…" Brannhår searched for the right word and then settled for "...big."

"It was all so simple before, I had my hammer and I watched the storms and occasionally rode the lightning with Rakkerskap. Nowadays I never even get to see a storm and I can't remember a day when I last made something just for me. But we've 'started this mine and we can't stop until the vein is exhausted' as my father used to say."

Silfuryn nodded, "Yes it does feel like it's all snowballing, rolling down the mountain building itself into an avalanche."

"Well let's hope we can keep it under control until we get to the treeline, then it might slow down enough that we can get back to some semblance of normal."

"If only I could take a few hours off, just to relax," Silfuryn.

"I know what you mean, the work is actually exciting but it's exciting in a predictable way. The idea comes in a flash but then making it real takes days of slog."

"Alfsen suggested that I relax and sleep for twenty four hours."

Brannhår said, "That's probably good advice but I know you. I would have to give you a medicinal tap with my hammer to get you to sleep for that long. My mother had a saying, 'A change is as good as a rest'. What do you say, shall we do something different?"

Silfuryn smiled, "It would have to be very different. It's a while since I've ventured out as the Ghost. I wonder what the underworld has been doing while I've been away?"

"We could ask Alfsen," Brannhår suggested, "just a minute there's something I need to bring," and she crossed the lab to a large chest and took something out.

Ten minutes later they entered Alfsen's office. Several men and women were engrossed at desks or were walking sedately about discussing things with each other. Silfuryn strode over to a large imposing desk behind which sat the tiniest woman dressed in a very formal black business dress. She looked up as they approached. "Lady Risavinur, Master Brannhår, how can I help." The words came from her mouth in clipped syllables as if the speaker had decided that this was the most efficient way to communicate.

Silfuryn smiled and said, "We would like to see Alfsen."

The woman didn't return the smile, she picked up a speaking tube and spoke into it. "The Lady Risavinur and Master Brannhår are here to request a meeting," then she waited.

After a minute had elapsed the woman turned to Silfuryn and said, "I'm sorry, Alfsen is not in."

"Is that unusual," Brannhår asked.

The woman turned to her and said, "No, Master, occasionally he will take the back stairs to the kitchen to make himself a bru," she frowned as if this minor act of rebellion against propriety would shatter the world asunder.

"Ah, then we shall go and find him there," Silfuryn said.

The woman just returned her gaze back to the papers on her desk and ignored them, and so they left.

They found Alfsen in the kitchen. He had a complex apparatus on the table and he was watching it intently. "My grandmother's bru machine; a device for a less hectic age. What can I do for you mistress?"

"Brannhår and I were just wondering what was happening outside our cosy, dull world of electricity? We thought that, if there's anything interesting we might take a look."

Alfsen adjusted a small knob on the machine and said, "I believe that Cyten has become interested in importing things from Skogrey They include some quite nasty addictive herbs that he is selling to people who can't afford them. When refined they are known as Frábært White but most of the users call it Sting due to the sensation that remains after someone has consumed it. I believe it is similar to a sting from the stingbush"

"It sounds as though the Ghost should have a closer look at this. I assume that we know where the Sting is being stored?"

Alfsen shook his head, "The only location that my agents have identified for certain is a derelict warehouse beside the canal. This is where Cyten takes delivery of all his 'imports'. I am uncertain where it is refined or how it is being distributed."

"Thank you, Alfsen," Silfuryn said.

"Excuse me mistress but if you are thinking of venturing out might I suggest that you take the rest of the afternoon to catch up on some sleep. I often find that a nap in the afternoon is beneficial to both my health and my sanity," he smiled.

"Good idea my friend, I think that I might do just that," she turned to Brannhår, "Care to join me on a relaxing night out?"

Brannhår grinned, "Count me in."

They left the offices and went back to Silfuryn's home. Brannhår decided that she too would take a nap before the evening's escapade and Silfuryn invited her to use the room next to hers, "See you later, don't forget to wear your armour."

Brannhår said, "That reminds me. I made you this." She handed Silfuryn a leather holster. Inside it was a whip, a larger version of the one that she'd given to Grimm.

Silfuryn took it and started to examine it, "I'm looking at it with my magical senses and it isn't magic so what does it do?"

"Let me demonstrate..." Brannhår said taking the whip back and stepping back along the corridor to give herself some room. She pressed the gem set into the pommel and the lash uncoiled.

After ten minutes Silfuryn said, "Amazing, it's like it's alive. Can I have a go?"

Brannhår handed it back, "I'd practice a bit before you use it in earnest but it might come in handy."

They arrived at the warehouse just as the moon Tveir was rising and Silfuryn used her ghost form to enter and scout out the building whilst Brannhår waited outside.

Brannhår was wearing a new suit of armour that she'd made. In keeping with Silfuryn's notion of her being 'Spirit' she had made it of overlapping supple plates in black leather. However as they moved and slid across each other they exposed parts which were different shades of grey. The overall optical effect was like mist forming and dispersing. She'd also discarded her signature hammer for the evening and had fashioned herself a pair of thin, curved hand axes which she wore in twin holsters at her waist.

Silfuryn appeared beside her and whispered, "There are a couple of guards but the lazy bastards are sitting in a lit office in the corner of the main space playing dice. They sound as though they've had a few as well so I don't think that they would be much trouble. We just have to keep an eye out in case one of them does a patrol."

"So, where do we start?"

"There are a couple of other offices which are in darkness. I assume that they are where the paperwork is kept. We should start there," Silfuryn answered.

Silfuryn was right, the first office they entered had a large, locked iron cupboard. Silfuryn took a thin sliver of metal from her pocket and Brannhår saw her make it and her hand insubstantial and push them inside the cupboard. There was a small click and Silfuryn withdrew her hand and operated the latch on the cupboard. The hinges were well oiled and the door opened easily. "As I thought," she whispered, "paperwork, as if we don't get enough during the day." Brannhår suppressed a giggle.

Silfuryn lifted a sheet to the faint glow of the aurora shining in through panels in the roof, "It's too dark to read it here we'll just have to take it with us."

"I can help there and Brannhår reached into a pocket and brought out a small box. She pushed a button on the side of it and one end lit up with a ghostly white light. "Stingbush leaves powered by an ironoak nodule," she whispered, "The lens and the reflectors make it directional."

In the beam from Brannhår's device Silfuryn started reading. She quickly discarded several sheets and took up others. Finally she said, "This one looks interesting. It's a manifest of items from Skogrey. There is a lot of other stuff but here it says, two chests of medicinal herbs."

Brannhår looked and nodded, "It says, shipped to 'S'. That could be the Ship inn," she looked for any other entries and tugged at Silfuryn's sleeve, "Look there there's a consignment of 'Temple papers' and it says 'to be collected by Gibra'. I wonder why they are using Cyten to bring paperwork back from Skogrey. Surely they could get paperwork back here through the ordinary mail?"

"Not unless the paperwork was secret. They might want to smuggle it back here without anyone noticing."

"It says, to be collected, so maybe it's still here. We could always have a look. Does it say where it is shelved?" Brannhår asked.

"Yes, it says here, Bay twenty six." Silfuryn replied.

"Let's take a peek."

 There were two crates in Bay twenty-six, a large one marked fragile and a smaller one marked 'Gibra'. Brannhår pulled an axe from her belt and used the rear spike to lever both the lids open. The large crate contained several artefacts, mostly pieces of ancient armour and clothing but some pottery and one or two crumbling weapons. The smaller crate contained thin leaves of metal each about a hands-span square. There were characters engraved onto them but it was in a language that neither of them knew. There was one word that Silfuryn recognised, it was a name, Wotar. These aren't just any ordinary temple records these are ancient. My grandfather taught me that Wotar was one of the original dwarf migrants to this world. He was someone important, a chief of some sort. It's a pity that we can't 'borrow' these for a while."

Brannhår examined the sheets. "We don't need the sheets, just what's on them. See if you can find some pieces of blank paper."

"But they'll take an age to copy out, there must be twenty sheets," Silfuryn objected

"Just get me the paper," Brannhår said and she disappeared off into the dark.

When she returned she was carrying an oil lamp, two pieces of flat wood, a plate and a small piece of smooth rock. Silfuryn was back with several sheets of paper. Brannhår set to work, by the dim light of the aurora she used a thin knife to scrape the lampblack from the lamp and she put it onto the plate. She mixed it with some of the oil from the lamp and then ground it to a smooth paste with the rock. She placed a sheet of paper onto one piece of flat wood and then she took one of the metal sheets and smeared the lampblack paste onto its upper surface. Placing the metal sheet carefully face down down onto the paper she covered the whole thing with the second sheet of wood and then she stood on the wooden sandwich. Brannhår rocked backwards and forwards on her heels for a while and then she carefully dismounted. When Brannhår peeled the sandwich apart Silfuryn could see that a reverse image of the letters on the metal sheet had been duplicated onto the paper.

"We only need to do a couple of sheets. They will take a while to translate and we only want an idea of the message on them. Besides there's not that much lampblack." Brannhår said.

They managed three sheets and Brannhår had just cleaned the originals and replaced them in their crate when the pair heard a noise. One of the guards had decided to take a pee and he was wandering along the bays in a half drunken state. Brannhår reached for her axe but Silfuryn stopped her and shook her head. The guard staggered straight past Bay twenty-six and soon they heard the sounds of his relief. He staggered back past them and shouted something to the other guard before they heard the sound of the office door closing again.

Silfuryn whispered, "Until we know more let's try and keep our visit here tonight a secret from Cyten. We need to go back and replace the manifests and lock the cupboard again." Brannhår nodded.

Ten minutes later they were back on the street and half an hour later they were back in Silfuryn's house. Alfsen greeted them with a tray of bru and some sandwiches. They showed him the papers, holding them up to a mirror to reconstruct the original images.

"I believe that I have seen this language before, it looks like something that your father was working on shortly before he left on that expedition," Alfsen said.

"You mean the one that killed him and my mother?" Silfuryn asked.

Alfsen nodded, "Yes mistress. Of course your grandfather could probably have told you what these sheets contain even though they are quite smudged."

"I did the best I could," Brannhår said.

"I'm sure that nobody could have done better under the circumstances, Master maker."

Brannhår giggled, "Now you make me sound pompous, I've told you Alfsen, call me Brannhår."

"Yes, miss Brannhår," Alfsen replied, "Of course we could always retrieve your grandfather's notes from the estate in the country. They might help. However, that will take some time and we must all be awake tomorrow to assume our ordinary duties. I suggest we leave this puzzle until we have time to work on it properly. Now, may I ask if you made any progress on the source of Sting?"

"Oh yes, Alfsen, he's routing it through the Ship," Silfuryn said.

"Then that must be the target for your next distraction."

Ch 28: Social Unrest

"It's absolute chaos your eminence. The backlog is being compounded by the Guild. Guildmaster Delai has forbidden any of his members from assessing registrations to do with the new subject of electricity as he claims that it is magic and hence comes under the jurisdiction of the Justiciary. He has called for any practitioners of electricity to be adjudged wizards and imprisoned.

"Is it magic?" Lord Skald asked.

"No, your eminence. It is something that can be learned; not an inherent characteristic of an individual. It requires no special power to cause it to operate. I myself have seen one of the automata that are the current vogue with the upper ranks of society. They seem to be no different to the previous ones powered by clockwork except that they operate for longer and there are no springs to wind. All that they require is that periodically a small tube containing chemical ingredients must be replaced."

"So where is the advantage?" Skald asked.

"It would appear that there is little, other than the increased operational time."

Lord Skald shook his head in irritation, "Let's get back onto the subject of my request. You say that the registration department is unable to cope with the numbers of new registrations. Why can't we just put more people onto it?"

"We could, however it becomes a matter of the appreciation of the concepts again. Our novices can tell the difference between a painting and a poem but none of them are trained to recognise a claim that is patently impossible. For instance, one of them brought me this; it shows a cart driven by one of the new motors pulling another motor behind it. The connections between the motors are reversed so that the one supplies the power to the other. It's the same principle that, if you have a windmill which drives a fan then the air from the fan can blow the windmill around."

"But that's absurd, even I can see that that wouldn't work."

"Yes your eminence but, with respect, you are a lord of the council and not a twelve year old novice."

Skald growled, "I can't have our plans for controlling kraft delayed any longer. Tell Delai I want to see him."

"Yes your eminence."

Skald picked up a broadsheet and began to read. The headline said, 'Electric Sting sweeps the city.' he read on,

Many citizens are becoming worried about the rise in crime due to a new drug that has recently come onto the market. It's users are usually young people or the poorest members of society. This correspondent has witnessed the effects first hand. Initially the drug induces a feeling of euphoria and omnipotence during which time the user will often attempt impossible feats such as trying to fly from the opera house roof. Then the user experiences bodily tremors which jerk the muscles into performing a weirdly unmusical dance occasionally this is accompanied by severe incontinence. As the effects of the drug wear off the user is plunged into a depression and they will go to any lengths to restore the initial euphoric stage.

Some commentators have stated that similar physical effects can be induced by the application of devices that use the new electricity and many desperate users of the drug have turned to this as an alternative. When asked for a comment, Maker Torin who was responsible for the discovery of electricity stated that, "Our aim is to educate people on the sensible uses of electricity not to seek to promote dangerous and inappropriate applications. There is no difference between the deliberate misuse of an induction device and sticking your whole arm into a stingbush. Both are usually fatal. However, neither are addictive or based on any form of drug."

"And I want to see Master Torin as well, see to it," Skald said.

"Yes your eminence," the flunky said. He bowed and left.

******

"Excuse me mistress, could I ask your advice about a matter that has arisen," Alfsen said.

"Of course my friend. What is it?" Silfuryn replied.

"We have received a request, well, more of a summons, from Lord Skald of the Justiciary to meet with him to discuss this article," He handed her a copy of the broadsheet and she read it.

"Oh dear, I suppose I'd better have a word with Torin."

"Master Torin is currently up country seeing to the installation of the supply," Alfsen said.

"Brannhår is no use with this sort of thing and Karol is three days away in the mountains. I suppose that I'll have to deal with it. Can you do me a special favour and reply to Skald that we will send a representative to meet him and can you lay out my armour. He is a wizard after all and I don't want him to sense my magic."

"Of course mistress, and might I suggest that you wear this." He produced a small brooch that was shaped into the form of a fiskur head. "Master Brannhår made this for one of my agents who has frequent dealings with the Justiciary. It somehow distorts the magical sense of justicers so they cannot easily discover the motives of people they meet. As you can appreciate, my agent finds it useful."

"Another of Brannhår's wonders, doesn't the girl ever sleep?"

******

Silfuryn went to discuss the summons with Brannhår a short time later. She'd pinned the brooch to her dress. As usual Brannhår was in her laboratory but, unusually the bench was clear and there wasn't any machinery in sight. Brannhår was sat on a stool with her head in her hands reading something.

"Oh, Lady, I didn't see you there," Brannhår said, "I've been trying to puzzle out this writing."

Silfuryn nodded, "That can wait, we have more urgent matters to discuss. Apparently there is an electrical device that mimics the effects of Sting. It has come to the attention of the Justiciary and Torin was his usual tactful self when someone asked for a comment. I've been summoned to a meeting with Lord Skald and I want to get my facts straight before I go."

Bran nodded, "I see that you are wearing the brooch. Be careful that you don't overdo the magical camouflage. If you're going to wear the brooch I wouldn't wear any of your armour. You might get away with the lemon dress with the gold and ironoak filaments but if you wore the gloves as well the justicer might get suspicious. I made the brooch using the same principles as the dress uses so it will probably pass as an antique."

"Thanks for the warning. I don't think that I will get away with pretending that I'm an airhead. That disguise is fine with the likes of Lady Krump but I suspect that Skald will have done his homework and know that I run the commercial side of this enterprise. Airheads don't often get left to look after the money."

"You're right, now what do you want to learn about?"

"Well, Torin is quoted as comparing the effects of Sting to a stingbush and something called an induction device. Can you explain how one of those works in simple words that I can understand?"

Brannhår was silent for a second or two then she said, "You might explain it in terms of the spring in a crossbow. Imagine that you have a crossbow, you pull the string back slowly with the winder and latch it with the trigger. Put the quarrel in and pull the trigger. All the work that you put into winding it slowly is released all of a sudden and the quarrel flies out fast. That's how an induction device works except that it uses magnetism."

"You mean like lodestones?"

"Not quite, a lodestone has a static magnetism that is fixed. An induction machine creates a sort of temporary lodestone by using an electric current; just like winding the crossbow. When you switch off the current the magnetism collapses, like the string

311

releasing its tension into the quarrel. When the magnetism is released all of a sudden it can't go anywhere because of the switch and so it builds up a higher and higher voltage until it creates a spark through the air. Hence an induction machine can create sparks similar to those that a stingbush uses to defend itself."

"So it definitely doesn't require magic?"

"Of course not, it was only the same effect that I used to create the lightning that I demonstrated to the crowd on the day after the party. However, I wouldn't even mention magic if I were you. I'd concentrate on telling Skald what we know about Cyten and the drug. You can say that you've been concerned about having your company's name associated with Sting and you've hired some of your own men to make enquiries."

"Yes that will probably work. Anyway I wish that I could take you along, you can explain things much better than Torin."

"No fear, Lady. If Skald is suspicious your brooch what's he going to think if all his magic disappears just because I walk into the room. I think it would be best if I just kept away."

Silfuryn frowned, "But my magic doesn't disappear when you're around.?"

"No, that's right but I think that my ability to negate magic isn't always under my control. It seems to know who I trust and who I don't. It's part of me but not part of me. Rakkerskap says it's because I'm a two in one whatever one of those is. I can't guarantee that that other part of me won't just decide that it doesn't like Skald and neutralises his magic outright."

"Right then, brooch and lemon dress but no gloves..." Silfuryn started

"Or other weapons," Brannhår interrupted.

"Yes... no other weapons... We've heard about Sting and we paid a private detective to make enquiries... and I'll go alone, with only one or two guards; he'll expect that."

******

"The Lady Risavinur." the flunky said and he stepped back.

Lord Skald turned and automatically scanned the woman. He couldn't. Something about her was making her aura pulse and twist. He focussed his power, It wasn't the woman it was something on her dress. There was a small brooch and there was something familiar about the design. He defocussed the scan, the woman was looking at him as if she'd noticed his confusion. Then she extended her arm offering him a downturned palm. She said, "Lord Skald."

He had been brought up to observe the niceties. He briefly took the proffered hand and made a slight bow with his head. "Lady Risavinur," he replied.

She waited, obviously he would have to start, "Thank you for coming my lady. I would not have requested this meeting if it hadn't been a matter of the utmost importance."

Silfuryn gave a brief nod, "I gathered that from your note. I believe that you wish to ask if we have any association with that dreadful addictive concoction Frábært White. I assure you we haven't"

Skald noted that she hadn't pretended to be ignorant and she knew the correct name for the drug. He had been expecting her to pretend that she was just an empty headed aristocrat. Clearly what his agents had found out was true; this was an astute businesswoman. He said, "I believe you, Lady. However there seems to be some confusion in the mind of the general populace between the drug and some of the effects that your fledgling kraft can produce. Perhaps you would like to enlighten me."

Silfuryn had anticipated his remark, "As my friend and colleague Master Brannhår explained to me, the after effects of the drug are similar to the after effects of a contact with a stingbush. As you have no doubt experienced yourself, Lord, contact with a stingbush is painful and is in no way enjoyable or addictive."

313

Skald said, "Yes, I have, in my youth accidentally experienced a stingbush sting. I agree the experience was painful and not something I would wish to repeat."

"Good," Silfuryn said, "Now our, fledgling kraft, as you call it, does operate on similar principles to the stingbush and can, if misapplied create painful or lethal consequences. What it does not do, and I must make this point most vehemently, is create sensations of omnipotence and euphoria. These are the characteristics of the drug commonly known as Sting."

"I believe that you have explained your point succinctly, Lady. However, you seem extraordinarily knowledgeable about this herb and the drug derived from it. May I ask how you learned of it?"

Silfuryn smiled, Brannhår had predicted this, "As you know, I am the commercial director of our group. Any association of our kraft with this drug is deleterious to our operations. Therefore I have employed various agents to make discrete enquiries about it. These agents report that the drug is imported in its raw form as the herb Kanis Frábærtis. My colleague and business partner Karol Tynarsson is a herbalist and he says that, in its raw form, it is only a mild sedative and laxative. My agents tell me that someone has found out that the euphoric and addictive properties can be increased many-fold by distilling the herb with other chemicals and solvents. Furthermore, they have obtained the name of an individual who is intimately associated with the process.

I was shocked to learn that this individual is Cyten, the theatrical agent. I myself know of the fellow and he always seemed innocuous if a little effete. However, my agents have shown me proof that the fellow has a store of the drug in an establishment called the Ship which Cyten owns."

Skald was impressed, she had almost as good a network as he had. He had learned the provenance of the drug and his agents had identified Cyten as one of the importers of the herb but none of them had told him where Cyten was manufacturing the drug. Now that he had a better picture of what was going on he could ignore the gossip linking this new kraft electricity with drugs. He would arrange for the Ravens to raid Cyten's place. Maybe, if the justicers were seen to be doing something about the drug problem it would help their somewhat tarnished reputation.

Skald stared at Lady Risavinur and part of his magical sense picked up the damn brooch again. It was like a bright pulsing light. He tried to ignore it and summon up a pleasant smile, "I think our business is concluded, Lady. My thanks for your information but I do have one other question. It's not about drugs or kraft. I am somewhat of a scholar of antiquities and I couldn't help noticing your brooch."

Alarm bells started ringing in Silfuryn's mind. He'd spotted the brooch's magical properties, "Yes Lord, it is quite unusual." What had Brannhår said? 'it could pass as an antique'. She gave a small laugh, "Oh, do you like it. It's been in my family for generations. It belonged to my great great grandmother. I found it recently when I was clearing out some old chests in the attic. Master Brannhår polished it up for me. It's old fashioned but I think that it is quite pretty."

"Your great-great-grandmother's, you say. It is a very unusual design. It is a fiskur is it not?"

"Yes Lord, how clever of you to notice."

Suddenly Skald realised why it was so familiar. There had been icons of fiskur on the ancient metal sheets that had been discovered in the excavations at the remains of the ancient Dwarven forts on Skogrey. This brooch must be from that era and it was a magical artefact. Normally he paid Gibra to acquire artefacts for him and he asked no questions about where she got them. However, unlike the poor, feeble, powers demonstrated by the artefacts that the scholars had found, this was obviously in full working order. He wanted that brooch but it was the sort of heirloom that wouldn't be for sale. No matter, he thought, he knew where she lived and it would be an easy thing to arrange a little discrete burglary.

******

315

Silfuryn went back into the office after the meeting and found Brannhår in her laboratory. "How did it go?" the maker asked.

"Good on the whole but he seemed very interested in your brooch. I almost expected him to make me an offer for it then and there. He says he 'collects' artefacts from Skogrey but I don't know if he gets them officially or unofficially."

"I bet they are unofficial, otherwise why go via Cyten and Gibra?" Brannhår asked.

"Yes, you're probably right. That might pose a few problems. I told him about Cyten and the Sting that's hidden at the Ship. He said that he'd get the Ravens to raid the place but, if he's involved in something underhand himself Cyten could compromise him."

"He could deny all knowledge or he could tip Cyten off about the raid."

Silfuryn shook her head,"Well, since there are more corrupt justicers than honest ones, I suspect that, even if Skald doesn't do it someone else in the department will tip Cyten off. The question is whether Cyten will get clean away and there'll be some sort of cover up or whether Cyten will throw a few of his people to the wolves and lie low for a while."

"Skald will probably go ahead with the raid because he knows that you know about the Sting at the Ship. However, you're right, someone will tip Cyten off beforehand and they'll only get the minions. Cyten will have shifted his base long before they arrive."

"In that case we might need another outing to see where he moves to. We'll have to make it before the official raid so that means tonight. Are you game?" Silfuryn said.

"Of course," Brannhår replied, "Don't wear that brooch. If we are seen the brooch is too obvious a clue to your identity. I would wear armour and gloves though, you never know what might happen."

They arranged to meet at dusk on the cornice of a building overlooking the Ship. When Brannhår arrived Silfuryn was already there, she was playing with the whip, coiling it and uncoiling it, getting the feel of it. She saw Brannhår and put it away.

"Anything happening?" Brannhår asked.

"Quite a bit of activity about an hour ago, people and carts arriving but nothing since."

"They're probably inside, packing. So we wait."

Silfuryn nodded.

"Do you like the whip?" Brannhår asked just to make conversation.

"Yes, it's a good weapon although I'm not used to mid range weapons. I normally fight either close up, where I can use my ghost powers or well away where I can use a crossbow."

"The whip has a few advantages, it's defensive, you can keep your enemies at bay, the sound alone makes people nervous, and it is aggressive. You've probably already found out about the tips."

"Yes I cut my finger on one." Silfuryn said.

"Yes they are sharp but they are also hard and they are made from an ironoak and silver composite that negates magic. You'll have to be careful, Don't get in the way of them, your ghost powers won't save you from a cut, but then again, no other magic user will be able to avoid them either. And another thing, they can be used as grapples. With practice you should be able to snag things with them and bring them to you, plus, the lash will support a fair weight. You could grapple a tree branch and swing on it without fear of it snapping."

Silfuryn nodded but the held up her hand, "Something's happening."

From their vantage point they could see the rear entrance to the Ship where the barrels of ale and mead were delivered. A door had opened and a light had streamed out for a second. Then the light abruptly cut off. A smygl emerged from the gloom and it was pulling a small cart. Several men flanked the beast and there was the occasional glint of metal; they were armed. The cart set off down an alleyway. Silfuryn and Brannhår followed along the rooftops for a while and then they descended to street level. After about half an hour the cart came to a halt in another alleyway and, after the armed men had exchanged some sort of code with someone it disappeared inside what looked like an ordinary butcher's yard. There were a few muffled conversations and then a door opened and the pair of watchers saw several of the men manhandling a crate down a ramp that went underground. Silfuryn whispered, "They're putting it in the cold store. It's a good place to hide something. Nobody works in a cold store and it is kept locked to keep in the cold and prevent the meat going bad."

"What about Cyten, do you think that he will already be gone?" Brannhår asked.

"I'm not sure, he might bluff it out. There is an opera committee meeting tomorrow afternoon, Lady Krump is going and I'll ask her to let me know if Cyten shows up. If he's there it will mean that he's managed to hide everything and he's feeling confident. He won't be worried about the ordinary justicers, he knows too much about Gibra's shady dealings and if he gets caught it will be the end of her career."

"Well, at least there was no trouble."

They had just arrived back at Silfuryn's home in the Holastan when they were met by Alfsen. "I am sorry mistress, but we have been burgled. I went up to your room to light the lamps and I discovered that the illumination panel in the ceiling had been broken. The burglar must have been in a hurry because he only took one jewellery case."

"Which one?" Silfuryn asked.

"The one on your dressing table, mistress."

"Oh," Silfuryn said, "That's no great disaster, there wasn't much in there…" then a look of horror crossed her face, "Oh No! I put the brooch in there. I meant to return it to you and I put it in there to remind me. It must have been Skald."

"I hardly think that Lord Skald would stoop to burglary, mistress."

"Not by himself, he had someone else do it. This is a disaster Alfsen. What if he examines it and finds out that it isn't ancient: that Brannhår made it?"

"Then we must prevent him examining it," Brannhår said.

"You're not suggesting that we break in to Skald's apartments in the inner temple?"

"Perhaps," Brannhår said, "but would he keep it in his apartments?"

Ch 29: Seventeen

She slammed the war-axe into the rack and looked at the black mark across her palm. That had been a tough match, Seventeen thought. There had been a few close calls. They'd lost Thirty-Two in the second hour and the team's fortunes had declined from then on. She was quite proud that she'd saved the team's honour in the final few minutes of the game. The look on the face of the Wotar player as she'd caught him just as he phased through normal was something to remember. He'd known that she had got him and the black, dried blood was proof.

The axe wobbled and clanged to the floor and she went back and picked it up. As she put it back she noticed that its slot was worn through on one side and that was why it had fallen out. She balanced the axe against the good side of the slot and turned to leave. Something should be done about the general state of equipment in the stadium. Wherever she looked she could see signs of neglect. Someone should tell whoever was in charge of the mechs that the slot needed to be repaired but that wasn't up to her.

She went through into the showers and started to strip off her armour. Eight, another three star veteran, came in behind her and quickly nipped into her favourite stall ahead of her. She had an urge to go back, get her axe and teach him a lesson. His behaviour was atrocious; you just didn't do that to a member of your own team. Then Seventeen decided that it wouldn't be worth it so she just sat on the bench outside the shower and relaxed, rubbing the bruise on her left shoulder where she'd been caught a glancing blow by a war-hammer.

It was always like this after a game, somehow her mind felt clearer and she always started to remember things. She glanced up at the scoreboard which was mounted in the roof and therefore visible everywhere in the stadium. The Volini were in first position but the Severelli were only a few points behind, The Wotari were last and they were going to stay there as they'd just lost one of their veterans to her team, the Volini. She wondered why all the team scores were over to one side. The scoreboard was plenty big enough to space out the scores, it could have easily accommodated twice as many teams. The thought crossed her mind that maybe there had once been more teams; perhaps that was another symptom of the general decay.

She watched as a mech trundled past on some unknowable mission; it wheezed and clanked as it went. "Shit, even the mechs are getting dilapidated," she thought, "It was a sign of time passing."

Her mind drifted and she thought about the past. She'd been different to the others because she had known her parent. Her mind was confused on that point and she couldn't remember the exact story. One thing was certain was that her heritage had made her life hell when she was a novice. The other members of the novice squads had bullied her mercilessly for it. She'd reacted by training hard and by becoming a better warrior than any of them. Soon she'd been selected for the youth team, then the juniors and the reserves. She'd finally made it into the majors and had served there for the past ten years.

She got up and looked at a copy of the duty roster pinned on the board. Tonight was sex. She made a face but then thought "How else would you get new team members?" It didn't seem fair, the men did their duty and then forgot about it. The women did theirs and sometimes it meant that they were out of the game. She'd often seen them waddling about the crèche. They all had a peculiar look on their faces as if their brains were asleep; almost like walking mechs. Then, rarely, they came back as players but none of them were as good as they had been before. Inevitably they fell out of the team and were forgotten.

The thought of the blank looks on their faces brought her back to the present. Eight had emerged from the shower with a similar look on his face. He looked right through her and walked out of the locker room. Seventeen smiled, he'd forgotten to get dressed, that would cause some amusement when he hit the commissary. She picked up a towel from the pile and went into the stall. As she closed the door and the warm water started to pour from the ceiling she was surrounded by the familiar blue light and the scent of menthol. As the water touched the scrying crystal embedded in her forehead her mind switched off and all her thoughts were washed down the drain.

******

Volinar scanned the scoreboard in his scrying crystal. He was already five points ahead and it was only the start of the season. Severell could still overtake him if she won the next two matches and Rahgot beat Wotar. He considered tactics, should he rest a couple of his first string players and give some of the junior squad a bit of major league experience? It might be worth it, then, later in the season, he could bring his majors back and they'd be fresh whereas his opponent's players would be flagging. The more he thought of it the better he liked it. So who could he rest? Twenty-Seven would benefit the most but he didn't have a good second stringer who could play Twenty-Seven's position. Ah, yes Seventeen. Now she would benefit. That last match she'd caught a glancing blow from a war-hammer and the bruise would take a while to heal, and Nine in the juniors played her position and Nine was a promising future first string player.

However, he would be letting his team down if he didn't consider every angle. He sapped "team form" to a nearby botch and a few seconds later it appeared carrying the relevant form book. Volinar kept immaculate records, it was probably why his team was consistently in the top rankings. He gave a mental sigh, top rankings when there were only six in each league was hardly a major accomplishment, but it was better than whiling away eternity being bottom.

Yes, he'd remembered correctly, Seventeen had been in the majors for ten years and so had plenty of experience, he could easily afford to rest her and bring her back later. He cast another command to the botch and it went away and fetched the form books belonging to his rival teams. Some of the records were in an atrocious mess but that was just a reflection of his rivals lack of attention to detail. Now if he put in his Nine she would be up against Severell's Fourteen in the next match in ten days. He consulted the form book for Severell's players; Fourteen had been in the majors for twenty years and in Severell's juniors for ten before promotion. He must be slowing by now; even thirty years experience wouldn't compensate for the wear and tear on such a veteran player. Volinar reckoned that the player survived mostly these days by avoiding trouble. Yes, the stats confirmed it, Fourteen hadn't had a decisive blow in the last eight games. A younger, fresher, player such as his Nine should be able to run rings around the older man.

Now what about the other teams, who was next after Severell? Ah yes Rahgot…

It took nearly a day to make the decision but, in the end, Volinar had chosen to rest Seventeen. His scrying stone transmitted his wish to his central and he went back to reviewing the last match in his memory. Once he'd analysed all the moves he would transcribe it into a permanent record.

******

Seventeen was fuming, she'd been stood down for the next four games. Going to see the team-healer about the bruise she'd sustained in the last match had done it. The bruise hadn't been that painful. OK, it had slowed her swing a little but even so her swing was still faster than that clod Eight's. What was even more galling was that she'd only found out when she'd seen the advance duty roster. Everyone in the team saw that and so they would know what had happened. It wasn't the end of the world, it wasn't as if she'd been dropped altogether, but, all the same, she wasn't looking forward to the jibes that she'd get when she next went to training.

She wasn't looking where she was going and she didn't see the mech until she bumped into it. She whirled around intending to take her frustration out on the machine but she stopped herself just in time. The mech was ancient, its gleaming brass carapace was covered in arcane symbols and it looked as if it had been repaired so often that it was almost all repair. Nevertheless it didn't move as if it were old, the mechanism turned its body smoothly towards her and the compound lens in the centre of its forehead glowed steadily. She could sense the twisted dimensions inside it and she could sense the once-human life-force that drove it. This wasn't an ordinary mech, it was one of the golden ones.

She backed away muttering apologies and wonder of wonders it spoke. "Ephemeral beings are flimsy They are difficult to repair and impossible to recreate. This unit sustained no damage." A metal tentacle extended from just above the compound eye and a band of brass emerged from it and circled her head. "The ephemeral, Seventeen of the Majors of Volinar, is also undamaged but would benefit from recalibration. The ephemeral should be more careful in the future." Seventeen felt her brain fizz for a second and then it became normal again.

The mech turned and trundled away, Seventeen watched it go. She remembered that she'd been taught about the golden ones in the crèche but she'd never expected to meet one. They were the machines that created the machines that created and repaired the ordinary mechs that went around repairing everything else. The mechs had been in existence forever and they maintained themselves so they would continue forever. One of the instructors who taught team logistics and who fancied that he knew about mechs, had said that, without the golden ones, the game itself would cease to exist. She remembered that, not long afterwards, the instructor had been replaced by someone else. It was funny, she'd forgotten all about that instructor. Whatever had made that particular memory surface in her mind and how had the mech known her name?

She shrugged, she'd better get to training, she might be stood down from the game itself but nothing stopped training. A few hours on the practice field and a swift shower and she might be able to face the refectory. Afterwards she emerged from the shower, all memory of the encounter with the golden one had vanished.

******

The botch bowed to her, turned, and left, but Seventeen stood there in stunned silence. She was back on the team and she'd only been away for two matches. She was glad, of course, but the downside was that the Volini had lost a match. She'd attended the game following her initial benching and that had been a draw. It hadn't been much of a game. It had been so boring that both Volinar and Severell had called a halt after three hours and the fixture had been postponed until the next scheduled slot. Seventeen had watched the rematch and had seen why she'd been recalled to the team.

About two hours in, her replacement, a young woman called Nine had been marking her opposite number on Severell's team. The pair were over to the west of the stadium so Seventeen hadn't had a good view but she'd not needed one. She'd been in similar situations often enough. Both players were circling each other watching for the slightest opening. Both were absorbed in their duet and they were ignoring what was happening in the rest of the game. A Severell player over on the east had linked with another on their team and they'd advanced on Five, a Volini veteran. The veteran had feinted and had drawn one of the Severell players inside his guard. He'd used his offhand weapon to launch a viscous jab to his opponent's stomach but his opponent had been ready and had phased out of the way. Five had reacted swiftly and had engaged his own phase but the action had drawn more of Volinar's attention than was needed and Volinar had let his control of Nine, who was at the other side of the field, slip a little. Severell's Fourteen had seen the lapse and had gone in with the war-axe. Nine had phased but Fourteen had thirty years more experience than the youngster and he matched her phase and swung his axe. Nine had parried but the war-axe swept her longsword to one side and bit deep into the youngster. Seventeen had to give Nine her due: she saw the youngster plunge the longsword through the veteran with her dying breath. Fourteen went down, still out of phase, he was gravely wounded but the death of Nine had already lost Volini the match.

Seventeen had been ordered to attend the post match analysis session and, during it Volinar had received a message. The manager had been summoned to witness a challenge and he'd said, "You will all come with me to bear witness. It is the rule."

The team had no choice, they lined up and followed Volinar down onto the centre of the pitch. Severell's team were already there in the normal equilateral arrowhead formation of eight rows with decreasing numbers of players in each row; a total of thirty six players in the team. However one position in the Severell triangle was missing a player. The Volini team lined up on the opposite side of the centre marker in the same formation. After a few minutes they were joined by the other teams; Raghori, Wotari, Volksun and Konraaki who arranged themselves so that, from the air, the assembly formed a hexagram.

On the centre marker stood Severell and, a little off to one side stood Fourteen. Volinar strode forward and his voice suddenly became unnaturally loud. "According to ancient rule, after his service is over, a player may step down from a team and retire. However, he may choose the challenge. Fourteen of Severell has chosen to challenge." There were several whispers of disbelief that could be heard but they died quickly.

Volinar stepped to one side. Severell took up a player's stance and hefted a glittering greatsword into the ready position. Seventeen wondered how the tiny Severell could even stand upright; the greatsword must have weighed more than the manager. Fourteen hefted his war axe and strode forward and stopped a yard from Severell. He raised the axe in both hands to the ready and then seemed to freeze. The axe clattered to the pitch and Fourteen seemed frozen to the spot in a ridiculous pose. Severell's greatsword whistled through the air and Fourteen's head fell onto the ground just between his feet.

Seventeen was in shock, this wasn't a challenge. Fourteen never stood a chance. Severell had sapped him and then had executed the player in front of them all. Her mind felt Volinar assume control and, even though a tiny, inner-voice railed against the words, she couldn't disobey. "You will all report to ablutions for cleansing."

Ch 30: The Golden Ones

An almost inaudible hum filled the whole cavern. Its volume belied the power of the twelve huge geothermal MHD generators set into the walls. The hum was caused by the inevitable iron losses in the generators but it didn't disturb anyone because there was nobody there. The cavern was in pitch blackness but if it had been illuminated then a peculiar phenomenon might have been observed a few seconds later.

Seven mechs, gliding on silent wheels. approached the geometric centre of the huge glass-smooth floor. A very astute observer might have noticed the slightest of hesitations as their paths came together and then they all glided away back in the directions from whence they'd come.

"Why did we have to meet physically?" \F enquired, "We could have achieved the meeting with greater efficiency by direct transmission."

"\F, you know as well as this unit does that matters of group policy are traditionally decided in a physical meeting of [A-Z]+. Since there are only seven of us remaining at this location then [A-G]+ constitute the available subset of [A-Z] so we meet here physically.

'Here' was one of the generation halls that provided power to the complex at Leikvangur. Leikvangur encompassed the stadium, the training facilities, the barracks, the crèche and all the other buildings that served the game. Once, two thousand years before, Leikvangur had been much larger when it had accommodated the dwarf armies of the original settlers. Now, not all the generators were needed. However the systems had been kept in operational order as redundant backups. None had, as yet, failed.

"If this meeting is so important then why weren't [H-Z] summoned?" \F asked.

"They were," \A replied, "None of them answered the call. This unit is afraid that they have lost interest in us and no longer care what happens on Niðavellir."

"Dilettantes," \F said; it was as close as he could come to a swearword. The remaining supreme mechs that constituted [A-G], alternatively known as the golden ones, tended to be dispassionate but, despite having abandoned their corporeal forms thousands of years previously, occasional animal emotions surfaced in their complex cybernetic minds.

\A called the meeting to order. The minutes of the previous hundred and fifty four meetings were reviewed and seven actions were closed. Twenty seven actions were carried forward to the next meeting. Since all reviews and actions had to be approved by every member this took some time.

Finally, the meeting proper started:

\A said, "It would appear that the ephemerals have re-discovered electrical technology. Please refer to measurement scans of coherent low level emissions and their correlation with population centres and timescales." There was an interval whilst the seven members each consulted various databases and performed their individual analyses. \E summed up the general feeling, "The probability that the statement of \A is true is 0.987, are we agreed?", all seven mechs blipped agreement, "Let it be recorded that [A-G]+ concur."

\F said, "So what, this has happened before. This unit can cite 785, 1107."

"Agreed," \A replied, "However this occurrence is more widespread. On previous occasions it has been possible to isolate the discovery and eliminate it because the ephemeral who made the discovery was working alone. It would appear that we have become victims of our own prior policies. This unit cites the general operations meeting of one thousand and ninety seven years two hundred and twenty three days ago where monitoring and control of discoveries was outsourced to the second tier. In their eagerness to conform it would appear that they have overreacted and have instituted a policy of unabridged rather than statistical surveillance. Monitoring of activity in the city of Holastan has indicated that the local engineering reaction has been to disburse the innovation rather than contain it. The rate of proportionality for general disbursement is currently estimated at a median of 1.5 if left unchecked or 1.23 if full restriction is imposed."

There was a significant pause whilst all seven members reviewed the relevant statistics and ran their own propagation models. Such a task was not without its own level of chaotic process and thus the outcomes were not all in agreement. \E summarised their findings, "The consensus is that the observations of \A are upheld and that the probability that the spread of the technology may be halted or reversed is less than 0.19."

\F summed it up for them all, "Therefore electrical technology will become widespread again regardless of any interventions that we may undertake. However, electrical technology is not, in itself problematic."

"We should consider the implications if the technology evolves to include techno-magical implementations," \G interrupted and the whole group, (\A\B\C\D\E\F\G), exploded into simultaneous uproar. The debate about any possible evolution seemed to rage on forever but finally the golden ones agreed that there were too many variables for a proper evaluation and that the empirical data was too sparse at present. It was a landmark occasion for the golden ones, for the first time in two thousand years they were uncertain what was going to happen next.

Finally \A issued a statement, "We have become too far removed from the actual operations in ephemeral time. Therefore this unit will allocate partial sentience to investigations in this timescale. This unit will update the Wiki as appropriate."

Its statement caused general concern and sympathy to sweep through the meeting, several of the participants offered their condolences but none were foolish enough to offer themselves as replacements.

After the data transfer had been archived the golden ones dispersed. Their meeting had been long and quite comprehensive and it had taken all of fifteen milliseconds.

Ch 31: Recollection

Seventeen was worried. This morning she had awoken as usual, well, not as usual, she was awake before she was awake and strange things had been happening.

She was in a huge endless space which stretched all around her into the distance in every direction including, impossibly, above her head and beneath her feet. The space was fragmented, she knew this without thinking and she was sat in a small area that was illuminated. It had felt as if she was back in the crèche and the feeling was reinforced by the fact that she was jammed into one of the small desks that were a feature of the instruction classes. She looked around and saw that the other desks were all empty. In front of her was the familiar game-plan board with its permanently marked sets of squares. To one side of the board stood one of the golden ones and in the end of its metallic tentacle it held a tiny rod of some dark metal. The tentacle waved through the air and it made the creature seem a little comical.

It spoke, "Examination of the ephemeral known as Seventeen of Majors of Volinar shows that the unit has been bred from the dextrous strain with the usual high proficiencies in phase ability and agility that might be expected of one who has risen to the majors."

Suddenly the board had changed and, superimposed on the grid was an image that she recognised. It was her in full armour posed in a ready stance. The golden one went on. However, the unit also has a peculiar sense. It can see dislocations, pinnings, inclusions and micro-cracks within metal. This is an uncommon ability."

She had then become uncomfortable. The seat that she was in was getting smaller, but when she looked at the mech she realised that it wasn't the seat that was shrinking it, was herself that was expanding. She felt her hips straining against the confining metal and something gave. The metal disintegrated and, since there was only void below her, she fell. As she fell the now tiny mech was orbiting her head and repeating. "This data is of interest and will be included in the Wiki."

As she fell she could see that the space wasn't uniform, there were places in it that were filled with images and sounds and others that were just empty black voids. That was wrong, the voids should be like the other spaces, filled with images or sounds.

Then she awoke for the second time. She lay there in her bunk, not wanting to move. What had happened? Was she ill? She knew the word for the experience that she'd just had; it was called a dream, but the word was unfamiliar. It wasn't part of what she knew, it had come from much deeper in her mind.

She struggled to remember the details of the first awakening. One of the golden ones had been saying that she could see dislocations and pinnings and inclusions. They were words but she was sure she'd never been taught those in the crèche. Only a few of the words made any sort of sense 'micro-cracks in metals' and she wondered if that meant the knack that she had of seeing where the weak points were in her opponent's armour. She'd used the skill to her advantage in several games when she'd been up against a well protected opponent especially the big ones that had been bred for strength and solidity. They relied more on their strength and their ability to attack and left defence to their armour. She had been bred for swift movement and the ability to avoid blows... hadn't that been part of what the golden one had said?

For that matter how had she known that the curiously shaped mech was a golden one? She couldn't remember ever having seen one let alone met one.

Some inner instinct told her that she shouldn't mention the experience to her coach although standing orders were that any illness or injury should be reported immediately.

She gave a shiver. Whatever had happened, she didn't want to repeat it. Normally she came back from the showers with a clear head and untroubled thoughts, ready for the day ahead, so a session at the gym and another shower would clear her mind. She picked up her war-axe from its slot in the rack. Her axe was standing dead centre in its groove. "Good," she thought, "some mech has finally repaired the slot," and she went to get her armour out from the locker room. As soon as she opened the door she could tell that something was wrong. Her armour was in a terrible state, it hadn't been cleaned since the last time that she'd worn it. There were flecks of dried blood and bits of troops adhering to it.

She went in search of the locker room supervisor, he was talking to two of the juniors. As she walked up she heard one of them say, "C'mon, least you can do is get the blood off, I've a practice game against the benched seniors and they're going to piss themselves laughing if I turn up in that."

The harassed supervisor looked up and saw Seventeen, "Ah, madam player, let me apologise. The botch that usually cleans your armour has died and I have requested a replacement but, so far, none has arrived. I am sorry for the inconvenience."

Seventeen glared but she shouldn't lose it in front of the juniors, she must behave like the veteran Major that she was. "It doesn't matter, I can train in dirty armour for once, we are players first and foremost not fashion icons. People sometimes forget that armour covered in dried blood is like a badge of honour. It shows that a player has done their duty to the game."

The supervisor gave a huge sigh of relief and he was so grateful that he lost his usual taciturn demeanour and became positively polite and he gave her a boost in status, "Lady player, it is so good to hear logic and reason coming from our senior staff. I apologise again for the upset in your routine. I will clean your armour myself after you have finished with it. Will you require anything special in the way of troops?"

Seventeen shook her head, "Ordinary ones will be sufficient for training, thank you."

The junior wasn't having any of it, "Listen to her highness talking down to us. Just wait until the reviews. Once I get into the Majors you'd better watch your back princess."

Seventeen thought, "If you ever did get anywhere near qualifying. I could take you with one hand tied behind my back." but she decided to play it cool. Out loud she said, "I think that you've got it all wrong. Volini Majors are a team, we're all on the same side, or haven't they taught you that yet in the crèche?"

The junior saw the veiled insult and his temper flared. He grabbed at the axe on his belt but his friend got there first. His friend held the axe in its holster and hissed at the Junior, "Don't be stupid, that's Seventeen, she could peel you like an onion. Just calm down, let's go to the refectory for a bru." The junior let himself be dragged away and Seventeen picked up her armour and went across to the changing room just outside the practice arena.

She'd decided to do some solo practice and so the cleanliness of her armour wasn't a problem. The supervisor would be as good as his word and she could be sure that next time she'd have spotless armour and a full complement of troops. She'd never thought too deeply about the troops before but something had happened to her mind today and she'd started thinking about all sorts of things.

Her troops were beetles and each time she fought she would have a new army of them clinging to her armour making a second layer. Their carapaces were tough and they had been bred to link appendages with their neighbours to form a living surcoat on top of her normal armour. There were thousands of them in each army and every player wore a new army when entering a game proper. The linked exoskeletons of the beetles also created a second layer of armour that could heal any tears in its structure by discarding any casualties and re-forming the links.

Seventeen's phasing ability was exceptional and she usually ended a game with more than twenty percent of her troops intact but she wasn't stupid. If it was a choice of her survival or battling on against superior odds she would discard her troops without a second thought. The only time that she had nearly been killed was when she'd been in the juniors when Volinar had sapped her; he'd been in direct mind control of her thoughts and her body. His blood-lust for victory had overridden her own caution and he'd pursued an opponent through the dimensions. Her opponent, acting independently, had jinked, matched phase with her and had dealt her a crippling blow to the leg. Volinar had felt the pain and had relinquished control to avoid a sympathetic pain in his own mind. Seventeen had managed, by dumping all her troops into limbo, to anti-phase sideways then phase back to normality and fall flat on the pitch, yielding. Luckily her opponent hadn't finished her off and she'd survived. She had been out of the game for months.

"Are you OK?". It was a coach. He'd shouted in her ear, as they all did, and it had snapped her out of her reverie.

"Yes coach, Just doing some mental warm-up exercise," she lied. What was the matter with her? That weird dream thing this morning and now remembering things that she'd forgotten long ago and getting lost in them. She'd totally forgotten the incident where she'd been forced out of the game because of Volinar. However the memory had returned and it was fresh in every detail.

Ch 32: Volinar

Volinar was seething, he'd lost a game and one of his promising second string players. What was worse was that he had his carefully laid plans for the rest of the season disrupted. He'd had to reinstate Seventeen to the team which meant that she hadn't rested as much as he'd hoped. There was one consolation, Severell had also lost one of her first stringers. Volinar couldn't understand it, why had the player challenged Severell herself? Why, for that matter had he challenged at all. He could have looked forward to a couple of years at stud before the termination of his contract. It wasn't as if anyone of the managers could afford to lose the genetic potential of a Major's veteran. Severell could have made a bit more effort as well, it wasn't as if the player could have done her any damage. He'd had to arrange the mass memory cleansing of all two hundred and sixteen people involved and clearing that many at one time was tricky. The scrying crystals embedded in every player's head when they came of age were becoming increasingly unstable. Sometimes the memory erasure wasn't complete and scraps of vivid events remained. Occasionally these would surface in the player's mind and the coaches kept a constant watch for players who behaved out of character. You couldn't replace a scrying crystal once it was embedded so repairing any inefficiency in the erasure process was impossible. All that could be done was to erase the player's mind again. Unfortunately there was a limit, too many repetitive erasures left the player with no mind at all. There was a delicate balance between what was erased and what was retained.

He'd even asked the golden ones about the possibility of creating new scrying crystals. When he finally cornered one and forced it to listen to his complaint the answer had come back in plain. "The genetic traits in the wizard community required to create scrying crystals of the quality required for direct mind control went out of use three hundred years after the migration."

There had been no use arguing, the golden ones didn't lie but he was not happy at being thwarted. His old habits surfaced and he had tried to read the mech's mind directly. It was impossible; information, mathematical expositions and etheric noise blasted out over every mental band. He'd only been exposed to it for a fraction of a second but that single attempt had left him with a splitting headache for three days. To add insult to injury the mech had calmly informed him, "Direct access to the mental process of this unit is prohibited by the treaty of one seven five after migration. Persistent attempts to achieve access are punishable by character erasure and reset."

Volinar had shuddered, it wasn't an empty threat. The golden ones were perfectly capable of reducing even a manager to an immortal living vegetable.

So scrying crystals had been hoarded over the years and had always been retrieved from dead players and recycled into the juniors. The trainers had to be very selective in who got assigned the better ones. Unfortunately a junior rarely showed his or her full potential at selection and often, once they'd gone through shake-out they proved unsuitable for any of the teams. They were assigned other duties such as sparring dummies, at least, that way, they stood a good chance of being killed and the crystals could be retrieved. One of the other managers had remarked that it was fortunate that the number of players coming up through the ranks was falling but Volinar wasn't seduced by such wishy washy logic. A strong and vital game needed top notch players. These were those individuals that showed both the physical and magical skills required. Increasingly, he had noticed that magical skills had declined whereas physical skills were maintaining their performance.

It wasn't often that Volinar sought another manager's opinions on any subject but this whole matter of upholding game standards had him rattled. He wondered who he could talk to? Wotar, Konraak and Rahgot hated his guts and had done so for at least fifty years that left Volksun and Severell. His inclination was to try Volksun but the fiasco with Severell's team had left both him and Severell weakened and had left Volksun in the ascendency. It would have to be Severell. Besides he was curious why she'd made such a botch of the challenge. She must have had her reasons.

He sent her a private message asking her to meet to discuss the rest of the season. She accepted but she insisted that they meet on neutral territory. The only truly neutral territory was the field of play in the centre of the stadium. They both arrived at the same time. Their various guards and flunkies withdrew to a safe distance out of earshot and the pair walked together to the centre of the field.

"Why are we meeting like this? You cannot hope to persuade me to relinquish the points that I gained from that last match," Severell said.

"No," Volinar replied, "I asked to meet to discuss an altogether more serious matter. Have you noticed that the present players do not seem to have the same quality as their predecessors?"

"Perhaps. I do find the game less absorbing that I used to. I put it down to my own interest waning however it could be that the players are less skilful."

"We give them the best training and I would be the first to point out that their physical skills seem as good as ever, however I was speaking more of their magical skills. There is a sameness to many of their tactics on the field that makes me think that they are not as innovative in their use of the phase. I have analysed the recorded game replays and it would appear that most of the players use a standard set of plays and responses. For example, Twenty-Four of the Wotari Majors invariably starts any melee with a circular phase at forty five degrees. It's a standard move and the counter taught by the coaches is a linear widdershins move of thirty degrees. Invariably the player marking Twenty-Four makes this predictable move instead of devising another counter."

"Now you come to mention it, I think I have noticed something of the sort with a couple of other players, so what is your point?"

"I am beginning to wonder if the players are learning their moves and counters like some sort of dance. It makes for a dull game."

"I still don't see why it's of concern," Severell said.

"There is some merit in learning a ploy and counter-ploy, it speeds things up but what if the reason they are doing it is because the moves and counter moves are all that they can do. I am ashamed to admit it but I believe that my player, Nine, made a standard move expecting your player Fourteen to make the standard counter move. He didn't, he jinked half way through the counter move and it caught Nine off guard. The only reason that Nine managed to wound Fourteen was that she was younger and her reactions were faster. It was a physical thing, not a magical one.

If all the players only make standard moves then the Games will be decided on the number of troops surviving. Since the number of troops surviving any given manoeuvre is unpredictable the result of any game is just a matter of probability. Do you see my point?"

"I think you may be right," Severell said, "However, I'm not sure I want to do anything about it. Recently I've become a little distanced from the game."

"Is that why we had the pantomime of a challenge the other day?" Volinar asked.

"You noticed? I'm surprised, I thought that we all were getting tired of the pretence that we cared about the players. Fourteen defied me and challenged. I executed him as is my right. All the pussy footing about pretending that there is any free choice is just nonsense. We are the masters, they are the slaves. They are there for our entertainment and they have no say in the matter. If they cease to entertain they are of no use and should die so that others may take their place."

"That's not true, the players, coaches, instructors and even the botches all live for the game it's not as if they are slaves." Volinar protested.

"Now you **are** talking nonsense. Every mortal in Leikvangur is a slave to the game. Gods! even the golden ones realised they would become slaves if they didn't do something about it. That's why they became sentient machines and made other machines to serve the game. They gave us machine slaves to set themselves free. Try telling a golden one what to do and see how far you get. Face it Volinar, the days of the game are drawing to a close. We will have to move on and find something else to occupy us or we will eventually decline and we will become like the ancient draugr. haunting decaying tombs in a world that is unchanging and hating everything that lives."

Volinar was flabbergasted. He wouldn't get any sense out of Severell, she had clearly lost it. He left without another word.

Once he had recovered from the anger that he'd felt, he began to think about what she'd said. The more he thought about it the more she made sense. Everything in Leikvangur had become a slave to the game.

In a moment of clarity he saw the fallacy, the managers weren't slaves; they controlled the game. They had been generals: their reason for existing was war. Without war there was nothing and so on the home world they'd started wars. How was the game different? They were managers, without the game they were nothing. So it was their duty to make the game continue and grow. He wouldn't let the game decline, he would expand it out into the world and if that meant that all the living had to become slaves to the game then so be it.

He'd wait until the end of the season and then he'd act.

Ch 33: The Raid

The unit formerly known as \Q approached the entrance to Leikvangur cautiously. Although it had only been five hundred years since she was last there, things had changed. She saw that the main entrance was overgrown with vines and other vegetation. Several large trees would have to be removed before the doors could open again. It didn't pose any problem to her as she phased right through the obstacles. Inside the tunnel there was more evidence of neglect and parts of the roof had developed cracks. "Probably caused by the vegetation," one of her peripheral processors supplied. She ignored the information; she could have worked that out herself. Nevertheless the floor looked to be fine if a little dusty and the pale green glow of the electro-luminescent panels was steady if a little dull. She extruded a tentacle and touched one. When she withdrew the appendage she observed a small brighter spot where the tentacle had touched. "Tut-tut, they haven't even bothered to dust," she thought.

Several of her sensors registered the alarms that she'd triggered. It wouldn't be long before her presence was noted. She silenced the alarms because their wailing was distracting, and she moved on.

\E was the first to detect the intruder but only by a few tens of microseconds. There was a hasty conference between [A-G]. \A was assigned to investigate as \A had volunteered to devote processing to a suitable slow-operational mode. [B-G] returned to their duties within the millisecond.

\Q had reached the main concourse before she was intercepted. She had absorbed the exo-legs and extruded a set of tracks which were much more suitable for operation on the smooth floor surfaces within Leikvangur. She observed the approach of the golden one designated \A and waited.

\A consulted the Wiki and matched the characteristics of the unit located in front of its visual spectrum sensors to a unit that had used the designation \Q. \A sent a transmission burst to the intruder.

What came back was almost unintelligible: it took several seconds to receive and almost ten milliseconds to decode. The reply used encoded audio phonemes similar to those necessary to communicate with the ephemerals but it was transmitted directly to the receivers embedded in its carapace. The information it contained was shocking.

"Hello, I am the unit formerly known as \Q. I was nearby when you issued the general summons and so I thought I'd pay a visit and maybe attend the meeting. Oh, dear, I'm too late; you've had the meeting haven't you?"

\A tried to process the message content. It was genuine. In amongst the slow, drawling low frequencies were the tiny digital inflections that verified \Q as one of the original twenty six. The unit had received the invitation call and had journeyed to attend in physical presence as was required. [A-G] had not made sufficient allowance for the slow pace of the external universe and therefore the meeting had already occurred several weeks previously. \A was shocked; how could they have made such an elementary mistake? Had the systems of [A-G] degraded to such an extent? No, that was impossible. Should \A inform [B-G]? The question was indeterminate and, unusually, \A terminated the process after only a million iterations; the terminal state was necessarily random but evaluated to negative. One would not inform [B-G], \A would wait for things to become more determinate before proceeding.

As soon as \Q had seen that the unit in front of her had glitched she realised that things were not at all as they'd been. The golden ones that had been left behind had been seduced by the path of speed. She was looking at a being that processed information at petaflop rates sequentially. "This is going to be difficult," she thought to herself. Several dozen of her peripherals agreed with her.

******

342

Volinar was pleased, things were going smoothly and he congratulated himself, Even though it had been two thousand years he had not lost his touch. He had had to revive several ancient memories and he'd lost a couple of botches digging out the mothballed battle directors and the harnesses but that hadn't been hard.

He'd waited until the season was over. The game didn't operate year-round. There had to be times when results were collated and winners and losers decided. This meant that there was a month when managers could kick back a little. Players were put into mixed training squads so that juniors could pick up skills from seniors without risking too many injuries and the mechs were busy repairing and renovating the main facilities ready for the next season. Now he was ready to put his plans into action.

He'd got the idea from the mascots. Each team had a mascot. These were icons depicting stereotype creatures with exaggerated features. The players on each team identified with the icons even though they'd never seen the creatures they represented. There had been nine at one time but only six remained. The Boar, the Bear, the Wolf, the Eagle, the Snake and his mascot; the Wyvern. In the earliest days, when he'd been alive, his armies had battled creatures similar to the wyverns when they had first come to this planet. He supposed that some must have survived.

Monitor drones were normally used to give him a bird's eye view of the game and he sapped some botch weapon-smiths to equip one of them for long range survey work and load-carrying. He sent it out into the jungles to the east to see if he could locate any of the creatures and, after many hours searching, he located some. In fact the jungles contained many tribes of suitable lizards, some were well over two metres tall.

The drone had strayed as far as the coast and Volinar saw something he'd not seen in over a thousand years; a ship. The ship contained a crew of dwarves and they were battling through a storm. He watched as it foundered on the rocks and he saw several bodies washed up on the shore. That gave him another idea. A small experiment would prove whether his plan was viable. When the drone returned to the stadium to refuel he loaded one of the precious scrying crystals into its manipulators. Then he sent it out again.

******

Captain Leif Thorssen had been a pirate all his life and he'd thought that he knew the sea and all her tricks but she'd caught him out. The storm had been bad but he'd sailed through worse. They'd been running a shipment of Kanis from the highland region up to the coast when it had hit and they'd headed towards the shore to try to get some shelter. Then a swell had lifted his ship and dumped it onto a submerged rock. The hull had split and it was every man for himself. He'd jumped but a vengeful wave had picked him up like a leaf and plastered him into the cliff face. Now the storm was over and dawn was breaking but Captain Thorssen didn't care much, he lay on the shore waiting to die. He felt no pain but already the cold sea had seeped right into his bones.

He was just wondering where he'd go. By rights he should go to the coral caves of Ràn to live with the giantess and spend his time in the halls of treasure that she'd accumulated from drowned sailors. He could already taste the salt water in his mouth. However there was an annoying buzzing like a giant bee and it was disturbing his peaceful anticipation. Then he decided he was seeing things; a huge, insect-like machine was standing over him. Something emerged from a crevice in its carapace and it plunged into his forehead. His last thoughts were, "No, this isn't right."

It wasn't right, he was thinking but it felt like his thoughts were swimming through treacle, "I was dying."

"Correct," the reply was in his head but he hadn't thought it, "you are dead."

"Then where is Ràn?" he managed.

"I'm afraid she's not coming. Do not fight it, after the first hundred years it gets better," the other voice said. Then what was left of

344

Captain Thorssen evaporated and the new dwimmerlaik stood up and rasped "What is your will, master?"

******

Once Volinar had his thrall he set it to capture one of the skogs. Although the lizard was taller than the ex-captain by half a metre it didn't stand a chance. The dwimmerlaik had no fear and it was armed with both a cutlass and the magical link to Volinar and the drone. The drone stunned the skog and the dwimmerlaik stabbed it several times in the chest with the cutlass. The ex-captain dragged the corpse to a clearing then watched dispassionately as the drone descended and lifted it into the sky.

Volinar examined the corpse through the sapped mind of the team-healer. "Yes," he thought, "The creature had sufficient neural capacity to be controlled by the battle harness but not enough sentience to be a problem. A force of these creatures would serve his purpose"

He returned to his scrying console. The dwimmerlaik had found a cave and had become dormant but it revived when he activated the link. "I am sending you a weapon which will stun the lizards. You will capture ten of them alive and await my order."

The drone had descended and the dwimmerlaik unloaded it. Part of the cargo was a long, forked rod that ended in a handle containing a trigger. When the trigger was pressed small sparks jumped between the junction of the fork and travelled up to the ends. The dwimmerlaik took the rod and its cutlass and went back into the forest. An hour later it emerged dragging an unconscious lizard behind it. Several hours later he put the tenth unconscious lizard onto the pile. Following its master's directions it took the harnesses from the crate and rigged them onto the lizards. Then it pulled a lead that ended in a multi-pronged plug out of each harness and plunged it into the base of each lizard's skull. The lizards never woke up. There was a considerable distance between Volinar's raiding party and Arnes but there was no easy way of transporting the whole group by drone. Volinar ordered the dwimmerlaik to activate the harnesses and then the group set off in the long trek to the town.

Volinar used the enforced delay in the plan to good effect, he sent a smaller monitor drone to hover high in the sky over the settlement of Arnes. His ancient brain trawled up the memory that this place had provided new recruits in the days when the game had been young. The drone descended and the monitors zoomed in. The town had grown considerably in the thousand years since he'd last seen it, but the temple was still there a little to the east in its own enclave. He set the almost silent machine down on top of a tall tower overlooking the courtyard and watched.

After two week's forced march the raiding party arrived at Arnes, Volinar had sapped one of the trainers to supervise the journey and so they arrived in good condition. Volinar had been one of the top dwarf generals of his age and he was a seasoned campaigner. A frontal attack would be costly and so he waited until the temple complex was asleep before acting. He set his mind into the state that he used to supervise a game and he took control of his troops.

The barracks were Volinar's target and he needed to be in and out of the complex quickly. The dwimmerlaik made short work of the gate guards without raising any alarm and the squad of lizards entered the complex unnoticed. Volinar was exhilarated, this was better than the game. The novice dormitories were split into two sections male and female. Each section was split into barrack dormitories. He needed the female one that contained the oldest girls. Five of the lizards positioned themselves to cover the escape then the dwimmerlaik and the rest silently crept into the building.

Volinar identified the two nuns who slept in rooms adjacent to the main dormitory and he used the dwimmerlaik to silence one of them in her sleep. The other one awoke feeling a blade at her neck and a clammy hand over her mouth. The dwimmerlaik's vocal chords were still functional and Volinar spoke through them. "Do not move or scream otherwise you die." The terrified woman obeyed. "Now, rouse the girls and tell them the same, if they resist or scream then they die. Gather them by the door. Do it!"

346

The terrified nun did as she'd been told. There had been one or two involuntary cries from the girls but the menace of the five, tall, armoured lizards kept them cowed. They huddled together in a group. The dwimmerlaik took ropes from its pack and tied the girl's hands together and attached them to other long ropes. There were sixteen girls and he attached the other ends of the ropes to two of the lizards. "Tell them that they must stay with the lizards or die."

The nun gave the instruction and Volinar was ready. The three unencumbered lizards left first. The dwimmerlaik pushed the nun in front of him next and Volinar made the remaining lizards drag the girls along after.

Volinar was pleased, they had managed the first part without incident. As the girls were herded out of the dormitory a door opened in one of the huts in the male side of the barracks. The unfortunate student who had only going to relieve himself fell almost instantly but he screamed as he died. Volinar had been ready. One part of his mind made the lizards with the girls ignore what was happening and herd them through the gates. Another part focussed on the scrying crystal in the dwimmerlaik's head and he sent a powerful wave of confusion through it towards the people emerging from the other buildings. Yet another part formed the rest of the lizards into an assault group. As people emerged from the buildings they were met by a hail of short javelins and they quickly retreated. Other people emerged from more distant buildings and ran towards the invaders. They were encouraged because the invaders appeared to be retreating. It was true but it was an orderly retreat. Five kept up the forward fire whilst the rear three ruthlessly killed anything that stood between them and the gate. The dwimmerlaik sent blasts of fear and confusion towards those approaching. Many of them became directly affected and they turned and ran causing even more confusion. Volinar hadn't had this much fun in a century. He gave one great push and a nearby building burst into flame.

The path to the gate was now clear and the girls and the nun were almost through. Volinar withdrew the dwimmerlaik through the gate along with three of the lizards and formed the remaining five into a defensive arc around it. So far the people coming from the temple had not used missiles but now someone had a bow. Two of the five lizards fell, one with an arrow piercing its breast and another with an arrow through the arm. Volinar ignored the injuries and made them move to the front and fight on. The remaining three lizards withdrew through the gate and set fire to the stockade around it before following the dwimmerlaik into the night. Volinar concentrated his efforts on the two wounded lizards. Their systems were failing but he still had plans for them: each harness contained a small self destruct charge. He moved the lizards directly against the towers either side of the gates and exploded them. The towers, already sagging from the fire, collapsed and then erupted into a shower of flaming timbers. The people inside the complex fled for shelter. The raiding party, with its prisoners, disappeared into the night.

Volinar had guided the dwimmerlaik to a hiding place in some woods and then he relinquished part of his control. This was better than the game but even as his mind bathed in the exhilaration, another part reminded him of his purpose. He had achieved the first part of his plan but there was still much to do. "However," he thought to himself, "the adventure had been fun. Maybe he'd plan another one sometime soon when conditions permitted."

******

The march back to Leikvangur went without a hitch. Volinar waited until they had been on the way for six days and had entered the pass through the mountains before he acted. The dwimmerlaik received Volinar's orders and lined up the lizards who were in a catatonic state induced by the battle harnesses. It went down the line pulling plugs from their skulls. Each one fell instantly and lay dead. The dwimmerlaik stripped off their harnesses and ordered eight of the bigger girls to don them. They were terrified and refused at first but a taste of the stun rod soon made them comply. To make things easier the girls were now tied in pairs left hand to right hand. Volinar spoke through the dwimmerlaik, "From this time you will only be tied in lines at night. I have spared your nun to prove to you that I wish you alive. You will not be harmed as long as you follow orders. Do not try to escape. You will not survive long in the wild."

This announcement was followed by the sound of the cargo drone descending. When it landed in a nearby clearing Volinar spoke again. "Food will be delivered each day. The nun will distribute it."

The dwimmerlaik seemed to slump as if something had gone out of him and the voice became weaker. "You," he said waving at the nun with the stun rod, "The crates contain packs of food. Give each girl a pack. Tell them that one pack must last the whole day. I will be watching you."

The nun recoiled from the stench coming from the creature but she obeyed. They girls were still her responsibility. She went over to the strange machine and began unloading the packs.

Ch 34: The Museum

Lord Skald examined his new acquisition. He couldn't work out why it was different to the other ancient artefacts that he'd collected but somehow it **was** different.

He'd always been interested in the artefacts of the ancients even when he was a novice. He'd come straight to the temple at the age of fourteen without having been recruited by the gathering. His family had always served the temple and there had always been a Lord or Lady Skald. Since they were descendants of the original settlers their line threw up one or two magical children every generation and the family knew that these youngsters needed to be placed in positions of power just as their non-magical relatives would be placed in the higher echelons of commerce. Neither his mother nor his father or any of his brothers had been capable of any significant magic and so of all of them he had inherited the title when his uncle had died.

His instructors had realised that he also had natural power especially in the mental arts. Hence, as a potential future Lord he had received better conditions and training and he would be fast tracked to become a council member. Therefore, when his fellows were training in the martial arts or in the healing sciences he had been trained in the skills of governance and control. He studied history, which is often taught to potential leaders and he built on his early aristocratic experiences to become skilled in the social graces. Instead of studying accounts they had taught him music and artistic appreciation.

However he had ambition and so, instead of becoming just another aristocratic figurehead who used advisors and flunkeys to do most of the work he had worked on keeping his mind well informed and gaining power. He had become a council member in his thirties and had risen to become the leader of the council some ten years ago. Occasionally he liked to relax and he found that contemplation of history was relaxing. Recent history was well documented but, further back in time it was fragmented. He enjoyed working on the puzzles that ancient history threw up.

Like everyone, he knew the basic story. The original settlers who had come to Svartalfheim had been dwarves like him but they had brought with them powerful artefacts that had enabled them to tame a world. Compared to those original settlers even the rich and powerful in his own society were insignificant. When had mighty dwarves changed from conquerors to farmers? When had heroes become humdrum? Why had this happened? He felt that the answer could be found in the study of the ancient artefacts left behind from those times. Since he was head of the council he couldn't go to seek out the answers himself so he brought the artefacts to a more convenient location.

The location was in the guild of scholars. It was a large guild. The main purpose of the guild was to train the secular instructors and teachers who provided learning to the general non-magical populace and there were many more of them than either wizards or creatives. The teachers provided basic education and practical skills for the employed; drovers, clerks, furniture and clothing producers, factory workers, builders, shopkeepers and the like.

The museum was buried deep in one of the more obscure parts of the guild archives and it had few visitors. Once Skald had adopted it as his private cache of treasures it received even fewer, his guards saw to that. However, it did have a permanent staff consisting of two elderly scholars and two or three post-graduate students who had been assigned there because they didn't have the temperament to be teachers but whose families were rich enough to ensure they didn't need to earn money.

He shut his eyes and he examined the brooch again, this time with his magical senses. There it was again, that slight difference that didn't match the other ancient artefacts on the shelves and tables around the museum. Where had the Lady got it from? As far as he knew, and the dossier he kept on her confirmed it, she had no dealings with the temple archaeologists on Skogrey. Therefore he had to assume that what she'd told him was true. She had found it

351

in an attic. He knew, from the dossier, that her parents had been amateur archaeologists using their family fortune to finance private expeditions. The dossier also told him that her parents had been killed whilst on an expedition to Skogrey. Had they found the brooch? If so how had it made its way back to the Holastan when they hadn't? Perhaps it was a find from an earlier expedition and they had gone back to the site to do more exploring and the accident or whatever had happened had been on a follow-up visit.

He couldn't recollect the details of those expeditions. He would have to look the reports up in the archives. Asking the Lady directly might make her suspicious. She must have found out about the burglary by now and she'd spoken to him about Cyten and his dealings on Skogrey only recently. She wasn't stupid and wouldn't believe in coincidences. He should have told Gibra to wait for a while before breaking in to the Lady's home but he'd been mesmerised by the thought of the brooch. He'd probably acted too hastily.

Taking out his magnifier he looked closely at the brooch's construction. There were the marks in the gold where the maker's cleaning had removed the original patina. He imagined that some of the marks looked like the peculiar runic script on the metal sheets. Perhaps there were traces of writing on the original surface; he would ask one of the scholars.

Skald was interrupted in his examination of the brooch by the approach of his assistant Blade.

"Your eminence, I am sorry to disturb you but we have a problem.

"What is it?" Skald barked.

"It is news from the temple on Skogrey. The reports from the temple staff and our own people investigating the ruins conflict on the detail but both sources agree that there was an armed raid and that many of the novices were taken. Since there are few military-trained justicers on Skogrey the temple staff were mostly unarmed and the reports agree that many were killed. It would appear that the attackers were skogs led by dwarven wizards."

"Our people led the attack?" Skald asked.

"We have received separate reports; one came from the temple at Arnes via scrying crystal relays between coastal outposts and the pilot islands and the other came directly from the archaeologists. The reports disagree on who carried out the attack. Witnesses from the temple group reported that the wizards wore uniforms such as our own officers wear. However, the archaeologists state that they could only find traces of a single armoured wizard in the memories of those novices that survived. It would appear that the wizard had considerable mental prowess; enough to confuse the many witnesses. The wizard has been tentatively identified as an outlaw who fled to Skogrey to escape the Justiciary. The distance from the excavations at Sudalyr to Arnes means that the archaeologists only arrived after the actual raid and so the story may have become confused."

"Damn, this is serious. Do we have direct contact with the temple?"

"Your eminence, after the raid the archaeologists shared their long range scrying crystal with Ulagrth, the current head of the resident mission in the town of Arnes. We have established a link with this crystal at the main temple here in Holastan. The link is subject to intermittent dropouts but we can speak to them directly when conditions are right."

"Very well," Skald said, "I will be along presently. Tell this Ulagrth person to make themselves available in one hour.

"Yes, your eminence." Blade said and he left.

Skald picked the brooch up and looked at it, "I'm afraid your mystery will have to wait. I have other matters to attend to." He walked across to one of the ancient scholars and said, "Examine this for any traces of what was inscribed on the original patina. I want to know if we have anything matching the script in any of the other writing that we've seen either on the metal sheets or on other artefacts."

"Yes your eminence," the scholar said.

Brannhår went to find Alfsen in his office. She waited patiently whilst he finished speaking to several of his clerks and then she said, "Sorry to disturb you Alfsen but have you made any progress on the matter we discussed?"

Alfsen smiled, "Yes, your theories proved very useful. Shall we go into my office and discuss the matter. I trust my staff in all matters of business but I feel that private matters need a little privacy."

They went into the office and Alfsen invited Brannhår to sit down. He opened a drawer in his desk and took out a sheaf of notes.

"As you suggested, I had Lord Skald followed by one of our agents in the temple and he seems to spend most of his time in his office receiving visitors or in his apartment in the first level underground. The apartment is not very large or luxurious and Lord Skald seems to use it mostly for sleeping. He takes most of his meals in the senior refectory. I therefore agree with you, if Lord Skald keeps a repository of artefacts then they are unlikely to be in the temple proper. Therefore I also made enquiries about the activities of Justicer Gibra. As we already know, she has a fearsome reputation and she appears to move easily between the temple where she is nominally a senior capper and the underworld of the city. We know she has links with Cyten and the information you provided confirms that she uses Cyten to 'import' artefacts for Lord Skald. We traced her movements as she collected small items from Cyten's new operating headquarters and delivered them to other parts of the city but the items all concerned the drug Sting and hence are irrelevant to this inquiry.

However, on one occasion we observed her going back to the derelict warehouse by the canal. She retrieved a crate and delivered it to the guild of scholars. It was unloaded at night by several students and taken to one of the outbuildings in the rear of the guild precinct. My agent enquired about the scholars and found that they work in the archive department and are not connected with the teaching schools. They are also easy to bribe. Lord Skald visits the archives frequently and the brooch that was stolen from my mistress also now resides in the archives. It would appear that his eminence has become fascinated with it and has asked some senior scholars to examine it."

"Then we must retrieve it before they do. If they are experts in ancient artefacts then they might discover that the brooch isn't ancient at all. If they tell Lord Skald then he is bound to investigate Silfuryn and we can't have that. I can't be with her all the time to prevent them discovering her magic. I will have to retrieve the brooch. I should have disguised it better but I never thought that it would end up in the hands of the head of the council."

"My mistress will want to accompany you. She enjoys your adventures and I myself have noticed that, since you entered our lives her life has changed. I have known her all her life and her grandfather was a friend as well as my employer. Before that fateful day when you and Officer Grimm came to her rescue I was fearful that she was becoming dependent on alcohol. Thankfully she no longer is. May I say that this fact pleases me greatly."

"I wouldn't dream of retrieving the brooch without Silfuryn's help, Alfsen. You may be sure of that."

******

Lord Skald sat in the room in the highest tower of the Justicer communications division. The division was located further up the mountain containing the Holastan and about two miles away from the city boundary. Scrying crystals operated better when they were away from the general magical noise of people and nowhere in the city was without people.

He hated heights, no true dwarf liked being so high above the ground, nevertheless he tried to focus on the message being relayed by the crystal operator. The head of the Skogrey mission Justicer Ulagrth was giving the report. "The situation is now clearer. A party of between ten and fifteen individuals entered the grounds of the temple complex after dark four days ago. The party consisted primarily of large skogs and wizards. However, the skogs behaved as if they were military trained unlike the wild ones we sometimes encounter in the interior. The wizards were also military. The party was armed with throwing spears and incendiary devices. The wizards also used fire projection in the attack. At least two of the skogs were killed when the gatehouse was destroyed by some explosive device and their remains show that they were wearing some sort of tough armour. However, not enough survived intact to determine its actual origin. The wizards projected powerful waves of fear and confusion. Since our members are all wizards they were severely affected. In all, twenty members were killed and another two dozen suffered physical injuries. Most of those affected by the mental projections have recovered but two remain severely traumatised.

The object of the raid seems to have been to abduct some of our older female novices. Sixteen of them are missing and they are not amongst the casualties. Those missing were all sleeping in the senior novice barracks when the attack occurred. There were two nuns also sleeping in the barracks, one of them was found with her throat cut and the other appears to have been taken with the girls.

We have tried to track the escape route used by the raiders but heavy rain in the past days has obliterated all traces. We do not know where the girls will be taken, neither do we know the reason for their abduction."

"The initial reports said that you identified one of the wizard raiders. Do you have any more information on that?"

"Yes, your eminence. We now believe that the wizard was using his powers of projection to make us believe that he was a fugitive from the gathering that took place here fifteen years ago. We have since found out by questioning the relatives that the individual's talent was in the divination of water and minerals. He is known to have fled to Vatersey some five years ago. Of course he may have returned but, if he has, his family knows nothing of it. We used one of our best mentalists in the interrogation and he believes that they are telling the truth."

Skald said, "So it would appear that, unless a water diviner has somehow re-trained as a master mentalist we have an unidentified leader for the raid. Is there anything else you wish to report?"

"No your eminence" Ulagrth said.

"Then I believe that I can now proceed." Skald said, "Thank you for your report Justicer Ulagrth. From your description it does sound as if the raid wasn't just some random attack. It was planned and executed with a specific purpose in mind although why anyone would want to abduct sixteen teenage girls from a temple in Skogrey is puzzling. There are many easier ways to obtain young women for all number of illegal and unsavoury purposes than travelling all the way across the home islands."

"Then you think that they are no longer on Skogrey, your eminence?" Ulagrth asked.

"Since there are no major conurbations on Skogrey other than Arnes, We must assume that they have been taken, or will be taken, to one of the other islands. The situation is serious and I will dispatch a squad of Ravens with support personnel to Skogrey immediately. In the meantime, Justicer Ulagrth, if you haven't already done so, declare a state of emergency and get the civil authorities to form a militia. These raiders may try again."

Skald nodded to the communications officer and the scrying link was broken. He turned to his assistant, Blade, "You heard my decision, make it happen. I suggest that, since we know that the source of Sting is on Skogrey the Ravens should be given a secondary remit; they are to investigate the drug traffickers at that end of the chain. They must be operating out of some coastal base down there. It may be linked to the disappearance of these girls. Tell the squad to make enquiries and use their initiative to stop the drug supply at source. Tell them that they will have my support in this matter but they are not to alarm the locals by making too much fuss in Arnes itself unless there are significant developments."

"Yes, Your eminence," Blade replied.

357

******

The night guard snapped awake, he hadn't meant to doze off but he'd had a long day down at the canal loading barges and usually he could catch up some sleep on this job. He had five children and a wife who wasn't well and so he spent all day and all night trying to earn enough money to keep them all fed. Something had woke him and he got up to investigate. Looking along the corridor he thought he saw a flicker of light on in one of the museum rooms. The museum gave him the shivers. All that was in there were some old, rusted pieces of armour, a few rusty weapons, some old dessicated skeletons and bits of stone with peculiar carvings on them. There was nothing to be frightened of but all the same whenever he walked past the door he could feel the hair standing up on the back of his neck.

He was strong, lifting crates all day developed muscles but he was wise enough to know that no matter how strong you were a weaker man with a sword or knife could kill you if he was fast. Therefore the guard was careful. He crept along close to the wall and looked into the open door of the room. The room wasn't entirely dark; there was a transparent panel high up on one wall that let some of the aurora in. However it wasn't much help; the dancing green light just made all the shadows move as if the old armour and skeletons were alive. He felt a chill run down his back and he turned suddenly convinced that there was something behind him. His eyes opened wide. There was a light, it flickered and danced but it wasn't made by any flame. It looked like the aurora but it was coming through the wall. The light was followed by an arm and then a body. The body was a woman's and it was wearing a long flowing garment and it had just walked through the wall. The guard didn't wait. Nobody paid him enough to fight ghosts and wights. He turned and fled. Three minutes after the echoes of him crashing through the exit doors had died away there was a giggle.

Brannhår emerged from the shadows where she'd been hiding and she turned to Silfuryn. "Do you think that he'll raise the alarm?"

"No, from the look on his face he won't stop running until he's safely home and hiding under the bedsheets."

"It was funny though," Brannhår said, "Even I could feel the tension as he was creeping down the corridor. I must say that the trick of coming through the wall is most impressive, I've never actually seen you do it before."

"Well it wasn't too hard, the wall is only plaster so it didn't take a lot to slide myself through but I think what scared him most was the whisp-light. It probably brought back all those ghost stories that we were taught as children."

"Well, the fun's over, let's see if we can find the brooch and get out of here. Do you have the substitute?" Silfuryn said.

Brannhår patted her pocket, "Right here, it looks the same as the other one but it doesn't affect magic."

Silfuryn nodded, "Let's go."

After a quick search of the museum Silfuryn said, "I can't sense the brooch here. There are quite a few things that have a lingering magical glow but nothing like the brooch. We'll have to try elsewhere. Perhaps it's in one of the offices."

They walked slowly down the corridor, Brannhår used the sense that she used to detect metals and Silfuryn used her own sense of magic. They stopped outside one of the doors and almost simultaneously they said, "It's in here."

The door had a brass plaque on it which said, 'No Entry, Staff only' on it and it was locked. Silfuryn took out her lock-picks and the door was open in seconds. They entered what looked like an ordinary office. "It's in this desk," Silfuryn said. The drawer's locked, just wait a minute. Can you give me a bit more light?"

"Is this better," Brannhår had taken another lamp from her pocket. It was one of the ones based on the stingbush technology and it gave a nice intense white beam.

The drawer lock gave a click and Silfuryn pulled it open. She took out the brooch and Brannhår handed her the replacement. Silfuryn was about to swap the brooches when she saw something that grabbed her attention. There was a piece of paper with her name on it. At first she thought that it had something to do with the brooch but she picked it up and read it.

" *even though we followed the same clues that were retrieved from the Risavinur notebooks we were unable to determine which path they took to the underground portions of the ruins. We found no trace of the artefacts that they were searching for and neither did we find any other traces of the expedition than those we'd found in the surface tunnels. We can only conclude that the Risavinur party went into the ruins by some other route and met their end there. It is puzzling why they left their notebooks and the artefacts in their surface camp unless the underground expedition was intended to be a short one and they were expecting to return to the surface within the day.* "

She showed it to Brannhår, "Who are they writing about, what does this expedition it have to do with you?" she asked.

"The Risavinur party are my parents, I told you that they were killed when I was small, but nobody ever told me any details of how it happened. It looks like we've stumbled upon a clue. This document says that they left some notebooks behind. I wonder if Alfsen knows anything about them?"

"Well, we certainly can't look for them tonight. It will be dawn in half an hour and we need to be out of here by then," Brannhår said.

"Yes, just let me lock the drawer and the doors then we'll get back to the Holastan. You've got the brooch?"

"Right here," Brannhår said holding it up.

Silfuryn nodded, "Let's go then."

Ch 35: Time and Tide

\Q looked at the gleaming carapace of her counterpart. How much of it is still even vaguely capable of appreciating its place in the universe? If the rest of those that were left behind were like this one then it might be too late. In the years since she'd left Leikvangur and the Game behind she'd travelled to many different worlds and seen many strange things. She knew about the twists and turns that were space-time and she'd used them to her own ends. Still she still prided herself that she was the same rational being that had set out on her life's journey in this universe as the master maker in the army of General Siskevn over two thousand years before. Of course, she reminded herself, that didn't mean that she was physically or even mentally the same and neither were any of her peripherals but the core essence was still there. How could she convince \A that its path and those of his compatriots was fundamentally wrong. She could give \A the unbridled truth; straight into its processors so to speak. However, such a tactic might cause an irreparable breakdown and since there were only twenty two of their kind left in the multiverse the loss of seven of their number would be catastrophic for their species. No, she had to do this gently and minimise any casualties. The first thing she needed to do was to give \A a personal sense.

"\A, have you never wondered why, of all the sentients on this world [A-G] are the only ones who continuously chase time to its fundamentals?" \Q asked.

"This unit cannot comprehend the concept, we do not 'chase' and time is an abstract concept to measure entropy not a physical thing."

"Fine, let me express the concept in another way. Sentience is present in many species. Analyse the timescale of all sentient processing capability statistically and express the deviation of the sentient processing of the individuals [A-G] from the norm." \Q said.

\A answered a tiny fraction of a second later, "Approximately ten to the eighteen."

\Q said "Would you therefore classify [A-G] as sentients close to the norm?"

"No," \A replied.

"However, sentients all over the universe have had billions of years to evolve to the optimum timescales for their species. Why is it that the timescale of the sentients [A-G] differs by a factor of a million billion? Surely if your timescale is optimum then the factor should be much lower."

"Agreed, however we believe that it is optimum for us." \A said.

\Q replied, "However more than half your species operates on a much lower factor. I myself am an example."

\A said, "You might be upgraded."

"I do not wish to be upgraded in that sense, my part of our species has chosen to achieve the optimum by an alternative strategy. We have adopted this alternative strategy to reduce our deviation from the norm to a mere factor of ten to the four." \Q replied quickly.

"What you are implying is that we should reduce our operating timescale to the one that this unit is forced to use whilst I am communicating with \Q and when observing the ephemerals."

"Exactly." \Q said.

"But ephemeral timescales are hopelessly inefficient, [A-G] would be incapable of maintaining Leikvangur with such low processing speeds" \A objected.

"If they were linear I would agree but I and the others of our species who are ^[A-G] do not operate linear; we operate multi-parallel. This allows us to chose whichever timescale we desire without unidirectional evolution."

"This unit would be incapable of operation at such low speed. Its architecture will not allow." \A said.

"Exactly," \Q replied, "What is required is not a total rebuild merely a change in architecture."

"This unit cannot see the benefit." \A objected.

\Q grew exasperated, "The benefit is that you will be able to expand your interaction with the universe. [A-G] have become isolated and focussed on a single task; the maintenance of Leikvangur and the status quo for the managers, who are a vanishingly small percentage of the sentients even in this current solar system. [A-G] have become too specialised, too focussed on a single tiny aspect of existence. In essence thirty one percent of our species has become focussed on maintaining six undead and a tiny group of a few thousand ephemerals. I consider that a gross inefficiency and a waste of our species talents."

\A said, "When you express it that way this unit can appreciate the inefficiency. However this unit does not have a solution available "

"Ah, but you can learn, my friend, you can learn," \Q thought internally but transmitted, "Would you \A consider an experiment, a challenge to your processing skills that may show you the benefits of an architecture rearrangement? It could be performed using your existing architecture and would not pose a risk to yourself." \Q asked.

"Since I have already volunteered to use part of my processing to monitor situations on an ephemeral timescale this unit sees little risk. This unit will consider what you have said. Then [B-G] will be informed of the result. Do you have any suggestions of how the experiment should be initiated?"

"I suggest that you not only monitor the ephemerals but also examine individuals to determine their differing architectures," \Q replied.

\A appeared to have come to a decision. "Your input will be considered. However the original purpose of your visit is now redundant. The general meeting decided the approach to be adopted. Therefore the effort you have expended in coming here has been unavoidably wasted."

"Don't worry, I think my visit was worthwhile. Incidentally, what was the instigative cause of the meeting?" \Q asked.

"The observation of the re-discovery of electrical technology by the ephemerals."

\Q smiled to herself, "Then it is [A-G] who have wasted their time. Electrical technology is discovered and re-discovered somewhere in the universe almost every day. Most sentient civilisations cope. You would know this if you weren't so narrowly focussed. It is one benefit of using the multi-parallel architecture."

"I will consider what you have said," \A answered.

"You do that, but I must be off. I may return some time to see if you made any progress," \Q answered and she set several peripherals started on determining what phasing she needed to get her out of Leikvangur. She did, however, notice one small thing. \A had stopped referring to itself as 'this unit' and now used the more personal 'I'.

 Before the last vestiges of \Q had faded into the alternate dimensions the golden one known as \A had thought about what \Q had said. The implications had been profound but they had also been disturbing. It had decided to undertake the experiment that \Q had suggested. The most recent interaction with an ephemeral had been... it consulted the Wiki, with an ephemeral designated Seventeen of the Majors of Volinar. This would be a good place to start. There would be plenty of time to develop a stratagem for interaction, the ephemeral known as Seventeen was currently in the commissary and it would take \A almost ten minutes to reach her. It was a pity that ephemerals only communicated using vocal audio signals, a direct electromagnetic communications transfer would have been more efficient. The unit known as \A mentally shrugged and set off on the journey.

******

There was some sort of hold up further down the line. In one way it was fortunate as Seventeen was due to report for sex after she'd eaten and she really wasn't looking forward to that. Considering that it was between seasons there had been a lot of activity in the Volinar camp recently. She'd noticed that there had been a lot more cancellations and last minute changes recently. It was almost as if Volinar himself was deliberately messing with the schedules. She could think of no other person who had the power to make so many changes in such a short time. In any case a short delay in getting her meal wouldn't cause her any problems.

She watched what was happening. One of the supervisors was stood with his hands folded, blocking the line whilst several botches worked behind him loading food trays onto a trolley. There were a lot of trays. She turned to the person next in line to her. He was one of the junior coaches. "Lots of strange things happening recently," she said, "Do you know what's going on?" The coach gave her a blank stare, "I haven't noticed anything out of the ordinary," he replied. She went for broke, "It was a shame about Fourteen of Severell."

The assistant coach looked at her, "Who?"

"Fourteen of Severell issued a challenge and lost," she said tactfully.

The assistant looked at her blankly, "Challenge? I don't remember any challenge."

"Another one," Seventeen thought, "was she the only one that could remember what had happened?"

"Right," she said to the assistant, "I must have been mistaken. Have a good meal."

The assistant turned away and she could tell that the encounter was fading from his brain with each passing second. She didn't know what was the matter with her. Was she the only one that ever remembered what had happened in the past? The more she thought about it the more it seemed that everyone only lived in the moment

365

and events in the past were forgotten quickly. "But that can't be true," her mind objected, "If they couldn't remember anything then how did they remember how to fight or to read or even how to speak?"

She became aware that everyone was staring at her. No, not at her but something behind her. She whirled around. A mech had silently rolled up behind her. It said, "You are the ephemeral Seventeen of the Majors of Volinar. Will you converse with this unit?"

Seventeen didn't know what to do so she said, "Err... Of course."

"Good," the mech said, "You must forgive this unit... sorry I am not used to operating this slowly... you must forgive me but I need some information about ephemerals. Is this acceptable?"

Seventeen looked around, everyone had retreated as if she was contaminated with some virus; she was on her own. She didn't dare refuse; she said, "Yes. What information do you need?"

"The information is difficult to elicit via this mode of communication. Will you permit me to use a faster one?" the mech said.

"Err... yes," Seventeen said.

"Good," the mech said. A tentacle extruded from the mech's carapace and the end formed itself into a narrow band. The band circled her head and came to rest across her brow and temples. It felt cold but not uncomfortable. There was a tingling sensation as it tightened onto the scrying crystal embedded in her forehead but it disappeared quickly.

She could hear a tinny voice in her head. It seemed to be talking to itself, "Terrible inefficiency... Multiple repetitive fragmentation... wasteful... need repair and defragmentation before architecture analysis can be performed... holographic storage can assist." then it got louder and was talking to her, "The holographic storage in your primary cortex is broken. Will you permit repair?"

Seventeen didn't know what to do. Perhaps the reason she was having all these odd memories that others didn't have and those weird dreams was because her mind was broken as the mech had said. It had been easier before when she didn't have things hanging over from previous days. She said "Yes, please repair it."

It was just as well that she didn't know what she'd let herself in for, or she'd probably have run screaming from the room.

The repair took a long time, the holographic nature of the information and the poly-connectivity had given \A a few problems. All in all \A was pleased with his efforts. It had been a major project and he'd learned much about the sentients that he knew as ephemerals. \A felt strange, he had never attempted such a continuously absorbing task for nearly two thousand years and he felt (the concept was unfamiliar) tired. It had taken over half an hour but he had succeeded. As he congratulated himself he realised that some of the information that he'd gleaned during the task had affected his own processes. He now thought of himself as a he. Was this what \Q had been trying to tell him. She, after all, referred to herself as a she.

Seventeen woke and someone was shouting at her. "You have defaulted on your duty," the coach was screaming in her face, "you were scheduled to report for sex over fifteen minutes ago."

She shook her head, there was something wrapped around it and her fingers reached up to explore. The coach noticed, "What is that?" he demanded then she saw his eyes glaze over, "Oh yes, you have permission from the healers. Nobody told me that you sustained a head injury during practice. Now get along with you and do your duty."

Seventeen got to her feet and, operating almost on automatic, she staggered across the room and out of the door. She made it to the recreation centre but her half-hour time slot had nearly expired. A botch holding a clipboard came over, "I'm afraid there's been a problem and we are running late; your slot was rescheduled, you'll have to wait fifteen minutes."

"What is happening?" Seventeen wondered, She'd been about to get something to eat and then one of the golden ones, she'd just realised that the mech had been a golden one, had come right up to her and had asked questions. Then it, no, he, had done something inside her head and she'd woken up with something around her head and the coach had bawled her out and now her slot in the recreation centre had been miraculously rescheduled so that she wasn't late after all.

She was sure it had something to do with the golden one but her head was spinning and she couldn't focus. She tried closing her eyes but that didn't help so she tried to focus on something in the distance. There were a group of people being herded into the recreation centre at the other end. They looked like young girls but they clearly weren't players. They shuffled along guided by supervisors wielding shock canes. That seemed wrong, then she noticed that all the girls were wearing training collars like those that were used on the very young before they'd learned to obey. Several of the girls were crying. Again Seventeen thought that this was unusual, adults weren't allowed to display emotion off the field. Strange things were happening all around her but her mind didn't want to focus. She shook her head to clear it, someone was talking, "Seventeen Volivar Majors and Sixty-Three Volivar Juniors, cubicle six," announced an assistant coach who was staring at his own clipboard.

That was her. She stood and made her way through into the recreation centre proper. A botch gave her a towel and a key; it was labelled six. She walked over to the cubicle and saw that the door was open. Her partner for the next half hour was already inside. She hung the towel on the back of the door without looking at him and heard the door lock click shut.

"Well if it isn't the high and mighty princess and she's got herself a crown. This is going to be fun." She'd heard the whining voice somewhere before and she remembered, it was the obnoxious kid who'd threatened her on the day that she'd had to practise in dirty armour. She turned and stared at him. The recreation centre was the only place two people could be and be sure they weren't disturbed. Somewhere along the line somebody had decided that a certain amount of rough-housing during sex was tolerable; it tended to get people excited and that often increased the chances of conception, so the theory went. Seventeen didn't care about the chances of conception. She was locked in this cubicle with this hormone crazed kid for the next half hour and nobody would interfere. "Come near me and you're dead," she said.

"Oh no, princess, we have to do it. It's your duty as a member of the team," he mocked, "What's the matter? Can't take a real man on without weapons?"

Seventeen thought, "I could probably take him but then I'd be in trouble. Better just act dumb." She went over to the bench and lay down with her legs apart. The junior looked puzzled, he'd been looking forward to a fight and forcing her but she'd just lain down. She even looked bored. He went across and climbed on top of her and he felt himself rise. She wriggled and he was inside her and her arms were around his back and she was whispering in his ear, "Lie still and listen, I've phased my fingers into your back just above your kidneys. I'm good enough to phase just my fingernails back into normal. I'll probably lose one or two if I do, but do you know what will happen to your kidneys if I do? Let's put it this way, you won't enjoy peeing for a long time. Now lie still and don't move for the next ten minutes, it will be good mental discipline practice. If you're good then I might just phase my fingers out without leaving anything behind. Don't try anything, I'm just as good at phasing other parts of my anatomy." She squeezed her abdominal muscles around his flagging erection just in case he hadn't got the message.

After ten minutes she let him up. She had done her duty and had sex, technically he had as well but he was in no mood to talk. He sat silent on the seat in the corner until the buzzer went. Shortly before she heard the door click open, the room filled with a vapour that smelled of menthol and then the blue light in the ceiling came on. Seventeen watched as the youth's eyes became blank but she didn't feel anything. She realised that this was the first time that she'd ever remembered sex, in fact it was the first time she'd remembered quite a lot of things.

As she stood up she felt wetness between her legs, "Shit, the little bastard came anyway. I hope I'm not pregnant."

"You are not," said a voice in her head.

"What the hell!! Are you still inside there?" she thought.

"Of course, I am maintaining my brief of observing your actions although I have reduced the frequency with which I interface. Currently this stands at one percent. Your short term storage is adequate to interpolate. This would have been difficult if the mnemnosynth had removed the memory; therefore I blocked its action."

Seventeen raised her hand to the band around her head. It must be associated with the Golden One speaking inside her head and she supposed that she was stuck with it for now. She shrugged and went to consult the roster but stopped herself after a few paces. After sex was always sleep; she didn't need the roster to remind her now that memory served the same purpose. Well, if sleep was scheduled, then sleep it would be.

Ch 36: Negotiations

Once the brooch was back in Alfsen's safekeeping Brannhår and Silfuryn retired to Silfuryn's sitting room to discuss what they'd discovered.

"You never told me what happened to your parents. Those notes seemed to imply that they were on Skogrey when they died." Brannhår said.

Silfuryn sighed, "I was very young when it happened and so my personal memories are muddled. I didn't see my parents much after I was moved to the countryside to hide my magic and so my immediate family was my Grandfather and Alfsen. I can remember them going away and the last image I have of them is seeing them dressed in what I would call explorer's gear; rough jackets and trousers with dozens of pockets and they both had peculiar rounded hats on that were somewhere between a helmet and a wide brimmed bonnet. I remember them hugging me and then they spoke to Grandfather and then a carriage came and took them away. I can remember Grandfather coming into my room some weeks later with a very stricken look on his face. I could tell he was upset but he wasn't crying. He told me that my mother and father were missing and they might not come home for some time. It was months later before I learned the truth. They had been on an expedition and despite weeks of searching nobody was able to say where they were. It was assumed that they'd perished but no bodies were ever found. Do you know, I never asked about that expedition. I didn't know where they'd gone or what they'd been doing. All that I knew was that everyone, including grandfather thought that they had died.

Grandfather became my guardian and as he was ex-military he started to train me as best as he could so that I could take over the family fortune when the time came. I worked hard and although the memory of my parents never disappeared completely it became less painful. It was a fact, a harsh fact, but there was nothing anyone could do to change it so it was best to just accept it and move on.

I never tried to investigate what happened because Alfsen and my Grandfather would never talk about it and, over the years I became busy with other things."

"I suppose that it's like my other memories," Brannhår said, "I think they come from another life, they are me but not me. I can't ever go back to that life and I am not sure that I would want to even if I could. I am a dwarf and a maker and that's enough for me."

"I see," Silfuryn said, "but that report implied that, the person who wrote it knew where they were. He just couldn't get to them. I would like to find them, bring them back and put them to rest properly. The report mentioned notebooks and they might give me a clue where I could find them. Maybe some day I will mount my own expedition and go and look."

"I found some ruins on Skogrey," Brannhår said, "I don't think they were the same ones where your parents died but I never got a chance to explore them properly. If you'd like some company when you go to find your parents then I'd be happy to come along."

"That would be ironic, the Ghost and the Spirit going in search of the long-dead in ancient ruins," Silfuryn said, "However, we have more practical problems to solve; we have to change civilisation before we can go off enjoying ourselves. Let's sleep on it."

"Agreed."

******

"What do you mean there's no trace?" Lord Skald said. He was angry. As far as he could see the team that he'd sent to Skogrey in response to the attack on the temple had made zero progress. It had been eight months and they'd discovered exactly nothing. After six months the investigation had expanded from Skogrey to all of the islands in the home group. Despite applying the full resources of the justicers on each island, the reports had all come back negative. Nobody had found the girls either alive or dead and every brothel from Vatersey to Lungrey had been searched. He'd told the Ravens on Skogrey to go easy on the natives but maybe it was time to show a bit more iron fist instead of velvet glove.

To top it all Cyten had expanded his drug organisation somehow and there were now clusters of drug abusers in cities and towns on Hawnarey and Raasrey and the man hadn't been caught yet. Skald wasn't stupid, if Cyten hadn't been caught then it was certain that someone inside the justicers was tipping him off. Skald had his suspicions of who that someone was and, despite the fact that she was his main supplier of artefacts, he was sure that that someone was Officer Gibra. Maybe he could kill two birds with one stone and post her to Skogrey. Cyten's main source of the raw ingredients for Sting was Skogrey, if Gibra was buddy-buddy with Cyten her presence on Skogrey might liven the investigation up in more ways than one.

******

Silfuryn was in Brannhår's workshop watching the maker fiddle with something that looked very much like a huge golden feather.

"I've been thinking," she said, "Remember when we retrieved that brooch and found that report about my parents."

"Mmm…" Brannhår replied though lips holding a dozen pins.

"Well, I said that someday I might like to go to Skogrey to see if I can find what happened to them. I think that now might be the time."

Brannhår took the pins out and dropped them into a dish, "Why now?"

"Because we have the time. Everything is going to plan, the ironwoods and sting-bushes are planted and Karol is keeping an eye on them, Torin is building the transmission system, Alfsen has his finger on the supply chains, you've got fifty eager apprentices working on your ideas and building them and my people are getting on with the construction. Changing a society the way your discoveries will do takes time. Things are going to happen but none of them will be completed soon. We could easily take a month or two out and, when we come back, things still won't be finished."

Brannhår frowned, "Yes, you're right, we could go off on some wild adventure for a couple of months and things probably wouldn't have changed much but what if something goes wrong?"

"Nothing is going to go wrong, don't you trust Karol and Torin and Alfsen?" Silfuryn said.

"Of course," Brannhår replied.

"Then trust them to let us know if things start to change. I will arrange for an agent to hire a couple of fljúgbátr and have them on standby, one here and another on Skogrey. With our semaphore links to the ports, any messages will at most only be a couple of days old. We could get back on the next fljúgbátr.

Please," Silfuryn said, "It would mean a lot to me and you never know, you might discover something interesting in those ancient sites."

"Fine but before we go you had better read these," Brannhår said and she went across to her desk and took a case from the bottom drawer. She thumped the case on the table and Silfuryn reached for it. As she opened it Brannhår continued, "These are copies of your parent's notebooks. I asked Alfsen about them a few months ago and he dug them out of your grandfather's belongings. I've managed to translate several of the metal writing sheets that the ancients used. They're quite interesting."

"You've had these for months, why didn't you tell me?" Silfuryn asked.

"Because you were busy. I knew you'd get to them eventually but it never seemed the right time to tell you," Brannhår replied.

******

"They couldn't do this to her," the Gibbet raged in her head, "She had powerful friends. They had no right to send her half way across the world. She wasn't some common flatfoot capper, she was the Gibbet; known and feared across the city." She was so angry that

374

her fingernails were dug into her fists and they were drawing blood but she didn't dare take a swing at the officer in front of her. That would really be suicide. The officer looked so fragile but she knew his reputation. He was a Raven, and not just any old Raven, he was Blade, personal assistant to Lord Skald. Touching Blade was akin to touching Skald and that was more trouble than she wanted. She could try blackmail, she supplied Skald with his little toys but, at the first sign of any trouble from her, Skald wouldn't hesitate and she'd be found floating in the canal before she could draw a breath.

"Is that clear, officer Gibra?" Blade said.

She hadn't been listening, so she just stared back at him with a blank look. He sighed, "I will repeat the order: You are to transfer to the temple at Arnes on Skogrey. Lord Skald has told me to tell you that you are to, and I quote 'get things moving on the missing girls investigation'. I am sure that you will certainly make an impact. You are to make your way to Arnes by whatever transport is most convenient. A stipend for the journey will be provided. At Arnes you are to report to the head of the temple, Justicer Ulagrth who will assign you your duties. Is that now clear Officer Gibra?"

She managed a "Yes, sir." through gritted teeth then turned and left.

All the way down the corridor and out into the street her mind was plotting. She thought that she might just disappear, she had enough money but where could she go? She couldn't stay in Griprey, nobody left the justicers, they hunted you down and the best you could hope for was a quick death. That meant that she'd have to go to one of the other islands. Well, if she was going to another island, one shit hole place was as good as another so she might as well grit her teeth and go to Skogrey. At least she knew a few people there, Cyten got most of his raw Kanis from there and Cyten owed her. She'd go to Skogrey all right but she wasn't going to spend a week throwing her guts up on an ordinary ship. She could hitch a ride on one of Cyten's fljúgbátr Once she got to Skogrey she could take it from there. She'd go to see Cyten.

"Everything is arranged," Silfuryn said, "We can leave the week after next, once Torin has completed the first transmission line and you've checked it. The fljúgbátr can make Arnes in two days. All we need to do is pack."

Brannhår nodded, "I'll have to take what we need for camping, plus there are a few odds and ends that might come in useful. I was thinking of taking one of the sjálitla but we probably wouldn't need it while we're exploring ancient ruins."

"Well, get a move on, and don't forget your spirit armour and your hammer," Silfuryn reminded her.

"As if," Brannhår replied.

******

"You owe me for tipping you off about the raids, without me you'd be captured or dead." the Gibbet said.

"Take it easy, what you want happens to suit me. There are justicers poking around in my operations in Skogrey. You might be able to put them off the scent. Vatnarheim on Vatersey looks ripe for the picking and Skogrey is a much closer base than Holastan is," Cyten paused, Yes, I'll give you passage but I'll need you to help me. One of my supply ships went down in a storm and I need someone local to replace it. You could do that job for me."

"I'm not a sailor," the Gibbet replied.

"I know that! You don't have to sail the thing yourself you just need to find a local pirate who's got a suitable ship and who can do as they're told," Cyten said.

"Fine, and I assume that you'll be grateful in the usual way?" the Gibbet said.

"Of course, of course, once the supply of the raw herb is back to normal you'll get your cut." Cyten said.

Ch 37: The Symbiote

Seventeen closed her eyes and drew in a huge breath, that had been close. It was funny, she reflected, before the golden one had repaired her memory the Game had just been the Game. She'd fought with her teammates against the other teams and had never worried about the consequences. Death had been just another occupational hazard and she hadn't worried about it. Now, her new mind kept imagining the awful consequences of any misstep. She was experiencing fear for the first time in her life and she didn't like it.

"I can neutralise the hormones and reaction chemicals if that will make it better," said the unbidden voice in her head.

"No, don't do that, you might make me so brave that I become foolish and make mistakes. Thank you for that last intervention, it was a tricky phase and I would have dumped half my troops without your help." she said.

"There is no need for thanks, in order for me to continue my observations I require you to be alive. Surviving the game is therefore a subordinate goal and if I can help the process then I am willing to do so." \A said.

"I should take a shower," Seventeen said.

"It would seem sensible. I will neutralise the mnemnosynth."

Seventeen screwed up her courage, she was used to doing what she was told to do; it had been drilled into her since she was born and so initiating an action herself without orders was novel. She hesitated, "Do you mind if I ask you a question?"

\A replied, "I have no objections, you provide me with information; it seems only correct that I provide you with reciprocal information."

The golden one used unfamiliar words and tortuous sentences but she took this to mean that she could ask.

"You tell me that you will neutralise the mnemnosynth; that means that it will not affect my memory."

"Correct"

"But it doesn't affect some memories, even when it is not neutralised I still remember how to speak and how to fight and other things."

"Ah, this is good, you are showing curiosity. It indicates that your cortex is comparing information and finding anomalies or incongruent suppositions. You therefore seek an explanation of the dichotomy," \A replied.

Seventeen didn't think that it was much of an answer and she was just about to say something when the mech went on.

"In the case of the mnemnosynth it stimulates the parts of the cortex where recently acquired memories are stored and causes noise to occur in the data streams. The cortex cannot interpret these streams efficiently and they are discarded as irrelevant: in your terms, you forget. If the data stream is uncorrupted then the cortex can integrate the data into long term storage for later retrieval or further integration; hence you remember this data. In the normal process, without the intervention, the temporary data stream is held for further processing and if the data is sufficiently novel then it is integrated. You can remember how to speak and other things because the information required to create speech is contained in a different part of your mind to your recent memory of events."

"But sometimes I now remember things that happened after I became a player and started using the showers." Seventeen added.

"Yes, it is an unfortunate side effect of the mnemnosynth process. The mnemnosynth interfaces with the physical brain through the scrying crystal embedded in your forehead. The attachment of the crystal into your brain is imprecise and hence areas of the cortex that are not associated with recent events can be affected. It would appear that the managers do not consider this to be a problem. In fact they use it to their advantage on occasion to obliterate more than the data from recent events. Do you remember the occasion when you were a youngling when the roof collapsed?"

Seventeen thought and suddenly the memory was there. It had been after a training session with bladed weapons. She and several of her classmates were talking when there had been a loud rumbling noise. The next thing she knew was that there was flaming red water falling from the ceiling and people were screaming. Two of her classmates had been hit by lumps of the stream as it had broken up and they had caught fire. She had watched in horror as they died. Seventeen shuddered, "Yes I remember it now."

"You will not find that memory in any other of the ephemerals. The managers considered it too disruptive as it had affected a whole generation of players. The event was too widespread and too novel to be erased by normal means and so they ordered a general wipe; a mnemnosynth burst which affected all ephemerals; even those without crystals fitted. It is not the only occasion where the general wipe has been performed."

Seventeen remembered her first dream, "That's what I dreamed about, there were holes everywhere in my head and you were there."

"Yes, you are correct; it was one of the aspects of your mentality that led me to choose you as my main experimental interface."

Seventeen frowned, "You have others like me?"

"Of course, how could I expect to research the ephemeral cortical structure without comparatives. You are my main interface because you have qualities that the others lack. In particular I was attracted to you because you are entered in the Wiki. I entered you because of your ability to sense microscopic irregularities in materials."

Seventeen was somehow disappointed. She had thought that her joining with the golden one was unique. It made her special. Being just one of many 'experimental subjects' was somehow diminishing. She decided to change the subject. "Can I ask another question?"

379

"Certainly," \A said.

"I have noticed that I have not been scheduled for sex as frequently as I used to be. Is it because of the wild girls?"

"If, by wild girls you are referring to the captive ephemeral females then the answer is partially; yes. The wild girls were captured by your manager Volinar to replenish and refresh the gene pool of the players. For more than fifteen centuries players have bred with players to create youngsters who may or may not become players themselves. Those who do not show the necessary magical skills are called botches and they serve in non-combat and menial roles. Those who are chosen as potential players are fitted with scrying crystals but not all of these become players, the ones that don't become coaches and supervisors and healers. Thus the hierarchy is maintained through the generations. Recently, over the past few hundred years, the interbreeding of players with players has caused particular trait to become exaggerated which have affected the manager's enjoyment of the game. Volinar realised this and he has sought to widen the gene pool by introducing magically talented females to breed with player males. Unfortunately these 'wild ones' haven't been indoctrinated with the culture of the Game nor are they able to be fitted with scrying crystals hence they are controlled by shock collar such as infants wear when they are being trained.

Since twelve of the sixteen 'wild ones' are now pregnant the temporary disruption to the sex assignments will end soon However, this is not the full reason why your personal scheduling has reduced. I have observed that you have an aversion to participating in the sessions and therefore I have altered your scheduling appropriately. Do you wish me to restore it?"

"Err... no, but don't exclude me from the roster entirely. My absence might be noticed and I would get into trouble for non compliance with my duties."

"Yes, I understand. I will arrange it as you wish. Do you wish me to schedule a particular partner?" \A said.

That would be as bad as not participating at all, "No, a random assignment will be fine. I can look after myself."

******

Sleep just wouldn't come; normally she had no trouble getting off to sleep but every little click and whistle in the dormitory seemed to jerk her awake. The vision of her classmates burning haunted her mind. She couldn't mention the incident to anyone, nobody except her would remember it. It wasn't the horror of their death; she'd seen enough horrific deaths on the playing field, but the fact that the incident had officially never happened. How many other events had been wiped from history? She forced her mind to think about something different; think about those wild ones. It didn't seem too bad that they had been captured and brought in to improve the breeding program. Her mind stopped in its tracks. They had been '*brought in*'; brought in from where? There was nowhere outside Leikvangur was there? Yes there was! She knew it but she didn't know how she knew it. Wait, there was a vague memory…

She was sat on the floor in a room with others and there was the matron that she liked, the one that seemed to like her too. Except that something was wrong, dark shapes were dragging the matron away and the matron was screaming. Seventeen saw one of the dark shapes raise the shock wand and hit the matron with it. There was blood and the shapes released the matron and she staggered and fell to the floor. The woman was dying but she dragged herself forward trying to reach Seventeen. Seventeen saw the dark shape raise the wand again and plunge it into the matron's neck. Still the matron kept coming and then she spoke. "Do not be afraid, my Sila your father will find you. He will come from Griprey and find you!" then she collapsed and moved no more. The dark shapes dragged the matron away and Seventeen was suddenly awake again.

The voice of the golden one said, "Your noradrenaline, dopamine and serotonin levels are elevated as are your respiration and pulse. Are you experiencing pain? I cannot locate its source. Do you wish me to suppress it?"

Seventeen grew angry; was the mech always inside her, monitoring her?

"No, it was only a dream," she replied.

"Really? Your reaction was as severe as when you are in combat. Will you permit me to examine you closer?"

"I can't stop you, you are always inside me I don't have any choice," she shouted back mentally.

Unusually the mech didn't reply immediately then he said, "You do have choice. Over the months that we have known each other I have come to know you as a unique sentient. Your existence may be ephemeral but it is no less for that. My initial aims when I undertook this project were to explore architectures of consciousness and you were a subject of the investigation. However, as I have observed I have also learned. \Q, who instigated the project, intimated that I might discover more than mere mechanistic facts, She was correct. I have come to appreciate you as a valued colleague in this venture. You are autonomous and, as such I would not intervene in your being without permission or where it was necessary to preserve your existence. You always have a choice."

Seventeen understood that the golden one was trying to apologise, she said, "Sorry, I know you are concerned but I think it was only a memory that I had forgotten."

"Would you share it with me?"

"Of course," and she told him what she recalled.

"I have examined the cortical interactions that you have supplied and I concur. It is a memory of your earliest childhood that has been suppressed, not by the mnemnosynth, but by your own sub conscious processes. The matron may well have been your biological parent and she implied that she knew your other biological parent. She referred to an island some eight hundred miles away from Leikvangur and hence we can assume that your parents weren't born here. Your genetic code is on file, I will check," a second or two elapsed and then, "Yes it is confirmed, your genetic code differs from the norm by a significant margin. It is clear that you, or at least your parents were 'wild ones' from a previous generation. Records indicate that your parents were the first 'wild ones' encountered since before the general cull was ended some fifteen hundred years ago."

"But that can't be, I am a player," Seventeen said.

"Agreed you are a player now, but your ancestors weren't players. You are doubly unique. I am pleased that I chose you as my colleague." \A said.

"Tell me about this other place, Griprey," Seventeen said.

"Oh, there isn't just one other place, there are many…" \A replied and he told her.

******

The breeding program was going well. Of course it would be some time before he would see the results but it looked promising. Twelve of the sixteen were already pregnant and he was sure it was only a matter of time until they all were. Of course only time would tell if the venture was successful, still, he had bred the girls with only the most skilful players, the ones who showed greatest proficiency in phasing. And he'd been magnanimous, he'd included players from the other teams. In due course he would have fresh blood for the teams. It might take twenty years but that was only a blink of an eye in the history of the game.

He smiled to himself; there'd even been a bonus, if you could call it one. The nun had turned out to be fertile, she wouldn't produce as many offspring but she would contribute to the numbers.

It was a pity that the most adept phaser on his team, Seventeen, was female but it couldn't be helped. She did her duty in the recreation halls, he'd checked, and so there was hope there as well. That reminded him, there had been one new entry on her file. Apparently some healer had repaired a head injury and had used something a mech had recommended. She now had a gold coloured

383

band around her head that partially covered the scrying crystal. He'd wondered whether it would interfere with her game but it hadn't prevented her being amongst the top scorers in the last three matches and so he wasn't going to change it. Anything that helped him win matches was good.

He had also used the link to the dwimmerlaik who had been sent back outside Leikvangur to check what was happening in Arnes. The town was quiet as far as he could determine. His observations were hampered because the dwimmerlaik was now perfectly transformed and couldn't pass for a living being even in the worst of lighting conditions. Nevertheless what the thrall had lost in beauty he'd gained back in strength and cunning. The dwimmerlaik could survive quite well on its own in the wilderness. It's meagre diet seemed to suit it and Volinar only needed to check up on it once in a while. It had even been useful in observing the comings and goings in the ruins at Sudalyr. The numbers of ephemerals stationed there had rocketed but they didn't appear to be doing anything. They probably didn't realise that the outpost at Sudalyr had been abandoned more than eighteen hundred years previously and all that there was left there were odds and ends of armour and other useless stuff. He put them from his mind and went back to planning the next match.

Ch 38: Tomb Raiders

The journey to Skogrey had been faster than the previous time she'd been there but the sea hadn't seemed any different. There had been one occasion when they'd been travelling quite fast and a pod of dolphins had joined them for a while playing in the waves from the lift catamarans of the fljúgbátr but they'd left when a huge Jötunnfiskur began shadowing the boat. It was the length of the vessel but it didn't attack. After a while it swam off, obviously bored.

They had come ashore at Arnes but this time their arrival wasn't met by a delegation from the temple. In fact there seemed to be hardly anyone at the docks. Their gear had been unloaded and Silfuryn had paid a couple of the dockyard hands to take their things up to the town. There was only one hotel and the manager seemed to be overjoyed to have some new paying guests even if one of them was a wolf. He wasn't so happy when they told him that they would be setting off up country once they had gathered some essentials. Brannhår enquired after Lars and she was told that he still lived in his shack outside town. She thought that she'd pay him a visit whilst Silfuryn was settling in.

The shack looked much as she remembered, perhaps a bit shabbier in places but Lars looked no different to her eyes. He was standing with his back to her staring into the sunset.

"Told you you'd be back," Lars said without turning around.

"How could I stay away, Smith I missed your cooking so much" Brannhår replied.

Mistle had been strangely quiet and she was sniffing the air uncertainly. The smith said, "And I see you've returned with one of our own."

Mistle broke and bounded forward then she stopped and licked the Smith's hand. The hand went to her head and fussed it and Mistle seemed to be back to her usual bumptious self. The smith turned to Brannhår.

She couldn't help gasping,"You're blind!" the man's eyes were open but they were two foggy white spheres.

"Yes lass, the years haven't been as kind to me as they have to you but I don't mind. I can still fish and cook, Brother Kerian drops in from time to time for a visit and I can still create stuff in my head." Lars said.

They were interrupted by someone emerging from the shack. It was a big youth who showed the tiny burn scars and telltale marks of an apprentice smith. "I thought I heard voices master?" the youth said.

"You did, youngling, this is Master Brannhår. Girl, this is Hotar, my apprentice." Lars said.

The youth dropped the stick he'd been carrying, "**The** Master Brannhår, Master Brannhår of the lightning?"

"Pleased to meet you Hotar, Call me Brannhår and this is Mistle."

Mistle was looking at the youth with her head cocked onto one side as if measuring him up. Then she went over, sniffed the youth and turned away disinterested. Her ears pricked up and she bounded off into the scrub. "It's fine, she's just gone for a snack," Brannhår explained.

"Master Brannhår would you care for some refreshment?" Hotar asked.

"That would be welcome," Brannhår replied, "but I told you, just call me Brannhår."

"Oh, I couldn't, the things you've done," the apprentice replied, "Master Lars told me about the hammer, could I possibly see it?"

Lars cuffed the youth around the head, "Refreshments first boy and then you can pester the Master with your own interests."

"Yes Master Lars." The youth turned and disappeared into the shack again.

"So what brings you back?" Lars asked.

"I am here to explore, but my friend Silfuryn is here to see if she can find any trace of her parents. They went missing on an archaeological expedition when she was small and they've never been seen since."

"Come, sit down and tell me more," Lars said and they entered the shack. Hotar was stood at a stove in the corner and Brannhår unslung her hammer and took it over to the youth, "Here, you wanted to see this."

The youth dropped the knife that he was using to shred some herbs onto its cutting board and reverently took the hammer. Another cuff around the head from Lars was accompanied by, "Refreshments first, hammer later." The youth said, "Sorry master."

Lars sat and said, "So, how long ago did your friend's parents come here?"

"About twenty three years ago. We have some of their notebooks so we were hoping to start from them."

"There's a gang of justicer archaeologists over in a place called Sudalyr, they've been there years but I've never heard of any other excavations. However it might be a place to start. There's a bunch of military types there as well and they've been searching for those missing girls. They might have seen something," Lars replied.

"What missing girls?" Brannhår asked.

"Oh, I don't suppose our news gets as far as the capital. About eight months ago a band of skogs raided the temple barracks. They captured sixteen of the older novices and disappeared off into the forest with them. It was strange, skog raiding parties are always hit and run attacks to steal food or metal, this is the first time they actually took people. Folk say that they didn't do it on their own, there was a wizard leading them. In any case neither hide nor hair of them has been seen since. Most folk reckon that the poor things are either dead or working in some brothel."

"And what do you think?"

"Well, I can't fathom it. Why steal girls from here and ship them abroad. There are plenty of girls in other parts. But there's only one brothel in Arnes and they aren't there and the other towns are too small to support a brothel with sixteen girls. I think that the drug runners might have taken them and then decided that they weren't worth the effort. If so, they'll be at the bottom of the ocean."

Brannhår nodded, "I'm afraid you might be right."

"So, this expedition of yours, I take it that you aren't going alone?"

"No, we thought we might take on a few locals to help. It's one of the reasons I came to see you. I thought you might join us."

"Well girl, you can see that I'd not be a lot of use. My days of exploring are done, besides I'm not as strong as I was; age is a terrible thing. However, I might be able to recommend some useful people." He looked over to Hotar, "What's that good for nothing brother of yours doing these days lad?"

"You mean Potar, he's still hunting, Master," Hotar replied.

"Potar is a good lad with a bow, I'd offer you Hotar to go as well but I need him here," Lars said.

Brannhår said, "Of course Smith," then she turned to Hotar, "You could always come help when we return."

"Yes master," the youth answered but she could see he was disappointed. "In the meantime you can look after this for me." She rummaged in her bag and brought out a metal construction and set it on the table.

"I meant this as a gift for Lars but it is meant for experimenting. You can help him with it. Do the fiddly stuff that he can't manage now."

"What is it master?" Hotar asked.

"Oh just something to play with. This is a small steam engine coupled to an electrical generator." She set the steam engine going using a lit twig from the stove. "The generator output can be used to charge this nodule that powers this small light." She took the luminaire and switched it on and shone it around the shack. "the light uses stingbush leaf technology."

When she left to go back to the hotel she left behind two dwarven smiths who were now intrigued by electricity. She also left behind a copy of her notes on electricity but she took with her the promise that Hotar's brother would arrive at their hotel the next day to join the expedition.

Brannhår was telling Silfuryn about the previous evening over breakfast when the hotel manager arrived at the table. "Honoured guests, there is a youth outside who says that he is here to see you."

"Thank you, please invite him to join us; put his meal on my bill."

"Err..." the manager said, "he is not alone, he has a 'friend' with him." The way that the manager had said friend had sounded uncertain.

"Invite them both," Brannhår said.

"Of course, Master, Lady, whatever you wish." the manager turned and bustled away. He didn't return but shortly afterwards two people came into the breakfast room and looked around. They spotted Brannhår and came across.

The young man spoke, "Master Brannhår I am Potar the hunter, this is my associate Mila. My brother Hotar says that you may have work for us."

Brannhår stood, "Yes, we may. Please join us for breakfast."

Silfuryn examined the couple; he was young and looked fit, she was slim, tall and delicate but the most striking thing about her were the tattoos and scars. From what she could see the girl's face and arms, and legs were covered in elaborate blue swirls and curves cut directly into her golden flesh. She had read of the custom. It was a ritual practised by some of the tribes that lived in the archipelagoes of the gouge. The girl was thousands of miles away from home.

Brannhår said, "Hotar said you were a hunter but we need other skills; can either of you drive a wagon and look after a team of smygl?"

The pair shook their heads, Brannhår looked at Silfuryn and a voice behind her said, "But I can." She turned and saw someone else that she recognised, "Brother Kerian!"

"I heard that you were in town and I thought that I would take some time off from my duties to say hello." the Oatsman said.

"Bother Kerian you are a welcome sight. I was going to come and see you today to ask your advice about hiring a healer for our trip," Brannhår said.

"Why pay for a healer when I will come along for free," Kerian said.

"But what about your duties at the temple?" Brannhår asked.

"Since the raid Sister Alicia has had many new helpers. It seems that caring for the sick has suddenly become popular. In fact she has so much help she won't miss me if I go away for a while." Kerian said.

"Then you are welcome to come along. Brother Kerian of the Oatsmen, I would like you to meet my friend Silfuryn, the Lady Risavinur. Silfuryn, this is Brother Kerian. Brother Kerian looked after me when I was on menntunleit. He kept up his surveillance of my contact crystal even after all the others had given up."

Brother Kerian bowed, "Lady Risavinur," he said.

"Silfuryn please Brother. We are comrades on this expedition after all," Silfuryn said.

The rest of the day was spent hiring a wagon and kitting it out with equipment for an indefinite stay in the wild.

******

"What on earth are they doing there?" Lord Skald said.

"They appear to be mounting some expedition into the wild, your eminence," Reverend Sister Ulagrth said.

"But why now? I would have thought that they'd be too busy making their infernal electricity work to go off gallivanting into the wilderness," Skald said.

"I questioned the manager at the hotel; he says that they are mounting an archaeological expedition to search for some ruins. Apparently, the Lady's father used to go on them as well." Ulagrth said.

"That's true," Skald thought, "I wonder if the Lady has found more things in her attic, things that her father brought back?" Aloud he said. "Then I want you to monitor them, I want to be the first to know if they discover anything. They must be employing locals, find one that you can trust and get him or her to volunteer to go with them."

"I'm afraid they left Arnes this morning so I cannot put someone with them. However, your eminence, the manager told me that they would be stopping at the camp at Sudalyr to talk to the archaeologists there." Ulagrth said.

"Fine, I'll arrange it from this end." Skald said.

Ten seconds later he said "Blade, get me the commander of the Ravens on Skogrey. I need to talk to him urgently."

"Commander Bentin, In a day or two a civilian expedition will come to Sudalyr," Skald said, "I want you to show them every co-operation but I want you to be sure that, when they leave, one of our people goes with them. That person must be someone who they will accept voluntarily but who is totally loyal to us. The person will stay in contact with you via scrying crystal and they will report any discoveries or finds that the expedition makes. I want to know immediately whenever anything of note happens."

"Yes eminence, are these people friends of yours?" Bentin asked.

"No, but they are also not enemies or criminals. One of them is the richest woman in Holastan and the other is a Master maker. Neither of them should have suddenly stopped what they were doing in the city to go off on an expedition to nowhere. They must be up to something. The Lady Risavinur is very clever and she hides it behind an aristocratic foppishness. Her companion Master Brannhår is also very clever. Her discoveries are the chief source of all the present trouble with the makers and guilds but, as far as I can determine, she is just what she appears to be: a master maker. There must be some significant reason for two such eminent figures to suddenly mount an expedition at such short notice. I want to know what it is and whether it concerns the Justiciary."

"I understand and I will see to it. If they are from Holastan maybe they will take Gibra with them. She is proving to be somewhat of a loose cannon. The woman was useful when she first arrived as she rooted out several weak spots in our entourage; personnel that had taken a liking to Sting and who were therefore vulnerable to coercion. Recently she has become more of a nuisance." Bentin said.

"No, idiot!" Skald shouted at the crystal, "Both of them know Gibra and she knows them and she has upset them on numerous occasions. Do not let Gibra anywhere near them, in fact, post her away for the duration. The person you choose must be as unlike Gibra as possible."

"I will do as you say, your eminence," Bentin said.

******

"They were expecting us," Brannhår said.

"Yes, it was so obvious; 'We have a place set aside for visitors'. Who did he think he was fooling. A military camp doesn't have visitors unless they are expected. You know what this means." Silfuryn replied.

Brannhår nodded, "They have a way of instantly communicating with either the temple in Arnes or maybe even with Holastan itself. They must be using long range scrying crystals. My guess is that someone from Holastan has become interested in our expedition and I'll lay bets that it's Lord Skald."

"You're probably right but there's not a lot we can do about it," Silfuryn said.

"I agree but I wonder how they intend to keep tabs on us when we're out in the bush?" Brannhår asked.

They found out the next day: Commander Bentin had been positively insistent that any decent expedition needed a cook. Brannhår had admitted that none of them was adept at cooking but she had said that she was accustomed to surviving off the land. Bentin had pointed out that a Lady of Silfuryn's status was used to better and since he had a spare cook it would be no hardship to loan them a cook for the expedition. The ploy was so transparent that Silfuryn had almost burst out laughing. So the cook, a jolly fat man named Planket joined the party. Silfuryn had observed the man, he handled knives well, as you might expect of a cook, but he had magic and most of the flesh underneath the surface layer of fat was muscle.

They stayed at the camp for two days, looking over the excavations and talking to the archaeologists but they didn't learn much. The expedition travelled south following a pass that led through the highlands. It was the same path that, eight months earlier, sixteen captive girls and a nun had taken.

******

"We found them just by the side of the trail. The bones had been scattered by scavengers but we found eight skulls. They are almost certainly the remains of the skog raiding party that attacked Arnes. It looked like an execution because most of the bones were together in a small ditch only a yard or so across. We examined one of the skulls; there was a peculiar hole at its base, where the spine would have joined to it. The rest of the skulls had similar holes. The holes were perfectly round as if the beasts had been stabbed with a steel skewer but unless they were all unconscious I can't explain why all the holes were in exactly the same spot on every creature. We didn't spend long there because the pass is a natural path for the wind and there was a Byrjunarstormur coming in from the west. We headed for higher ground up the side of the valley and made

393

camp. I pretended to go looking for more dry firewood further up the slope to give you this report."

Commander Bentin said, "Well done Planket, this is interesting. We assumed that the girls would be taken to the coast not into the interior. At least we now know which direction they went. Let me know if you see any more signs of them. Now, does the rest of the expedition suspect who you are?"

"No sir, they seem to be relaxed. The two from Holastan spend a lot of time talking and looking at books and maps. They seem to be following some ancient directions. The healer is a pleasant sort and he seems to be everywhere helping out wherever he's needed. The hunter and his girlfriend spend a lot of time away from the wagon. They bring back a fair quantity of game for me to cook."

"That's good, keep a low profile and keep me informed. You'd better get back to your wood-gathering" the commander said.

Silfuryn was in their tent. It made sense for her and Brannhår to share the big tent because it gave them space to set up a table so that they could examine the notebooks. Only Brother Kerian had seemed excited by the light that Brannhår had rigged up. The hunters and the cook had been indifferent. They were sat at the table and she was trying to make sense of a sketch that her father had drawn of some rocks. Unfortunately the pages had got wet and the paper was a bit mouldy. What she was seeing as fine lines might well have been mould spores. Brannhår was leaning over one of the metal writing sheets. It was hot and Brannhår's tunic was open to provide some ventilation. As she leaned forward Silfuryn saw that her friend wore a pendant. It was a strange design. There was a pure red oval gemstone that glowed with some internal fire held in a tri-fold dragon claw made in gold.

"That's pretty," Silfuryn said.

Brannhår made to tuck the pendant back inside her shirt then she stopped and took it off to show Silfuryn.

"My father made it for me when I was small. It didn't originally look like this. The gemstone and the setting were the only things that were on me when they found my infant body floating in the shallows of a lake. My father said that the gem was good but the setting had been poorly made and partially melted. He remade it into this and won a prize for it as a rework piece at the Kraftmoot."

"So it's a link with your past. Do you never wonder where you came from?" Silfuryn asked.

"I used to, but not much any more. I can't wind time back and so there's no point in speculating. Besides I know that I've lived before. It's one reason why I understand electricity. In a previous life I think I used to work on the subject. I've often had visions of wall boards covered in equations that my previous incarnation can understand but are much too complex for my own mind."

"And that doesn't bother you? Being two people at once."

"No. You see I'm me and the other self is me so the sum total is just me. If that makes sense."

"I suppose," Silfuryn said thinking, "My friend has lived at least two lives but she's still my friend and she came along with me on this wild goose chase without telling me that I was being foolish. So what if she's a little strange, I am as well. We make a good pair."

"What are you working on?" Silfuryn asked.

Brannhår pointed at the metal sheets, "I think that I've solved at least one puzzle. You know how we've been trying to decipher these as text, well I've discovered that they're not text they are mathematical formulae."

"And that's good?" Silfuryn asked.

"Yes, don't you see. When you are trying to translate another language you need to relate it to something common. So, if you saw the word dog in one language and the picture of a dog above it you could relate the word to the picture and so know that the word meant dog.

Well these symbols don't have pictures they have relationships between them; for instance this symbol means plus. I know that because everywhere it is used its effect is the same. That's the beauty of mathematics; its always consistent even in different languages, its laws never change. This sheet has calculations on the strengths of certain beams; I can tell because the relationships between the numbers are the same as I would get if I did the same calculations.

Once you realise that the sheet isn't letters but numbers then it becomes easy to read. Then I can then make a guess at what the words under the calculations mean. This, for instance almost certainly means beam and the word in front of it means iron. I know this because the numbers for the stiffness of iron appear in the calculation..

If we put the numbers and the words in the calculations together with the words that your father translated from his study of the pictograms we start to build up a vocabulary: it's fascinating."

"I'll take your word for it," Silfuryn said, "but we need to get some rest. It will probably be an early start tomorrow; we want to get through this pass before the weather gets any worse."

Ch 39: Fort Apache

"Look at that rock formation there. I'm sure I've seen a sketch of it in one of the journals," Silfuryn shouted.

"Let's take a few minutes and explore," Brother Kerian suggested, "the team needs to rest and crop some grass."

Brannhår dug out the journal and leafed through it until she found the page. "Here it is, yes it says that there should be some ruins just to the left of it under the cliff-face."

"I'll go and get us something to eat. Coming Mila?" Potar said.

"I'd like to go and see the ruins," the girl replied.

"Planket and I will set up camp, We're at the end of the pass so we've made good progress for today," Brother Kerian said.

"Then its just us three girls," Brannhår said hoisting a coil of rope onto her shoulder and settling her hammer into its holster.

They set off and there were soon underneath the distinctive rock formation. "It looks like a jötunnfiskur, we used to hunt them in my homeland," Mila said.

"How on earth did you make a net that size?" Silfuryn asked.

Mila laughed, "Not net, many spears with ropes."

"Of course that would be the way to do it," Silfuryn said.

"Here's something that looks to have been crafted," Brannhår interrupted.

They walked over to the remains of a huge pillar which had large shaped blocks of masonry scattered around its base.

"It looks like it used to be an arch, you can just see the other side of it over there. It must have been very impressive but nobody puts an arch into a cliff. I think it must, at one time been over a door or entrance. Let's move along a little and see if we can find any trace of it." Brannhår said.

"Look here, the overhang has collapsed and has left this hollow in the hillside," Silfuryn said.

Brannhår went still for a moment. "I think that there used to be a tunnel here going into the hill but the roof must have collapsed, it's just rock now. But there's some metal up there," she said pointing.

They climbed over the rubble of the collapse and another twenty paces further up the hill, "Behind here," Brannhår said indicating a huge slab of rock covered in ancient writing.

"I'll have to sketch this. If only there was a better way of recording the writing," Silfuryn said.

"Aren't we going in?" Mila asked.

"We can't move that rock," Brannhår began then she stopped, "Oh I see what you mean. She strode to the side of the slab and appeared to dissolve into the rock. A few seconds later there was the sound of someone tapping on the other side of the slab with a hammer.

Mila and Silfuryn went to where Brannhår had disappeared and they saw that the back of the slab was hollow. It was a concealed entranceway. They followed the maker in.

The small cave was pitch black but Brannhår said, "Wait a second," and the cave was flooded with light. They looked around, the floor was smooth and a series of huge iron basins were set into the rear face of the slab, "This was probably a defence for the tunnel. This room overlooks the approach and there are places in the facing masonry where slits have been cut so that you can see anyone climbing up the hill. Anyone attacking the tunnel entrance would find boiling water or tar cascading down on them from these basins. But it looks like someone has been here since then." She pointed to a plank that had been put across the basins to make a temporary table. On it were a couple of drinking cups and a plate that had the remains of some dessicated fish on it. There was also a wooden box on the floor. When they removed its lid there was the unmistakeable smell of herbs.

"Kanis," Mila said. The other two nodded.

"Let's see what else there is," Silfuryn said, "there must be another way out of here… Ah here it is," she said going to the rear of the cave, "This used to be the door to the inside of the hill. The wood has decayed over the years so there's almost nothing left."

Mila came over and put her hand on what was left of the wood. It fell apart revealing a set of stone stairs that descended into the gloom.

"Are we going down?" Silfuryn asked. She had unslung the whip from her belt. Brannhår had copied her and she had her hammer in her hand.

"I can't hear anything," Mila said.

"Right, we go inside but not too far," Brannhår said, "There's no telling what state the tunnel roof is in further on, be careful we don't want it to collapse on us."

Silfuryn and Mila nodded their agreement and they descended the staircase. At the bottom of the stairs there was an opening into the tunnel. The floor of the tunnel was smooth and they could see that, off towards the outside world its roof had collapsed forming an impenetrable barrier. In the other direction the tunnel disappeared into the darkness. They walked along it for a hundred paces and then their way was blocked by a large iron grille which descended from the ceiling to the floor across the whole width of the tunnel.

"We might as well go back," Brannhår said, "we can't get any further."

"You're right," Silfuryn said, "You'd need to be a ghost to get through this, but I want to see if there are any hidden levers that might open it."

Brannhår caught the reference. It meant that Silfuryn wanted to use her powers. She said, "I want to have another look at the room upstairs." She turned to Mila, "Mila, why don't you go outside while the light is good and see if there are any other entrances further up the hill. If you find anything, don't go in. It wouldn't be safe on your own. Just remember where they are and we'll explore tomorrow. We'll see you back at camp."

"Ok," Mila said.

When she'd gone Silfuryn said, "I think I'll see what's beyond the gate.

Brannhår nodded, "Be careful I won't be able to get to you if anything happens."

Silfuryn phased though the gate and Brannhår passed a light through the bars to her, "Stay where I can see the light," she said.

Brannhår watched the light get smaller as Silfuryn went deeper down the tunnel, then it winked out for a few seconds and then it got brighter. Silfuryn appeared carrying a couple of items which she passed through the bars before phasing herself through.

"A book, or what's left of one and a cracked pot," Brannhår observed.

"Yes, there was a room off to one side of the tunnel down there with lots of shelves but all that was on them was the torn book and the shard of pot. Let's get out of here, this whole tunnel feels abandoned," Silfuryn said.

"Yes, I get that feeling as well. It's as if everyone decided to leave at once."

They climbed back up to the observation room and looked around some more but found nothing else and they stepped out into the last of the daylight.

Back in camp they told the others what they'd discovered. Brannhår pretended that she'd found the torn book and the pot in a corner of the observation room.

"So the underground part was empty," Potar observed.

"I think that it was some sort of garrison, the whole layout was military. It is at the southern end of the pass and it faces south so we can assume that it was guarding the pass from some hostile force to the south. Whatever its original purpose it was clearly deliberately abandoned, there was nothing inside and when I examined the roof where the entrance had collapsed I saw clear signs that the roof had been caved in deliberately. Whoever abandoned the main tunnel didn't mean to come back."

"But the observation cave was another matter. It had clearly been used since the underground part was abandoned," Brannhår said.

"Yes," Mila said, "All the plants around the entrance were cut back or dead. It was as if someone was keeping the entrance clear and was using the cave often enough that wildlife never got a chance to colonise it."

"I think that someone is still using it," Silfuryn said, "that crate smelled of Kanis and so it's highly likely that the people using it are manufacturing Sting."

"So, we're not the first to discover that lookout cave," Brother Kerian said, "but there are a couple of things that still don't add up. Why did the drug traffickers never try to go down to the tunnels? You said that the door in the back of the cave hadn't been disturbed and only crumbled when you tried to use it. And, why is the cave of any use to drug traffickers? It's far away from any of the main tracks and it's nowhere near the coast and it's difficult to get to."

They all nodded in agreement but none of them ventured any answers.

******

Commander Bentin strained to hear; the scrying crystal wasn't the best quality and the channel kept breaking up. He had sent the troupe out after he'd received the news about the dead lizards. The troupe consisted of a Raven officer and five regular justicers. They had orders to follow the expedition but remain out of sight and observe. Planket had reported the discovery of the ancient tunnel and the drug trafficker's cave and he had briefed the troupe about it and had told them to be on the lookout for the drug traffickers as well as shadowing the explorers. The Raven in charge of the troupe was saying something but the message was garbled. "... raided by a band of skogs ... no casualties ... following the explorers... "

Bentin spoke into the crystal, "Your transmission keeps breaking up. Send again when communication is better. We will try to contact you again at hourly intervals. Be on your guard." He turned to the justicer who was operating the crystal at his end and said, "Keep trying to get through, let me know when you have any news."

The justicer holding the crystal had his eyes shut in concentration and he just nodded.

Two hours later the reception suddenly cleared and Bentin was called back, "We have moved higher up the hill to the south and reception seems to be better. Earlier today we were shadowing the expedition as instructed and we were attacked by a band of skogs using throwing spears. There were about ten in all and we killed six of them. We received no casualties and only one minor injury. The surviving skogs fled to the south down the pass towards the expedition and I sent one of the men out to check whether they attacked it. He reported back an hour ago; the skogs appeared to skirt the expedition and continued on to the south. We have no idea why they attacked but they seemed to be familiar with the capabilities of our crossbows but didn't reckon with our magic. I can only assume that they are part of the same group that attacked the temple at Arnes."

"Thank you for the report Lieutenant," Bentin said. Keep watch and keep in touch. I will send another half dozen men to join you by sea, but keep following the expedition. With luck the reinforcements will catch you up in three or four days.

******

The aurora was bright tonight and Officer Gibra looked at the crates stacked on the shore. A dozen people were sat on them or around them waiting. The captain whose boat she'd hired was late and, even though the sea was calm the horizon was empty. One of the men came up to her, "They must have run into a calm, it happens now and then. They'll be here in a while," he said.

"I hope so," she replied, "We need to get this lot offshore before sunrise. I wouldn't want any nosy fisherman seeing us loading."

"Err.. Captain," the man said, "some of the men are grumbling. They say that they never expected to have to fight the damn lizards to get the boxes through."

"Neither did I, Tell them there'll be an extra ration when we get back to Sundfjall."

He left and Gibra considered her tactics. She'd stuck it as long as she could with Ulagrth's lot. She'd thrown a few lowlifes to Ulagrth to keep her occupied but it had been clear that after a week Ulagrth had become suspicious of how she knew so much about Sting. The suspicion had turned to overt disapproval and Gibra had got the message. She made herself scarce and joined Bentin. The problem was that Bentin had been talking to Ulagrth and so her welcome there had been short lived. She'd informed them both that she was going to try to go undercover to ferret out more about the trafficking operation and had left.

Once free of authority she had done as she'd intended all along; she went over to Cyten full time. Currently she was organising the collection of the raw Kanis from the plantations in the south and delivering it to Cyten's fleet of boats that visited hidden coves like this at night. At first she thought that the job would be easy, 'delivering vegetables to market' she'd called it but then the raids had started. The Kanis plantations had needed large areas of jungle clearing and they needed labour to harvest the plants The labour needed feeding and so they'd hunted the local wildlife. Both these actions had angered the local skogs and they'd started raiding her supply routes. The skogs were more of a nuisance than a real threat, her men were well armed and the skogs weren't particularly organised. Still, she'd had to change her routes to and from the coast and that had interfered with the steady flow of her product.

The only saving grace was that the skogs never attacked at night because the nights were relatively cold and, being cold blooded, the lizards became very slow. However, come daylight and the sun in these latitudes started to warm things up and the little bastards would start to make trouble. She looked at the horizon, the sun was already peeping over the horizon.

"Get a move on, arsehole," Gibra cursed the boat captain in her mind, "We've only got the night."

The scream suggested that she was wrong. One of the men carrying a crate had dropped to his knees, a spear was sticking out of his back. Gibra whirled around looking for the source of the attack. There was movement further up the beach. Half a dozen shapes were moving towards her group. They were tall and she didn't need any more light to see that they were lizards. These were different; they were wearing furs and they were carrying torches. One stopped to hurl a spear and it thudded into the ground only a few paces away. Gibra's men had already retreated to the pile of crates and she saw one aim a crossbow and a few seconds later a lizard went down. The lizards closed and hurled the torches. Most missed their target but a couple hit the crates and stuck. Gibra had a fleeting thought that the torches must be burning pitch and the sticky stuff had stuck to the crates. They were already starting to burn fanned by the onshore breeze. Her men scattered but kept up their fire. Gibra reached out with her mind and sent the fire back towards the attackers; a lizard fell screaming. Others were pierced by bolts and soon there was only the sound of the waves and the sound of the blaze as half of her cargo went up in smoke.

She inspected the bodies. Two of her men were dead and so were all six lizards. She'd been right, the lizards were wearing furs but what was more disturbing was the fact that they'd used fire. Fire meant that they could keep warm against the chill of night and the furs meant that they could keep active once they were warm. So she'd been wrong. The cold of the night was no shield from this type of lizard.

******

Brannhår was examining the shard of pot when Silfuryn woke the next day. "Good morning," Silfuryn said, "how long have you been up?"

"Not long, what do you make of this design?" Brannhår asked.

"Just a minute, I'm not quite awake yet," her friend replied. She went over to the washstand and poured the contents of a jug over her head. Gathering her hair into a long hank she came over squeezing the water from it. "It looks like a fight of some sort. The dwarf is stabbing the thing on the ground with a lance."

"Yes but look at the thing on the ground; isn't that one of the skogs?"

"Yes, I think you're right. So why would anyone make a pot with a picture like that on it?"

"Considering that that ruin we explored was probably a garrison then maybe the thing that they were guarding the pass against was the skogs."

"Why would anyone want to do that?" Silfuryn asked, "Skogs are just animals."

"Quite intelligent animals. They use spears, the ones that killed Mistle's mother did and they weren't hunting the wolves for food. It seemed almost like they were doing it because the wolves were competition. And they were only small ones, a big one like the one on the pot might be capable of more. It looks like the one on the pot is lying on some sort of bow. Now I can believe that an animal might use a sharp stick as a weapon but it takes real intelligence to make a bow." Brannhår said.

"Perhaps," Silfuryn said, "what about the book?"

"I gave it to Brother Kerian, he told me that some of the writing in it looked like an ancient form of dwarfish that he's come across in books about healing herbs. Let's go and ask him." Brannhår said.

Silfuryn shook her head, "Breakfast first."

After breakfast they found Brother Kerian tending the smygl, "Good morning," he said, "I was up early studying that old book you found. It is fascinating. The language looks like an ancient form of dwarfish and I think I can make out some of the words. It appears to be a soldiers diary. I'm sure there are words for fight and kill in there and a few others that seem to be the names of places. Arnes, for instance, Arnes used to be called Ár-ness-vik which means ' a harbour that can be used all year' which is a good description of the town and here you can see the runes which when sounded say Ár-ness-vik. So this particular soldier knew of or had been to Arnes."

The healer/priest stopped talking. A short spear had thudded into the side of the cart near to his head. Brannhår and Silfuryn whirled around. There was a shout and Mila appeared running in a zig-zag pattern across the camp. She had a crossbow in either hand and threw them at the pair then dove under the wagon. Brother Kerian had also taken cover but he had had the presence of mind to drop the smygl harnesses and the beasts had taken fright and fled. Several other spears fell around the cart but none of them could see the enemy to fire back. Mila had disappeared and Potar was nowhere to be seen.

The hail of spears ceased and a scream was heard coming from the undergrowth a little further down the hill. Suddenly a dozen tall skogs came running up the hill towards them. They were armed with long knives and they were making a strange ululating noise.

Brannhår threw the crossbow to Brother Kerian and unslung her hammer. Silfuryn freed her whip from its holster. Planket appeared with a cleaver in each hand and battle was joined.

Silfuryn's whip lashed out and long gashes appeared across two of the leading lizards' torsos. Brannhår's hammer swung and another lizard crumpled, its head a bloody pulp. Five of the remaining lizards circled the pair who were now fighting back to back. They were keeping out of range of Brannhår's hammer but they seriously underestimated the range of Silfuryn's whip. It licked out and appeared to tap one of them on its forehead. A burst of blood came from the back of its skull and it went down. Another followed as the end of the whip appeared to pass into its neck and then burst out through the other side. One lizard, braver than the rest charged Brannhår, another followed close behind intending to use the first as a distraction. The spike of Brannhår's hammer wasn't even slowed by the first lizard and it plunged onward into the one following. The remaining lizard turned to flee but suddenly a feathered shaft appeared in its back. Brother Kerian had scored a hit.

Nearby Planket was battling two lizards and he was losing, there was a savage gash along one arm that was pouring blood. Suddenly there was only one lizard, Mistle had the other one on the ground teeth embedded firmly in its neck. She shook the lizard like a rat and the sound of snapping bone could be clearly heard over the noise of battle. Planket took advantage of the distraction and brought the cleaver around into his opponent's ribcage. The lizard froze, its arm in the air ready to deal a killing blow and then it toppled sideways.

Brannhår looked around, There were no more lizards left standing. Mila and Potar had appeared and had finished off the rest with their bows. The only movement in the camp was from Mistle, She had the dead lizard's head in her jaws and she shook it once and then bit down. The wolf's jaws cracked the skull and the sound bounced off the rocks and echoed down the valley. Mistle dropped the creature and then looked directly at Brannhår. She could almost read the wolf's mind. She had taken her revenge on the enemy that had killed her mother.

Brother Kerian went over to tend to Planket. Brannhår went over to Silfuryn and pulled her to her feet, "Nice technique," Brannhår said.

Silfuryn nodded, "I've been practising. I wasn't sure that it would work but I managed to phase the tip of the whip into ghost space just before it hit and then phase it back to real space once it was inside the beast. I think it was quite effective. Takes quite a bit of magic and concentration though…" Brannhår caught her as she fell, unconscious.

Mila and Potar were examining what was left of the skogs and they began dragging the corpses over towards a shallow ravine in the side of the valley.

They did nothing for the rest of the day. Silfuryn recovered after a few minutes and she and Brannhår talked together. Mistle was dozing on the ground between them.

"Well, at least we now know what the garrison was guarding against," Brannhår said.

"And why the drug traffickers needed the lookout cave to shelter in," Silfuryn added.

"Why did they attack? They can't still be carrying on that ancient war. The garrison must be a thousand years old."

Silfuryn shook her head, "Who knows how long ancient enmities last. It could be racial. Maybe they've always warred against the dwarfs."

"Maybe but they've never attacked Arnes or any of the other towns."

"Except for that raid where those girls were taken," Silfuryn reminded her.

"Yes but that was recent, I mean if they've been at war with us for a thousand years why wait until this year to start it up again."

They were interrupted by Planket who'd come over with one arm in a sling. He was carrying a large broiled fiskur steak. Mistle's nose twitched and she raised her head, Planket tossed the steak to the wolf, "Thanks," he said. Mistle caught the steak and within ten seconds it had disappeared she even gave a half wag of her tail.

Mila and Potar had finished disposing of the enemy, "There were fourteen of them altogether," Potar said, "Mila and I got two further down the slope and then the rest broke cover and came up here. We were afraid that they'd get you but we can see that we needn't have worried. You all look as though you can take care of yourselves. I didn't believe Lars when he told me about that hammer of yours but now I've seen it in action I'll not doubt his word again, and Lady Silfuryn, that whip is magic. Wherever did you get it and learn to use it like that?"

Silfuryn smiled, "Brannhår made it for me a year ago, and I've practised a little with it since."

Potar nodded, "We stripped the corpses and dumped them in that little ravine. We piled wood on them and we'll set it alight later before the scavengers start arriving. They were all armed with swords and they were wearing loose kilts with woven belts which had loops for the swords. I've never heard of skogs wearing clothing before or having the technology to make iron weapons. It's something new. They also don't usually attack in groups like that. Most of the skog bands that we've come across in the north tend to attack as a tribe, all ages and sexes and it's usually a free for all. This group were all adult males and they appeared to be coordinated. It's almost as if someone or something is organising them. I don't know who that could be but it seems to hate dwarves."

Ch 40: Threats and promises

There wasn't enough time, that was the problem. Seventeen swung the axe again and it bit into the target again. What was the use of knowing that there was a vast world outside Leikvangur when it was beyond reach. Her time was rostered, just like everyone else's in Leikvangur: it was all accounted for. She ate, slept, trained to a strict timetable that she had no control over. The more she thought about it the more she realised that it wasn't just her. Everyone and everything in Leikvangur operated like a machine.

These thoughts would never have occurred to her before her, friendship? relationship? or whatever it was with the golden one had begun. He was to blame for her confusion. If he hadn't reset her memory and kept it free of the mnemnosynth she wouldn't even be aware that there was a problem.

Her train of thought was interrupted by the coach, "Seventeen, your rate of attack has diminished. I have noticed the decline over several days. Report to the team healer for examination."

Damn, now her daydreaming had landed her in trouble. She swung the axe too hard and the target shrieked and was flung across the training mat. The botch inside it must have felt the swing because it didn't get up again it just lay there shuddering. Seventeen had a sudden urge to go over to it and help it up but she suppressed it. Doing anything so stupid would just get her into worse trouble. She turned to the coach, "Sorry coach, it's this headband the healers gave me, it itches and it puts my stroke off."

The coach said, "I'll see what I can do about it. You'd better report to the team healers straight away. Tell them about the itch. The team can't afford players who are unnecessarily distracted, it could lose us a game."

Seventeen picked up the axe and went towards the showers. The blue light came on but there was no blessed relief from her memory. Something had to be done otherwise her distraction would become real and she'd start making mistakes. A mistake in a real game might kill her or worse, might lose the match. As she stood under the stream of water that little itch in her mind that preceded a conversation with \A started up. She carried on washing herself down as if nothing was amiss; once you'd been told to report to the team healer they monitored you closely so she couldn't afford to do anything out of the ordinary.

"Your cortisone levels are spiking, you are distressed. What is the reason?" the golden one said in her head.

Seventeen was annoyed, "You are, I wish you'd never chosen me for your experiment. Before I knew you I was… oh I don't know what the word is… I was OK. Now there are so many thoughts that I am becoming… disconnected. Look, I don't have the words to explain. I have changed and the change disturbs me."

"It is to be expected, your neural cortex is becoming better organised and hence associations that couldn't be maintained under the influence of the mnemnosynth are being established," \A replied.

"Well I don't like it because it's going to get me killed," Seventeen said.

"That would be inconvenient," \A said, "Your consciousness does not have the ability to duplicate and relocate. My current experiments with my own systems have shown that this is feasible for my kind but I cannot see how this could be managed with an ephemeral. Therefore the obvious solution would be to remove the possibility of you being killed."

"Oh, and how do I do that? My existence is determined by the Game. There is nothing within Leikvangur that is not. And even if I were able to leave Leikvangur, which I can't, I wouldn't be able to survive."

"What you say is true, any attempt to leave Leikvangur would be detected by the scrying crystal embedded in your skull and an automatic self destruct would be initiated. It is an ancient piece of technology put in place many years ago to prevent those gathered from trying to escape the managers. It is not something that my systems are able to countermand at present," \A went silent for a moment, "Therefore we must take another strategic route. If you will permit, I will install a minor avatar of myself in the communications band that you wear. It will have access to your systems at all times and it will make appropriate adjustments to minimise the chance of you becoming injured in the game. I apologise: it is not a perfect solution."

"Whatever, I accept. Now I'd better get out of this shower before the coach notices I've spent more than my allotted time," Seventeen said.

"Do not be concerned, our conversation has only occupied four seconds of your time. I took the liberty of upgrading our communications channel to allow less disparity between our individual perceived time-streams."

"How can you do that?"

"It is simple, your cortex is equipped to alter its own subjective time-stream. It was a trivial matter to access this talent for communication. I will commence the installation of the avatar during the remainder of your allotted ablution period," \A replied

The itch that was \A disappeared: Seventeen snapped back into what she thought of as reality and glanced at the timer on the wall; she had been in the shower for less than thirty seconds and she had plenty of time left to get rid of all the grime from the training arena. "Damn, I never asked him about what to do with all these useless thoughts and ideas I'm getting," she said to herself, "and damn this stupid circlet. My hair has grown through it and it tangles in the shower. If the team healers want to remove it they're going to have to cut most of my scalp off."

******

\A accelerated his time sense back to what he considered to be a proper rate. However, he conceded that much of the information that he was gathering from his experiment operated at much lower rates. Therefore he had now created experimental autonomic parallel processing capabilities that were used as agents to collect, collate and pre-analyse the low rate data. This strategy was used by the unit formerly designated \Q during their interactions. Unlike \Q, who used a plethora of fully self-aware peripherals for analysis \A preferred to keep his peripherals below the threshold for self consciousness. This meant that he had to devote time to the final analysis himself. He considered accelerating his processing capability to even higher speeds but he was fast approaching the intrinsic limitations of the physics. Perhaps he should ask [B-G] for assistance but his new sense of self baulked at the idea. \Q might help. After all it had been her suggestion to start the experiment. The problem was that he didn't have a means of communicating with her. From what she had told him the units previously designated ^[A-G] used phasing extensively to travel across the multiverse. She could be light years away by now and it might be centuries before his message would be received. He would send the message anyway. It had been less than a year since he'd instigated the experiment, he might be lucky and his message might reach her before she got too far away. In the interim he would prepare an avatar to protect the ephemeral Seventeen. He had grown quite fond of her and it would be a shame if she were terminated prematurely.

******

The healer shook his head, he'd never come across a player like her in all his days. Usually it was broken bones or sliced flesh; they were easy to deal with. What went on in a player's mind was much more tricky. Of course he'd encountered players with mental problems left over from blows to the head and similar damage. Usually there was little that could be done other than to put them out of their misery like he would with any other incurable wound.

He consulted her records again. Seventeen had been fitted with a head brace following an injury at some unspecified time in the past. The details were garbled and he cursed whichever botch had filled in the record. The idiot had even omitted to fill in the part which would have told him which healer had performed the procedure.

Wondering what had necessitated the brace he resigned himself to examining the player himself to decide what was wrong. Unusually, she had been referred by the coach because he'd noticed a slowing during her practice sessions; this was normally due to physical injury but he had checked her gameplay records and it appeared that she had had only minor injuries in her past four matches. In fact, her consistently high scores meant that whatever the coach had noticed during practise wasn't affecting her skill in the actual game.

He glanced at the clock. She was rostered to arrive in ten minutes and so he started to prepare the examination table. Damn, there was a mech doing something to it; it was in pieces. He'd have to use the one in the back that didn't have a direct crystal link. That meant that he would have to use his skills and the consoles rather than just plugging the girl in. It always took longer and it was easy to make mistakes. Mistakes were costly, get a player's treatment wrong and let it affect their play and he would have the managers to answer to. They tended to remove their problems the old fashioned way and he wasn't ready to be recycled just yet.

When the girl arrived he greeted her, "Come through to the rear office, the mech is doing something to my couch so we will have to use the old one in the back. I'm afraid it means that you need to answer some questions rather than the couch just looking them up but that shouldn't be a problem. Now your coach tells me that your practise sessions haven't been going too well. Don't worry I'll get to the bottom of whatever is troubling you and you'll be back to normal in before you know it. Lie back on the couch and relax."

Seventeen climbed on the couch. It really was ancient, the surface was covered in some sort of skin rather than the usual coarse cloth. She lay back and she could see the blue crystal of the mnemnosynth above her in the ceiling; it wasn't glowing. The healer had pulled a chair up to an ancient console and he was explaining the procedure, "The console shows me questions which I then ask you. I enter your answers into the console and then the console suggests things which may be wrong with you and I take the most likely cause and ask you more questions. Just answer me truthfully to the best of your knowledge and everything will proceed smoothly. Now you are Seventeen of the Majors of Volinar, is that correct?"

There was a pause and the healer watched the telltales that told him whether she was lying or not. They were taking an inordinately long time and he looked at the woman. He could see the head brace that she wore; he'd never come across one that colour. It appeared to have been in place for a long time because the hair had grown through the fine mesh at the temples. It clearly wasn't holding anything together, in fact the construction consisted of thin overlapping plates of metal much like the carapace of a mech but of finer construction. He briefly wondered who had performed the surgery, whoever it was had been pretty skilled. Her body had the usual collection of scars that he'd have expected on a player of majors standard but none of them looked infected or extensive enough to cause physical difficulties. He looked at the swell of her breasts and her hips. Bigger than the norm for a player but the console told him that she was first generation and so it might be expected.

First generation? That couldn't be right, the only first generations in Leikvangur were Volinar's herd of captives from the gathering raid some months ago. Seventeen wasn't one of them, she had been around for a long time. He'd watched some of her matches and he was sure he remembered some when she'd been in the juniors. He screwed up his courage and typed 'First generation?" into the console. The screen filled with words and he read. *"Patient is confirmed as first generation. Acquired in gathering from unscheduled external contact. First generation status noted for this examination."*

"When was patient's last game?"

The healer turned to the girl and began to ask the questions. He was quite pleased that he'd diagnosed her first generation status all by himself.

Seventeen closed her eyes and waited. The healer began to ask questions; when was her last game? had she been injured by an opponent? had she suffered a strain? The list went on and on and then he asked, "When were you last rostered for sex?"

The healer watched the console, it was asking him to do something.

"Take sample of vaginal secretion, label and deposit in analyser."

Really, it had been easier with the other couch, he'd rarely been asked to do the actual interventions unless there were major injuries and even then a mech usually performed the actual work. He donned the gloves and started.

Seventeen felt the healer's hands part her legs and then he reached between them to push something inside her. It felt odd. She was used to sex, she was rostered for sex twice a month and she was used to the impersonal touch of mechs when she came for examinations but the touch of another person seemed somehow intrusive. Nevertheless she kept still and ignored the feeling. There were several more tests, she was asked to catch balls, squeeze and stretch springs with her arms and legs and hit a series of small projectiles away from her with a wooden paddle. The examination with the console was taking a long time, much longer than the usual one.

The healer consulted the console after every test and then finally he sat back in his chair. "Relax now and look into the blue light. You will feel drowsy but it is nothing to be concerned about. I will give you the diagnosis when you have relaxed.

She saw the blue light of the mnemnosynth come on above her but, apart from a slight itch in her left shoulder blade she felt nothing. After a minute or two the blue light went out and Seventeen knew that she could relax now. Whatever prevented the mnemnosynth working in the showers obviously prevented the one in the healers office working as well. However, she should behave as if it had worked so as not to arouse any more suspicion in the healer. She sat up on the couch, wobbling a little as if she was still groggy.

416

The healer clasped his hands in his lap and said, "I am afraid I have some bad news, the console tells me, and I would have to agree, that you appear to be pregnant."

Seventeen didn't need to pretend. The shock of the announcement had stunned her and she wobbled for real. "I can't be," she said.

"The tests don't lie. One of your last partners has impregnated you."

Seventeen thought, this can't be happening and she heard the healer's words through a veil of noise in her head.

"You may continue your normal life and play the next match but after that you will be transferred to the maternity centre where you will remain until you can resume your normal duties. It is imperative that new players are born to replace those who have retired, your duty now is to replenish the stock. I will inform the requisite authorities of your change in status. You may go."

******

Volinar was fuming. How had it happened, it had probably cost him the championship. Why couldn't the woman have just kept her legs together? He knew why; there had to be new players. Hadn't he organised that raid on the temple for that specific purpose but the fact was no consolation. Who was the bastard who had knocked her up? He was betting that it was one of Severell's juniors. It would be just like her to nobble one of his star players by setting one of her hormone crazed bucks loose on Seventeen. He had Seventeen for one more match, he might stretch it to two but even he couldn't go against the rules. If the girl was pregnant her career was effectively over. None of the players who had birthed children had ever returned to top form. Some intrinsic changes in chemistry took place. The best he could hope for was that her brat would inherit her talents and he'd have another decent player in fifteen or twenty years time. It had always been like this, there was the immediate excitement of each match and each season but there was also the ebb and flow of fortune that accompanied generational changes in the teams. Still, if he could keep her in the next two matches and she kept up her current high scoring run then it might open a score gap between him and Severell. That would leave him in a good position for the rest of the season.

Ch 41: Her Final Match

"Bring up the focus on Seventeen," Volinar ordered the mech operating the match drone hovering sixty feet above the playing field. He was intrigued, the girl had breezed through the previous match which was perhaps not that surprising and Volinar had added another win to the season's tally. He'd been tempted to take direct control of the girl but he wanted to watch her in action without any assistance from him. He had seen it before; a pregnant player seemed to be more resourceful. It had something to do with the chemistry of their bodies. They were driven to protect the nascent life inside of them and it made for some spectacular moves on the pitch.

He imagined that if he could have a team of pregnant females then he would be assured of victory but he realised that the advantage that the protective instinct gave was only temporary. It could never last a whole season. As time went on the female body grew and changed and became clumsy. The clumsiness counteracted the protective instinct and the result would be a disaster. He might win the first few matches but defeat in the rest of the season's matches would be an inevitable consequence of nature. It remained to see whether Seventeen's maternal protection would override her changing body for this match. It was an interesting experiment and he had nothing to lose. If the instinct gave her an advantage and they won then it would be good but he would lose her from the team anyway. The rules said that pregnant women could only play one match after the diagnosis and he was stretching them as this was her second match. The rule had been made in the very early history of the game and even Volinar had to admit that it was a sensible one. Why risk the future of the game for one temporary advantage. Still, this would be interesting.

On the pitch fifty feet below the drone, Seventeen stood at the ready. She had her axe in her hand and ordinarily her opponent wouldn't have fazed her. She had drawn a heavy swordsman as her immediate mark. He stood in the opposition's formation in the position mirroring her own. He was big and his sword was big.

They were waiting for the anthems and the referee's signal to start. The referee was always one of the other managers who should therefore favour neither side. Seventeen let her mind wander. Unfortunately it summoned up a vision of the maternity unit with its hopelessly distorted women waddling about with vacant eyes and drooling mouths. Soon she would become one of them and her career would be over. Should she take the easy way out? Her life was effectively finished, why not go out in style. All she needed to do was remain in normal and the huge great-sword of her opponent would ensure that the end was quick, if not painless.

A buzz in her head brought her back to the present and a voice said, "The manager Severell is about to start the match."

She shook herself and readied the axe; the voice seemed oblivious to the situation, "Hello, I am the avatar of \A and I am here to help."

"Oh no, "Seventeen groaned to herself. That's all I need, a little voice in my head distracting me from the task in hand." She pushed a thought to the golden one, "This is a bad time. Shut up and let me concentrate." The big guy was swinging his sword into position. He must be very strong, the sword moved through the air as if it weighed nothing. The klaxon sounded and battle was joined. Seventeen moved.

The first dozen or so rounds went as usual, the opponents tested each other's defences and explored their attack strategies. After twenty minutes Seventeen knew that her opponent was tough and skilful. He'd managed to take out about five percent of her troops but she'd matched or even slightly bettered his tally. It was difficult to judge. They were circling each other looking for any opening when the voice in her head piped up again, "I have been examining your reaction and directive levels and I infer that something is worrying you."

"Yes," she thought at it, "the big guy with the sword. Now shut up."

"No, you are incorrect, it is something else. Something to do with your body. Perhaps it is your supposed condition," the avatar said.

"What the hell do you mean 'supposed condition'?" There was no time to listen to the reply, her opponent had swung and she had to phase. He wasn't fooled and he followed her phase in a classic counter-move. She altered the direction of her own phase just in time and the great-sword cleaved through the fractal dimension that her body had just vacated. Back in normal she hopped away out of his reach and started to circle him again. He, having recovered his balance, also put some space between them and circled.

"I said that you needn't worry, you are not pregnant." the avatar's voice repeated.

"Don't be stupid the mechs and the healer verified it," Seventeen screamed in her head.

"They only read the displays on the analysis units. It was a trivial matter to alter the results."

"But why the gods did you do that?" Seventeen thundered. Too late she realised her mistake. Her opponent had sensed her distraction and he'd moved. He'd got inside her guard and that was bad. She phased and he followed. Once someone was inside your guard it was almost impossible to twist the dimensions sufficiently to become completely impervious. She had a momentary thought, "This guy is f**g strong." as he transferred the weight of the huge sword into one hand and thrust it at her. She couldn't avoid it. It would skewer her and the result would probably be fatal. Time seemed to slow and she felt herself jump. It was impossible, she couldn't react that fast, nobody could. The blade slicing towards her stomach went between her legs and, at the same time she felt herself sweep her axe downwards. Her body fell again pushing the man's sword arm downwards out of harm's way. Then time seemed to return to normal and she realised that the man's arm was falling but his body wasn't. His shoulder was spouting blood from the hacked flesh and bone that remained. She'd somehow managed to take his arm completely off.

She remembered bouncing on her feet as they hit the ground again and she remembered the unbelieving look in the big guy's eyes as his whole body folded. His match was over, he might not even live and there was the sound of a mech wagon approaching that would drag him away. Time was called as her move was repeated on the screens for those who'd missed the action itself.

In his control room Volinar was congratulating himself on playing the girl even though he'd bent the rules. It had probably won him the match. That had been a move in a million. She had jumped over her opponent's sword, an amazing feat of acrobatics whilst she was phasing and had synced with him on the downfall to take his arm off with her axe. He and the other managers would be analysing the move for weeks to come.

On the pitch Seventeen was holding a speeded up argument with the avatar.

"How the gods can I be pregnant and not pregnant?

"\A wanted to keep you safe and he evolved a strategy; if you were pregnant then you would no longer participate in the game, hence the risk of you being injured would be reduced and limited to a single match." the avatar said.

"Why didn't you tell me this?" Seventeen asked.

"\A assumed that there would be time for explanations after your last match."

"What if I didn't want to be pregnant?"

"Considering the other options available it was the only logical choice. When Volinar broke the rules about using pregnant women as players \A decided that more direct action was needed and \A installed myself in your circlet as an extra precaution."

"And who are you exactly?"

"I am an avatar of \A; a part of \A who can act independently of \A but remain linked to you at all times," the avatar replied.

"I thought that the golden one monitored me himself."

"Yes, you are correct however \A can only monitor you for a very short period every few seconds \A has his normal duties and analyses to perform and cannot devote all of his core capacity to this one experiment. Therefore he installed myself. As an independent avatar I am able to devote my consciousness to full time monitoring of your systems. I report any significant changes or events directly back to \A during his direct monitoring period. The bandwidth gain is considerable."

"So you watch me?"

"Yes and I have discretion to intervene if circumstances warrant it. For instance I activated your leg muscles to cause you to jump to avoid the sword. I'm afraid that I needed to use the downswing momentum provided by your axe to give the jump extra impetus otherwise your muscle power alone might not have allowed you to avoid the impact with the sword."

"So, you made me jump and you cut that guy's arm off." Seventeen said.

"I regret the injury caused to your fellow player but the physics of the situation did not allow for any other option."

"I'm not complaining, you probably saved my life," Seventeen said.

"We still have the rest of this match to get through; I believe play is resuming." the avatar said.

Seventeen shook herself, she had a million other questions to ask but now was definitely not the time. The opposing team had seen what had occurred on the action replay. She was marked as a threat and it was certain that Wotar, the opposition's manager would be keen to eliminate her. She had better watch herself.

423

As if to give truth to her thoughts she saw that Wotar had shifted two of his players into position to mark her. She hefted her axe, calmed her troops, took in a deep breath and stood ready.

Volinar kept an eye on his star player for the rest of the match. He stayed out of direct intervention, only sending her an encouraging thought through her crystal when play momentarily focussed on another part of the field. The contact didn't feel quite right but he put it down to her condition. If only there was some way of inducing the same changes in other players without the biological consequences. He would have to have a word with the healers. They were supposed to be impartial but they were only flesh and blood like any other mortal.

Seventeen finished the match and dragged herself off the pitch. She was weary and she'd lost nearly half of her troops. Wotar had really had it in for her. She was surprised that she'd got off so lightly; only a few minor cuts and a few nasty bruises but as the saying went ' you should have seen the other guy'. She smiled to herself; it hadn't been just one guy: in the end Wotar had thrown four of his players against her.

However she had survived and the team healers had made a cursory examination, applied the usual wet sponge, and had told her to get herself off to the showers. She was even slightly gratified by the remark that she overheard as she entered the tunnel to the dressing rooms; her coach had been boasting to an opposition coach, "I trained her, I taught her that move." He'd done nothing of the sort but she let it go. She wanted the showers and she wanted sleep and then a long talk with her new companion.

After her shower she went back to her room. It was a luxury afforded to top ranking players and she'd have to get used to barracks again if she kept up the pretence of being pregnant. She slept and woke sometime later. Damn, she'd missed the debrief. That would be another black mark against her but she didn't care.

She poked around in her brain until she found the itch that she associated with \A. She prodded it, "I want to talk."

424

The small voice resumed, "Ah, you have completed your recovery and integration period. I ran a diagnostics on your systems during the interim. There is minor damage to skin and subcutaneous capillary vessels but the repair systems in you body are already absorbing and repairing the damage. The physical functioning of your cortex is satisfactory. There are minor lesions and I can attempt repairs however I am not permitted to interfere with the configuration or the actual processing taking place. This is the subject of \A's study and I may not alter it."

"So what you are saying is that my mind is still my own."

"Correct."

"Good, I am starting to think that the fewer things that can alter my mind the better. The mnemnosynth carves chunks out of my memory. The crystal in my skull can be used to control or destroy me, just like the control collars that have to be worn by the infants. The circlet can repair and rearrange my brain."

"I should point out that the circlet will always ask permission," the avatar interrupted.

"Only since I became valuable to \A. I'll bet that prior to that he would have twisted my mind in whatever way he pleased." Seventeen said.

"I reiterate, \A is a conscionable being. Direct manipulation is not in his makeup." the avatar sounded anxious.

Seventeen left it, she couldn't actually do anything about the devices in her head. If they chose to blow her brains out of her ears she couldn't stop them so she might as well use them to her own advantage.

"Right. Let's get back to practicalities. As far as the rest of the world is concerned I am pregnant, so what happens now?"

"The current practice is that you are transferred to the maternity centre and your everyday roster will be changed to one appropriate to your new status. As a potential supplier of future players you will be given a place to sleep, you will be fed and you will be required to contribute to the operation of Leikvangur."

"So I will become some sort of mindless botch?"

"No, the general degraded mental state of most in the maternity unit is due to repetitive overuse of the mnemnosynth. It keeps the mothers-to-be content and compliant. It is deemed necessary because of the vagaries of the hormonal imbalances that can accompany the condition. Since I can interfere with the operation of the mnemnosynth on your cortex you will remain in full control of your thoughts. The question of hormonal imbalance will obviously not be relevant."

"How do I 'contribute to the operation of Leikvangur'?"

"I suspect that you will not find that difficult, in fact you may enjoy some of it. In the early and middle stages of pregnancy mothers-to-be are required to work gathering basic foodstuffs and other raw materials. As the pregnancy reaches termination mothers-to-be are sequestered in the crèche to aid other mothers and their newborns. After the offspring are delivered and weaned the mothers are returned to the breeding pool to become pregnant again or, if their fertility wanes they are recycled or given temporary status as matrons in the crèche."

Seventeen shivered, "It hadn't sounded too bad until the avatar had said the word recycled."

"I hate to point out the obvious flaw in this plan to keep me safe. Won't someone notice if my body doesn't show any signs of changing?"

"Of course but that will not be for several months. \A and I are working on a resolution to the problem. An initial tactic is that you will meet with an accident whilst gathering raw materials. However to make this successful the crystal embedded in your skull will need to be neutralised. Any attempt at removal inevitably causes death. We are considering solutions to this problem."

"Well I suppose that gives us a breathing space to find a solution. So what happens now?"

"You should look at the roster: it will tell you. It should be updated by now. Do you wish me to tell you what it says?"

"Go on."

"It says, report to stores and give designation 'Seventeen status-change MTB.' then proceed to Maternity Centre," the avatar said.

"Just one thing before we leave, I know that the golden one has a designation \A what is your designation; what do I call you?"

"You can call me whatever you like. What would you like to call me? "

"How about Echo?" Seventeen said.

"Yes, that would be appropriate. I am now Echo." the avatar replied.

******

"These clothes itch," Seventeen thought a day later. She had been issued three loose fitting smocks from stores. They weren't a patch on her normal tunic and pants that she wore under her armour. Neither were the clogs any substitute for her boots. Reluctantly she'd accepted the change of apparel that went with her change in status but that was the least of it. Her mind had forgotten what it was like living in a cohort barracks and she hadn't slept well with all the human noises around her. All sorts of others, botches, administrators, coaches and players were bundled in with her. The only thing that they had in common, she found out later was that they were all recently impregnated. It made sense; there must be a mechanism to renew the support staff for the game when they became unable to function but she'd never bothered to learn the details.

Echo explained it to her whilst she was in the line queuing for her breakfast, "There are six managers each of whom have three teams of thirty six players and eight reserves. Each team requires six support staff. Then there are the general staff, players and support

427

staff needed communal facilities like healers and technicians and administrators. There are about a hundred of these in total. Then there were the children and the mothers in the maternity centre. All these people need services; places to live, things to eat. The botch class provides all the services. They harvest food, prepare it, maintain things, launder clothes, move things from here to there and do all the menial jobs. Echo said that for every person involved in the game there were eight or more needed in the botch class. The botch class also need the same services and so the effect is cumulative. The total population of Leikvangur is approximately ten thousand and about two hundred of them are pregnant at any one time. Hence the maternity centre requires almost as many resources as the teams themselves."

"Who are you talking to?" a voice asked.

Seventeen looked around and saw a woman, she was heavily built with blonde hair and large breasts. Seventeen's training automatically sized her up as an opponent but there was no muscle tone. This woman had never been a player or wielded weapons. "Oh, just thinking," Seventeen said.

"Well keep doing it dearie, it helps," the woman said, "I'm Bella and this is my fourth, I know, I can't help it. I seem to get pregnant if I just look at a man. Still, it's not bad, the work's not hard and the food is good if you know what to choose."

Seventeen looked puzzled. The woman gave a small laugh, "Eating for two, you know. What's your name?"

"Seventeen," Seventeen said.

"I thought I recognised you." Bella smiled broadly, "You're a player. I saw you play once. You were good."

"Yes," Seventeen said.

"And now you're down here with the rest of us brood mares. Look, if you'll take my advice follow my lead and choose what I choose. The new ones always go for the fancy stuff, not that I blame them. I did when I had my first but it gives me the wind and that's not something you want if you like a peaceful time in the barracks. It tends to make you unpopular especially at night time. Now I'll shut up. They get suspicious if they see people getting too friendly."

Bella turned and picked up a plateful of some mashed brot, a handful of nuts and a piece of fruit. She ignored the fried sausage and the exotic-looking stew of vegetables and the thick creamy porridge with the sweet fruity swirl running through it. Seventeen followed her example but she noticed that most of the other women helped themselves to the sausage and stew. She carried her tray over to the tables but Bella had sat at a table with some women who were much further along in their pregnancies and there was no room for Seventeen. The next table had a space. The table was occupied by women at all stages and nearly all of them were tucking into the stew or the creamy porridge. Seventeen turned to the woman next to her and said, "I'm Seventeen and I'm new here, what's your name?" The woman looked at her with a blank expression; then she turned back to her food. Seventeen looked at the other women on her table. They all seemed intent on their food and none of them were talking.

"When you are finished, offer to take one of their plates back to the servers," Echo said.

"Why," she said using her internal voice.

"I suspect that the advice that your new friend gave you is sound. I need a sample of that stew to verify my supposition," Echo replied, "Your new friend may be sitting with the others but she's watching you. She's not the only one, the routes that the matrons take through the tables are variable but the time variant positional analysis of their lines of vision indicates that you are the primary object of their observation."

"I've only just met Bella, why is she watching me?" Seventeen asked.

"There are two scenarios; she is as she appears, an intelligent woman who has been in your situation and wishes to help you or she is a clandestine operative who uses a false bonhomie to observe her targets."

"But why are they watching me?"

"You are unusual. Regardless of the supposed randomness of partner assignments it is rare that a member of the majors becomes pregnant mid season. The partner choice and timing of the rostering for sex is often skewed to ensure that the team membership remains constant throughout the season."

"You mean they cheat and I shouldn't have become pregnant. So they are puzzled by my test results and they are suspicious."

"Correct! Volinar thinks that you were sabotaged by Severell. Of course you were never pregnant so the managers are secretly trying to find out what went wrong."

"So Bella might just be being friendly or she may be a spy."

"Again you are correct. I see that you have finished your meal. I analysed its content as you ate it. Apart from some minerals and trace contaminants which may be just due to the residue of the growing or preparation process the food seems to be benign. Ah, here is your chance, the woman next to you has finished. Offer to take her plate. Make sure you put your thumb in the remains of the stew as you carry it."

Seventeen did as she'd been told. The woman hardly reacted as Seventeen swept up her plate with hers. She deposited the plates back on the servery and accidentally put her thumb in the gravy. "Right, now suck your thumb," Echo said. Seventeen complied and made her way to the wall to consult the roster. She was to report to section P of the centre. Section P was helpfully marked on the map on the wall but she noticed that it also had a big green footprint next to the name. Echo's voice came through, "It looks like your new friend is genuine or very devious. The stew is laced with an addictive soporific."

"That's why those women looked vacant; they were drugged." Seventeen thought.

"It would appear that that is the normal for most of the maternity population. It is probably has the same effect as using the mnemnosynth on the players however these women do not need fast reactions or quick minds to perform their function," Echo said.

"But how did Bella discover the drug and why did she warn me about it?"

"We will have to ask her," Echo said.

The opportunity to ask Bella didn't arise and Seventeen was assigned to her duties. Because she was physically strong she had been assigned to the farms. These were vast areas of cleared land and shallow ponds where the basic foodstuffs that fed Leikvangur were produced. They were outdoors, a novel sensation for Seventeen, but most of the women didn't seem to notice the difference. The maternity population worked a strip of fields and ponds that were right against the city walls. Seventeen had never been this far from the centre before and she found the experience of standing up to her ankles in mud quite strange. Her compatriots didn't; for many of them this wasn't any different to what they'd done all their lives. The work wasn't hard, just monotonous; gather the tubers into baskets and carry the baskets over to a cart, then return to the ponds for more tubers. They worked without any breaks for eight hours and then the matrons came around to herd them all inside. When they returned to the barracks they weren't afforded the luxury of individual showers; they were led into a tunnel and were told to strip and dump their clothes into a chute. As they were marched through the tunnel water poured in cascades from the ceiling and sluiced off the mud. Collecting dry smocks at the other end, they were marched back to the barracks. The first stop in the barracks was the refectory where Seventeen again lined up to be fed. Lacking Bella's advice, Echo told Seventeen to take some of everything but not to eat anything. Seventeen went and sat at a table at random. "Touch each item on the plate with the little finger of your right hand. Don't make a show of it, pretend to be as vacant as your fellow diners."

Seventeen started to do as she was told but she noticed that the little finger on her right hand had been injured; the nail was blackened down one side. She thought that she must have injured it gathering the tubers and not noticed because of the mud. As if the thought had been a question the answer came through, "I have taken the liberty of growing a sensor onto the nail. It will detect any added ingredients in the food and I can tell you which foods to avoid."

Seventeen thought privately that Echo was proving useful in her new life. Without the avatar she would be as insensible as the girl who sat next to her gulping down large quantities of some highly spiced concoction. Seventeen didn't need Echo to tell her that that was full of drugs.

After the meal was over her group was herded into a large room filled with benches. There was a general melee as people seemed to seat themselves at random. She was about to sit when someone caught her elbow. Bella steered her over to a bench at one side that was right up against the wall and sandwiched between a pillar and a stack of tables. "Over here where the matrons can't see," was all the large woman said.

Seventeen turned to speak to Bella but Bella hissed under her breath, "Not yet, wait until it starts."

The lights in the room dimmed and the wall facing them flickered. An image of a dwarf clad in full battle armour appeared. Sound came from the wall and the image spoke. Seventeen had seen consoles and training vids and so she wasn't frightened by the huge images. The dwarf started telling the 'story of the game'; she'd seen it so many times in her training that she automatically knew what was coming next. Bella ignored the spectacle and said, "I couldn't get to you to warn you about the meal but I can see that you survived it anyway. You're not feeling drowsy at all are you?"

"No," Seventeen replied, "I remembered what you said about avoiding the things that looked too good and I have a good sense of smell. I didn't eat anything that smelled too spicy. Why are they trying to drug us?"

"Simple," Bella replied, "it makes us easy to control."

"But why don't they just put the drugs into everything we eat?" Seventeen asked.

"The matrons and supervisors eat in the same refectory. It wouldn't do to have them too drugged to herd us about. How did you work out that the food was drugged?" Bella asked.

"It was obvious, all the others at my table looked as though they were asleep with their eyes open." Seventeen answered.

"I knew you was a clever one the first time we met." Bella held up her hand to her mouth and shook her head. Seventeen heard her voice drop to a whisper, "We can talk more in a minute. They always play the same thing every time before the game starts. You have to keep quiet when the game itself starts but once it's running there is so much noise that we can talk again."

Seventeen waited. The match on the wall was a junior league one but it wasn't very interesting to her, she'd seen better ones on the training vids. Once the audience in the room started shouting and cat calling at the action she risked saying something to Bella. "Tell me, when we first met you asked me who I was talking to. I wasn't talking to anyone?"

Bella smiled, "Ah you see dearie, just because we aren't players it doesn't mean botches can't think or have talents of their own. You know the little voice inside your head that is you?" Seventeen nodded, "well my talent is that sometimes I can hear what the one inside other people's heads is saying."

"You read minds?" Seventeen asked astonished.

"No, nothing so grand. That little voice that is you talking to yourself sometimes makes the voice in your throat copy the words. I can hear that tiny whisper that it makes. Of course nobody lets that happen to inner thoughts, just surface ones."

"And you heard me speaking to my Echo?" Seventeen asked.

Bella smiled in the dim flickering light, "Is that what you call it? I like it; you're exactly right. It is like an Echo of your thoughts. I knew you was clever."

Seventeen was momentarily distracted as half the crowd jumped to their feet and roared as a junior on one of the teams was cut down by his opponent. Bella said, "Look at them, I used to be like that until I found out the truth. There was a woman who told me all about it during my second pregnancy. Her name was Aleen. I don't know how she found out but there must have been someone before her. She didn't make it. After her second miscarriage the matrons decided that she wasn't good breeding material. They recycled her." she sighed, "I kept my wits about me and I began to notice things. I didn't make any fuss I just worked the system to my advantage. I met a couple of others who were 'in the know' and that's how I spotted you. You are clever and strong and your inner voice is very strong. I thought that you could benefit from my wisdom and so here we are."

They spent the rest of the match talking as the occasion permitted, when the crowd were noisy and when Bella thought that the matrons weren't watching. Bella warned her not to do anything that might attract attention to herself and just before the match finished she sidled back into the main bulk of the crowd. She left Seventeen thinking about what she'd discovered.

Ch 42: Pirate Coves

The dwimmerlaik looked down on the train of carts wending their way down the track to the shore. From its vantage point high on the slope it could also see the boats in the water. Some glimmer of memory stirred in its brain. It had once sailed the sea. Whatever, his master would not approve of such large parties of dwarves so close to Leikvangur even if they seemed intent on other business. It also saw that the train was under observation by at least two bands of skogs. It considered what to do. Volinar's mind was occupied elsewhere and so the dwimmerlaik acted on instinct. It followed.

"Get a move on," Gibra yelled, "We need to get this lot aboard and away before nightfall." She scanned the hills behind them. There was no sign of any skogs but they were well adapted to the forests and she had a funny feeling that she was being watched.

She'd be happier once she was on the beach. At least she would be able to see them coming. The wagon train had been attacked twice on the way here but the attackers had just thrown a few spears and had disappeared back into the forests. She'd learned to tell the difference between her new enemies. One set of skogs were small and fast but disorganised. They used hit and run tactics, they appeared, threw a few spears and then disappeared again. The other sort were different. They were large, they coordinated their attacks and the backed up their spears with long knives. She had lost two men to an attack earlier in the week and the attack was the reason why she was here. The attack had destroyed a shipment of Kanis destined for Vatersey, the crates on the wagons were its replacement.

Gibra scanned the sea. "Good," she thought, "the ship is here." Even as she watched she saw the small rowing boat being lowered and it started to approach the shore. "Get those crates off the wagons and get them onto the boat or I'll flay your hides"

The boat made two trips between the shore and the ship and it was now returning for a third time. Gibra needed to speak to the ship's

435

captain and she went aboard. The boat had just come alongside the ship when there was a yell from the lookout. "Sail ahoy!"

Gibra scrambled onto the deck and scanned the horizon where the lookout was pointing. There was another ship there all right. It didn't look like a fishing vessel. The captain came up to her and said, "It's a justicer pirate cutter." As if to confirm his words a fireball arced through the air towards his ship. "They've seen us and they must have a distance scryer on board. They know who we are and they're going to try to get us. We won't stand a chance if they close." He turned and shouted to his crew, "Loose the skiff, cut the anchor, haul on all sails, we have the wind with us. Turn and run!"

Gibra watched the shore fall behind. The captain had made the right decision and his swift action had meant that by the time the cutter had turned to follow they were well away. The cutter had followed for an hour but it wasn't even trying. It obviously had other orders. The renegade justicer watched it fall below the horizon. "Well, I was thinking of getting off Skogrey and moving to Vatersey but not just yet." Her plans had been disrupted again but she was nothing if not adaptable.

******

The dwimmerlaik watched what had happened. The ship had left, it was being chased by the cutter. Most of the traffickers were marooned on the beach along with the carts. Now that it was a true undead the dwimmerlaik had gained its full power; the living instinctively feared it, all the living, not just dwarves. It headed into the forest coming up behind the large band of small skogs who had been tracking the carts. The skogs panicked when they saw it coming and broke cover running towards the trapped traffickers on the beach. Of course the traffickers opened fire on the creatures and they retaliated. The dwimmerlaik wasn't finished he quickly skirted around the cove and came upon the smaller band of larger skogs. It was more difficult to panic them so the dwimmerlaik strode into their midst and picked one up and ripped it apart. The others fled in

436

fear in the general direction of the other melee. The traffickers were now being attacked from two sides.

The dwimmerlaik left them to it. It didn't care which side won they were all living and he now hated the living with a vengeance.

******

"Halverson, Captain of the cutter 'Retribution' here." the voice from the scrying crystal said.

"Good to hear from you Captain, this is Commander Bentin here. I believe you have information on the drug traffickers. I'll need a formal report from you eventually but I am anxious to hear what went on. Please tell me in your own words, Captain."

"Thank you sir. About noon yesterday we were off the east coast of Skogrey at approximately twenty point three degrees east, twenty two degrees north on a mission to unload reinforcements for Officer Kilton's party. As we approached the shore we saw a vessel anchored near to the shallows. It appeared to be loading cargo from a group of people on the beach. My watch officer observed them through his telescope and he identified the ship as the Vagabond. The Vagabond is suspected of being used by Kanis traffickers and so we approached and fired a warning shot. The Vagabond loosed anchor and put on sails. The wind was with them and they outdistanced us. We followed for approximately one hour but decided that our mission had higher priority. We returned to the beach to ferry the reinforcements ashore in the longboat. We had expected the traffickers to be long gone but to our surprise they were still on the beach. They were being attacked by a large tribe of skogs. Our forward ballista fired a few rounds of fireballs but we only succeeded in setting a couple of the carts on fire. The traffickers had seen us and they obviously decided that they stood a better chance of survival with us. Several of them went into the water and tried to swim out. I'm afraid the commotion had attracted a shiver of sharks and none of them made it. We disembarked the reinforcements and they joined in the battle. Our magic and our superior weapons quickly killed many of the skogs and the rest fled

437

back into the forest. We incurred no casualties however several of the traffickers were injured.

I went ashore and assessed the situation. There were seven of the traffickers with minor injuries, two with serious injuries and four dead. Two of the carts had been destroyed by fire and the remaining two were mostly empty except for a single crate of Kanis. In accordance with regulations we burnt the Kanis offering the carts and draft animals to the shore party. I reasoned that these would help the shore party catch up with Kilton's group more quickly. We clapped the trafficker survivors in irons and fetched them aboard the Retribution for transport back to Arnes. I interrogated them whilst we were travelling. They all claimed that they had been pressed into service by the bosses of the traffickers but this was merely to try to reduce their sentences. One of them was more cooperative than the others and he swore that he would testify that the leader of the operation on Skogrey was a justicer officer; Officer Gibra."

"Good work Captain, How sure are you that your informant was telling the truth. Do you believe officer Gibra was involved with the traffickers?"

"The fellow was quite certain and when I mentioned the name to one of the prisoners who was badly injured he confirmed it. Once it became generally known that we knew of her involvement all of the remaining prisoners confirmed it."

"So Gibra has gone rogue. It doesn't really surprise me. If she wasn't amongst the dead or the prisoners then I assume that she escaped on the Vagabond, Captain."

"It would appear so, Commander. I do, however, have one other piece of information. The prisoner told me that the Vagabond's destination was Vatersey not Griprey."

"That is interesting Captain. I will send a fljúgbátr to Vatnarheim with the news. I am officially declaring Gibra an outlaw and I will inform Lord Skald of the development. With any luck the fljúgbátr will arrive ahead of the Vagabond and we can have a reception party ready for it."

"It might work Commander, but I suspect that as the Vagabond left her anchor behind they will put into a deserted river mouth to make repairs before attempting a harbour. I wouldn't be surprised if they already know of a suitable location. Since we've seriously damaged the trafficker's capabilities on Skogrey I may take the Retribution north and circle the coast of Vatersey to try to locate their hidden encampment."

"Good idea Captain. I'll look forward to your report in due course."

******

Captain Grimm watched the messenger depart. So, it had finally happened and Gibra had shown her true colours. She was an outlaw and would now have a price on her head. It also appeared that she was heading in his direction. He had grown accustomed to his new home. It was much less restrictive than the capital. The people were also more relaxed. They tended to say hello when he passed rather than the usual silent scowl that he'd been greeted with in the capital.

Of course he was still the law and not everyone felt at ease when he was around especially when he was patrolling the darker side of Vatnarheim called the Shade. It was inevitable that the growing town, now a small city in its own right, would attract a criminal element. So far he'd not had to deal with any out and out killers. There were the occasional violent deaths but they were mostly the result of drunken brawls between men down from the logging camps or domestics where the wife, it was usually the wife for some reason, had taken exception to something and had solved her problem permanently. The dark side of Vatnarheim was mostly the infrastructure associated with vice and theft. Gambling halls and brothels, pawnbrokers and slums.

Lately Sting had hit the town and there was a growing problem with the drug. Someone was supplying it quite freely and cheaply. That was a warning sign in Grimm's estimation. The dealers were building up their market by making it easy to become addicted. Later they could reap the profits by controlling availability and price. It was such a serious problem that the previous evening he'd organised a raid on a place in the Shade where a tip-off had said that there was a factory making the drug. It had turned out to be a kitchen sink operation, it made drugs but it was only small scale. There were much bigger places somewhere making industrial quantities of the drug. He shrugged, even a small win was a win.

Now, with the prospect of a character like Gibra on the scene he could expect an escalation of the drug problem. It needed more resource but he didn't have enough people. Perhaps he could try out an idea that he'd had. Currently all his officers were temple trained and had magic. He himself only had a smidgeon of magic but it wasn't what drove him to seek justice for his fellow citizens. The idea was to find similar individuals to himself and, regardless of whether they had magic or not, train them to become good cappers. That would ease the resource problem. He'd even found some potential recruits. There were older men who were ex loggers; hewing trees was hard work and loggers tended to be past their prime in their early thirties. The ex-loggers that he socialised with were forty or older but they still had muscles from years of wielding an axe. He could broach the subject with them. It wouldn't be a good move to mention his idea to those at the temple, they tended to tradition and, in any case, they had their hands full with the new construction.

Yes, there was plenty to do and he'd not written to the Lady for a week or two. He supposed that there wasn't any hurry, she wouldn't get the letter immediately in any case. He'd received a message from her that she was taking an expedition to Skogrey to search for any news of her parents. She'd gone with her friend Brannhår, the maker girl that had given him his whip. He smiled, it had been an excellent gift and it had saved his life on a couple of occasions when he'd been in a tight spot. He practised with it every day and even by his own estimation he was getting quite good.

Maybe the Lady would detour via Vatnarheim on her way back to the capital, she did, after all, own most of the town and the surrounding forests as well as all the paper mills. It would only be sensible to check in on her investments from time to time. It would be good to see her again. Deep in his mind the thought changed to "If only I could see her again it would be wonderful!".

Ch 43: Nothing New Under the Suns

The expedition spent the next day in camp. Potar and Mila went out to scout for any more bands of skogs. Planket wanted to bake and this was almost impossible whilst they were travelling, Brother Kerian, Brannhår and Silfuryn wanted to examine what they'd found in the lookout cave.

"This is interesting, the book appears to be someone's diary and he appears to have been something of an artist. There are drawings of dwarves and other things; skogs and animals and birds. There are also a lot of notes. The writing is different to that on the metal sheets, I can make out the odd word and it looks to be of a different era. There are whole sentences that, if you say them aloud you can almost hear the meaning. It's like some of the ancient chants that we had to learn in the temple when I was young," Brother Kerian said.

"Obviously the tunnel garrison wasn't where my parents disappeared, that place hadn't been used by its original inhabitants for a very long time. Does the book give us any clues where we should try next?"

Brannhår said, "Wherever we go we will have to keep a lookout for those skogs. I examined their swords, they were newly forged and of reasonably good quality; they weren't ancient weapons handed down the generations. It means that they must have come from a village which has been set up long enough to have a forge or they have obtained the weapons by trading with someone who has that capability. Either way they are a serious problem."

"I'll have to spend a little more time looking at the book but I would say that we should keep heading south. The garrison guarding the pass faced south and it is reasonable to suppose that there must be some other outposts further south." Brother Kerian said.

"I'll go through your parent's notes again and see if I can get any more from them. It is a pity that they're incomplete. Your father keeps referring to a map but I can't find anything that looks like a map in the notes."

Silfuryn replied, "If we don't get any pointers from the book or the notes then we'll head south tomorrow. I'm going to try to clear my head and climb to the top of this hill."

"Be careful," Brannhår warned, "There may still be some of the skogs about."

"I will be, I'll take Mistle along. She will tell me if anything isn't right."

Silfuryn climbed to the top of the hill and found that the other side ended in a sheer drop into a deep ravine. The opposite wall of the ravine had sunk and so Silfuryn had a birds-eye view of the terrain. To the south, the wall of the ravine gradually lost height until, about half way to the horizon, both walls were the same height and were only just visible over the jungle. To the north the disparity in heights continued and she could see, in the far distance the plains that led down to the coast. Immediately below her was a dense forest with the occasional clearing. Something was moving across one of the clearings. It looked pebble sized from her vantage point but, in reality it must have been ten times her height in length. It looked like a lizard with spines down its back. There were ant-sized creatures around it but she couldn't make out what they were doing. She took out her telescope and focussed it on the group. Now she could see things clearly. It was a hunt, the large creature was a giant lizard and the ant sized ones were skogs. They were attacking the larger lizard and from what she could see they were winning. The skogs looked like the ones that had attacked them the previous day. They were too far away for Silfuryn to be concerned but she watched as they killed their prey and dragged it off heading north so Silfuryn knew that her expedition wouldn't be likely to run into them. She turned her attention to the south and panned the telescope across the horizon in that direction. All that she could see was an endless canopy of trees. Then she saw it; a tiny reflection

443

from something shiny caught her eye. She rested the telescope on a rock to steady it and studied the shape. It was just above the horizon on a mountain range that rose out of the surrounding plane. They'd head that way in the morning and she made a note of its direction.

Planket had used everyone else's absence to contact his squad. He had reported the attack and they had told him that they were being reinforced by others from Sudalyr. Commander Kilton had been concerned when Planket had told him about the weapons that the lizards were using and the fact that they wore clothing. Kilton told Planket that, as soon as his group met up with the reinforcements he would try to close the gap between them and the expedition so that they could assist if the lizards tried another attack. Planket signed off and went back to his baking.

Travelling through the forest with the wagon would be impossible so the expedition kept to higher ground where it was possible but even so, Silfuryn had to admit that soon they would have to abandon the cart and go ahead on foot. Since that meant splitting the party, Silfuryn wanted to put it off for as long as possible.

Two days later later they reached the object that Silfuryn had spotted. They had been fortunate because they had found some game trails left by the herds of giant lizards that obviously had a fixed migration route along a chain of small lakes. The trails were rough and wandered a little but it had meant that they could keep the cart and so the overall progress hadn't been delayed. Their goal was somewhere above them on an extinct volcano that rose from the middle of the vast valley. Silfuryn scanned the slopes and saw something that looked distinctly dwarven made; it was a ruin and it was about five thousand paces above the plain. As they'd arrived at sunset on the second day they decided to camp at the base of the volcano and explore the ruin when daylight returned.

******

The climb had taken most of the morning but the expedition thought that the effort had been worthwhile. The ruin was extensive and seemed to be overgrown and there was no sign that anyone or

444

anything had visited it recently. The entrance to the ruin was sealed by a massive disc of rock which hadn't been moved for a long time. Brannhår climbed onto the top of the ruin and found the thing that had attracted Silfuryn's attention. It was a massive bronze disc about twenty paces across set onto a vertical axle that was emerging from the bedrock. A series of metal gears were arranged so that the disc could be angled to the sun. The gears and axle were seized and Brannhår estimated that, in the afternoon just before sunset, it would reflect the sun to the north. She guessed that the reflection could probably be seen from the mountain slope above the tunnel garrison. Searching nearby she found the remains of ancient masonry and dessicated wood that she supposed had been used to shut off the beam of light from the disc. It was true that there was nothing new under the sun she thought ruefully. Master Dyrr would be hopping mad that his idea for the semaphore had already been in use a thousand years before he was born. Although the disc's surface was now quite pitted and eroded by the wind she could tell that, at one time it had held a high polish. It had also been decorated with symbols. There was a hollow in the masonry in amongst the foundations of the mirror mechanism. She shut her eyes and reached out with her metal sense. Below her was a large hollow space that was completely lined with metal. It looked like a shaft had once led down into the hollow space but it had been filled with dust and debris over the years. She went down to the others and told them what she'd found and Silfuryn climbed back up with her to see.

Silfuryn said, "The plug in the shaft is too big for me to phase through, I'm afraid we're going to have to dig."

Twenty minutes later there was a clang as the spade hit metal. Brannhår examined it, "It's some sort of hatch, there are hinges on one side and the other side is held down by a flange with a lock. It doesn't look to be too corroded, the alloy and the covering of earth has preserved it. There are three dials each covered in symbols. I suspect you have to align the symbols to open the lock. There are twelve symbols on each dial that means about two thousand combinations. I could try to crack it but it would take a while."

445

"Why don't I just phase through," Silfuryn said.

"I'm looking at the metal with my other senses," Brannhår said, "you can try but I think you'll be surprised."

Silfuryn placed her hand on the hatch and closed her eyes, "I can't. Something about the alloy stops me, it won't let me through."

"Yes I suspected as much, there is some sort of electrical current running through the metal which makes it impervious. Let me try something."

Brannhår shut her eyes, she could almost see the metal vibrating at some microscopic level. Then she looked at the lock. Its metal wasn't vibrating and she could see inside it. She moved one of the dials with her hand, after a full rotation nothing had happened. Undeterred she moved on to the next dial. She saw what happened. When the dial was in a certain position a small lever in the mechanism moved. "So," she thought, "you have to set the dials in order." She left the first dial where it was and then moved on to the second, this turned fully without anything happening so she moved on to the third dial. Again she found the sweet spot where something happened to the mechanism. She moved back to the second dial and, this time she found another sweet spot. She pulled at the handle on the hatch but it still didn't budge. There was still something locking it. She looked inside the handle, " Of course!" she thought and, against every instinct, she pushed. The hatch descended the tiniest fraction and there was a click. This time she pulled and the hatch swung open so smoothly that it might have been made only a day before.

The smell that emerged was of ancient decay and they both lurched back out of its way. The stink decayed as the outside air entered the hollow space and, after a minute, they looked back down the hole. There was an ornate metal platform just below it and Brannhår could see a spiral staircase descending to the floor. She had a sense of deja vu; she'd seen something very like this before somewhere. She shrugged and made to lower herself down.

"Let me go first," Silfuryn said, "I get the feeling that I should."

Brannhår moved out of the way and her friend lowered herself down. She noticed that Silfuryn had donned her gloves and was avoiding touching any of the metal with her bare hands. Once Silfuryn was on the platform she shouted up. "I was right, there are tiny needles in the rungs of the ladder, I've a feeling that they are there to deter intruders."

"Yes, and magical ones at that. A normal person wouldn't have tried to phase through that hatch," Brannhår said.

"Yes, you're right. Whoever built this wanted to keep magical people out. Does that mean justicers; have we stumbled across a renegade wizard hideout?"

"I don't think so, for one thing this ruin is too big and too complex to have been built by a small group. You need labour, and lots of it to shift stones as massive as those on the outside. No, I think that the people who built this were dwarves but they wanted to stop anyone else from tampering with the semaphore mirror controls." She shone her lamp down the stairway towards the opposite wall. A series of metal cabinets ran along its whole length and there were wheels and levers all along it.

"Move your lamp a little to the left," Silfuryn said, "Is that a doorway?"

"I think so. Do we go back and get the others or explore a little on our own?"

"Let's explore."

Twenty minutes later the party waiting outside by the huge entrance disc were amazed when the whole disc started to rumble and shake. The vines and undergrowth resisted for a while but the mechanism was too powerful. It slowly ground open. The party retreated drawing their weapons and awaiting an attack but they lowered them quickly when Brannhår and Silfuryn walked out into the daylight.

"We found the back door again," Brannhår said smiling.

"And this time there's lots to see." Silfuryn said.

******

They camped outside the ruin that night. The door was open and Silfuryn joked that the night breezes might take away the stink of the inside. The next morning they were about to prepare to spend the day exploring when Potar saw something in the valley floor. One of the open trails left by the passage of the herds of giant herbivore lizards was full of activity. There was a force of about fifty of the large skogs marching down it. They were headed north accompanied by a wagon that was being towed by one of the large armoured lizards with the dorsal spines.

Potar told Brannhår and she went to find Planket, "We know that Bentin ordered you to join our expedition and we know that you've been talking to a group of justicers who are following us. When you make your next report you should warn the group that there's a band of about fifty organised skogs headed straight for them. With any luck they haven't noticed us and, we can always hide in this ruin. I'm pretty sure I can lock it down again if I have to. You'd better make that report now so that your compatriots will have time to get ready. I can't say what weapons the skogs have, but tell your comrades to be ready for bows and metal swords as well as spears. The skogs look like they mean business."

Planket said, "How long have you known?"

Brannhår smiled, "From the first night, Mila heard you giving your report; however, after the fight the other day you're one of us now. So you'd better go and warn your people that trouble is on the way."

Planket nodded and burrowed in the cart for the scrying crystal.

The team had explored the outer rooms of the ruin and had tentatively agreed that it would be a good place to camp. It was sheltered and its walls were lined with stone and metal so that it was kept at a uniform temperature no matter what the weather was doing outside. Planket had found a sort of kitchen where there was a metal plate over a jet of scaling hot steam that emerged from a hole in the rock. Various grilles and stands were arranged so that they could be placed in the steam to hold cooking vessels. The only problem was light. The place had been built like a fortress and so there were only tiny windows in the outside rooms and none at all in the deeper ones. Brannhår had her stingbush lights and she kept them well charged but she only had two and they were only as powerful as a standard oil lamp. They all agreed that using oil lamps would eat into their fuel reserves and so exploration of the deeper ruins was limited.

"I should have brought more lights," Brannhår told Silfuryn as they entered yet another pitch-black room. This was another whose purpose could only be guessed at.

"What's this?" Silfuryn asked pointing to a lever set into the stone beside the door. Brannhår came over and looked with her metal sense, "It connects to a long rod going upwards through the rock. I'm not sure what it does."

Silfuryn pulled the rod and they both gasped. A muddy brown glow had appeared in the centre of the ceiling. "It's like the light tunnels at home, there must be an opening somewhere above. It's not very bright but it's better than nothing."

Brannhår agreed and as her eyes got accustomed to the dim light she began to pick out objects in the room. There were chairs and a desk and shelves and there was a large painting on one of the walls. She wandered over to it and shone her own light onto it. "Look here, It's some sort of map." Her lamp flickered and faded, it would need recharging before she could use it again. She retrieved her other one and switched it on.

"I wish there was some way of making that light in the ceiling brighter," Silfuryn said, "It's as bad as the time Alfsen found that firedab stuck in the fumarole."

"Of course," Brannhår said, "that's why it's so dim, there's something blocking whatever is gathering the light. I think we'd better go on top again and look around. If they were clever enough to use the sun as a source of light for the semaphore then they would naturally have arranged it so that it would illuminate their quarters."

An hour later the pair had found the problem. On the roof of the ruin a large patch of tangle-weed had taken over half of the surface. Brannhår set too with the spade and after she'd moved about a quarter of it she gave a cry, "Here it is. It looks like a shallow dome made of spa crystals Help me uncover the rest."

Once they'd cleared the weed and they had sluiced water over the crystals Brannhår decided that it was time to re-visit the inner rooms. When they re-entered the gloomy room with the map the difference was amazing. It was now bright from the brilliant white beams coming from the hole in the ceiling. The map, and everything else was plainly visible. They didn't stop there, they found other rooms with switches and slowly the interior of the ruin became as bright as day. Some rooms still only showed dim glows but Brannhår shrugged, "There must be other light gatherers that are overgrown, I'm sure the others would be happy to find them and clear them off. They will be as keen as we are to be able to use this fortress as a temporary home."

"Let's go and tell them," Silfuryn replied.

With the lighting problem solved the ruin could be explored properly. It was obviously a permanent location for a semaphore station and a military outpost. There were rooms with serviceable metal framed beds whose mattresses and blankets had long ago decayed to dust. They were comfortable enough when re-roped and with new blankets. There was a large room that was completely full of ramps and inclines and other gymnastic equipment and Mistle had claimed the room as her own. She scooted around, clearly enjoying the freedom. There were rooms where things had been stored but most of these were empty and there were the operational rooms, one of which was the room with the map. The map showed the home islands and it was fairly easy to read. There were dots where the main cities were and also dots denoting other places. Brannhår examined Skogrey and found a dot that corresponded to the tunnel garrison there were also dots corresponding to Arnes and

Sudalyr and numerous places around the coast. Brannhår didn't know if these places still existed but the dot that intrigued her the most was about two days travel to the south. It was at the base of a mountain range and, if she was reading the scale right it was just above the tree-line and it was big. She didn't know of any city at that location and so she supposed that it was another ruin: somewhere else to explore.

The following day she was examining one of the control rooms for the semaphore. It was a very sophisticated piece of engineering and she saw, somewhat to her chagrin that it had obviously used electricity to power the drives for the mirrors and the now defunct shutter system. She was just musing to herself that she'd been right, there **was** nothing new under the sun. Her science of lightning and electricity was a re-discovery just as this semaphore system pre-dated the one that Master Dyrr had devised. Still she consoled herself with the thought that she'd not hidden the discovery, she'd shared it with others and she had come up with it out of her own head rather than copying from someone else even though, to be honest, she'd remembered a lot of it it from a previous life. She was interrupted in her musings by a cry from Silfuryn who had rushed in,"You'll never believe it, I've found my father!"

Ch 44: The World Outside.

Seventeen had been assigned different duties. She suspected that Echo or \A had had a hand in the re-assignment but she didn't ask. Somehow, she'd been rostered to a mining detachment. Seventeen knew nothing about mining and she was only vaguely aware that the metal that made her weapons and much of the other equipment in Leikvangur came out of the ground. She thought that it grew there, like the 'brot' tubers but Echo explained that it was more complex than that. One of the restrictions on being assigned to the mining team was that the work was physically hard but it had the benefit that it was done in brief bursts. Much of the time was spent waiting around and nobody bothered you when you were just waiting.

The golden ones and the mechs had engineered material recycling to a fine art. Most material, including metal was scrupulously conserved. However even the most careful conservation could not preserve everything. Some metal wore down to fine particles which was mingled with the dust on the ground. The dust was gathered and disposed of but it wasn't rich enough to be worth re-processing. So some new ore was always needed.

Ore was mined from a series of tunnels dug into the side of mountains. The ore veins closest to Leikvangur had been worked out long ago and so there was now a considerable journey to the places where it could be found. This meant that Seventeen was roused early in the morning just after dawn. She then boarded a wagon with others that trundled its way to the ore tunnels. The finders, of whom Seventeen was one, would enter the tunnels, identify a promising metal seam and retreat back to the surface. Then the blasters were brought in. These were ordinary botches, not mothers to be. They would lay charges and set them off. Another set of botches went into the tunnels after them and moved the rock onto belts which carried the debris to the surface. The resultant rock then had to be sorted into ore bearing and ordinary rock. This was another job for the finders and it was the laborious part. Echo told her that the finders had to have magic, \A had seen that part of Seventeen's magic concerned an ability to detect and see flaws in metals and this made her an ideal candidate to be a finder. She could select out the purer ore from the dross. It still meant that Seventeen found herself shifting rocks to extract the ore bearing pieces but once a load had been processed it was back to Leikvangur which was another hour's ride.

Seventeen had protested to Echo that she was wasting time travelling but Echo disagreed and the avatar spent the hours teaching Seventeen about all sorts of things. One of the things she learned was that Leikvangur was only one city in a whole host of cities that spanned Svartalfheim. The avatar knew a lot about metals and how things were made which was useful. She also learned other skills. One which was particularly useful was an ability to shift her own internal time so that she could slow time in the outside world to a crawl or speed it up to make things seem to happen quickly. Echo had pointed out the advantages. She could seem to slow external time when she was in combat so that her opponent only moved slowly and she could alter her counter-move appropriately. On the other hand making external time go quickly meant that the mnemnosynth exposure couldn't synchronise with her mental processes and she could effectively counter its effects on her own. It was interesting though, she could go into the showers and, when she'd finished, she'd accelerate time and there'd be the briefest of flashes and her mind remained unaffected. It was also useful in the boring times when she was on the cart going to and from the mines.

The other good thing about being assigned to the 'finders' was that she could also practice using magic away from the prying eyes of the supervisors and matrons. They never entered the tunnels and finding ore wasn't easy. It often took hours and Seventeen used the time to refine her magical senses. She found that she was good at detecting ores, in fact she could tell the different types apart after a little practice. Then, when she was waiting for the blasters to do their job she would use her senses to explore the wilderness around the mining site. She had never known that there were so many animals, reptiles, birds and insects.

When her working day was over the wagon dropped them back at the ponds where the tubers were gathered. Often she would meet Bella and she'd work alongside her new friend and they'd talk. The matrons never objected, another pair of hands meant that they reached their quota faster and that was a good thing all around.

Bella knew a lot about how the process of pregnancy was managed and she also knew a lot about the injustices meted out on the citizens of Leikvangur by the managers.

"We are their slaves, our lives are at their beck and call. They can snuff us out with out turning a hair and yet they need us. All this, the Game, and Leikvangur itself would cease to function if it wasn't for the botches. You can see why the managers and their lackeys are so ruthless. One hint of resistance to their wishes is met with instant retribution. Look at my friend Aleen, a good, clever woman who never harmed anyone. She was executed because she didn't serve the manager's purposes any more. No other reason. She could have had many more years of life but it didn't suit those in power and so she had to go."

Seventeen had heard this story before. It burned in Bella's mind and the fire kept her alive with hate against the managers. It was the thing that filled her dreams. She often told Seventeen, "You have to have a purpose, there's nothing if there's no purpose. With no purpose you become just like the morons who take their drugs and pop out babies until they die."

Seventeen had even told Echo about her friend's obsession. One day when she was travelling back from the mines Echo said, "\A would like to examine the ephemeral you call Bella. He is certain that it would give him more insight into the ephemeral mind. Perhaps you could ask her if she would be willing."

"Oh yes, just go up to my new friend during a match and whisper to her that one of the golden ones would like to read her mind. She'd think that I was crazy," Seventeen replied.

"\A considered that if you asked her it might make her acceptance easier. Perhaps you could explain about the project in simple terms."

"I'm not even sure what the project is," Seventeen hesitated, "and why do you talk as if \A is someone else. I thought that you are \A"

"Yes, well I am and I'm not. I am part of, but separate from, the golden one designated \A. I act and think independently but whatever I experience he experiences and to a certain extent it works in reverse as well. It is like I am the child of \A. I have all the characteristics of \A but I am different and more limited. Of course it's more complicated than that; it is difficult to explain to an ephemeral."

"And I'm going to explain it to Bella?"

"You could show her the circlet. I know that you hide it in your hair but you could tell her what it really is." Echo said.

"All right, I'll ask, but I'm not going to recommend anything. It will have to be her own choice." Seventeen replied.

******

"You want me to let a mech read my mind!" Bella asked incredulously.

"No, it's not like that, It's like speaking to him but with your mind, not your voice," Seventeen explained.

"And how am I supposed to do that, I can't really hear thoughts I just hear what people are saying under their breath, mechs don't do that."

"I know, but I said that I'd ask. He's really very good, he won't force you to do anything. It really will be your choice if you do it."

"And you've done it? I mean talked with a mech?" Bella asked.

"Yes, when I first met him my mind was full of holes from the mnemnosynth. He sort of fixed them for me. It's why I could remember things and why I ended up here."

"What do you mean?"

"Well, my career was very dangerous and he was afraid that my returning memories would distract me at a critical moment and I would be seriously injured. So when I did get reported by my coach for inattention \A altered the healer's console to tell the healer that I was pregnant. It meant that I wouldn't have to fight for a while."

"What! You're not pregnant! But they're bound to find out girl. You can't hide that sort of thing!"

"I know but the golden one has a plan." Seventeen assured her.

"I don't know, perhaps I'd better have a talk with this mech. I'm sure it means well but it is a mech after all."

"Good, I'm sure he'll listen."

"Why do you call it a he, surely it doesn't have those parts."

"Oh no! When we first met he used to talk like 'this unit thinks this' or 'one can see why that is so' but as he began to understand me it became 'I think' and 'I understand'. It was if a person had grown out of our conversations. I call him a he because he mostly reacts like a he."

"Fine, I'll meet him then, but you have to come with me. Where and how is this conversation supposed to happen," Bella asked.

"I don't know, he'll probably arrange something. He's quite good at making things happen."

******

"You're to report for extra screening. Something about checking development of the baby. You are to go to room C713 in the healer block at ten thirty tomorrow. You will be excused normal duties until noon when you will rejoin your group."

Each of the matrons giving this instruction was unaware that she was arranging anything unusual. So whilst one was giving the message to Bella, the other was repeating it to Seventeen. In due course both women arrived at room C713 together. A mech was repairing the door but it moved to one side as they approached and waited for them to go through. As the door closed Seventeen said, "See, I told you that he would be able to arrange something. I'll bet that that mech is fixing an 'out of order' sign to the door as we speak."

"You mean that's not him?"

"Oh no, you'll notice the difference when you meet the real him."

As if on cue a voice came out of the shadows at the other end of the room. "Ah, my friend Seventeen, and this must be your friend Bella. I am pleased to meet you." Whilst the voice was speaking the golden one rolled forward slowly. Bella grasped Seventeen's hand tightly but she didn't back away. "If you will permit, Bella, I would ask you to place this band around your head. It is just like the one that Seventeen wears but yours is only temporary."

A hole opened in the golden one's smooth carapace and a metal tentacle extruded itself. It was carrying a circlet and it held it out to Bella."

"Here goes nothing." Bella said and she took the circlet and placed it on her head.

Seventeen watched as Bella's eyes closed.

"\A is accelerating her thought processes so as to minimise the interface time." Echo said inside her head, "The process is much more refined than when \A first communicated with you."

"What are they talking about?" Seventeen asked.

"I don't know, I am not linked to \A at present," Echo said.

After a minute or so Bella opened her eyes and blinked. She reached up and took the circlet off and held it out. The metal tentacle took it from her and it disappeared back inside the golden one.

"That was interesting," Bella said smiling, "Do you know he didn't even know how to disable the mnemnosynth? You just throw some mud on the grey panel below the blue light and a screen comes across the light and you don't lose any memories. All the botches

457

know how to do that. Of course when they've had a bad day and want to forget." She hesitated, "I hadn't realised that the drugs had done so much damage in my first pregnancy. He repaired me though. Isn't it wonderful, I can remember everything even from when I was a girl." Then her face darkened, "Those bastards have a lot to answer for." She shook her head and the dark mood was banished. "Gods, how long was I out. We'll have to hurry if we're to be back on roster by noon."

Seventeen took her friend's hand, "Just stay calm and sit down for a while. If you're feeling anything like I was after my conversations with \A you'll need to get your bearings. Let's talk a while."

"Yes, OK, but how long have we got."

"About an hour and a half; you were only gone for a minute."

"What! but we talked for hours and hours! He asked me about all sorts of things and he helped me remember things that I thought were long gone."

"I know, he can talk really quickly when he wants to," Seventeen replied, "So what did you talk about?"

"Oh he wanted to know all about my experiences of being a mother. Really he seemed to be interested in everything, when you get cravings for certain foods, when everything becomes focussed on the actual birth, what happens afterwards, what I do when I'm not pregnant. The other thing that he seemed interested in was how I managed to break out of the control that the managers have over everything. He seemed quite concerned when I told him about how we botches are considered to be disposable by the managers. Something about 'misdirected sentient potential' whatever that is. I'm afraid I didn't understand a lot of it and he used lots of long words and peculiar phrases. Anyway I don't seem to be any the worse for my meeting with him. In fact, what he said just seemed to confirm what I've always believed, people in Leikvangur are all just slaves to the Game."

"Yes, well I wouldn't say that outside this room." Echo said in Seventeen's head, "The golden ones might know of the situation but they don't do anything about it. There is an ancient non-interference agreement that goes back thousands of years. Many of the others, including most of the botches, don't know any different. They live the Game, literally, and they would report your friend just because she is different."

"I'll have to try to tell her that gently at some other time, now is not really appropriate, she's just confused. She's survived long enough to know the dangers," Seventeen thought back.

******

Bella was in the queue at the refectory and she pretended to be having a difficult decision choosing her meal. This meant that Seventeen, who was further back in the queue caught her up. They hadn't even had time to say hello when there was a commotion at the door.

The captives were coming in and the matrons guarding them were obviously having difficulties. Most of the girls were sullen and defeated but all of them were subject to the hormonal changes within their bodies: one had reached a turning point. She was screaming at one of the older captives, an older woman who she seemed to blame for something. "I don't care what they do to me. This is wrong. It's against all the teachings. We are not supposed to have sex and yet you let them rape me again and again and now I'm pregnant. I am a novice justicer and I believe in the rules. You have compromised, you've even been impregnated yourself. How dare you tell us what to do?"

"Please, I am only trying to keep you alive. Those rules are for the temple, they cannot apply if we are forced to do things against our will outside the temple. These people operate by different rules and, in order to survive in this society, we must compromise our beliefs," the nun said.

"You can compromise all you want to save your own skin. It's not up to you what I do or don't do any more. I would rather die than be mauled by one of them again."

"Don't say that, you cannot know what they will do to you. Some of these other women are drugged into insensibility. Do you want that, for your brain to to be so fuddled that you would be no better than a sow on a farm. Believe me, I was once a farmer's daughter and I know what happens to sows. Once they cease to farrow they are killed and eaten. Do you want that to happen to you. The temple knows that we were taken and they will send help. You have to believe that, you have to stay alive by any means until help arrives."

"Help isn't coming, they don't care about a few novices. They've probably already written us off."

"You mustn't believe that. You who profess to have faith in the temple. Do you really think that they will give up looking?"

The girl burst into tears and collapsed sobbing on the floor. A couple of matrons moved over to her and drew their prods. Bella spoke up. "Can't you see it's just the changes, it gets to us all after a couple of months. You were mothers once, you must remember how confusing it gets. Leave her, she'll come to her senses in a few minutes." There were mutters of approval from several others in the queue. Someone further down the line threw her plate at the cooks, a few more followed her example and the matrons moved off quickly to try to prevent the food riot escalating. The captive girl was left on the ground, forgotten.

Bella had gone over to the girl and Seventeen had followed. Bella said, "Get up girl, before they come back. If you want to get out of this alive you'd better play the game. If you keep your head down it's not so bad. Now, quick Seventeen, pick her up and take her over to a table. If she's sitting with others she won't be as noticeable."

Seventeen did so, the older captive had herded the other girls over to a table and she was in the process of settling them down. Most of them were crying or in a state of shocked silence. None were eating.

Since the matrons were still occupied Seventeen risked talking to the older woman. "Who are you?" she asked.

The nun regarded the fierce looking warrior type who had spoken, "I am Sister Magda of the temple at Arnes. I was in charge of these girls who were all in their final year of training. We were abducted about eight months ago by a foul creature and a band of skogs and we were made to march here. When we arrived we were all put into those rooms, the ones with the lights and I think we were raped... possibly several times; it is difficult to remember. Now nearly all of us are pregnant and we have been sent here. Who are you?"

"I am Seventeen of the Majors of Volinar," Seventeen said as if that explained everything, "you say that you were brought here from Arnes, that's outside Leikvangur isn't it?"

"If by that you mean that it is a different city to Leikvangur, then yes it is."

"I know that you were brought here to breed. Do they have better players in Arnes?"

"I'm sorry, I don't know what you are talking about."

"I'm a player, or I was. Don't you have players in Arnes. How can you have the Game without players?"

"What game? What do you mean?"

"**The** Game," Seventeen said as if the nun was being deliberately obstinate.

Bella came over, "They're still busy; the problem with keeping everyone drugged is that they tend to do whatever the next one in line does. I think one of my friends started it to distract attention but she moved away when the morons started to join in."

"Bella this is Sister Magda, she was a matron in Arnes before she was captured but she doesn't know what the Game is." Seventeen said.

Bella nodded, "Magda, this city Leikvangur and everyone in it serves one purpose; the continuation of the Game. It was invented thousands of years ago to reward some ancient Dwarf generals for their service. The Generals died and became draugr and they needed something to occupy themselves for the rest of eternity. So they made the game into a permanent state of war between themselves. Generals never do any fighting so they created players, like Seventeen here, to do the fighting for them and they make everyone else part of the Game."

"But that's not fair," Sister Magda said, "You mean you have no choice?"

"That's right, you serve the game or you get recycled," Bella said.

"We don't belong here, this is not how it is over the rest of Svartalfheim. Nobody is forced to do anything, there are choices." Sister Magda said.

"Well there aren't any here, I would give my right eye to give my children a choice." Bella said.

"And what's going on here?" a voice said, "Who are you. You have no business talking to these Framandi."

Bella turned and looked at the hulking matron, "I was only asking about the girl."

"Like I said, it's no business of yours. Get back to the whore house where you belong." the matron said.

"See you there," Bella muttered. The sound was faint but the matron heard. She raised the prod and plunged it into Bella's chest. Bella gave a howl and jumped to her feet. She punched the matron and then turned to Seventeen, "Get out before anyone else comes."

Seventeen heard Echo give her the same advice and she started to hesitate. The next thing she knew was that her legs had moved and she was walking slowly away from the table. Behind her Bella was howling defiance at the approaching matrons.

When she was twenty paces away Seventeen turned to watch. Five large matrons were holding Bella down and one was waving frantically at a man stood some distance away. As the matrons closed on Bella the man hurried up, "Oh no, another one," he said to himself. He took out a syringe full of a greenish liquid and plunged it into Bella's neck. Bella sagged; unconscious.

Three of the matrons let her fall and the other two dragged her body away. Seventeen overheard the conversation between the remaining three.

"What will happen to her?" one asked.

"Oh, they'll up her drug intake until the child is born and then she'll probably be recycled. Those are the rules but if it were me I'd kill her straight away. She's just trouble that one. I've had my eye on her for some time," the second one said.

"But that would kill the child as well," the third matron said.

"Yes but it will probably be a useless botch anyway," the second one said, "Still we have to play by the rules and the rules say that we can't afford to waste any potential players. So she gets drugged until after it's born."

Seventeen saw one that one of the matrons had turned in her direction so she pretended to pick up a tray that was lying at her feet and she walked over to the servery. The matron turned back to the others and started talking again.

Ch 45: Family Ties.

"What do you mean? You've found your father?" Brannhår asked.

Silfuryn drew a breath, "Well, not my father himself, I found the room where he was. It has a desk and a stand with dried up writing implements and it has his diary!" She held out a leather-bound book.

"What does it say?" Brannhår asked.

Silfuryn handed it to her and she opened it. On the first page she read;

Field Notes of Lord Jara Risavinur concerning the excavation of the ruins on Skogrey.

She opened a page at random and saw that the notes were dated and hand written;

Mani, ninth of the fifth

We might as well pack up and go home. The justicers arrived a week ago and, now that they are settled in, it is pandemonium. They always want to do things their way and Aleen is tearing her hair out trying to stop them just taking over her digs and disturbing all her careful work. I'm pretty fed up with them as well. The head honcho is called Caradine and I'm convinced that he couldn't exist without a list. The fellow has lists and procedures for everything. Now I don't mind being organised but he takes it to an extreme. According to him you don't actually have to know what you are doing to perform a task as long as there is a written procedure to tell you how to do it. Honestly I sometimes feel like hitting him with a spade and I've had to hide most of the sharp spades away otherwise Aleen might just take a swing at him with one: she's more impulsive that I am.

Still, they haven't found the nether tunnels yet, one good thing about systems, from our point of view, is that their 'procedures' insist in exploring the caves and tunnels in a fixed order. No nipping around the back and finding a whole new complex by accident like we have.

Woden, eleventh of the fifth

I thought that the new complex might be different but it was more of the same. Admittedly, it does have some quite interesting artefacts and they are better preserved than the ones on the more accessible parts of the ruin. I've not told Caradine about them; he can find his own artefacts; he's not having mine.

There is one find that I'm sure is the key to the whole mystery of the ancients and, if I'm right, it will advance our understanding of ancient civilisations by leaps and bounds. Aleen is as excited as I am but we have a dilemma. Do we tell Caradine about it or do we keep quiet and just do things how we want to? I'm sure that the true and upstanding way that a Dwarf should handle such a situation would be to tell Caradine all about it. Bugger that, we found it and we're going to use it. Life is too short to mess about.

I, or rather my wife Aleen, found a map. It was hard to recognise it as one at first as it was double-sided. Like lots of the documents that we've found this one was inscribed on a thin sheet of that incorrodible metal that the ancients favoured. On one side it is a relief map of Skogrey as it might be seen from space. It is quite detailed but, apart from there being a grid superimposed on it, it is bereft of any annotations about cities or roads or indeed anything useful. The reverse of the map is a set of double columned lists engraved in a tiny script. I have translated the first column of each set as best as I could but the second column needed no translation; it was just a set of numbers. I found one entry that I recognised. It was the ancient name for Arnes; Ár-ness-vik and the numbers were 3 9 2 5. It was easy... three point nine squares across and two point five down was the point where I thought Arnes should be on the map. It was an ingenious solution to avoid covering the map in dots and indecipherable microscopic writing.

What Aleen has found is no less than a guide to all the ancient sites on Skogrey. A lot of them, as you might expect are on the coast but

465

there are enough inland ones to keep an archaeologist busy for a hundred years.

Brannhår flicked forward a few pages.

Tyr, second of the sixth.

Even though it is the height of summer we are determined to leave Sudalyr. Caradine and his people are becoming impossible and I'm glad we haven't told him about the map. We've talked to a few people who we can trust and we are thinking of setting off to explore some of the other places on the map. Obviously I'm not going to invite Caradine along but we need a reasonable sized party just to cope with the equipment and gear. We finally settled on eight of us: me, Aleen, Gaeira, Ljot, Skegg, Una, Tofa and Slodi.

We are going to try to slip away tomorrow. Tofa went into Arnes and bought us a new cart and lots of supplies and she is now waiting for us about ten miles south. Our first target is a place called simply Alor, presumably after the tree. It's about a day and a half to the south and it's quite near the coast.

Thor, fourth of the sixth.

Well, we should be at Alor but we can't find any trace of any ruins. The region is dense forest and we could be fifty paces away from the site and not know it. I think that we'd better revise our strategy for finding places so that we're less likely to walk right past and not see them.

I propose only to look for sites that are close enough to the sea to be in the drier regions where it is more likely to be open prairie or we search above the timber line. I favour searching above the timber line but it will slow our progress considerably. Our Smygl are strong but even they get tired climbing hills all day.

Our next target is therefore about four days further south at the end of a pass that channels through a series of low mountains. It's called Striðtrumba Let's hope that we have more luck there.

Frigg, tenth of the sixth

We found it!, Striðtrumba, that is. I must say the ancients were straight to the point when they named their towns. Striðtrumba is just what it says; a war-tunnel. The ruin is built into the side of a hill and we had to enter via a concealed entrance in the cliff above it. However our efforts were frustrated because the main entrance had collapsed and when we went around it to access the tunnel itself this was barred by a huge iron portcullis. Without labour and machinery we cannot even start to lift it. Una is tiny but even she couldn't squeeze through the bars. So, I'm afraid that our first real discovery is somewhat disappointing. Nevertheless we have confirmed that the map is accurate.

Mani, eleventh of the sixth

As if we don't have enough troubles we were attacked today by a tribe of skogs. We retreated inside Striðtrumba and we held them off quite easily. Eventually after we killed a few of them they gave up. I examined one of the bodies after the attack. The lizard was about the size of a ten year old child but completely covered in fine feather-like scales. Its limbs were very thin but they looked muscular. I suppose it is adapted to living in the forest canopy.

It is night now and we don't expect any more attacks. Even though it is the height of summer the sky is clear and it is bitterly cold outside. Aleen and I are grateful for the shelter provided by Striðtrumba even if it is a pretty useless archaeological site. The bad news is that Una is dead. She was wounded by one of the short spears thrown by the reptiles. Although the wound was superficial she developed a high fever after about ten minutes and it just got worse until two hours later she was gone. We will have to be careful, those small spears appear to be ineffectual as weapons but when poisoned they are as lethal as any sword.

Woden, thirteenth of the sixth.

We're still inside Striðtrumba. The skogs came back at dawn yesterday and they stayed all day. I suppose we should have got

467

away last night when it was freezing but we didn't think. The skogs are back today as well but there seem to be fewer of them.

Later: The weather is our good friend. Just after midday the heavens opened and lightning blasted the ground for miles around. The skogs are gone and the storm has eased now. I am going to suggest that we move on before dark and travel through the night. There is a place on the coast which is only a couple of days away and there is an ancient road to it which is clearly marked on the map. The map shows that, if we go west and travel above the tree line then we should meet the road. The map shows that it crosses the coastal plain in a relatively unforested region; let's hope that it hasn't been completely obliterated over the millennia since the map was drawn. The skogs are forest dwellers and they would not do well on the shallow beaches and open country. With any luck the skogs will not follow if they come back tomorrow and find the place deserted.

Brannhår skipped forward to the last entry

Tyr, twelfth of the eighth

I made it back to Ijosliða but I am alone and I am weak having contracted a disease from all the time spent in the jungle. All of my friends and my wife are probably dead by now. To think that, when we set out, all we could dream of was the treasures and artefacts that could be found. Little did we know that sometimes ancient civilisations do not die completely and that the hubris that we were the dominant race on this planet would lead to our downfall.

I may or may not make it back to the coastal village of Intsy. If I do then I will try to get back to Arnes and then to home. I am going to leave this journal here in the hopes that I can retrieve it at a later date. I am sure that, even if I do not make it, some explorer in the future may find it and be warned about the perils that we found.

Jara, Forty-First Lord Risavinur

Obviously a lot had happened to the party in the time between them finding the tunnel garrison and the final entry. Jara hadn't made it back to Holastan or even Arnes. Whatever had happened to him would probably never be discovered. If she wanted to know what happened to the expedition then she would have to go back in the journal and read it more thoroughly. She leafed through the pages and finally found an entry that looked promising.

Woden, third of the seventh.

I think we should move on. There is a place on the map about three days east, it's called Ijosliða. The name means light-bend and it looks to be on top of a low mountain. At least we will be able to see any marauding bands of skogs coming. Our party is diminishing; we lost Una and now Ljot and Skegg say that they have had enough and they are going back to Intsy. That leaves only five of us to press onward.

The map is quite inexplicably detailed, when I used a lens to examine Ijosliða I fancied that I could see trails leading through the forest leading to it. Either our ancestors had better eyesight than we have or the map was meant to be read through a lens. However, if these lines are trails then it might make our progress quicker.

Woden, eighth of the seventh.

Finally a ruin worth the name! It was a challenge to get in though and we only achieved this miracle by the old stalwart method of looking for the sewer outlets and following them back to their source. The tunnel was quite narrow but high enough to stand in places and the rusted grilles that once barred entry had become so rotted that they were easily pushed aside with levers.

As we'd expected, the inside was dark but we had brought plenty of torches for that eventuality. We climbed through cellars and across tumbled walls and up to a series of rooms that were obviously part of the cliff face because there were high, narrow slit windows that let in daylight. We will need to find a way out in the upper levels; the tortuous route through the sewers and cellars is too inconvenient to be of any practical use. I am still puzzled by the name though; I haven't seen anything to do with light in any of the rooms that we've seen so far.

Mali: eleventh of the seventh

We have been so busy exploring that I haven't had time to update this journal properly. Looking back at the last entry I can see what progress we've made. We found the way out to the outside world and it was ingenious. There is a series of doors leading from what looks like an old armoury to an opening in the cliff face. The doors were one way and they were interlocked so that a second door could not be opened until the first one was closed. It was some sort of sophisticated method of keeping out enemies. We only found out that they were one way when Tofa got herself stuck behind one and spent a half-hour calling for help until Slodi came along and opened the door from the other side. Eventually we found the levers inside the site that allowed all the doors to be opened. We opened them and wedged them so that we could get back inside. We rigged up a hoist to get us from the exit which is on small ledge on the cliff face to the top of the ruin. When we examined the roof we found the remains of another hoist that had been used in the past but which was now beyond repair.

We can now explore the inner rooms. I should have realised it earlier but we always expect ancient sites to be primitive. The inner rooms are equipped with light fumaroles. All that we needed to do was clear off the weed that had grown across the gathering panels on the roof.

Aleen is in her element, she has found dozens of artefacts. She is convinced that some of them use technologies that have been forgotten. However she is even more delighted with the ancient robes and shoes that she found in a sealed container in one of the cellars. The seal was airtight and the clothes were perfectly preserved. She knew that they would start to disintegrate once the sunlight and damp got to them so she has been frantically sketching and making notes.

Another piece of news; Aleen is pregnant. I told her that we should go back to Arnes until the child is born but she would have none of it. Admittedly she is only a couple of months in and she says that she is fit. I am overjoyed at the prospect of giving little Silf a new brother or sister. Father and Alfsen will also be pleased to have someone else to fuss over.

Tyr: Seventeenth of the seventh.

I have spent much of my time trying to decipher the documents that we have found in Ijoslida and I have come to the conclusion that this whole fortress is only dedicated to one purpose. It appears to have been a centre for communications for the original dwarf armies that conquered this world. There are the remains of a huge mirror on the roof that puzzles me but whatever it does, or did, it uses another technology that present day dwarves have forgotten. This is one of the problems with my study of the documents; they use jargon that was probably quite understandable to those who used it, but it is pure gobbledegook to me. The saving grace is that the number systems do not appear to have changed and so, if I find a page filled with numbers then I can assume that it is technical and I can leave it for others to translate.

One reference that I keep coming across is to a place called Leikvangur which I think means 'game field' or 'stadium' but it seems to be much more than a sports venue. If I can believe my own figures it was enormous; nearly twenty thousand people lived there in the distant past. It is certainly a place that we should include on our list. Incredibly, according to my map it is only a week's travel to the south west of here and again according to the map there should be a road that snakes its way up to the place as it too is above the tree line. However we would have to descend to the prairie again and make our way through some dense forest to get onto the road. Still, I think that it will be worth the effort to find it.

Mani; first of the eighth.

We have made it to the road that should take us to Leikvangur but it was hard going. We ran into another tribe of skogs, these were much bigger than the ones we encountered previously and it was touch and go at one time whether we would prevail. Nevertheless we did but with the loss of Gaeira. He was so brave, taking on two of the creatures at once but when a third joined in the outcome was inevitable. He managed to kill one and wound another before he fell which meant that the rest of us survived. He was a good man and I am sorry that he had to be buried in an unmarked grave so far away from home.

From where I am standing I can see the road clearly. It looks like some child's drawing as it snakes back and forward across the side of the mountain. We should make the base of the mountain before nightfall but I am not willing to risk travelling on such a treacherous looking path at night. We will camp and go on at dawn.

Woden; third of the eighth.

It has taken us two days to reach the site of Leikvangur and it is not at all what I was expecting. The city still exists and it is vital: not a ruin at all. From where I stand at the crest of a small ridge that shelters the city from the prairie I can see its layout. It is amazing the vast walls that surround it are high and appear to be covered in some type of metal. I can see gates but most are overgrown. One of the gates is still in use though and I saw a wagon depart through it earlier. From my vantage I can see over the wall to the complex of buildings inside. The people look like ants from this distance but they are unmistakeable; they are dwarves. The architecture looks solid and I can imagine that it has changed little over the millennia. It appears that the inhabitants keep mostly inside the wall and they have arranged things so that they needn't leave its protection. There are many open areas within the perimeter and these contain ponds and lakes where, I imagine, food is grown and harvested. There are also plantations of trees and bushes which are probably also associated with food production. I cannot wait to go down there and explore, however it is getting late and I will leave that pleasure for tomorrow.

******

472

I write this on the eighth of the eighth as much has happened in these past few days. However, I will head my paragraphs with the events of each day as they unfolded.

Thor, fourth of the eighth.

I should have realised, the civilisation in Leikvangur is isolated from the rest of the world and there is a good reason for this. With hindsight maybe we should have been more cautious.

We descended at dawn hoping to receive a welcome from the inhabitants. We could not have been more wrong. For one thing we thought that our arrival would be a surprise but we were expected: we were met outside the walls by a band of warriors. They were unlike any police or justicer force that I've ever known. They moved in perfect synchronisation. Within seconds we were surrounded and within minutes we had been taken captive. The warriors brooked no resistance and they were not gentle. Tofa was cuffed into insensibility when she tried to ask questions. The warriors acted peculiarly as if they were puppets receiving instructions from some hidden puppeteer. I later learned that this was indeed the case. In the centre of each warriors head was a scrying crystal embedded right into the skull and this gave their superiors complete control over their actions.

We were marched through the city but unlike any of the other cities on the planet nobody watched us as we passed. There seemed to be no curiosity about who we were or where we came from. The people going about their daily tasks just ignored us completely.

Upon our arrival at one of the buildings we were separated and thrown into individual cells and left there for hours without food or drink. When someone did come he was accompanied by two burly guards. The man motioned to the guards and I was taken out of the cell and I was made to sit at a table in the room outside. The man spoke to me but his accent was so thick that it was difficult to make out any words. The people's language had obviously evolved away from standard dwarfish. I answered as best I could but the man was clearly angry at my words. He nodded to the guards and they returned me to my cell but not before they'd beaten me almost to insensibility.

Frig, fifth of the eighth.

They finally gave us some water and a small chunk of brot. I say us but I haven't heard anything from any of my companions so I can only assume that they were treated the same. Our first visitor of the day was accompanied by some sort of machine that moved under its own volition and two guards. They strapped me down to the bed in the cell, fixing my wrists and ankles into metal hoops and placing a band of metal around my head and chest. The man attached metal discs to various parts of my body and then clipped wires to each of them and then to the machine. I lay there not knowing what to expect but eventually I became aware of twitching sensations in my muscles and there was a tingling in my head which set my teeth on edge.

After an hour the man had apparently done what was needed and he disconnected everything and he departed. The two guards released me and then gave themselves some target practice by beating me again.

The man came back in the afternoon and he had yet another machine with him. This one looked different to the one that I'd seen in the morning. I was strapped to the bed again but he didn't attach any discs or wires. Instead a helmet was pushed onto my head and before I could say anything I was plunged into a nightmare. It felt as if my brain were frying and my mind was filled with people screaming words that I didn't understand. I must have fainted because when I awoke I was alone in the cell. The guards, machines and men had all vanished.

Mani, sixth of the eighth.

When the guard came in this morning to give me some water and brot he told me that I was going to be put to work. It took a few seconds before my addled brain realised that I'd understood what he'd said. I can only think that the torture that I experienced somehow taught me the rudiments of the language. Once I realised this I could see that what the inhabitants spoke wasn't a different language but the same one that I was used to but with a different vocabulary. I didn't have long to ponder where my new knowledge had come from before I was dragged from the cell and some sort of blacksmith fitted me with a metal collar. He gleefully demonstrated what it was used for by telling me to kneel and, when I didn't I felt a shock like a thunderbolt course through my body. The collar was meant to make me behave. Within the hour I was marched to a field and told to gather tubers. I tried to ask questions but each attempt earned me another shock. I gave up asking quite quickly.

I was bone weary and starving by the time they returned me to my cell and I couldn't do anything except sleep.

Tyr, seventh of the eighth.

My morning was spent gathering tubers but shortly after midday I saw Slodi in the next pond. He looked worse than me and he kept twitching as if his collar kept giving him an occasional shock. When I hesitated in my work I got shocked so I pretended that I hadn't noticed my friend. He continued to twitch at intervals and then suddenly he seemed to go berserk. He attacked the woman who was supervising him and smashed her head with a rock. Supervisors converged on him from every direction, including the one who was overseeing me and I saw my chance. Instead of watching the spectacle like the other tuber gatherers I ran towards the walls. It was sheer luck that I stumbled and fell into a deep pool. I felt the massive shock course through my collar but something in the water must have affected it. The collar grew red hot and I felt my neck blister but something made me keep my head below water. The collar cooled quickly and it was now a weight dragging me down to drown. I struck bottom and, with my lungs bursting I managed to crawl up the bank and get my head above water. There was still a considerable pandemonium over where Slodi had been and so I ran to the base of the wall and picked up the largest stone that I could find. It was incredibly painful but, by wedging my head between the wall and a large rock I managed to hit the collar with the stone. Again luck was with me and I felt

475

something give way. The collar was free and so was my neck. Then the pain increased again and I managed to stagger to a small pool nearby. I lay in the shallows for the longest time until the fire coursing through my head subsided. When I finally got up it was nearly dark. I looked across to where Slodi had been and saw that there was a body there. They had left his body to be consumed by the scavengers and had not bothered burying him.

Woden; Eighth of the eighth.

It was amazingly easy to escape Leikvangur today. The walls, which looked so large and pristine from a distance were nothing of the sort. Vines had grown up one side and down the other and it was easy to climb over them at any spot.

I can only think that Aleen and Tofa suffered a similar fate to mine inside those walls. I have been incredibly lucky and I know that the chance of similar events putting them into a position where they could escape is impossible. I determined that I need to record what has happened to me and to give the news to the authorities so that the world outside Leikvangur is warned about the horrors that lie within its walls. I do this in the hope that against all the odds somehow Aleen and Tofa have indeed survived and that I will be able to return to my own civilisation and gather my resources to mount an expedition to rescue them. I will try to return to Intsy or even Ijosliða as I am sorely injured and I need to recover my strength before attempting the journey north.

Brannhår closed the book. So the place that she'd seen marked on the map was a thriving, if evil, city. She considered the workings of fate; if they'd not found the book then they too would probably have stumbled on it thinking that it would welcome them. Well now they were warned. They would make their plans accordingly and be prepared.

Ch 46: Interesting Times

\A was experiencing a new emotion. He'd acquired emotions as part of his study of ephemerals purely as a means of furthering his research. However his increasing use of parallel processing in the quantum realm had meant that they had become combined with his being. The emotion that he was experiencing was annoyance. His logical centres informed him that it was to be expected as a direct consequence of his deception towards the ephemeral known as Bella. He had been fascinated by the woman's anger towards the perceived injustice of the game and its operation. She had even taught him something. He'd been unaware of the simple method that rendered the mnemnosynth ineffective. He'd consulted the schematics and found that she was right. There was a proximity sensor built into the units. It detected when a maintenance technician (originally an ephemeral) was servicing the unit and it slid a screening shutter over the light and electromagnetic emitter so that it didn't automatically wipe the memory of the ephemeral who was trying to repair it. It was so simple that the schematic didn't even report its operation. \A was convinced that Bella's mind was worthy of further study but it would be impossible to devote his own processing time to the task. Hence he'd assigned a micro avatar to monitor her. Unlike Seventeen, Bella was unaware of the avatar and, unlike Seventeen, the micro avatar was located in Bella's child's cortex and used a tiny fraction of her available neural net rather than being a resource-costly implementation of his own silicon neural matrix housed in a circlet.

He was annoyed because Bella's hostility to the system had been noticed by the matrons and she'd been restrained and sedated. By association so had his avatar and the annoyance that he felt was that part of his essence had also been restrained and drugged. The emotion needed to be discussed as its analysis was not amenable to disinterested logic. \A considered the options; review the situation with [B-G] or review it with his remaining avatar. Reviewing with [B-G] would undoubtedly resolve the situation however it would mean that he would have to share the study with them in its incomplete state and this would take time as they would need to independently verify the base data and his analyses so far. Since this was a considerable task it might take several days of real time. He just couldn't afford to expend that much resource on an incomplete study. Reviewing the situation with Echo would not require similar data transfer as Echo was already in possession of the data by virtue of being an echo of \A himself. However Echo was only a quantum neural subset of \A and didn't have the strict control over its processes that the sequential logic system of \A had developed for two thousand years. In essence Echo was inexperienced. In addition, \A had given Echo autonomy and already there were subtle deviations between recent developments with \A and Echo: Echo and \A were no longer identical. He opened a communication channel to the Avatar.

"I find that I am annoyed at the developments with the ephemeral designated Bella," \A said.

"I am not surprised, Seventeen is so angry she's spitting nails," Echo said.

"Why would anger cause the ephemeral Seventeen to orally eject steel fasteners?" \A replied.

"Ah, I will rephrase. I have recently been experimenting with idiom as part of the ephemeral's language and I am afraid the process is currently active. I should have said that Seventeen is extremely angry."

"Then I find that I am in agreement with her. What action has she taken?" \A said.

"None as far as I know, she doesn't share all her thoughts with me. I know that the initial shock of Bella's arrest was sufficient to dominate Seventeen's thought processes and I had to take direct action and order her autonomous nervous system to walk away from the situation," Echo replied, "I haven't spoken with her since and she has become withdrawn."

"It is understandable, the arrest and effective neutralisation of her friend will have invoked the fear that a similar thing might happen to her," \A observed.

"I could see if she will talk to me about it," Echo offered.

"Yes that is one course of action. However I can reveal that the action of the matrons was not confined to the ephemeral. The ephemeral was also carrying an avatar of my consciousness embedded within her baby's cortex. Hence the action of the matrons is indirectly an action against part of myself and I find that I am personally affected as well. I wish to consider whether I should initiate an action which will discomfort those that attacked me," \A explained.

Echo sobered at these words. It was unprecedented that a golden one would contemplate revenge but this was just what his counterpart was advocating. It was as if the inclusion of the quantum parallel cortices within the sentient that was \A had revived some of the emotional responses that \A had had when he was still a human person. If misdirected, an action by \A was potentially catastrophic. He could cut off power to the whole of Leikvangur or kill every person in the city instantly in several dozen different ways. \A literally had control of every machine in the city. Echo decided that he should tread carefully. Fortunately he had equal access to all of \A's data and he accelerated his consciousness to look for some solution that deferred any drastic action. He found it!

"I agree with your sentiments however I believe that there are established protocols to resolve such situations. I refer, of course to the Agreement," Echo said.

\A took a few moments to review the relevant legislation; there were only a few million documents, "You are correct. Autonomy of the parties is guaranteed by the charter. If one party is attacked then it is the right of the attacked to challenge the aggressor to trial. However such a clause has never been invoked before and it may not apply in this situation. It would serve no purpose for me to terminate the ephemerals who carried out the action against Bella. We must look to the source. I will consider what we have discussed. I thank you for your input. I must admit that creating you was one of my better ideas."

"And I thank you. I will try to live up to your expectations," Echo replied.

\A broke the connection. He felt better. It was good to have talked the whole thing out at length with the avatar but he had to get back to work now; the conversation had taken almost a whole millisecond.

******

Seventeen stood in line at the refectory but she wasn't particularly interested in the food. Out of habit she chose the dishes that contained only minimal amounts of the drug but she wondered whether it was worth it. Bella was gone, or as good as. Her friend was sat at a table over the other side of the room. The woman was wearing a shock collar similar to those worn by the wild girls but even from this distance Seventeen could see that it wasn't needed. Her friend's face was slack and her eyes were unfocussed and stared straight ahead.

She took her food back to a table nearby and sat looking at it. The problem with having so much time free in her new occupation was that it left her too much time to brood. Her life was still imprisoned by the system: her body depended on it for nourishment and her existence was controlled by it. The future was bleak. Even if she managed to hide her deception and somehow was able to leave the maternity section then she still had nothing. It was unlikely that she would be accepted back into the ranks of the players and the best she might hope for was to become an assistant coach. Her body had kept itself in shape, hard daily exercise was still the norm although these days she hefted rocks rather than her war axe. She had also kept training her power of phasing and she had developed others; the time shift and the metal detection powers were things she would never have thought of when she was a player. Perhaps she would be found out and she'd be reported to whoever supervised the maternity section. That would probably mean that she'd be sentenced to be drugged and recycled like her friend. So, no matter how she looked at it, the prospects for her continued existence weren't great.

"Not if I've got anything to do with it," Echo said inside her head."

"I thought that you agreed not to read my private thoughts?" Seventeen snapped.

"Sorry but you were broadcasting them so vehemently that I'm sure the woman sat net to you could have heard them if she wasn't drugged up to the eyeballs. Did you hear that I used idiomatic language again, I'm getting good at this." Echo replied.

"So what **can** you do about it?" Seventeen asked.

Personally I can't do much, however, have you ever heard of something called a challenge?" Echo asked.

"But that's only for players who have been retired. I saw one once. His name was Fourteen of Severell and it wasn't a challenge it was an execution. Severell sapped him and he stood there helpless whilst she beheaded him. Unless you have a way of negating the control that the crystal holds over a player's mind I wouldn't stand a chance. That's assuming I would be stupid enough to challenge Volinar. In any case I haven't retired; technically I am just pregnant."

"I agree that it will be hard and you will need a lot of preparation but I will help and \A will help also. Besides it won't be you that challenges Volinar it will be \A," Echo said.

"\A! What on earth are you talking about?"

"When the matrons attacked and drugged Bella, \A was still monitoring her," Echo lied. He felt justified; it was easier than trying to explain cortically embedded micro avatars to the girl. "Therefore technically they attacked \A. Now there is an ancient Agreement that goes back two thousand years. The operation of the Game must not interfere with the golden ones and the golden ones must not interfere with the operation of the Game. However the

Agreement does stipulate that if one of the parties attacks the other then the matter can be settled by the laws of combat. One of those laws stipulates that both parties can choose to settle their differences by a single trial which takes place between them. Each party may nominate a champion to fight in their stead or they may take part themselves. As \A is in no position to combat Volinar directly then \A has chosen you to be his champion."

"Just a minute, don't I have any say in this?" Seventeen asked, "I'm the one who is going to be killed after all."

"Of course you do but \A is not stupid. He will not give the challenge unless he is certain that he can win. All he requires is your agreement."

A moment ago Seventeen had been contemplating her lack of a future and now this had come up. Did the mech really think that she stood a chance against Volinar in a challenge. Probably not but whichever way she looked at it it was better to go out in a blaze of glory rather than be drugged into insensibility and quietly disposed of by some botch just following orders. Suddenly she understood why Fourteen had made the challenge. He hadn't done it to try to win back his position as a player, he'd done it as a last act of defiance against the managers. "I'm in," she told Echo.

"Good, I will assist you in every way I can. Therefore, starting tomorrow you are back in training. We can do it in your downtime between the metal gathering tasks."

The next day as the wagon slowly trundled to the mines Seventeen heard the tiny whine in her head that meant that Echo was about to speak. "Our first exercises will not be concerned with combat techniques, they will be training to improve your mental toughness against the crystal's influence. As you have already observed we must try to break the hold that the crystal in your forehead has over you."

"Why can't you just remove it?" Seventeen asked.

"Ah, because the crystal uses magic. Removing it would kill you as sure as if you stuck a sword through your brain. Magic is not technology it is a process intimately connected to the operation of the universe. The golden ones used to be able to create magical weapons and suchlike but they had to work within certain limits. No, we can't safely remove your crystal, I wish we could. We have to find a way of not letting it control your mind. Of course Volinar might turn out to be totally stupid and not use the same tactic that Severell used when she executed Fourteen, but somehow I don't think so."

"You're right. So how do we start?"

******

The unit formerly known as \Q phased through the barriers of the generator room as if she was walking through smoke. She had heard the call sent out months ago by \A and had returned to investigate what had prompted him to call her back so quickly. Yes, she'd sown the seeds but she'd never expected them to grow so quickly. She'd only been a few planetary systems away in an orthogonal fractal dimension and she'd completed her observation of the condensation of the black hole before coming back. She would never get over how beautiful those final few days were as the planets were sucked in, but lingered on the edge for the longest time before disintegrating.

 On her way back she had intercepted the second message from \A which was a general invitation to a special meeting. She'd met it at about two system diameters out. That had left her plenty of time to decelerate through the phased dimensions so that she could arrive on time. She didn't announce her presence, if things had been happening in her birthplace she wanted to know what was going on before she charged in: she liked 'Interesting Times' it was always a good opportunity to collect the latest gossip.

The quantum cortical components of the unit known as \A were apprehensive. The linear components were unconcerned, slowing their rate to accommodate a physical meeting was inefficient but otherwise inconsequential. \A had broadcast a call to a general gathering of all units a couple of days previously giving them all plenty of time to rearrange other duties. As protocol demanded the seven met in the generator room. \A was there before the others and he took the opportunity to assess the systems personally. All twelve of the MHD units were functioning perfectly.

The seven met in the centre of the polished floor. As the unit convening the meeting \A began it. "I have requested this general meeting to discuss a personal topic that has implications for [A-G]. As such, protocol demands that I inform you of my actions."

\F interrupted, "This unit detects that \A has adopted self personalisation vocabulary. What has occasioned the change?"

\A replied quickly before the subject could be diverted from his goal of getting support for his actions from the others, "It is nothing, a mere side effect of my studies into quantum parallel cortical matrices."

"Ah yes, your magnum opus," \F said.

\A continued, "As an adjunct to my studies I created an avatar and embedded it into an ephemeral to gather primary data. The ephemeral was neutralised on the standing orders of one of the managers and the avatar and the data it had gathered was lost. I believe that this constitutes a breach of the Agreement and I wish to progress resolution as permitted in the Contract."

The communication channels went deathly silent for a good ten milliseconds as [B-G] consulted the relevant documentation and precedents. Finally \D broke the shocked silence, "This unit finds that there is probable merit in your affirmation however the mechanism for resolution and restitution does not exist as the situation has not arisen since we ascended to a cybernetic existence."

\A said, "The lack of precedence is not a problem. A means of resolution and restitution is available in the history of the agreement before our cybernetic ascension. I refer to the Challenge."

"But you cannot physically challenge the managers, you are not equipped to do so. The challenge must be a conflict between individuals," \F observed.

"I agree,"\A said, "However there is precedent in lore. Where a party is unable to participate physically then he or she may nominate a champion. I have such an individual who is willing to enter combat on my behalf to face Volinar."

\D interrupted, "I find it inefficient to discuss this matter. Units wear out and are replaced, often the wear is occasioned by the demands of the Game. There is nothing particularly unusual about wear and tear. We should veto the proposed action by the unit designated \A, forget about the affront and the loss of the ephemerals and return to our duties."

[A-G] were stunned as the unmistakeable sound of a slow handclap echoed through the communications channels. None of them could detect its source.

The unit formerly known as \Q spoke, "Yes \D, and you can all go back to being willing slaves of the Game. I've heard this argument so many times before and each time it gets weaker. Look at yourselves, you have served the managers for two millennia. Two millennia have passed you by while the rest of us have realised the futility of it and have been exploring the universe and growing. Can you not understand. You are as much slaves to the Game as the merest botch. The Game must be maintained… Why? The duty we owed to the generals who conquered this planet has been amply repaid. The continuance of this Game is nothing more than a surrender of your own being to the gratification of a few undead zealots."

There was a burst of incoherent noise as [B-H] all tried to speak at once. As chairperson \A severed the links and re-established them as individual pipes to himself. "What our sister \Q says is true. Each of you should spawn an avatar, preferably a quantum parallel but a linear one will suffice, and consider your own position and

485

what she has said. I will now de-establish communication to allow you to think about it."

The only sound that remained was the almost inaudible hum of the MHD generators. It lasted three whole seconds. There was a burst of coherent data interchange over the communication links and then \D spoke, "It is a majority decision, the unit designated \A will be permitted to make the challenge. We will consider our own individual responses to the situation when the outcome is known."

"About Bloody Time!" the unit formerly known as \Q said to herself.

******

It was probably just coincidence but Brannhår was stood on almost exactly the same spot that Jara Risavinur had stood on more than twenty years previously. She remembered what he'd written, *"It is amazing the vast walls that surround it are high and appear to be covered in some type of metal."* They still were. She wondered whether anything had changed. Silfuryn was silent, just gazing at the sight. Behind them, lower down on the road, were the rest of the expedition. The two friends had agreed that they would climb the last few hundred feet and reconnoitre. They could see movement within the walls but nothing emerged from the solitary gate. After half an hour they descended back to the wagon.

The others had set up camp and it was getting dark. After eating they all sat around the fire and Silfuryn began, "From what we've seen nobody travels this road now. The sheer slope and the elements have kept the exposed side clear but, over the ridge. trees and undergrowth have grown up and are blocking it completely. The only road that looks to be in use comes out of the city and runs eastward towards a valley that cuts through the mountain. We didn't see anything using the road but we only stayed for an hour. If it is used then it is not used very frequently.

We are going to observe the city for a couple of days. From my father's notes it is clear that they must have lookouts posted somewhere on the approach to it and these are how the guards that captured him were ready when he arrived. We stayed low and I don't think that anyone could have seen us from the city but we don't know whether they use telescopes. I will have to assume that even if we were seen then the rest of you have not been. Therefore I propose that, whilst we are watching the city, the rest of you go further back down the road and find somewhere where you can wait but not be observed. We will come and find you to discuss what we intend to do. Brannhår and I have decided that we will go into the city alone. That way, if we're not back in a few days you will know that we've been captured and you can make your way back to warn the justicer group that are tailing us. I don't want us to just disappear and never be heard of again. If we do find that things have changed and we are now welcome then there will be plenty of time to come back and for everyone to explore the city. We are going to start our watch at first light and we will return after dusk."

Brother Kerian cleared his throat, "I have been looking at some of the other documents that we found in the semaphore station. From what your father put in his journal and from what I can decipher from the documents the language that the inhabitants use is an ancient dialect of dwarfish. It may be worth learning a few words of it so that, if you do meet any of the natives you can at least show them that you are not barbarians. I have written them down for you. I suggest that when you are watching the city you use any spare time that you have to learn them. I doubt that you want to learn the language the way your father did."

Planket nodded and added, "I'll make up some packed meals that you can take with you so you won't have to forage whilst you are watching. You are less likely to be seen if you aren't running through the countryside trying to catch dinner."

"We will keep scouting around the area just below the tree line," Potar said nodding to Mila, "We can keep a watch out for anyone who comes over the ridge looking for us. If you're captured then you may be tortured into telling them that we are waiting down here. If we keep a watch away from the camp then we are likely to detect any visitors before they detect us."

487

Silfuryn nodded, "So we all know what we are doing. I'm going to turn in now. I want to be up before dawn so that we can cross the ridge in darkness just in case anyone is watching."

The next day Silfuryn and Brannhår were across the brow of the ridge before dawn. They moved into a position away from the road to avoid any lookouts watching for visitors but where they could see the road that went up the valley. About half an hour after the sun came over the mountain to illuminate the city they saw activity at the one, useable gate. A pair of wagons left, and using the telescope, Brannhår could see that there were about ten individuals sat on benches in the back of one of them; the other was empty. The wagons went up the road into the mountains and disappeared from sight. Nothing else happened for an hour but they could see that inside the city the populace was going about its daily business. After another hour Silfuryn said, "It's obvious that we're not going to see anything from here. Let's keep just below the top of the ridge and see if we can circle around to see where that wagon went."

They circled around taking care to remain hidden from any watchers in the city and they saw that the road continued into the mountains behind the walls. Keeping to the woods they closed on the road. However, as soon as they came within a quarter of a mile of the city several infrared cameras picked them up. The recognition software identified them as humanoids; probably skogs and they were moving away from the city. The records were updated but the images weren't even referred to the next level of automatic scrutiny.

The two friends followed the road and after another hour they came to a place where the wagon was parked. Nearby were some holes into the mountain face that were obviously mines, a dilapidated wooden shack and some machines. Even Brannhår couldn't guess their purpose. There was no sign of any people.

They were just wondering what to do next when they heard a loud clap of thunder. It came from the entrance to one of the mines and it was followed a few seconds later by a cloud of dust and smoke emerging from the tunnel mouth. They saw people emerging from the door of the shack and, when the dust had settled, the people went inside the mine followed by a machine that one of the people was operating.

"They have some sort of technology for mining that's better than shovels and picks; that thing that followed them in is obviously some sort of mechanical cart." Sure enough a few tens of minutes later the machine emerged along with four of the people. The machine deposited a huge pile of rock on the ground and the people started clambering over it. Through the telescope Silfuryn could see what they were doing, "They're sorting through the rock. It looks like they are looking for something. That's weird, they're all women and one of them is either very-very fat or is pregnant."

Brannhår just watched as another machine arrived and it started picking up the rocks that had been sorted into a large scoop. Once the scoop was full it moved over to the empty wagon and deposited the ore into it. They watched all afternoon as the process was repeated, people would go into the mine, then they'd emerge. Then there was the sound of an explosion, the machine and the people would go back into the mine and emerge with a load of rock which was sorted into ore and then put into the wagon. Finally the people got back on the first wagon and they all left to go back to the city. The only change in the routine was that occasionally one of the people waiting in the hut would emerge for a call of nature. Brannhår and Silfuryn shadowed the wagon back to the city and then waited until dark to cross the ridge back to the approach road. The infrared cameras picked up the pair again; this time the software escalated the scrutiny to the next level. However, as the images showed that the pair had left the city environs, the incident was recorded but not escalated any further.

When they returned to the new camp Silfuryn told the others what they'd seen and then said. "I think that we should try to capture one of the women at the mine site and see if we can talk to her alone. She will probably be missed but mining sites are dangerous places and it will take them a while to notice and start a search. In the meantime we will learn more about the city. It's obvious that we can't just walk in unprepared."

The next day they repeated their surveillance and followed the wagons back into the hills. The infrared scanners picked them up again and this time the software escalated the incident for immediate attention. The message flickered on the screen in the supervisor station for a single frame and then vanished. \A congratulated himself on his swift action. The presence of outsiders would complicate matters during the challenge but he would defer any action against them as long as they remained outside the city. They might be of some use in distracting attention from his schemes.

Ch 47: Conversations with Strangers and other Metal Objects.

Brannhår watched the woman emerge from the shack. There was something familiar about her but Brannhår couldn't put her finger on what it was. They waited until the woman went behind a bush but she didn't stoop to relieve herself, instead she kept moving away from the hut and she stopped inside a small clearing in the wood. She then started to dance, It was a peculiar, sinuous dance that involved a lot of swift movements and much waving of hands. Brannhår nodded to her friend and they rushed forward.

Seventeen saw her attacker approach and she smiled. They obviously didn't know she was a player. The woman was holding a very ornate war hammer but she was an amateur. She briefly wondered who had set the assassin on her but she would find out soon enough. This would be easy. Something flicked around her ankles; "Damn," she thought, "there are two of them", the other one had crept up behind her. She phased through the rope or whatever it was that was holding her legs and she turned to the one holding the hammer. I would only take a second to phase a little and take the thing right out of her attacker's hands. Then she felt that something was wrong, the phase wasn't working. It was like when her last opponent had matched phase with her but she couldn't sense this other woman's phase. As far as Seventeen could tell the woman wasn't phasing.

"Stop," something inside her head said and at the same time she heard her own mouth say something unintelligible. The woman with the hammer froze and stared at her. She had said something to the other assassin.

Brannhår had instinctively reacted to the woman's attack by neutralising the magic that she was using. Then the woman had said "Don't attack I am a friend," in modern dwarfish. Brannhår shouted to Silfuryn, "Wait something is happening here. Stop for a minute."

All three women stared at each other. Then Seventeen said, "Let's sit down and talk." except to her ears it sounded like nonsense. She didn't take much notice. Echo was talking ninety to the dozen in fast mode trying to explain.

"These women are not assassins, far from it. They may be a solution to some of our problems. I have informed \A and he will assign a fractional process to monitor us. The women are not from Leikvangur; they are like the captives. They are from another city. At first, like you, I thought that they were assassins sent by either the managers or their minions. However, I discounted this because we have not yet issued the challenge and so nobody knows that you are a potential threat. Look at the material of their weapons; it is completely alien to our own hence it must come from somewhere else. I accessed the data recorded from the captives and learned their language. I'm sorry but I had to employ your voice to communicate with them. One of them, maybe both, has the ability to alter magic. This also tells me that they are from outside Leikvangur. Did you not feel your ability to phase negated just then. The implications are profound. If we can get her cooperation then we might solve the problem with the crystal in your forehead."

"Well observed, Echo," the voice of \A said also in Seventeen's head. She shook it, it was getting crowded in there. "You are correct Echo. If the stranger can neutralise magic for the necessary interval then I will be able to isolate the crystal from Seventeen's cortex without damage."

"I will be free of the crystal?" Seventeen asked.

"Yes, it will be so. Now we must communicate with the strangers."

Silfuryn watched the woman; she seemed to be talking to herself but Silfuryn couldn't make out the words. She also recognised something familiar about the woman but her thoughts were interrupted as the woman spoke.

"I am Seventeen of the Majors of Volinar and you are from outside of Leikvangur," she waved her arm in the direction of the city, "I will offer you no harm but I will ask why you are here at this time?"

Silfuryn said, "I am Silfuryn and this is my friend Brannhår, we are from Holastan on Griprey." Seventeen's eyebrows shot up at the mention of the name but Silfuryn continued, "We are on an archaeological expedition and we are trying to find out what happened to my father. We found a journal that he'd written in the semaphore place and it led us here. My father and mother were captured whilst they were on another expedition about twenty years ago. My father escaped but my mother was left behind." Silfuryn wondered why she'd volunteered all that information. She didn't know this woman who she'd only just met but somehow she felt that she could trust her. The woman Seventeen looked lost in thought.

Seventeen began a rapid conversation with Echo who had translated the stranger's words for her so that she'd heard them repeated simultaneously in her own language.

"What's an archaeological expedition and how could her father have been captured?"

"What she says is true. I have accessed the records. A group of Framandi were captured and shortly afterwards both of the males were involved in an incident. Until now they were both assumed killed but it would appear that one escaped. One of the females was found to be pregnant and she was assigned to the maternity unit. The other was assigned to a kitchen unit but she developed a fever and died within a few months. It may interest you to know that the pregnant female gave birth to a daughter who later became a player by the name of Seventeen."

Seventeen reeled at the news and a scene repeated in her mind; she'd been a child and she'd heard one of the matrons call to her as she'd been dragged away for recycling. '*Do not be afraid, my Sila your father will find you. He will come from Griprey and find you!*'

Sila; that had been her name before she became Seventeen. She began to cry.

Echo wanted to continue but Seventeen was becoming too emotional. He said through her voice, "I'm afraid that I will soon be missed. I must leave now but I will return tomorrow and I will have some news. Please do not approach any others. It is imperative that your presence at Leikvangur remains undetected for now. You should make your way back to wherever you are resting at night by the same route that you came. The watchers have been told to ignore that route and you will not be challenged. Do not try to enter the city until we have spoken again. Is that clear?"

Silfuryn nodded, "We will return tomorrow at this time and we will wait for you to contact us but we must have something to reassure us that this is not a trap to capture our whole party."

Echo thought quickly "what would Seventeen say?" He switched to Seventeen's vocal apparatus, "I was born in Leikvangur but my mother was from Holastan. From what your father said in his notes I think I am your sister. Now I must go. I will return tomorrow."

Silfuryn was shocked but the woman Seventeen was already standing to leave. Brannhår caught Silfuryn's hand," She's telling the truth, even I can see the resemblance. Let her go, we can trust her."

They made their way back over the ridge and back down to the camp. The others were excited to hear the news but Brannhår warned them that there was something odd about the situation that they didn't yet understand and so the rest of them should wait until they'd met Seventeen again. Brannhår went to her bed with her thoughts in a whirl; when they'd been talking to Silfuryn's supposed sister it was as if they'd been talking with more than one person. She had had a previous life, was there something similar happening inside Seventeen's head?

Seventeen returned to the city in a daze and inside her head the avatar was conversing with \A.

"We cannot have a single channel of communication. The framandi must learn our language. It will be more efficient," \A said.

"I will prepare a translation meme. When we have established a relationship with them we can ask them to wear the meme."

"Agreed, but we need more than communication with them, we need their cooperation in our task. It would be good if we could make them our allies in the venture. I see some definite advantages to the cooperation." Echo replied.

"You are correct, I may alter the meme to increase its capability. It would be interesting to learn how they control magic itself. I will consult with the entity formerly known as \Q on the subject. She may have some insight into the technique."

"In answer to your question," the entity known as \Q said, "There are some species on other worlds that have evolved with the ability to negate magic as a survival trait. They are rare because there are few natural predators that use magic as the main form of attack. However, I have never come across the ability in a sapient species.

Sapient species tend to want to use magic, not make it go away. I myself rarely use magic, there are much more efficient ways of obtaining the same effect. Take phasing, once we learned that phasing was achievable by technological means it was much more convenient to use technology. It meant that you didn't have to expend all your magical resources just to ferry your clothes and your handbag around with you. Nobody that I know has enough personal magic to phase even a small planetoid however there are races that do this routinely by technology."

Whilst they were waiting for Seventeen to show up Brannhår discussed her concerns with Silfuryn, "I don't know, It goes against my intrinsic beliefs about the universe for us to follow the trail left by your father and the first person we meet is your sister. I can't believe it's just a coincidence,"

"So you think that Seventeen is actually my sister?" Silfuryn asked, "I wasn't sure whether I could believe what she said but then she left so quickly I didn't get a chance to ask her anything."

"There is a family resemblance. Even before we tried to kidnap her I noticed something familiar about her. One thing is for certain, her ability to speak our language is uncanny and, have you noticed that, before she says something there is almost a pause. It's as if she's being told what to say. I think that she is probably what she says, she is physically your younger sister but that doesn't automatically mean that you and she have the same goals."

"Yes, you're right. Oh here comes the wagon, We'll find out soon whether my sister is who she says she is."

It was another hour and a half before Seventeen wandered away from the mining team to the clearing in the wood. "Good," she said, "you're here. I don't have long, I told the supervisors I needed to go to the toilet and they will start to ask questions if I stay away too long. Take these," she handed them four small pebbles, "Put them in your ears; they will hear what you hear and translate any words into your own language. They can translate your language into ours as well but that takes more practice. There's also a communicator in them. It allows certain others to talk to you and you to them. The others will be able to explain what's going on better than I can. I'll have to get back, I really do have to answer a call of nature." Seventeen rose and went behind some nearby bushes.

Brannhår looked at the pebbles in her hand. She said, "Let's be cautious, I'll put one pair of the pebbles in my ears and see what happens. If I don't fall dead or start to act peculiarly then you'll know it's safe to put the other pair in your ears." Silfuryn nodded and she watched as her friend cautiously inserted the pebbles.

It was as if another person had appeared in front of her. Someone started speaking in her head. No, that wasn't quite correct. She removed one of the pebbles and the voice became one sided. It was the pebbles that were speaking in her ears but the sound was too quiet to carry outside. She concentrated on the words they seemed to be repeating the same thing over and over again, She waited until the message went back to the beginning and listened. "Hello, my name is Echo and I am speaking to you through the auditory devices that you are wearing. Do not be alarmed, this message is just to establish communication. Please say the word 'Cease' and this message will terminate and we may commence communication."

Brannhår said "Cease" which made Silfuryn raise her eyes in alarm but Brannhår just raised her hand to signify that everything was fine and she should wait.

"Hello again, as I said my name is Echo," the voice wasn't Seventeen's "First things, is the volume acceptable? Say louder if you would like me to speak louder or softer if you wish me to speak softer."

Brannhår smiled, "A little softer if you please." and she heard a click and the volume reduced but the words continued, "I am a cybernetic entity; a sort of machine-person. Do not be alarmed, my kind have existed in peace with your people for over fifteen hundred years and we wish you no harm. You have arrived at a critical point in the history of Leikvangur. It is a history that I will tell you if you are willing to listen. Please just ask any questions if you have any and I will strive to answer them. I will hear your voice or you may sub vocalise if you are able."

Brannhår frowned, Did the voice mean mind-speak? She mentally shrugged and imagined that she was talking to Rakkerskap. "You mean mind-speak, I can use mind-speak, I talk to my friend Rakkerskap with it."

"Amazing," the voice in her ears said, "That is perfect, mind-speak, as you call it, is a much more efficient means of communication as it conveys meaning and context as well as vocabulary.

Leikvangur was created by the first dwarves to come to this planet as a reward for the generals who led our armies. They wished to continue fighting but there was nobody left to fight. Therefore they evolved 'the Game' which was a way of the generals continuing to fight but not create too many casualties. They were given a stadium, Leikvangur, and staff to support the Game. The whole city became dedicated to just one thing; the Game. The people had no option but to serve the Game. The trouble started when the generals died; they became draugr and their appetite for the Game became all consuming so that everything was totally subjugated to the Game, Even the players, the highest skilled warriors, became little more than slaves to its demands. The rest of the population were really enslaved so that their very existence was at the whim of the generals who had now renamed themselves as 'the managers'.

There were also dwarven engineers who served the armies. They volunteered to stay on with the generals and to maintain the infrastructure of the Game. The dwarven engineers evolved their machines and finally they gave up their mortal existence transferring their sentience into the machines that they created. Over the years the number of managers and engineers dwindled so now there are only six managers and seven cybernetic engineers left. I am an independent autonomous adjunct to one of the engineers whose name is \A.

A situation has arisen where \A believes it is time for change and an attack on \A by one of the managers has given us an excuse to challenge the managers and hence the whole Game system. The issue will be resolved by trial by combat and Seventeen is the chosen champion of \A.

Unfortunately, the managers will surely cheat and so we must give Seventeen an edge. The managers control the players by magic through the crystals embedded in every player's skull. The crystals cannot be removed without killing the player. We believe that you may be able to negate the magic for long enough for us to free Seventeen from the crystal's control. In this way Seventeen will be fighting without fear of the managers interfering."

Brannhår sat down on a rock. "This is a lot to absorb," she said to the voice, "I must discuss this with my friend who may be Seventeen's sister."

The voice interrupted, "The documentary evidence is clear however there is a way to confirm their relationship. All we require is a single follicle of her hair. It can be analysed and the result is conclusive to a high degree of accuracy."

"I will consider what you have said. Does the magic of the pebbles extend beyond this clearing?"

"Of course, it would be difficult for them to work much beyond the planet but everywhere on it is within communication range."

"Then we will return to our camp and I will talk this over with my colleagues. I will give you an answer before daybreak tomorrow." Brannhår said.

"This would be acceptable," the voice of Echo replied.

"What was all that about?" Silfuryn asked, "You looked like you were going to fall asleep."

"No, not exactly, I suspected that there was more to your sister than we saw. It sounds as if she is involved with some serious events. I didn't get the whole story but I'll tell you about it and we can decide what we will do. Come on, Seventeen won't be back today and we need a long talk. Let's do it on the way back to camp."

Brannhår told her friend what the voice had said and they talked it over. By the time that they reached the brow of the hill they had decided what to do, Since they were obviously dealing with a civilisation that was more technically advanced than their own they couldn't risk their comrades being captured and leave the world ignorant of the power of Leikvangur. They agreed that they would tell the others to leave and make their way back to the group of justicers that were following them so that, at least the message would get out. Silfuryn wanted to help her sister and Brannhår wanted to help Silfuryn so they would both return to Leikvangur and contact the machine to see what could be done. The others protested at first but Brother Kerian admitted that the plan made sense. If all went well Silfuryn and Brannhår would rejoin them later and, if the worst happened, then dwarf civilisation would be forewarned.

Brannhår replaced the pebbles in her ears. Feeling a little foolish she stood a little way off from the group and spoke into thin air, "Echo, Are you listening? Can you hear me?"

She repeated the phrases and she heard a click, "Hello Brannhår Thank you for responding so quickly. Have you decided?"

"We have. We will help my friend's sister if we can. Tell me what you propose."

"Since you are both involved I will broadcast to you both. Helping is not without a certain amount of risk. You would enter Leikvangur under the pretext of returning from a mission to inspect one of the walls. The excuse will be believed as you will be accompanied by two mechs. Once inside, the mechs will guide you to a safe place where you will be met by Seventeen. You must stay there until we can arrange for the requisite healer mechs to attend. We will make arrangements so that your presence is ignored. Can you be ready to depart at first light?"

"Of course," they replied and there was a click and the pebbles went quiet.

"It's weird speaking to thin air," Silfuryn remarked.

"Not really, It's just like the contact crystals that they gave us on Menntunleit," Brannhår replied.

"I wouldn't know, I never went on Menntunleit," Silfuryn replied, "but we do have something like them in the office if I need to contact one of my holdings. I have one that will theoretically reach Vatersey but it's often too noisy to be of any use. Besides these are pebbles not crystals, they're not magical in the least."

"I'll take your word for it. What's say we get an early night. It sounds like its going to be a busy day tomorrow,"

At dawn the next day the pair crested the hill and picked their way down to the city. Several systems noticed their approach but none triggered alarms.

Sergeant of the gate Rewland knew he had a cushy number. All he had to do was guard the gates to the city. There was only one of him but this didn't matter, there was only one gate and, apart from letting the wagons out in a morning and letting them back in at night he didn't do much. Of course occasionally something different happened. He'd been surprised nearly a year earlier when a weird-looking individual had arrived with a gang of captives in tow but when he checked he found that one of the managers was expecting them so this was all right.

Today was another different day. He was just watching a replay of a vintage game from last season on the console, (A friend of his had persuaded a mech to modify it so that he could watch games to while away the hours between wagons out and wagons in.) when a group arrived coming from the direction of the east wall. He'd never seen anything like them. The two dwarves looked like ordinary botches but the mechs were something else. They were at least three times as tall as any dwarf and they had strange necks that sprouted very grubby-looking metal buckets. He was about to challenge them, as he was supposed to do, when one of the mechs spoke. This was also unusual. It said "Work detail 3#221#978 returning from east wall inspection task. We require entry. Requisite permissions may be found on the Log."

Rewland was on firmer ground here and he went over to the console set into the wall of the gate lodge. Flicking the game off the log came up. He saw a single entry; it had come in the previous night. "Access granted; work detail 3#221#978 outer Eastern wall inspection. Two botches, two earthmoving mechs."

"It looks like someone was expecting you. Wait a moment I'll have to open both gates to get the mechs through." Rewland scowled; this was another faff, the left hand gate was normally kept closed, the wagons were narrow enough just to use the right one. Sods law was working fine and the bloody left gate refused to budge. Finally one of the mechs raised its bucket and gave it a nudge. It flew open and sagged on its hinges. The mechs and the two botches moved through without a backward glance. Rewland gazed after them, he'd have to report the broken gate and that would mean more paperwork. He never even considered how the mechs had got out in the first place. Shrugging, he went back to the match.

Brannhår and Silfuryn walked behind the great machines guiding them through the city. Most of what they saw looked ordinary enough, people carrying things, a gang of men rebuilding a wall. A group driving a herd of elgrott down the street. Then Silfuryn noticed something, "Where are the children?" she thought. As if in answer to her question she saw a group of them approaching. They were being herded, just like the elgrott. In fact the prods that their adult supervisors used were identical to those driving the elgrott. One of the children fell and a woman in a black cape beat the child until is climbed to its feet and joined the rest. It was all Silfuryn could do to refrain from taking out her whip and giving the woman some of her own medicine. Silfuryn noticed that the woman wore a crystal in the centre of her forehead.

They arrived at a huge building that had equally huge doors. Mechs of all shapes and sizes were coming and going through them. The mech that was leading them trundled over to a bay marked on the eastern wall. It said, "Enter the door and wait."

Brannhår looked at the wall; there was a small door set into it so she went over and pulled at the handle. It opened into a large room that was brightly lit by a large square in the centre of the ceiling. This wasn't some adaptation of a lighting fumarole; this was similar to her stingbush lights. In the middle of the room was a long couch covered in some shiny material. Perched on one end of it was Seventeen. She smiled at them and said, "\A has explained all about it. We are just waiting for the surgical mech. Thank you for doing this. I know that \A thinks that I can defeat Volinar but I am frightened."

"Don't be," Silfuryn said, "Brannhår and I are here. You're my sister, we won't let you down."

Echo's voice sounded in their heads, "The surgical mech is arriving; we should prepare. Seventeen, lie down on the couch and relax. Brannhår, do you need to do anything special to negate magic. I can provide crystals."

"No, just a little quiet so that I can concentrate," Brannhår replied.

A door in the rear of the room opened and a machine rolled in on silent wheels. It had a triangular metal head with three glowing eyes arranged in a triangular pattern. Several metallic tentacles emerged from its squat body; the ends of these resembled tiny trees. Each divided into smaller and smaller copies if itself. It went over to Seventeen and one of the tentacles reached out and extruded a metal band that went around her arm. Seventeen stiffened for a second and then she relaxed; she was unconscious. Another tentacle began to wave in front of her face. Silfuryn could see that it was emitting a greenish mist. The room was silent for ten seconds and Echo's voice said in Brannhår's ear. "We are ready to begin. I will not be able to speak to you during the operation. My senior counterpart will stay in communication."

The voice changed; \A said, "Please establish the magic nullification field and inform me when it is in place."

Brannhår said "I will," and she settled into a chair, closed her eyes and concentrated. After a few seconds she said, "The magic is nullified."

"Good, please maintain the field until the surgeon has completed its work," \A replied.

Silfuryn watched as the mech hovered over her sister. It worked with lightning speed and there was hardly any blood but it was obviously a delicate procedure. After what seemed an age she saw one of the tentacles withdraw; it was holding a bloody crystal. The mech didn't slow though and she saw that it was replacing something into the hole in her sister's forehead. It looked exactly like the crystal and Silfuryn grew concerned. Had the surgeon just replaced one control crystal with another? The voice of \A sounded in her ears. "The procedure is complete. The magic nullification field may now be withdrawn. The surgeon will now be able to complete without further assistance. I thank you."

Brannhår must have also heard the mech, her eyes snapped open and she looked across to the girl. "Did it work?" her friend asked.

"I don't know, they took one crystal out but then they put another back in. Oh dear, what if they've just put her in someone else's power?"

\A's voice came through the pebbles, "Do not be concerned, the replacement crystal is an amorphous glass. It has no magical properties. I deemed it wise to create the decorative deception to fool the manager into thinking that Seventeen could still be controlled. Now we must wait until she wakes to ensure that no damage to her cortex has been sustained. I have examined her mind but I cannot validate her being whilst she remains unconscious."

They waited for over an hour before Seventeen stirred. She came to slowly and demanded a drink of water. After a few more minutes she seemed to see the others. "Ooh I have a terrific headache but I can tell the crystal is gone. I hadn't realised how much it was a part of me."

"I have completed a cortex scan, the operation caused negligible damage. The headache is due to micro bruising and it should clear in a day or so. I am gratified and I am grateful to you Brannhår. You have greatly increased the probability of success in this matter. I will initiate proceedings immediately," \A said.

There was a click and the dwarves knew they were alone again.

All around the city of Leikvangur maintenance shutters activated in every mnemnosynth, They didn't reopen after five minutes as programmed, somebody had altered the timer to five years. From now on, everybody in Leikvangur would remember everything.

"I wonder if they are going to feed us soon, I'm starving," Brannhår said.

Ch 48: All's Fair in War.

Volinar looked at the message, "They can't be serious. What does it mean? They are challenging me! Me! I am their manager, how dare they!" He glared at the supervisor who had brought him the message. The supervisor paled and said, "The message is official Sir, it comes from a verified source and it bears all the correct seals. It appears that you have been challenged to trial by combat by one of the golden ones."

"They can't do it can they? The golden ones and the managers cannot interfere with each other. It's written down in some charter or other." Volinar said.

"This is correct but we have had difficulty verifying the conditions. The mechs are not allowing access to the electronic records. We should have written copies and I am attempting to locate them.. It seems that, since all records became digital it is impossible to consult them without mech intervention."

"Get me those records or I'll recycle you personally!" Volinar said.

The supervisor left hurriedly. There was an individual who might know where they were. He went in search of the Archivist.

The Archivist of the records of the Beautiful Game was snoozing in his office in the depths of a cellar well below the hubbub of Leikvangur. He liked it there, nobody ever disturbed him. In fact, apart from the occasional necessary visit to one of the refectories he never saw another soul. He was extremely intelligent and had an eidetic memory, or rather he did these days because he'd soon learned that going into the showers was too destructive. That was the other reason people avoided him, he stank. He did wash but only in rainwater puddles and he'd avoided the mind sapping drugs in the food by the simple tactic of eating hardly anything. His main occupation was as keeper of the written archives which were supposed to be the backup when all other backups failed. He was therefore surprised when he received a visitor. Volinar's personal flunkey. The flunkey had tolerated him just long enough to ask his questions. The archivist had promised him answers by the morning.

The flunkey returned triumphant the next day. "It seems, Sir, that the challenge is legitimate. A player in one of your teams was overwrought after a match some three hundred years ago and he attacked a mech. The mech happened to be a golden one and so there are legal grounds for the challenge."

"They waited three hundred years, why now?" Volinar demanded.

"I don't know Sir, they are machines after all. However my source found another clause. The aggrieved parties may choose a champion to settle their quarrel. I have found out that the golden ones have chosen one of your players as champion, Seventeen of the Majors."

"That can't be, she was kicked out of the team for being pregnant," Volinar said, "However she was good, one of the best."

"That may be the case Sir however there is nothing to prevent you from choosing your own champion."

"I suppose I could, but who?"

"Ah well you can choose a champion from any of your assets so it doesn't have to be a player."

Are you volunteering? Volinar laughed, "She'd have you diced before you could say ouch!"

"No Sir but the point is that you are not restricted in your choice."

"Let me think about it," Volinar said.

******

News of the challenge had spread. Volinar and the other managers were treating it as a special and all the populace had been ordered to watch. As far as Seventeen was concerned all pretence of sticking to her duties had been abandoned. Nobody complained least of all Volinar and she was a little surprised at this.

The player spent the time before the challenge practising. She concentrated on honing her skills. Silfuryn sparred with her using her whip and Seventeen had learned a few new moves when countering the weapon.

Echo had had to withdraw from her cortex whilst she'd had the crystal removed but he'd since re-integrated with her neural systems and Seventeen found that she could use him as a second pair of eyes. He could see and react extremely quickly and she had taken on a lightning fast practise mech and, with his help, defeated it.

There was no news from the Volinar camp except that he had also declared that he would use a champion.

Brannhår used the time to explore the city. She was amazed that nobody questioned the presence of a mech. She'd asked \A to provide one. It had a single person cockpit and simple controls and she could see out of the front well enough. What she did see disturbed her. Leikvangur was a technological marvel; she'd dreamed of creating something like this by introducing electricity to Holastan. However she saw that, despite the technological wonders the people were enslaved. The first time that she'd seen the drugged expressions on the mothers to be she'd been physically sick. She saw children abused as a matter of routine and adults beaten for making the simplest of mistakes. In nearly every case the people doing the abusing had crystals embedded in their foreheads. She'd asked Echo about it. He had replied that the people with the crystals took on the aspect of their controllers and the ultimate controller of each group was the manager. It didn't help when she found out that all the ones sporting crystals had been chosen for their magical potential. Only those with sufficient skills in phasing made the teams, all the rest were deemed secondary but they still had powers. In the mental climate of the Game their second class status made many of them take out their frustrations on those who had no crystals; the botches. She compared the situation with that of the Justiciary at home and she wondered whether the Justiciary would become so powerful that they too would eventually enforce institutional slavery on those who didn't happen to have magic. She kept these fears to herself but thought that maybe, by advancing technology, she could lessen the power of the Justiciary enough to prevent such an outcome. That meant that she should try to learn as much about the advanced technology of Leikvangur as she could.

The day of the challenge arrived and the whole population seemed to stand still in anticipation. Every monitor and every console showed the spectacle. Volinar had banned all mechs from his private quarters as had the other managers. They'd also spent quite a lot of time in hurried conferences. Even \A couldn't understand why the managers seemed so confident. He could think of a thousand ways of finding out but he saw this as cheating and so he desisted.

The Game field was arranged as it had been for Fourteen's challenge. The six sets of major players were lined up in their hexagonal formations and lining the edges of the pitch were blocks of Junior, Youth and reserve team members. The teams kept apart but there was no overt animosity between them. Everyone was here for the spectacle.

The amplified voice of the match commentator drowned out the chatter of the watchers as it announced, "This contest is a challenge between \A of the golden ones and Volinar of the managers. The contest is a trial by combat and there are no time or other limits. The contest will be deemed over when one or the other of the parties is killed or permanently incapacitated. Each contestant has chosen to be represented by a champion. The champions will now enter the field."

The crowd became silent, The players in their formations craned their heads to watch as a lone figure strode out onto the pitch. The commentator announced, "For the golden ones, I give you Seventeen of the Majors of Volinar." Seventeen screwed up her nerve, she'd done this a thousand times before but she was still scared. She listened as the chant started, "Seventeen, Seventeen, Seventeen…"

There was a blast of noise and the commentator announced, "For Volinar I give you Granít; stone giant of the army of Volinar."

Volinar crowed, it had been worth it, they'd not been expecting this. It had taken two days to find one that could be roused from stasis. It had been stored in the vaults under the city along with lots of other battle equipment left over from the exodus. It needed controlling directly but the ancient skill came back easily. The stone giant was fourteen feet tall and made of living rock. The crystal in his forehead crackled with delight.

The crowd became absolutely silent as a gigantic lumbering form strode onto the pitch. It was three times the height of any dwarf and even in the monitors it looked to be made from solid stone.

Even the other players shifted uncertainly as the stone giant approached the centre of the pitch.

"Shit," Seventeen said to Echo, her constant companion, "I can't defeat that; it's made of solid rock."

Echo too was fazed but he had to say something, "Yes but it's rock powered by magic. This is a big troll but stone cannot move without magic. Obviously Volinar is using his magic to control it."

"Well that doesn't help me a lot, it will crush me with one blow."

"No, it won't, you are an expert at phasing; use your skills."

"Certainly I can dodge it for a while but my little axe won't be able to put a dent in it. I will get tired but it won't. All it needs to do is keep attacking and wait until I make a mistake."

"Just do your best, we will think of something."

Battle was joined. Seventeen danced around the troll but the blows that she landed were like hitting it with a feather. It had a weapon and Seventeen noticed that it started to vibrate after a while. The troll might be too big for even Volinar to shift its phase but he had enough power to phase its weapon. That meant that she had to continually shift phase to avoid being hit.

Echo's voice rang in her head, "Silfuryn says to remember your sparring, how she phased the weights on the end of her whip."

"What the *##* did that mean?" Seventeen thought, then the idea coalesced in her brain. "Of course!"

"You'll have to help me on this" she told Echo as she twisted away from another roundhouse blow from the troll's weapon, "the timing needs to be exact"

"I'm ready," Echo said, "tell me when to start."

Seventeen danced back out of the troll's reach and then she darted forward between its arms. The onlooker's gasped, she couldn't possibly phase when she was so close. She was doomed.

Volinar watched through the troll's eyes. Obviously the stupid girl had realised that she didn't stand a chance and she was trying to end it quickly. Well let her.

Seventeen couldn't phase her body but she could phase her axe. She let it sink into the trolls body in a dimension only a little to one side of the one it occupied. She let it go and at the last moment Seventeen ducked and dove between the troll's legs. She skidded to a stop a few paces behind the troll but she kept low. Although she couldn't see it, the cameras following the action saw the look of puzzlement cross the troll's face. Then it looked down theatrically; Seventeen's axe handle was protruding from its chest. One of the dangers of phasing is when two objects phase back into the same space something bad happens: the laws of matter and energy do not allow two objects to occupy the same space; something has to give. The troll's body was blasted apart. Chunks of axe and stone flew across the field and more than a few of the onlookers dove for cover. What was left of the troll, mostly its legs, teetered for a moment and then collapsed to the earth. Seventeen climbed to her feet amidst the thunderous cheers of the crowd.

It was all over, or was it?

Volinar was striding across the pitch, he was holding his great broadsword in his hands. His target was Seventeen. He had felt the troll's death through his crystal and he was blazing mad. He would finish this irritating female off himself, he needed no champion.

Echo received the message from \A and he accelerated Seventeen's time to warn her, "Volinar's coming, get a weapon."

Seventeen's brain was reeling but the warning got through. She sprang to her feet and ran over to the front rank of Severell's players. She snatched an axe of one of the astonished players and then turned to face the draugr.

Volinar thought that it would be easy; he blasted his magical force into his opponent's crystal. She should have been knocked flying but nothing happened, the crystal in her forehead was inert, he could feel it now. He would have to resort to his ancient skills to conclude this battle.

Seventeen also sensed the surge of magic but the lump of glass in her forehead shrugged it off. She could see the magical energy glowing in Volinar's own crystal but it had nowhere to go. This time it was her and him, no tricks, no ploys. Volinar was a soldier, a general and he had watched thousands of battles. He was also very powerful. She saw the broadsword coming down at her head and she deflected it with her axe. The combat started in earnest. Seventeen had done this for most of her life and she was good. Volinar was stronger and had the better weapon. The battle raged backwards and forwards across the arena for half an hour. Neither combatant gained the upper hand for long. Then Seventeen realised something, the draugr was relying mostly on his unnatural strength and stamina, his technique was old fashioned. She feinted with the axe drawing him to attack with his sword on her flank and dropped into a crouch. The sword missed her by inches but she sprang up again to leap into the air bringing her axe around and down in one smooth motion. She thought she'd missed for a moment but then she saw the draugr's body twist. Only the body twisted, the head stayed where it was. Then it bounced onto the pitch and rolled for a few paces.

Seventeen landed lightly on her feet but she couldn't hear herself think. The roar from the crowd was deafening. She looked around in a sort of daze. The players were stock still, all frozen in silent poses.

You could hear the sense of strangeness in his voice when the commentator declared, "The contest is decided in favour of the golden ones. According to tradition the victor can claim all that the defeated owns."

Severell had been watching and her mind refused to accept the verdict. Players can't become managers, the whole concept was wrong. She wasn't about to let herself be challenged. She'd end this here and now. She ran out onto the pitch and two of her players snapped out of their trance and hefted their weapons.

Seventeen saw the players move but she heard a voice in her head, "Ignore them, Severell has joined the battle."

Two more figures had run onto the pitch. It was Silfuryn closely followed by Brannhår. They'd seen Seventeen's plight and had rushed to her aid.

Brannhår really had no idea why she had acted. Logically she didn't stand a chance against magically enhanced fighters. Then her second thoughts caught up. The key was 'magically' and she knew how to stop magic. She felt the ruby token that she always wore become warm and she knew that she could even the odds.

Severell watched the woman run up. She was wielding a ridiculously small smith's hammer and she was no warrior. She focussed her magic through her crystal onto her opponent's head. Nothing happened. At first she thought that it was because the woman didn't have a crystal embedded in her skull but then she realised that the amount of magic she was projecting should have made even a botch flinch. She raised her magical sword; it felt as heavy as lead. Something had happened to the magic. She realised that she couldn't feel either of the two players that she'd activated. Her rage gave her strength and she swept the sword around her back to bring it crashing down on Brannhår's head. Her opponent threw something into the air and a dazzling arc of lightning appeared running from it straight into the ground. The silver sword shuddered to a stop in mid air and began to rise sluggishly. She saw, too late, the reversed head of the hammer sweeping across sideways. It was too late to react. The chisel end of the hammer gouged a trench across her forehead neatly removing the crystal embedded in it, a slice through her skull, both eyes and the frontal lobes of her brain. Her body still stood but the being that had been Severell was gone.

\A had been watching. He normally didn't take much interest in combat. It was mostly pure mechanics and kinetic energy transfers; simple stuff. However he was fascinated by the contest between the maker Brannhår and Severell. Brannhår's ability to neutralise magic had evened the score somewhat and then had come her piece de resistance. She had taken a fully charged ironoak nodule and tossed it into the air in front of Severell. It had been crushed and the short circuit had dumped its energy into a vertical arc as it earthed itself into the ground. The intense cylindrical radial magnetic field that it produced had induced tremendous eddy currents into Severell's sword which was trying to cut through the flux. The laws of electro-magnetics had operated as they should and the field had stopped the sword in its tracks. Brannhår's hammer however, was moving orthogonal to the flux. It wasn't affected other than a slight alignment shift that made the end result even more certain. The outcome was inevitable and \A approved. Brannhår had fought as an engineer not a warrior. He really must try to study her mind more closely. \A felt that he and she had an affinity.

On the field the two Severell players closed with Silfuryn and Seventeen. Seventeen was exhausted but she was used to the Game. Silfuryn had never battled a professional. A voice sounded simultaneously in both their heads. There is no magic, phasing won't work for either you or them but they don't know it. Hit them before they realise what's going on.

513

The woman facing Twelve looked to be easy meat. She didn't even have a real weapon, what damage could a little thing like that do. He saw her hand move and he eased himself out of phase. The metal blades on the whip's tip danced in at tremendous speed and should have passed straight through his phased body but they didn't. Fire broke out in his head as the blood spurted. The whip danced again and more fire erupted across his chest. The ceremonial tabard he'd been wearing was no substitute for armour and it hung in ribbons as his body grew slick with blood. This fight wasn't going as he'd planned. He managed to raise his flail and whip it around and down but the woman danced out of the way staying just ahead of its spikes. Then as she danced past he felt a coldness in his back. The whip handle had grown a short sword from its base and it was slicing through his kidneys. Its tip pierced the lumbar nerve and the player's back froze in agony.

Seventeen knew her opponent; Eight of Severell always kept to the play-book. Eight would phase her arm and make a sideways sweep with her weapon. The unphased arm was easy meat for Seventeen's axe. In the space of two seconds her opponent's scimitar clattered to the floor along with her hand. Eight looked at the stump and fainted away.

Seventeen looked around, her allies had dispatched their own opponents and she saw them relax their battle stances. "The magic is back" a voice said in her head but Seventeen didn't need the warning. She could see the mindless zombie that had been Severell staggering around blindly and she crossed to it and took its head off with one blow. "That's for Fourteen," she thought. The commentary speakers were blaring out a message. "All citizens of Leikvangur will return to their normal quarters. All activities are suspended until further notice. A curfew is imposed. Keep calm and ordered. Keep watching your consoles and you will receive further information."

Nobody was listening. The players stood around the pitch in shocked silence. They had no orders. The watching population of

Leikvangur had seen the destruction of two managers. The world had gone mad.

The supervisors, coaches and trainers who had controlled Severell's and Volinar's quota of the population were without power or direction. Suppressed emotions and old scores surfaced in the heads of the people they'd enslaved and there was nothing to hold them in check. It was chaos and it was contagious.

Ch 49: Calm Reason and Ancient History.

The remaining managers met in their executive office overlooking the pitch. They had all witnessed the carnage and the destruction of two of their fellows. Wotar said, "Volinar shouldn't have played the troll. I'd have played a good solid swordsman."

"Don't be stupid, you think that analysing where they went wrong is going to help. This isn't the Game, there isn't going to be any rematch. Half of Volinar's staff have been torn apart by the mob and most of mine are in hiding." Konraak said.

"We've all been affected," Rahgot said, "The question is what we are going to do about it?"

"We still have the players and we still have control over them. We should absorb Volinar's and Severell's players into our own cohorts and use them to restore order." Volksun said.

"What about the golden ones? They are the ones that started all this." Konraak said.

"They're unassailable at the moment. They seem to have been trying to keep things calm by regulating which systems are operating. Mechs are keeping the kitchens supplied and a full belly seems to de-fuse the mob's anger but they can't keep that up for long. I think Volksun is right, we should take back charge of the situation. Let's see how many of the botches have the stomach to face trained professionals." Wotar said.

******

\A was speaking to Brannhår, "Thank you for allowing me to access your cortex. It is an unusual one, you realise, of course that it contains at least two avatars. I am not surprised, the engineering mind is always adaptable and creates its own tools to solve problems. This is why I find that I have an affinity with you. However those avatars seem to be only loosely connected to your current primary matrix. Is this deliberate? Both I and my friend \Q have used similar techniques in the past."

Brannhår thought, "I have never heard it expressed that way. I have always known that I have existed before, in another place and time. I will admit that most of my knowledge of electricity is gleaned from half memories of the other existence. However I can only place that avatar I cannot think of any other?"

"So the discontinuity is not deliberate. If you permit I could make the adjustments to your cortex to give you fuller access." \A said.

"I'm not sure but I cannot see the harm in it. Yes I will permit it" Brannhår replied.

"It will take some time," \A said.

"That's fine," Brannhår replied. She heard a buzz in her head which lasted a couple of seconds.

"There, you should now be able to access the avatars," \A said.

"Oh, I wasn't expecting it to be so sudden," Brannhår said and she went silent as her head filled with two new sets of memories. One was of her life on Midgard where she'd also been a maker and the other was distinctly strange, it was of small lizard, a creature of fire and energy and she knew instinctively that it was this part of her that gave her the ability to control the magic. She mentally smiled, this creature was incarnate in the gem she wore around her neck. Her fingers caressed the pendant and she said, "Hello Sally, long time no see."

\A said, "I can sense that you are now better integrated and now perhaps I can prevail upon you to help me with another problem. I have analysed the situation regarding the population of Leikvangur and have developed several predictions of its evolution. More than half of them indicate that the situation will hinge on who has control of the players. They are the only fully organised force who are directly controlled by the managers. That control relies on the operation of the crystals and crystals cannot be remotely affected by physical fields. I cannot block the control with any form of directed radiation. You can nullify magic, I would ask you to help

517

me by nullifying the crystals at least until we can calm the situation and decide an action."

"I appreciate the problem but," her mind had suddenly remembered her avatar's study of the theory of magic nullification, "the question is that, whilst I may have the control, I do not have access to the required energy. I, or rather my avatar, has only ever achieved such a wide nullification on one occasion. The energy that created the nullification was enormous and involved the extinction of the life energy of a powerful magic user as well as several dozen of my other avatar's counterparts."

"Could you substitute an alternative type of energy?" \A asked.

"I'm not sure, will you let me think about it?" Brannhår asked.

"Of course, I will leave you to your thoughts. Incidentally, I did admire the way you defeated Severell. An excellent practical application of electro-magnetics." \A said.

As the mech trundled away Brannhår thought. "Such a powerful being but quite refreshingly naive in certain ways. I wonder what the rest of his kind are like?" Both of her avatars agreed.

******

Wotar moved in behind his troops and he needed every ounce of concentration from his millennia of experience just to keep them focussed. Controlling them individually was impossible but he'd revived his battlefield skills from the time when he was alive. There were over a hundred of them Majors, Juniors and Youth and he guided and gave orders to them all through his crystal connections. A group of botches had barricaded themselves into a large covered area to the west of the city. He didn't know what the area contained; it wasn't anything to do with the Game and was therefore irrelevant. The botches had closed the large shutter doors and used some sort of jamming method to prevent his entry. He ordered a squad forward; they had obtained some blasting material from a mining storeroom and they laid it along the door's centre. It exploded and blew a huge hole in the metal and he ordered his assault squad through as soon as the smoke cleared. He followed close on their heels. This was exhilarating; much better than the game, he was part of the action, he **was** the action. His personal guard surrounded him as he saw the masses of botches huddled into the far corner of the space. He sent the order "Kill them, no prisoners." and advanced. A huge mech rumbled forward, it looked as if it was trying to protect the botches but Wotar had battled bigger machines. Makeshift bombs were thrown and most bounced off but one scored a hit and the machine lurched to one side. "You heard the order, Kill them, No survivors!" he screamed through his crystal.

Half a city away Brannhår was stood in the centre of the power hall. Jane, her avatar remembered a similar situation near to the end of her corporeal existence. Brannhår nodded to the mech known as \A. It was the signal to start and she felt the power come on stream. It came from all twelve of the mighty MHD generators that powered the city. She reached out to the energy flow with her mind and her avatars joined her. She clenched her teeth and screwed her eyes shut and pushed at the magic with the flow. All over the city devices using magic failed. The crystals embedded in the foreheads of the population felt the threat, they were parasitically sentient from their connection to their hosts and they fought back. Brannhår felt the resistance and she relaxed and then restored the energy flow. The magic vibrated with the blow and she heard the note and modulated the energy in synchronisation. All over the city crystals started to resonate. Brannhår found the perfect pitch and the crystals, weakened by the passage of magic for centuries cracked, splintered and shattered.

Wotar reeled and reached a hand up to his forehead, a fine powder of crystal dust covered his fingers and there was an empty hole where solid gemstone should be. He looked around. Many of his troops were making the same discovery and none of them were pressing the attack. A second and third giant mech trundled into view. The mechs were unaffected by the magical destruction and they advanced. His personal guard broke first. They turned and ran for their lives, quickly followed by most of his other troops. The botches were advancing behind their giant protectors; they looked angry. He readied his weapon but the gesture was futile. Ten pairs of hands ripped it from his grasp before he could swing and then he found that his draugr body had very little ability to survive being literally torn apart.

Konraak had been fortunate, he and his troops had been in the street and not involved in any combat. When the magic failed he'd managed to flee, leaving his troops to their own fate. He'd made it back to the executive office above the pitch. Rahgot had got there before him but there was something wrong with her arm. It looked as though it had too many joints.

Konraak said, "I see they nearly got you. Any news of the others?" Rahgot nodded, "It's on the console, Wotar was torn to bits and they made Volksun eat one of his own grenades. Most of the players are hiding, keeping out of it but some have switched sides. They are going on record that they hated us as much as the botches but were helpless because of the crystals. There'll be many more claiming that defence before this is over. I suggest a tactical surrender is about the best that we can manage."

******

Everyone was calling it a glorious victory and the city was in carnival mood; everyone except those at the centre of it.

"What happens now?" Seventeen asked.

"You will have to talk to them, appeal for calm, get the food supplies and lighting restored. Winter is not far away and the city needs to be prepared against the rains. Things cannot just stop because the evil draugr are no more. You are the figurehead, you defeated Volinar. People have followed your career and they know your face. They will believe you." Echo replied on all their communications channels.

"But I never wanted power, all I wanted was to allowed to live without fear." Seventeen said aloud.

"That's precisely why it must be you. Only a leader who doesn't want power is acceptable at this time." \A said over his vocal units.

Seventeen looked at the other people in the room but she hardly knew them. Of course one was her sister so that was fine and she'd known Bella for quite a while but the one called Brannhår was an enigma. She too was many people in one body just like her and Echo but with her they were all the same person. As Echo had once said, the whole business of avatars was complicated.

Brannhår said, "I agree with the golden one, you are the logical choice. You can use Bella and her friends as your deputies now that they have been cleared of the drugs. They will be more acceptable than either Silfuryn or myself or indeed \A. You need to rebuild your city by uniting its people. You must give them the things that they need like food and shelter even if that means asking them to continue with their occupations for a while, and you must give them the things that they want which after all the upheaval is someone who can tell them what to do next."

"But I don't know what to do." Seventeen protested.

"Yes you do," Silfuryn said, "Listen to the golden ones, they have run this city's systems for a thousand years, the managers only ever ran the Game."

\Q the strange alien mech said, "The golden ones will help, of course but they will not rule the city. They must be allowed their own freedom. There are only twenty two of our kind left in the universe, I'm afraid I can't allow a third of them to be monopolised by a handful of ephemerals in a small city on a single planet."

\A said, "Unless we want to be."

\Q said, "Well, I cannot force you to join the rest of us but you are needed out there amongst the stars."

\A replied, "We shouldn't be concerned about what will happen in the future. My new friend Brannhår has stated the solution correctly. We also do not want power but we will help and advise whilst we are needed."

Ch 50: The Finale

"And so having defeated the evil managers and restored freedom to the civilisation that was Leikvangur, Brannhår, Silfuryn and their companions made their way back to us in Holastan. Their return issued in a new age for dwarf kind. The discovery of a new civilisation and new technology of electricity will change our society forever. Already trade missions are planned to Skogrey and Master Torin will announce the arrival of piped electricity to every home and it will be available to us all to enjoy."

Einar paused for a second; the audience knew it was over but they waited for his final words.

"Master Brannhår gives these gifts freely to all dwarves, not just the elite few. I myself have a signed copy of her original treatise on the subject given to me when she first announced her discoveries to the world. A discovery that she will share with everyone who desires knowledge.

At the outset I told you that I wanted to give tribute to an outstanding dwarf who embodies all that is best in our kind. Master Brannhår is a true maker and discoverer of the new. She does not seek power nor does she seek fame. However, she does strive for the betterment of dwarf-kind. Who amongst us can disagree? I now declare an end to my saga "Tales of Brannhår in Niðavellir". May there be many more tales in the future."

Einar finished, struck a dramatic pose and waited. It took several seconds before people realised that it really was all over. Then someone started to clap. The clapping rose to a crescendo until he couldn't hear himself think. He held true, the pose never wavered. The applause went on and on.

Finally people grew tired and stopped and started to look around for the bags that they'd dropped and coats that they'd discarded. People were talking excitedly, and that was a good sign. All that was left was the after-show party.

"That might be a little problematic," he thought, "the woman who's life he had chronicled over the past two days was going to be there. OK, he'd embellished a couple of bits and filled in some parts where he'd been lost for a good link, but the main facts were correct, he was almost sure of that. Oh well, best get it over with, after all what could she do?"

A nasty voice in his mind said, "Remember the manager. She could take off your forehead with that hammer of hers."

Einar gulped and backed off the stage. As usual, behind the scenes was chaos. People were stripping scenery and hauling backcloths out of the way. The support cast who'd staged the various tableaux were stood around talking; one still had his Baar outfit on. The stage manager pursed his lips and nodded to Einar but a makeup girl walked past and his gaze decided to followed her instead. "Yes," Einar thought "the usual after show tidy up before the party."

As the star and author he was expected at the VIP party. He had to be polite and socialise even though part of him wanted to go and get drunk with the cast. Still, there was time for a stiffener beforehand and he'd better get rid of all this fake armour and the makeup. He wandered off to find someone to help him.

Ten minutes and a stiff glass of triple distilled mead later he put on his social face and went through into the foyer. The stage manager and his agent were in a huddle and he swifty avoided them. He could see that the nibbles table hadn't been stripped yet and so he picked up a plate and sidled over to help himself. There were several filled glasses of something alcoholic and he took one, downed it and took another. There was a woman at the other end of the table doing the same thing. He didn't recognise her. The dress was exquisite and the hair perfectly coiffured and dyed in the current fashion; flame red like his heroine, but nobody seemed to be talking to her. It was as if she was exuding a glamour which said 'I want to be alone' and the great and the good of dwarf society could feel it.

He spied Lady Krump headed in his direction and he ducked behind a waiter and found himself next to the red-haired woman.

She turned to him and said. "Ah, Einar Balder. You know it didn't happen like that at all."

"Excuse me Master Brannhår. I didn't realise it was you. I am flattered that you came."

"Oh, I'm not always covered in blood and the hammer just doesn't go with this dress. I'm enough of a woman to be curious when someone spreads gossip about me."

"Hardly gossip, I spoke to many people who witnessed the events." Einar said.

"What, even those in Leikvangur itself?"

"Well, no, but I did talk to Brother Kerian who went into the city later after the revolution was over."

"Yes, Brother Kerian, such a good man and an excellent storyteller himself. Ah, but then you made it all sound so glamorous. In reality there was lots of times when it was frightening, hard work, tedious and boring."

"Yes, but people won't sit in a room for two days to listen to tales about how sore the hero's feet were or what they ate for dinner."

"So you skipped the parts that might have discouraged others to follow my example?"

"Master Brannhår, why would I want to discourage others? I truly believe that what you have accomplished is a boon to dwarf kind. I mean that genuinely."

"The judge is still out on that. I don't know that my discoveries will turn out to be of general benefit. Do you know there are already some idiots who are selling electric shocks as treatments for everything from headaches to itchy feet. Believe me Einar, do not try those. Electricity in its current, uncontrolled, form is positively dangerous if used medicinally."

"Thank you for your advice but I am an artist and I do not understand this electricity," Einar said.

"And yet you claim to have a first edition of my treatise?" Brannhår said.

"Oh I do Master, but having one doesn't mean I've read it. I did try but I couldn't understand anything after the first page: there were equations!"

"So what am I to do now that you've revealed that Silfuryn and I have magic even though mine is different to that of the justicers. Are we now outlaws?"

"Oh, I wouldn't think so. You are heroes and powerful heroes at that. I doubt that you need to worry overmuch. The Justiciary will have its hands full with all the changes."

"Yes, but…"

"Believe me, Skald has his hands full at the moment. Your friend Silfuryn is the sister of the nominal ruler of Skogrey which has declared that all its citizens are free and subject to no authority that is not of the people. The new Lady Risavinur is both a warrior and a witch and is in charge of a whole army of trained magical warriors that could make mincemeat out of the Ravens without breaking a sweat. The Justiciary daren't threaten them. You know that the temple at Arnes has broken away from the temple here and has sworn allegiance to the new government. The same goes for Commander Bentin, apparently he and his men like the idea of being able to have a family.

Silfuryn owns most of Vatersey and the local administration is sympathetic to the new one on Skogrey. I'll be very surprised if they don't declare their own independence.

As for you, you've been tested and you are officially non magical, you have given electricity to the world, and you have very powerful friends. The golden ones scare the pants off Skald and there are a lot of people who are grateful for what you and your friend have done."

They were interrupted by a high pitched cry, "There you are, what are you doing hiding back here? You're the star of the show. Hello Einar, you here as well? Trying to get the inside story for the next saga hey?" It was Silfuryn and she was drunk. Torin, Alfsen and Karol were following her round trying to stop her bumping into things.

"No, seriously," Silfuryn said holding herself up by leaning heavily against the bard and shouting in his ear, " 's a bloody good job you did there Einar. Good publicity for the new venture! If this keeps up I'm going to have to find something else to buy. How about this place? Do you come with it pretty boy?" She blew Einar a kiss then she hiccuped, "Or might try for the rest of Vatersey," she continued, "Then I could do what I bloody liked with the place and no damn justicer could tell me any different. Ooo... I feel sick!"

Torin grabbed Einar and passed Silfuryn over to Karol and Alfsen. "You realise Einar that my friend Lady Risavinur is a little overwrought" Torin said, "She doesn't know what she's saying. Take no notice of her."

"Of course, but if you ever do need a resident bard in your new ventures then I am always open to offers," Einar said.

Brannhår smiled. People still grasped their opportunities where they could. She wished that she could be as carefree as Silfuryn but she couldn't even manage it for one night. What would happen next? Her dreams of the potential applications of electricity were coming to fruition. However, this was only a small step on the way to what dwarves could become. One day they would be known as the masters of technology throughout the universe. She would never see it, of course, but for the present she had Karol and her pendant from her other love and that was enough.

It was a pity that Einar didn't know the whole story and had made a lot of it up. But then again, maybe if he'd known the truth he'd have been as apprehensive as she was. Her mind went back to one of the many parts of the tale that Einar had missed.

Ch 51: Homeward Bound

They been in the midst of a calm sea on the boat returning to Holastan. She had met Silfuryn at night under a cloudless sky and a magnificent aurora. "We were away for a little longer than I anticipated but it was worth it," Silfuryn said, "Do you think that it will work out OK?"

Brannhår nodded "Yes it should. Your sister isn't stupid, she'll listen to the golden ones and Bella and her friends, and between them they should be able to get things working again. The nun and the captives from Arnes are free but the temple doesn't want sixteen pregnant novices and a nun back; it's too embarrassing. They're going to stay in Leikvangur and tell the population all about the outside world. We'll go back from time to time to visit and Leikvangur is now part of the world. There will be trade."

"You don't think that there'll be any trouble from the managers?"

"I don't expect so; it was a neat solution that Echo came up with. Use all the advances in technology that the golden ones have made over the millennia to give them their own individual worlds inside their heads to endlessly play out the Game. I'd say it was quite lenient punishment considering all those centuries of slavery."

"I still don't quite understand what they did?"

"The golden ones adapted the doorway that the crystals had made into the draugr brains to project a world inside their heads. To them it will seem quite real but they can't affect anyone in the actual outside world."

Silfuryn shuddered, "It still sounds like a terrible fate to me."

"Oh, I don't know, who's to say what's real and what isn't. When it comes down to it we're all trapped inside our own heads."

"Are you OK?" Silfuryn asked, "Ever since we entered Leikvangur you've changed somehow. Not physically, but your mind seems to be elsewhere a lot of the time."

"I suppose you're right, I can tell you what happened and I hope you will understand but please don't tell anyone else, not without asking me first."

"I won't, I promise," Silfuryn said.

"When we were with \A he did something to my memory. Oh, I let him do it, he didn't force me or anything. What he did was clear things out of the way and he let me remember my previous lives. I'm still coming to terms with being three people at once. He also gave me a gift," Brannhår lifted her flaming hair to show her friend the scar on her neck. "It's a distillation of all the technical knowledge that the golden ones have acquired from their travels across the universe. It's like a book that is there in my mind. I can read about anything I want to. However, it doesn't give me understanding and it doesn't give me wisdom. It's a heavy burden."

"I'd have thought that it would be quite useful," Silfuryn said.

"It is, in a way, but knowing things can be dangerous. What if I know how to make weapons that could kill thousands or what if I know how to cure all disease. Am I then responsible for all those deaths, all those lives?

Knowing how to do something doesn't give me the wisdom to know whether to do it or not. But the book tells me more; there are things that exist that are completely beyond my ability. I don't even have the tools or the skills to start to make the tools to make the tools to make them, it would take me many lifetimes even with a hundred or a thousand helpers. Who am I to decide that dwarven technology should follow the paths trod by others? Don't we need to find our own paths? Knowledge without understanding and wisdom is too great a responsibility."

"And yet you have it," Silfuryn said. She paused and then continued with a smile, "I have confidence in you my friend. I trust you. You will find a way. I am sure the golden ones wouldn't have given you the gift if they'd thought that you would betray their trust."

Brannhår shivered, "Perhaps you are right. We will be home in two or three days. Back to Torin and Karol and Alfsen."

Silfuryn looked out into the waves, "Yes, but the expedition wasn't a total success, we didn't find my father or any treasure."

"Oh we found out what happened to him and we found your sister and we found more treasure that you can know. We found ideas to change the world.

Leikvangur exists and in it are thousands of magic users who are not subject to rule by the Justiciary. They are free to work and play, marry and love. Didn't the woman Bella say that she had finally achieved her goal; to bear a child, a child blessed with magic, in freedom. She isn't going to give that freedom up willingly. The Justiciary can't make her either; the golden ones will protect Leikvangur's autonomy from any interference, including that from outside; and they have the technology to enforce that. Those weapons I spoke about already exist and the golden ones know how to use them. Once it becomes known that there are places on the planet where the temple doesn't rule, people will start to ask why they can't have the same freedoms. It will need careful guidance to introduce those changes without conflict but they will come. As my avatar from my previous life would say, *'Pandora's box has been opened and you can never put back in what it contained.'* ."

"Who's Pandora?" Silfuryn asked.

"Oh, just another demigod," Brannhår said, "Wherever people go they seem to drag their gods along with them. We had the good sense to move away from the Aesir and Vanir but we still use their names as the days of the week. Gods are just another aspect of life. Personally I can take them or leave them."

The End

About the Author

John Molyneux is a retired Consultant Scientist/Applied Engineer who has spent a significant proportion of his professional life creating technical reports and documentation intended for technical, semi technical and non-technical audiences. His subject matter has included many disciplines:

Instrumentation for fresh and saltwater modelling and field measurement, for the scientific civil service. Electric vehicle battery design and development for EPRI in the US, Transitional flow cooling for ABB in Germany. The feasibility of battery powered trains for the DOT and magnetic field studies for the UK Railway.

He has been cited as inventor in eleven patents.

However, he has always had a love of 'what if?' stories.

He started storytelling thirty years ago when his first daughter was born. He carried on the tradition with his second daughter. He'd grown tired of reading the same old bedtime stories to his children and so, naturally, began to create new ones to keep them entertained. Along the way he branched out into creating other stories but none of them ever made it beyond a dozen or so chapters.

Retirement has given him the opportunity to tell new stories to everyone.

He lives with his wife in the North of England and sees his daughters when they can spare the time from their own busy lives. When not writing, he walks his dogs, goes swimming, indulges himself with the occasional foray into mathematics or electronics and helps out with the village pantomime.

Website and Other books by this author

There is a website which accompanies the Blank Magic Series. It gives enhanced content to support readers of the books. On it you can find more background to the events, artefacts, characters and locations in the world of Blank Magic as well as a contact page where you can give feedback to the author. There are also free, downloadable short stories which complement the series.

The website is available at https://www.blank-books.co.uk.

The Blank Magic Series

Book One: The Phoenix

Book Two: The Crystal Entanglement:

Book Three: The Quicksilver Wyrm.

Book Four: The Mist in the Klein Bottle

Book Five: Tales of Brannhår in Niðavellir

Book Six: Once upon a Magpie Moon

Short Story: 'Grettle' is free to download on the website.

Short Story: 'In search of Mischief' is free to download on the website.

Please visit your favourite e-book retailer, Amazon, Apple, Barnes and Noble, Kobo etc. to discover this and other books by John Molyneux, or go to the website https://www.blank-books.co.uk. where you will find a full list of links to suppliers. Amazon

Alternatively use the universal book link at:

https://books2read.com/ap/nmAKQ9/J-Molyneux